Across
the
Ages

Books by Gabrielle Meyer

TIMELESS • 4

Across *the* Ages

GABRIELLE MEYER

BETHANYHOUSE

a division of Baker Publishing Group
Minneapolis, Minnesota

Published by Bethany House Publishers
Minneapolis, Minnesota
BethanyHouse.com

Bethany House Publishers is a division of
Baker Publishing Group, Grand Rapids, Michigan

Printed in the United States of America

Library of Congress Cataloging-in-Publication Data
Names: Meyer, Gabrielle, author.
Title: Across the ages / Gabrielle Meyer.
Description: Minneapolis, Minnesota : Bethany House Publishers, a division of
   Baker Publishing Group, 2024. | Series: Timeless ; 4
Identifiers: LCCN 2024010436 | ISBN 9780764244209 (paper) | ISBN 9780764244216
   (casebound) | ISBN 9781493448234 (ebook)
Subjects: LCGFT: Religious fiction. | Novels.
Classification: LCC PS3613.E956 A63 2024 | DDC 813/.6—dc23/eng/20240314
LC record available at https://lccn.loc.gov/2024010436

Cover design by Jennifer Parker

Published in association with Books & Such Literary Management, www.booksand such.com.

Baker Publishing Group publications use paper produced from sustainable forestry practices and postconsumer waste whenever possible.

24 25 26 27 28 29 30   7 6 5 4 3 2 1

To my twin boys,
Judah and Asher.
Thank you for all the adventure
you've brought into my life
(though I could do without the ER visits).
I love you with all my heart.
—Mama

The Lord is not slow in keeping his promise, as some understand slowness.

Instead he is patient with you, not wanting anyone to perish, but everyone to come to repentance.

2 Peter 3:9

1

MAY 21, 1727
MIDDLEBURG PLANTATION
HUGER, SOUTH CAROLINA

My bare toes dug into the hardpacked earth as I beat the rug on the back line, watching the dust melt away into the setting sunlight. It moved through the drooping Spanish moss on the ancient oak trees overhead, making me long for my troubles to fade away so easily. My arms burned from my task, and yet the anxious thoughts did not disappear, nor did the work calm my fearful heart.

No matter how hard I tried to forget, the reality of my life was still with me—or rather, the reality of my *lives*. I didn't know what to call my existence or why it happened to me. When I went to sleep tonight in South Carolina in 1727, I would wake up in Paris, France, in 1927 tomorrow. And when I went to sleep in Paris, I would wake up in South Carolina again the next day—with no time passing while I was gone. I had two identical bodies, but one conscious mind that moved between them. And I had been going back and forth since I could remember. Perhaps from the very beginning of my strange life.

My breath came hard as sweat beaded on my brow.

If only I could release the secrets my heart kept hidden, just as

I released the months of dust and dirt from the rugs. Everything about my life was one secret built upon another. A fortress of mysteries too high to breach.

Some were the secrets I kept, and others were the secrets kept from me.

"Caroline!" Grandfather's stern voice drifted through the oak trees and magnolias on our small tobacco plantation. The Cooper River sparkled in the distance, but the fields of ripening tobacco, and the indentured servants who worked there, were hidden from my view.

"I'm here," I called to Grandfather, just around the corner and out of sight from the back porch of our simple two-story plantation home. I lifted the apron from the front of my homespun gown and wiped my brow as I made my way over roots and rocks toward him.

Grandfather stood on the porch of our white clapboard house, his arms crossed in disapproval as he waited for me. Middleburg Plantation was a prominent property, and my grandfather, Josias Reed, was well respected. He'd come from England, by way of Massachusetts, to South Carolina. He was pleased with the home he had built, but the future of his pride and joy was uncertain, as I was his only heir.

"What have you been doing?" he asked as I slowed my steps.

"Beating the rugs."

His gaze fell to my bare feet and then lifted to the dust covering my face as his disapproval deepened. "We have servants to do the menial tasks, Caroline. The mistress of the plantation should be tending to the indoor work."

"I like beat—"

"Our guests have arrived," he interrupted. "You should have been prepared by now. Governor Shepherd is an important man, and he will not look kindly upon his oldest son marrying a hoyden."

"His son?" I frowned, confused. "I am not marrying the governor's son."

"What do you think this meeting is for?" he asked, his frustration mounting. "Really, Caroline. Your naiveté will be your undoing."

"I've heard he's old and lazy," I protested.

Grandfather took a step forward and lowered his voice, no doubt worried that the governor and his son might hear. "Elijah Shepherd will inherit five thousand acres of the best rice plantation in America one day." He shook his head with disappointment. "I could make nothing of your fickle mother before she ran off with that worthless sea merchant. But I will make something of you."

I had heard this threat my whole life. My mother, Anne Reed, had been a hoyden, as well. A motherless child with a penchant for recklessness and rebellion. She'd run off with the first man who had shown interest in her.

She'd only been thirteen.

A year later, she'd left me on my grandfather's doorstep. Her recklessness had led to Grandfather's poor opinion of me, so I vowed to never be wild and thoughtless like her. I was twenty years old—seven years older than her when she ran off—and I had done nothing to earn his poor regard. Yet, he let me know I could *still* turn out like her if I didn't follow his plan for my life.

"I do not want to marry Elijah Shepherd," I said, trying to appeal to his compassion, though I'd not witnessed it often. "I do not love him."

"Love." He said the word with such disdain it made me wonder if he'd ever been in love. He'd never spoken of my grandmother and rarely spoke of my mother, unless he was comparing my inadequacies to hers. The only things I knew were the rumors I'd overheard the servants whispering.

Witchcraft. Adultery. Abandonment. Betrayal.

"If I can secure a marriage between you and Elijah," he said, "and we can join our plantations, we will be the richest planters in South Carolina. I will not have you thwart my plans." He opened the back door. "Come. Nanny will help you dress for supper."

I had no choice but to slip up the back stairs to my room. The house was long and narrow, with three rooms on the main floor and three above. Grandfather slept in one room on the far end of the upstairs, and I had the middle room. The room on the opposite end had belonged to my mother but had been locked my whole life. I walked by the closed door now, a reminder of all the secrets kept from me. Twice, I'd tried to break into that room to see what Grandfather was hiding, but both times I had been discovered and thoroughly disciplined with the rod.

Nanny was waiting for me when I entered my room, my best muslin gown in her arthritic hands. She had been with me my whole life, coming to Middleburg when my mother was an infant. She'd been old when I was young and was almost too old to be of service now. But I would not hear of her being displaced. She was one of the only connections I had to my mother, though she told me little more than Grandfather.

"Off gadding about again?" she asked, tsking me with a smile in her voice. "Your grandfather is in a state. We must hurry." She began to untie the lacings at my back.

"I was not gadding about," I told her as I slipped out of my gown. "Did you know the purpose for Governor Shepherd's visit today?"

"Aye—and I suspect you did, too."

"Grandfather has told me nothing before now."

"Are you that naïve, Caroline?" she asked. "Surely, you knew that he would marry you to his advantage." She turned me to look at my image in the mirror as she helped me into my muslin gown. "Look at how pretty you are. 'Tis a wonder someone didn't scoop you up before now."

My brown eyes stared back at me from a face that some called beautiful, though I saw all the flaws. A square jaw, thick eyebrows, a petulant mouth, and a rebellious gaze—one I tried to quell.

I shared some similarities with my parents in 1927, but neither of them had brown eyes. Did Anne, my mother in 1727, have brown eyes? Or were they the eyes of her sea merchant husband? The man with a name I'd never been told.

Nanny helped me restyle my hair as I used a wet cloth to wipe the sweat and dust from my face. When I was young, I tried telling her about my other life, but she had shushed me, threatening to whip me for speaking such blasphemy and lies. She had put her trembling hand against my lips and said, "Speak not such things. You're already marked by your ancestors." She had moved her hand to my chest where I bore a sunburst birthmark, the same one she said my mother had possessed, and perhaps my grandmother before her. "Do not give them a reason to destroy you as they did them."

Her words had further terrified a frightened child. For years, I had lived in fear and uncertainty, wondering if I was insane. Perhaps my two lives were a work of my imagination. But, if so, which one was real, and which was made up?

I wanted to ask Nanny who had destroyed my ancestors, but my questions would go unanswered, so I heeded her words and spoke no more about the second life I lived as the fortress of secrets grew around me, holding me captive. Over the years, I had come to accept that somehow *both* of my lives were real, and there *had* to be an explanation—one that was being kept from me.

One that perhaps my mother could answer.

Moments later, as I walked down the stairs and into the central room of our home, I felt all eyes upon me.

My gaze met Elijah Shepherd's, and my heart filled with dread. He looked me up and down, assessing me with a coolness that was all business. He did not smile or offer any warm welcome but analyzed me as if he were purchasing livestock or seed.

"Caroline," Grandfather said as he lifted a hand to beckon me. "May I present Governor Shepherd and his son, Mister Elijah Shepherd?"

I curtsied as I'd been taught, and the men bowed.

"How do you do?" I asked them, trying to hide the revulsion from my face and voice.

Elijah was at least ten years my senior, and he did not bear the look of a man who worked his own land. He was thick about the middle, and his skin was pale, telling me he spent his days indoors. There was no depth to his gaze, no sign of intelligence or character.

More than anything, I longed for a man with fire in his eyes.

"'Tis a pleasure to finally meet you, Miss Reed," Governor Shepherd said. "We've been working through the details of the betrothal, but I believe we've finally arrived at an agreement."

"Indeed we have," Grandfather said with a smile.

I could think of no greater prison or worse fate.

I left the men to their cigars and brandy the moment I could be excused. It had been an unbearable supper as Elijah stared at me. Grandfather and Governor Shepherd spoke of farming and politics, though neither man included Elijah in the discussion. The longer I sat in his presence, the more I worried Elijah was simple-minded. Was he even capable of inheriting such a large plantation? Or taking a wife?

I didn't want to find out.

My pulse thrummed as I left the room, needing to be free of the confines of my life and the expectations placed upon me. I shivered just thinking about Elijah Shepherd touching me or living with him day after day.

I wanted so much more from this life. Freedom, the opportunity to make my own decisions, and most of all, I wanted to know my mother.

But paramount to all of that was the need to know why I lived two lives.

I felt breathless as I raced up the stairs to my bedchamber, an oil lamp in hand. Tomorrow I would be in 1927 and could have a reprieve from this life—yet I would wake up here the next day, and it would be waiting for me.

I thought of my mother and wondered if Grandfather had tried to force her into a loveless marriage. Was that why she had fled South Carolina at such a tender age?

There had to be an answer—a way out of this nightmare.

I stopped at her bedchamber door, curious to know what Grandfather was hiding from me. Perhaps my mother was still alive and the answer to all the secrets was behind this door.

I didn't think twice but went into Grandfather's bedchamber in search of the keys. My heart pounded so hard, I could hear the beating in my ears.

Finally, I found a key ring and then quickly replaced everything I had dislodged in my search. I returned to my mother's bedchamber door, and with shaking hands, I slipped several keys into the lock until I found the right one.

When it clicked, time felt like it stopped.

Tossing a glance over my shoulder, I slowly turned the knob and then slipped into the dark room, closing the door behind me.

My breath was shallow as I looked around, holding my lamp high. The room was nondescript. A four-poster bed, a bureau, a washstand. I wasn't sure what I was expecting—but nothing so normal or . . . simple.

Perhaps Grandfather wasn't hiding something.

Disappointment weighed down on me. I had hoped this room would reveal the answers to my questions, but there was nothing. I opened each of the drawers and looked under the bed, but it was all empty. Nothing remained of my mother.

My legs felt heavy, so I walked across the room and sat on the bed, holding the lamp in my hands. I wanted to cry, but I had learned at an early age that it didn't make anything better. I wanted to pray, but I wasn't sure that God would listen. Did He hear the pleas of a marked woman?

The lamp cast a shadow over the wall, and I noticed a slight variation in the wainscoting. Frowning, I set the lamp on the nightstand and moved across the room. When I reached the wall, I ran my hand over the boards and felt a piece shift.

Slowly, I removed the panel and sucked in a breath.

There was a hole behind the wall, and within it was an envelope.

With trembling hands, I lifted the envelope and brought it back to the bed. Sitting next to the lamp, I opened the envelope and pulled out the thin paper within.

My mouth slipped open as I skimmed the page.

It had been written by my mother, and she had dated it December 1706—three months after I was born and about the time I had been brought to my grandfather.

I leaned closer to the lamp to see the words my mother had penned twenty years ago.

> *I suspect you will hate me, Caroline. As much as I hated my mother for abandoning me and leaving me in the care of my father, Josias Reed. He tells me she died in Salem in 1692 but refuses to tell me how or why. There can only be one reason a woman of her age died there that year and it is kept a secret. She was a witch. Did she curse me? Is that why I must suffer through two lives, because she hated the child she bore?*

My pulse thrummed in my wrists. My mother also had two lives! I continued to read, filled with both panic and exhilaration to know I wasn't the only one.

> *I hate myself for leaving you with my father, but the difficult life you'll lead with him will offer you more advantages than the difficult one I've chosen for myself. You might wonder why I don't abandon my life in Nassau, but that is the trouble with love, isn't it? We give up anything that makes sense to be near the one who makes us feel the most alive. That is what your father does for me. That is why I am returning to him. I left before my pregnancy was obvious and will never tell him of your birth. You would not be safe if he knew you existed.*
>
> *I write this to you now because I wish my mother had left me something. A morsel, a grain, even a speck of correspondence. But, mayhap this will only make you angry*

when you read it one day. If you read it one day. I wish I could explain why I've left you—why I left South Carolina in the first place—but it will only hurt you more. I've never told anyone the truth about my lives, and I wouldn't expect you to understand it, either. I shall carry the secret to my grave, though that inevitable day feels closer and closer. I might only be fourteen in this life, but I've lived for twenty-eight years. Mayhap when you read this, I will no longer be alive. But that might be best for you and anyone else who knows me.

The letter ended on that final, fatalistic note.

My mind spun with all the implications. My mother had two lives, just like me. She'd brought me to South Carolina to protect me from my father. Would he have harmed me if he knew she was pregnant? And who *was* my father? Grandfather said the sea merchant my mother ran off with was a cowardly, weak man. Surely, he wouldn't have wanted to harm his own daughter. More importantly, she said she was returning to Nassau. The only thing I knew about Nassau, Bahamas, was that it was the Republic of Pirates until nine or ten years ago—and it still had a reputation for depravity and crime. Pirate leaders like Benjamin Hornigold, Blackbeard, and Charles Vane had either been pardoned by the king or killed, but there were still some pirates who plied the Caribbean.

I looked away from the letter, the possibilities endless. My mother could have been associated with the pirates. But was she still living in Nassau? I desperately wanted to understand what was happening to me, and she was the only person who might have the answers.

I heard a footstep on the stairs and quickly blew out my lamp. It was Grandfather's tread, slow, heavy, deliberate.

His footsteps didn't even pause or hesitate by Mother's room, and a few seconds later, I heard his door open and close.

I let out the breath I was holding and slipped the letter back into the wall before closing the panel. After waiting a few moments, I left Mother's bedchamber and locked the door.

Nanny would be asleep above the kitchen, and the house would be settled for the night. I would need to work fast if I was going to get away without notice.

Nothing would stop me from finding my mother.

2

MAY 21, 1927
PARIS, FRANCE

The next morning, I awoke in the Hôtel Westminster in the heart of Paris, but my pulse was still hammering from my escape in 1727. It would be dangerous to travel as a single woman for the thirty miles from Huger to Charleston, so I had borrowed a set of the stable boy's clothes from the wash line behind the kitchen. He would miss them, but I was desperate.

Most men wore their hair shoulder-length and clubbed at the back with a ribbon. My hair went past my waist, so I had cut it with trembling hands and wore a red handkerchief under the leather tricorn hat I borrowed from a hook in the kitchen. I'd also taken a pair of buckled shoes from the back porch that belonged to one of the servants. They were a little too big for me, but they would have to do.

Before I left, I slipped my diamond necklace into my pocket. It had been a gift from my grandfather on my eighteenth birthday, and I would sell it for passage to Nassau.

With nothing but the clothes on my back and the necklace in my pocket, I set out on foot, walking and running as far as I could throughout the night until I fell into an exhausted sleep hidden in a cover of trees about a mile outside Charleston.

But now I was in Paris again and would have to wait an entire day to wake up in 1727 and continue my escape. Grandfather would come looking for me, so I had to get onto a ship as fast as possible. It was my one chance to learn the truth about my mother and see if she could help me understand the strange existence we shared.

The Paris street was already loud and busy outside my hotel window as I quickly threw back the covers and got out of bed.

"Wake up, Irene," I said as I chose a simple, modest dress with long sleeves and a dropped waist. The dress might not be as glamorous as the dresses I admired on others, but it was much more comfortable than my stays and heavy skirts in 1727.

My cousin Irene was in the bed next to mine and moaned, "Leave me alone, Caroline."

My first name was the same in 1727 and 1927, something that always amazed me. But my last names were different. In 1727, I was Caroline Reed, the daughter of young Anne Reed and her sea merchant husband. Even if Grandfather knew the name of Anne's husband, he had chosen to give me his last name. In 1927, I was Caroline Baldwin, the daughter of the Reverend Daniel and Mrs. Marian Baldwin. Passionate reformers, prohibitionists, and devout Christians.

"We can't make Father late," I told her, tired of the game we played every morning. She was just a few months older than me and had been invited along on our trip to be my companion—yet I knew the truth. Irene's father had passed away last fall, and since then my cousin had become reckless. She'd cut her hair short, wore provocative clothing, began to smoke cigarettes, and went around with a loose crowd. My parents had hoped to reform her on this trip. So far, nothing had changed, and I had spent most of my time trying to keep her from embarrassing my father. But I'd quickly come to realize she didn't need reforming. Her heart was grieving, and she needed time to heal. The rebelliousness distracted her from the pain.

I shook her shoulder. "Irene," I said with a little more force. "Today is an important one for Father—perhaps the most important. You must hurry."

With another groan, she rolled onto her back and yawned. "I thought coming to Paris would be fun."

"You knew we were coming to attend the conference."

Irene lifted herself onto her elbows and blinked away the sleep. Her short blond bob was in a net to protect the marcel waves while she slept. Mother and Father refused to let her wear makeup, but there was a hint of color on her lips and rouge on her cheeks.

Neither had been there last night when we went to sleep.

"Did you go out last night?" I asked.

A saucy smile tilted her lips. "I had to have some fun, Caroline. I couldn't go back to Des Moines without something to tell my friends. And boy, was it the cat's pajamas!"

We'd been in the City of Lights for two weeks and had spent most of our time sitting through boring lectures, meetings, and sermons. Father had been invited to speak at the World Conference of Christian Living. It was a summit that included leaders from denominations all over the world, seeking unity and understanding amidst the social chaos of the Roaring Twenties. As one of the most prominent and outspoken preachers in America, Father had been asked to attend. He was known for his fiery sermons and the large tent revivals he hosted across America. But it was his ardent support of Prohibition that had made him famous, by friends and enemies alike.

Some called Prohibition a failed social experiment and were advocating for its demise. Father was working hard to ensure its success—and he'd enlisted my help, though I'd been given little choice.

"What if you were seen?" I asked her, whispering so my parents wouldn't hear in the connecting room. "What would people say if they knew Reverend Baldwin's niece was cavorting on the streets of Paris—at night?"

Irene tossed her covers aside and sat up to stretch. "Don't spoil this for me. I had so much fun last night at the Dingo Bar—and I plan to go back." Her blue eyes were shining. "Do you know who I met? You'll never guess. Ernest Hemingway! The author. And he said that F. Scott Fitzgerald and his wife, Zelda, would be there tonight! Can you imagine? *The Great Gatsby* is the bee's knees. Fitzgerald is one of the greatest literary minds of our time, and I'm going to meet him."

A longing filled my heart that surprised me. Books were one of my favorite pastimes, and to meet an author like Ernest Hemingway or F. Scott Fitzgerald was a dream. But I could never take the risks Irene had taken. Fear of disappointing my parents, and bringing shame to our family, was always on my mind. I was supposed to uphold the ideals and morals that Father preached—no matter how much pressure it created. "You can't return. If someone sees you—"

"No one cares." Irene stood and touched her hairnet. "They don't care about your father or what he has to say—they don't really care about any of the old rules that used to matter. There are no pretenses with this crowd. No right or wrong. The war changed everything—it woke people up, and now they're living their lives however they want. And that's what I'm going to do, too. We're leaving Paris tomorrow, and I won't miss an opportunity to meet F. Scott Fitzgerald—even if your father locks me in this room."

The door to the connecting room creaked open, and Mother appeared, a pleasant smile on her pretty face. "Good. You're up. We'll be heading down to breakfast in twenty minutes. We mustn't be late."

"Of course, Aunt Marian," Irene said with a placating smile. "We'll meet you down there."

Mother closed the door again, and I faced Irene. "You're not returning to the Dingo Bar."

Just like 1727, there were expectations placed on me here. The only difference was that I didn't have to marry a man I didn't love, and I had more opportunities and comforts in 1927. Beyond that—my life was not my own.

What would it be like to live a life of my own choosing—both here and in 1727? I was almost too afraid to wonder. Reaching for something I couldn't have would only bring disappointment and regret.

Irene dismissed me with a bat of her eyelashes as she entered the bathroom and closed the door tightly, humming loud enough for me to hear.

By the time she left the bathroom, I had to rush in to finish getting dressed, and then we raced to the hotel restaurant where my parents were already eating. After a quick breakfast, we exited the building and entered the vehicle waiting to take us to the conference.

Father was silent as he looked over his sermon notes, encouraging other countries to follow America's lead and abolish alcohol. He was a handsome man in his late fifties. Tall and athletically built. He'd been a baseball player in his early twenties before turning his life over to Christ and pursuing a ministry as a pastor and reformer.

Mother was small and gentle in comparison, but her size was no indicator of her strength. She stood passionately alongside my father, supporting every move he made and advocating for her own beliefs and opinions. They were an admirable couple whom I respected deeply, even if their ministry felt too heavy for my shoulders. I often wondered if I hadn't been born with the uncertainty that came with two lives, and the possibility that my grandmother was hanged as a witch in Salem, would I have been more confident in my role as their daughter?

Irene looked out the window as we drove down the Avenue de Friedland and around the Arc de Triomphe. She'd washed her face and was wearing a modest dress, but I suspected she was thinking about her escape the night before, making me curious as to how many other nights she had snuck out.

We finally arrived at the Bois de Boulogne, a magnificent park in Paris that housed several venues that had been used for the conference. Hundreds of people were enjoying the beautiful morning, strolling through the landscaped park, riding the merry-go-round, and fishing in the ponds.

The driver opened the back door for our family.

Father stepped out first, Mother followed, and then I exited after Irene.

"Lindbergh! Lindbergh!" A bedraggled newsboy ran up to us, holding a newspaper aloft in our faces, his hands smudged with ink. "*Aviateur Américain!*"

"What is he saying?" Father asked Mother.

The boy was speaking quickly in his native tongue. Since Mother spoke French, she listened and nodded several times.

"Another American pilot has attempted to make a flight from New York to Paris for the Orteig Prize," Mother explained to Father. "He left New York yesterday and, if he makes it, will land in Le Bourget airfield just outside Paris tonight."

Irene's eyes opened wide as she tried to peer over Mother's shoulder at the newspaper she couldn't read.

"Please purchase the paper from him, Caroline," Father said as he offered his arm to Mother and led her toward the amphitheater.

I pulled five centimes from my purse and purchased the newspaper, but before I could tuck it under my arm, Irene grabbed it.

"This is so exciting!" she said. "Imagine if he makes it."

I said, "*Merci,*" to the newsboy and wrapped my arm through Irene's to tug her along as we caught up to my parents.

Mother, Irene, and I were ushered to seats at the front of the amphitheater as Father went behind the stage to meet with the organizers. I felt hundreds of eyes upon us as we took our seats. Mother kept a placid smile on her face, but I felt fidgety. Not only because we were the center of attention, but because I was anxious about my escape in 1727. As soon as I woke up there, I would need to work quickly.

I longed to speak to Mother about what was happening in 1727, but just like Nanny, Mother had hushed me as a child, admonishing me not to lie. But when I insisted my second life was real, she brought the matter to my father, who threatened to discipline me if I didn't hold my tongue. I hadn't breathed a word of it since then.

Mother took the newspaper from Irene as she said to me, "Stop fidgeting, Caroline. Do you want the others to think you're nervous? They might wonder why the daughter of a preacher would be nervous. We don't want them to think you're hiding something."

Irene's smug smile made me stop trying to get comfortable in my seat. Why did she seem so calm about her secrets? How did she not feel condemnation and guilt, knowing she had run out last night to spend time in a bar?

It was just one more secret I had to keep from my parents and from the teeming masses who either wanted to elevate Father to sainthood or ensure his complete demise. The responsibility to appear perfect on such a worldwide scale was suffocating. My brothers had folded under the demands and chosen their own paths, though my parents had no idea the double lives they were living. Just like Irene, they showed no signs of guilt or shame.

I, on the other hand, felt smothered under the weight of the smallest transgression. Everything I did was scrutinized. Father's calling to serve God had placed me on an unwanted pedestal. And, if that wasn't enough, his vision for evangelism was grand and impressive.

Was it not enough to serve God with an ordinary and humble life?

Mother glanced at the newspaper as she was about to set it aside, but then she paused. "This Lindbergh fellow is from Minnesota."

"Minnesota?" Irene's interest was piqued again.

I looked closer at the paper, surprised, because we lived in Minneapolis. We would board a ship tomorrow to make our return trip to America, arriving in New York and then going by train to Minneapolis and home. Irene would return to Des Moines and her fretful mother.

When the program finally started, the amphitheater was packed.

All eighteen hundred seats were full, and hundreds more were standing around the edges.

Father motioned for me to join him.

I trembled as I took the stage. Though I'd done this dozens of times, it never got easier.

"We'll sing 'Rock of Ages' and 'Come, Thou Fount of Every Blessing,'" Father said to me.

I nodded and then took my place in the center of the stage where the microphone had been placed.

"Please join me in singing 'Rock of Ages,'" I said into the microphone.

As I began to sing, the amphitheater filled with my voice, and the audience joined me. Mother's eyes lit up with pride and joy.

Ever since I was young, people had praised my voice, and Father insisted it was a gift from God. To me, it was another burden. If I could sing for pleasure alone, I would love it. But singing for an audience who judged each note robbed me of joy.

After both songs were finished, I took my seat next to Mother again, my cheeks warm and my heart pumping with relief.

"Before I hand the microphone over to Reverend Baldwin," the organizer said in English, while a translator interpreted in French, "I want to make a special announcement. Reverend Baldwin has just agreed to host a weekly international radio broadcast program. It will be the first of its kind, and, we hope, will further our mission to eradicate alcohol use around the world."

The audience cheered enthusiastically as Mother and I looked at each other in surprise. I didn't know of any other pastor who had an international audience.

My heart started pounding for a whole new reason. It terrified me to think about my brothers' secrets getting out. Father's entire ministry would come crumbling down, and thousands of people would be disillusioned.

After all, what good was a pastor's preaching when one of his sons was a gangster and the other was a crooked cop, taking bribes from criminals?

The lights of Paris sparkled as the sun set on our last day in France. I had left the window open to allow the fresh air to flood our room, filling it with the fragrance of spring and the sounds of people at sidewalk cafés or passing by on the street. I wasn't ready to go to sleep in Paris—to face my escape in Charleston. I wanted to lie for a few minutes and enjoy this moment of tranquility. This breath between my two lives.

Ever since I was young, I could choose when I wanted to fall asleep. I would simply lie down, close my eyes, and fall into a deep slumber. If midnight came and went while I slept, I would wake up in my other life. But if I stayed awake past midnight, as was common while at a tent revival with Father, I would not cross over until I went to sleep. If I wanted to nap during the day, I would remain in whatever life I was in, as long as I woke up before midnight.

Somehow, I woke up refreshed in body—if not in soul or spirit.

The room was dark fifteen minutes later as I heard the rustle of Irene's bedding. When I turned, I was shocked to find that she had been under her covers fully dressed—shoes and all—and she was sneaking out of our room.

"Irene," I said in a loud whisper.

She opened the door and stepped into the hall. "Go back to sleep, Carrie. This doesn't concern you."

And, with that, she closed the door and was gone.

I tossed my covers aside and quickly began to dress. I put on the same clothing I'd worn earlier that evening to the farewell dinner. My gown was modest, but it was probably the most fashionable thing I owned. With layers of black silk and lace, it extended to my mid-calves and had a dropped waist. But it was the shawl, made of the same black lace, that had made Mother approve. She had not let me cut my brown hair short, like Irene's, so I had found a way to roll it up to make it look like the shorter styles, with marcel waves framing my face.

As I made my way toward the door, I slipped my black heels onto my feet, but I left my hat and purse behind.

I needed to stop Irene before she left the hotel.

Thankfully, my parents' connecting room had been silent since nine. I just prayed they wouldn't wake up and discover neither of us in our beds.

I didn't see Irene in the hallway or on the stairs. She wasn't in the lobby or just outside the hotel, either.

Traffic moved past the Hôtel Westminster as people walked toward the Place Vendome, a large public square nearby. I moved in that same direction, my eyes scanning the street as I neared the large obelisk in the center of the plaza. Nightclubs, cabaret shows, and jazz clubs beckoned on this cool night. If Irene hadn't told me she was returning to the Dingo Bar, I would have thought of looking in one of them.

I caught a glimpse of my cousin as she took a left to head toward the Jardin des Tuileries, a beautiful garden along the river Seine.

"Irene!" I called out to her, heedless of the French men and women who turned toward me as I began to jog in her direction.

"Irene," I yelled again.

Finally, she stopped. When I caught up to her, she asked, "What are you doing, Carrie?"

She was wearing a dress I hadn't yet seen. It was ruby red and shimmered under the glow of the lamps. The hem was at her knees, and the décolletage dipped dangerously low. She wore no brassiere or undergarments and was covered in long, black necklaces, earrings, and a black headdress with more dangling jewels. Her outfit was so shocking, my mouth slipped open.

"What am *I* doing?" I stared at her. "What are *you* doing?"

"I told you." She continued to walk with determination toward the Jardin des Tuileries. "I'm going to meet F. Scott Fitzgerald."

I raced to keep up with her, wishing I had the same courage as Irene—or was it foolishness? To the left was the famous Louvre Museum, and to the right, at quite a distance, was the Champs-

Élysées. I could glimpse the top of the Eiffel Tower, though it was shadowed in the night sky.

"You can't go—"

"There's no use trying to stop me," she said as we walked through the Jardin des Tuileries, toward the Pont Royal bridge. "You can come with, if you want." She looked me up and down and wrinkled her nose. "Though you look like a frump in that getup."

I paused for a second, my heart longing for something my head knew was reckless. Irene was going, whether I liked it or not. I could either return to our hotel and pray she got back before my parents woke up, or I could go with her and try to get her back at a reasonable hour.

I had a feeling that either way, I would regret my decision.

"Wait for me," I said.

She slowed her pace and grinned as she wrapped her arm through mine. "I knew you'd come to your senses."

"We're going to regret this," I told her, feeling both excitement and guilt. I couldn't believe I was going to a bar. Even though alcohol was legal in France, if anyone found out where I'd been, it wouldn't bode well.

"Maybe you will—but I won't. What can Uncle Daniel do to me? Send me back to my mother? I'm heading that way tomorrow anyway."

She hailed a taxi just over the bridge to take us the rest of the way.

When we got into the back seat, she told the driver to take us to the American nightclub called the Dingo Bar at 10 rue Delambre in the Montparnasse Quarter.

"It's open all night," she told me as she pulled a tube of lipstick and a pocket mirror from her purse. With the aid of the street-lights, she began to apply it liberally to her lips. "It's a popular gathering place for the Lost Generation. You know who they are, don't you?"

I sighed. "Of course I do." They were Americans disillusioned after the Great War, the Spanish flu, and Prohibition, who saw their lives as fleeting. Too short to waste. They were grasping hold of the fragility and opining about its faults in their novels, poetry, and artwork. "I hope none of them recognize us."

Irene offered me the lipstick, but I shook my head. It wasn't that I disagreed with the use of lipstick, but that I would be in enough trouble with my parents already.

She applied her rouge next and rolled her eyes. "If you need to use an alias, I won't stop you. But I'm telling you, none of them care about you or your father."

"I can't take any chances."

We arrived at the Dingo Bar a few minutes later. It wasn't remarkable or even attractive. Nothing like the Moulin Rouge, with its red windmill atop the roof. Instead, it was a simple building in a row of buildings, with an awning that said Dingo American Bar and Restaurant. The windows were covered with curtains, not allowing us to see inside without entering.

Irene paid the taxi driver as I left the vehicle. She joined me a moment later.

"Ready?" she asked, her blue eyes lighting up with excitement.

I'd never been to a nightclub—had no idea what I was doing there—but Irene didn't give me time to think about it. She pulled open the door and sashayed into the bar as if she'd done it a dozen times—and perhaps she had.

"They say Lindbergh should have landed by now," a man said to another in an American accent as I followed her in. "I'd lay odds that he crashed in the Atlantic and no one will remember his name a month from now."

"I think he still has time," said the other. "We'll be hearing about his landing any second."

The room was long and narrow with a dark paneled bar on one side and a small stage at the back. There were dozens of tables, some in the middle and others along the outer wall. Pillars were interspersed throughout, giving people a little privacy. Were any of these men Hemingway or Fitzgerald?

"Lindbergh, Lindbergh, Lindbergh," Irene laughed. "That's all I've heard today. We should have gone out to the airfield to watch him land."

"What are we supposed to do now?" I asked Irene as she scanned the room.

A smile tilted her red-tinted lips. "We mingle and wait for Fitzgerald."

Several people looked in our direction as cigarette smoke swirled over their heads. They couldn't possibly know who I was by looking at me—and I wasn't going to tell them. They would recognize my father's name as part of the problem with America, but I was rarely in the newspapers. If I kept my identity to myself, my parents would never know I'd been there.

"There you are," a man said to Irene as he approached. He was probably in his late twenties, handsome, with intelligent eyes and a dimple in his left cheek when he smiled.

"Mr. Hemingway," Irene said in a voice that didn't sound like hers. "I was hoping to see you again."

This was Ernest Hemingway? My pulse pounded as I tried to remember to breathe.

His gaze slipped to me, and he took me in from head to toe, a curious look in his eyes. "Are you going to introduce me to your friend?"

Irene hadn't needed the rouge, since her cheeks were bright with color. "This is my cousin, Caroline B—"

"Reed," I said. "Caroline Reed."

"You sound Midwestern, too," he said with a chuckle.

I lifted my eyebrows, his easy demeanor relieving my nerves. "You could tell from three simple words?"

His grin was infectious. "You've got that innocent, wholesome look about you. Not to mention, I'm from the Midwest, so I know one when I see one." He put out his hand and said, "Ernest Hemingway. It's nice to meet you, Miss Reed."

"My pleasure." I wanted to tell him how much I'd enjoyed *The Sun Also Rises*, even though I'd had to read it in secret since Father shunned anything that came from this so-called Lost Generation. But I couldn't find the words.

"Jimmie," Mr. Hemingway said, rapping on the bar. "These girls need a stiff drink."

"No." I quickly shook my head. "No, thank you. I don't drink."

"I'll take one," Irene said with a giggle.

After Hemingway ordered a drink for Irene, he turned back to us. "Fitzgerald isn't here yet, but he should be along shortly."

Disappointment lowered Irene's shoulders and caught me off guard, too. I shouldn't have been so eager to meet these men—but I couldn't help it. Their books were popular because they reflected the thoughts and feelings of this generation. Even though my parents tried to shelter me, I was still intrigued. Perhaps even more so because I felt foolish not knowing what others knew.

"Don't fret," Hemingway said. "We can have a good time while we wait." He glanced at the empty stage. "If we had some music, we could even dance."

"Caroline sings," Irene said, much too eagerly. "She sings all the time."

"Is that right?" Hemingway's face filled with interest. "We haven't had music in here for days." He took my hand and led me through the maze of tables, laughing as he bumped into people, leaving me to apologize in our wake.

"Really, Mr. Hemingway," I protested as I tried to pull away. "I'm not going to sing here."

"Sure you are. And I'll accompany you." He led me up a short flight of stairs to the stage. "My mother is a musician, and she forced me to learn the cello. It comes in handy now and again." He motioned toward a cello sitting on the stage. "It hasn't been played nearly enough. What do you want to sing?"

"I *don't* want to sing."

"Come on," he said, his handsome smile almost blinding. "You're young, beautiful, and, if your cousin is right, talented. Life is too short to be bashful or modest. If you have it, use it. What'll it be, Miss Reed?"

He was still holding my hand, probably afraid I'd bolt if he let go.

People had noticed us on the stage, and several were watching with mild curiosity. Irene had found a table and was waiting with expectation.

But I couldn't do it. I only sang in public because I felt obligated to Father. I had no such obligations to Ernest Hemingway.

"I'm sorry," I said as I shook my head and pulled away.

"Miss Baldwin," Hemingway said as he stepped to the edge of the stage to address Irene. "Can't you convince her?"

Irene jumped up from her seat and met me at the base of the steps. "Please sing, Caroline. I'll do anything for you. I promise."

I paused. "Will you leave this place when I'm done? Return to the hotel with me?"

Her face fell. "I don't want to leave yet."

"Then I'm not singing." I began to move around her.

"Come on," Hemingway said.

"Please don't embarrass me in front of him," Irene begged.

"Promise me we'll leave as soon as I'm done," I told her, even though I wanted to meet Fitzgerald. The longer we stayed, the more we risked getting in trouble.

Most of the occupants of the bar were now watching, since Mr. Hemingway made no attempt to be discreet.

"Fine," she said, almost angry. "We'll leave when you're done."

"Good." I climbed the stairs again as Mr. Hemingway whistled his approval.

The crowd clapped, and Irene returned to the table, shooting daggers at me with her eyes.

"What'll it be?" Hemingway asked me as he took a seat behind his cello.

"I suppose you don't know 'Amazing Grace' or 'Rock of Ages,' do you?"

He laughed, hard. "I do," he said, "but I don't think this crowd will appreciate either one. How about 'Downhearted Blues'?"

It was a popular song, one I'd heard Irene sing several times since our journey began.

"Alright." I gripped the microphone like an anchor, trying not to look as nervous as I felt.

Almost every gaze was on me as Mr. Hemingway began to play.

I closed my eyes, trying to block out the room and remember the lyrics that I'd only heard a few times.

The entire room was silent as I sang. I slowly opened my eyes and found their attention was riveted to me and the stage. Several of them were smiling and tapping their toes.

There were no judgmental stares, no one whispering behind their hands, and the weight of my father's reputation was nowhere to be found.

A smile lifted my cheeks, and for the first time in my life, I didn't hate singing in front of an audience. It was a strange and liberating feeling.

When the song came to an end, there was a brief pause, and then the room erupted into applause. They cheered and stamped their feet, calling for an encore.

I grinned. I couldn't help it.

The door of the Dingo Bar flew open, and a man ran inside shouting, "Lindbergh did it! He made it to Paris! *Vive* Lindbergh!"

The Minnesota boy had made it across the Atlantic Ocean all by himself.

Everyone left the bar to join the celebration in the street.

Mr. Hemingway was at my elbow, a smile on his face. "Come on, Miss Reed. Let's go commemorate this amazing feat of mankind. The first person has flown an airplane across the ocean. For better or worse, our world just got a whole lot smaller."

I didn't care about the world. All I cared about was finding Irene and returning to the hotel before my parents knew we were gone—and before I could think too hard about what I had just done or why it had felt so good.

3

MAY 22, 1727
CHARLESTON, SOUTH CAROLINA

Before I opened my eyes the next morning, I was aware of the cold, wet earth beneath me. Slowly, I blinked awake and found myself in the cover of trees just off the main road into Charleston. I'd come this way with Grandfather several times and knew I was less than a mile away from the heart of the city.

I sat up and winced. My neck and back were stiff from lying on the hard ground. The cloth I had used to bind my chest was loose, and my shoulder-length hair had fallen out of the ribbon. My clothing and skin were damp from the dew, but I would soon dry.

Urgency pushed me as I stood and unbuttoned the vest I had borrowed and then untucked the cotton shirt underneath. The linen cloth covering my chest was long and narrow, so I had to wrap it around several times, as tight as possible. It was uncomfortable, but no worse than a corset, which I had left behind. When I lowered my shirt and tucked it into the knee-length breeches, then buttoned up the brown vest, I felt confident I could pass as a thirteen- or fourteen-year-old boy. I had feminine features, but so did a lot of younger boys. I carried myself with proper, ladylike deportment, but I could change that, too.

I slipped my leather tricorn hat over my hair and buckled my shoes, ready to continue my flight to Nassau.

I pushed thoughts of the Dingo Bar and Irene out of my head. She'd protested all the way back to the hotel the night before, but we had made a deal. I couldn't risk getting in trouble—or worse, hurting my father's reputation. My brothers were trying to do a fine job of that already. Andrew had left his work at the bank to bootleg alcohol from Canada into Minnesota, and Thomas was getting paid to cover up criminal activity in Saint Paul. If my parents knew the truth, they'd be devastated. If their enemies knew the truth, they'd be ruined.

Instead, I focused on today as I stepped onto the road. The sun had not yet crested the horizon, and I suddenly realized something important was missing.

My diamond necklace.

I stopped and searched every pocket, every crevice, and every hem of my clothing, but the weight of the necklace was not there. Running back to the forest, I looked all over the ground where I had slept, behind the boulder where I relieved myself, and along the trail I had taken in and out of the covering.

But the necklace was nowhere to be found.

Panic seized me, and I tried to think. How would I book passage on a ship if I didn't have money? Part of me wanted to follow the road back the way I had come, but there was no time. Grandfather would wake soon, and he'd be on horseback looking for me. I didn't have a moment to lose.

With one final, desperate glance, I raced back to the road and continued toward Charleston.

My mind was spinning as I came into the outskirts of town and saw the harbor in the distance. The large masts of the ships beckoned me. There were dozens of them anchored in the harbor, representing freedom and answers. I had to find one heading to Nassau.

I moved quickly toward the wharves, remembering to walk like a boy, and stopped several people. "Are any of those ships going to Nassau?" I asked one person after the other.

I received shrugs and disgruntled scowls, but a haggard seaman finally nodded and said, "I believe the *Adventurer* is headed that way. Captain Frisk is signing on new crew members as we speak. Hop to it if ye're wantin' to be employed, boy."

I hadn't even considered the possibility of becoming a crew member, but the thought made my pulse race. I could get to Nassau without passage if I was employed by the ship's captain.

"Which ship is it?" I asked.

He pointed to one of the largest ships in the harbor. "The captain's overseeing the loading of cargo, but they'll be pulling anchor soon, so you'd best hurry."

"Thank you," I said as I started to run.

The freedom of trousers was a thing to behold. Not even in 1927 was I allowed such liberties, though other women had begun to wear them.

The smell of the sea turned my stomach as unwashed sailors yelled instructions to dockworkers and cargo was being loaded and unloaded from ships. The sun had just crested on the horizon, past the harbor, and made the ocean come alive with color.

I finally arrived at the place where I assumed they were loading cargo onto the *Adventurer*. The ship was in the harbor, so the dockworkers were moving boxes and barrels from a nearby warehouse onto a large boat to transfer to the ship. The man who appeared to be in charge was probably in his midthirties and wore a well-made frock coat over a silk waistcoat. His breeches matched his frock coat, and he had shiny brass buckles on his black shoes.

"Pardon me," I said, trying to make my voice sound less feminine as I glanced over my shoulder to make sure Grandfather hadn't already found me. I doubted he would know where to look right away, but he might eventually discover the truth. "Is this cargo meant for the *Adventurer*?"

He glanced at me but didn't look long. "Aye." He took a step forward and motioned for one of the dockworkers to stop. "Not that barrel," he growled impatiently in a British accent. "I want the beer brought to the ship first, then the victuals. I won't say it again."

I waited, swallowing my nerves. If I couldn't find work on the ship, I might never get to my mother. I couldn't stay in Charleston long enough to work for passage. Grandfather would find me.

"I heard you're looking for crewmen," I said.

He turned to me, irritation in every movement. "You have experience?"

I wanted to say yes, but it wasn't true, and he'd learn it soon enough. "No, sir. But I'm a hard worker and I learn quick."

"I have no desire to take on inexperienced boys. The Caribbean is fraught with danger, and I don't need someone who will cause more trouble than he's worth." He moved around me and started walking down the dock.

I ran to catch up to him. "Please, sir." I tried not to let my voice shake with my fear. "I need the job. I'm willing to work night and day for my keep." I didn't have the kind of skills necessary to sail a ship, but I had some skills. "I can sew, haul water, cook, clean—anything you need."

He paused so abruptly that I almost ran into his back.

"How old are you, boy?" he asked as he looked me over.

"Four-fourteen, sir," I said, though I hated to lie.

He grabbed my upper arm and circled it with his fingers. "There's nothing to you."

I fought the urge to pull away. No one touched a refined woman in such a manner—but I forced myself not to flinch or react. He thought I was a boy and was treating me thusly.

"I'm strong," I said as I pulled from his grasp and lifted a barrel. It was heavier than I expected, but I heaved it onto my shoulder—desperation making me bold. "I need the job."

He squinted at me. "What are you running from?"

I couldn't say a loveless marriage to a simpleminded man, so I said, "A future I don't want, sir."

As I set the barrel down again, I stood before him and waited.

"I could use a cabin boy. It'll give you time to put some meat on your bones and learn the ropes. In a year or two, if you work hard, you could be a rigger or an able-bodied seaman."

I swallowed the excitement and nodded quickly.

"What's your name?"

I opened my mouth to say Caroline, but that wouldn't do. Grandfather had often told me that he needed a male to inherit his life's work and that he wished I had been born a Carl instead of a Caroline, so that was the name I would use.

"Carl Baldwin," I told him, taking my last name from 1927.

The captain nodded. "Help load the rest of the cargo onto the launch, Carl Baldwin. We'll pull anchor soon."

"Thank you, sir." I nodded quickly and then turned to help with the cargo. The sooner we left the harbor, the sooner I could breathe easily that Grandfather wouldn't find me.

I was on my way to Nassau—almost.

The sun was high as the ship left the harbor. I stood on the main deck, watching Charleston slip away as the crew set sail.

I had never been on a ship in this life and was surprised at how tight it was packed with cargo, livestock, and crewmen. Ducks, geese, and chickens squawked from their coops at the front of the ship, while piglets wandered the main deck uncaged. They squealed as the ship started to heave in the water and make its way out to sea. Cattle lowed in the ship's hold, and goats were tied up on the main deck, bleating their anger at leaving shore. I'd already seen two cats parading about the ship, one orange and the other black, and had been told they were there to catch the rats that inhabited the hold.

How long would it take for this vessel to smell like a barn? I had only been on the ship for a few hours, and I was already tired of the smell of pine tar, wet wood, tobacco smoke, and unwashed bodies. But I wouldn't complain, not even to myself. I was free of Grandfather's plans and on my way to find my mother. I could put up with unwelcome smells for a few weeks.

"Baldwin!" the quartermaster called to me from the quarterdeck where he was standing with the captain. "You're needed in the galley."

I shaded my eyes as I looked up at him and nodded.

My gaze roamed the ship for the galley as I tried not to appear inept or nervous. I had warned the captain that I was new to sailing—but I didn't want the rest of the crew to know the truth.

"It's in the bow," a sailor said as he stood beside me, pulling ropes hand over fist.

I turned to him, trying to remember I was supposed to be a boy and not a young woman. "Where?"

"There." He nodded his head toward the front of the ship. As he spoke, I noticed several of his teeth were missing. His skin was tanned dark from the sun and had a leather quality about it that spoke of the sea. "Through that hatch and down the ladder, ye'll find the cook in the galley." He chuckled. "I started out as a cabin boy meself. Ye'll find yer way, soon enough."

"Thank you." I nodded my appreciation and then made my way across the main deck, avoiding a collision with a piglet, and tried to stay out of the way as the crew raised the sails. It felt like I was listening to a foreign language as the crew yelled words I'd never heard before. *Bowsprit*, *forecastle*, *mizzenmast*, *capstan*, and *ratlines*.

The hatch was open, so I stepped onto the ladder, thankful again for my breeches.

More smells assailed me as I entered the galley. Woodsmoke, grease, and sweat among them. It was hot, and the ceiling was low. Barrels, cotton bags, and wooden boxes filled the room from floor to ceiling, so there was little space to move around. A large cookstove and a worktable were the central pieces of the room as utensils, pots, pans, and more swung from the rafters.

"So, they've found me some help, have they?" a man asked as he snarled at my arrival. He was a short fellow with a white apron covering his dirty clothes. Sweat dripped from his forehead, and his face was greasy. "Are you any good, is what I want to know. Do ye have experience in a kitchen?"

"Aye, sir," I told him. I learned to cook and clean at a young age at the plantation. I could butcher chickens, pigs, and cows. I had planted and oversaw the vegetable gardens and knew how to harvest and preserve food, make cheese and butter, and cook or bake. In my 1927 life, I was taught many of the same basic skills, though we lived in Minneapolis and bought most of our meat at the butcher, the produce from the grocer, and the bread from the baker. Our milk was delivered once a week, and we had a hired girl who lived on the third floor and helped with the cooking and cleaning.

"We'll see if yer experience is good enough. I'm Harry," he said. "And ye'll be working for me when ye're not running for the captain or the quartermaster, ye understand?"

"Yes, sir."

"Have ye been told where ye'll sleep?"

I shook my head. "I haven't been told anything."

"Ye'll sleep with the crew in the forecastle."

I opened my mouth to inquire about the location of the forecastle, but he wasn't finished.

"'Tis just above us, at the front of the ship," he said. "Ye'll hang yer hammock between the cannons. The men have four-hour watches throughout the day and night, so they will be coming and going. Ye'll report for duty each morning at six bells, and we'll begin preparing the first meal of the day. The men get a gallon of beer a day, four pounds of beef a week, which they eat on Tuesdays and Saturdays, two pounds of salt pork . . ." He continued his litany of rations, but I could hardly keep up, wondering if I would need to know all this.

He began to work as he rambled on, instructing me to tote fresh water from a cistern to a barrel where we added several pounds of salt pork. It would have to soak for hours before he would boil it for the midday meal, which I was told was the largest meal of the day.

It was arduous work, and I began to sweat. The binding at my chest made it hard to take deep breaths, and it itched.

As the ship made its way out of the harbor and into the open water, it began to list slowly from side to side, making my head swim and my stomach turn.

I needed fresh air.

And, more importantly, I needed to relieve myself. But, for the first time since leaving the plantation, I realized the issue that this might be on a ship full of men.

A new sort of panic overcame me as I thought through the implications of this problem. Not only on a daily basis, but as a female. I would have monthly needs, as well.

Why hadn't I considered this issue?

I needed to at least know where to relieve myself, and then perhaps I could make a plan from there.

When I told Harry what I needed, he said I could use the head. "'Tis at the bow of the ship. There's a tow-rag hanging in the water if you need it. But be quick about it."

I wasn't sure what a tow-rag was, but I nodded nonetheless. I climbed the ladder to the main deck and looked left and right, trying to orient myself. The ship wasn't nearly as big as the one I sailed on to reach France in 1927, but it was bigger than most I'd seen in the harbor at Charleston. Harry had told me there were three dozen crewmen aboard, and most of them looked like they were busy getting the ship underway.

I wasn't sure what I was looking for, but there was a door at the front of the deck, so I opened it and found a room with hammocks hung between the cannons. This must be the forecastle where I would sleep later.

It was empty—though I couldn't find anywhere that could be confused with the head.

There was another door on the opposite end of the room. I gingerly opened it, hoping no one else was using the toilet.

Thankfully, this area was empty, as well, and offered a little bit of privacy since it was behind the forecastle and at the front of the ship. There were holes cut into the wooden head for the purpose I sought and a long rope nearby that dangled in the water. It didn't take long for me to realize what that was for, though the thought of using the same tow-rag as everyone else was disgusting.

What else hadn't I considered? Surely, I would be shocked and appalled at each turn.

If they discovered I was a woman, I wouldn't be safe in their company, and I would probably be abandoned at the closest port of call.

A dozen thoughts mocked me—but I wouldn't let them deter me. I had to do this. I couldn't go the rest of my life without talking to my mother. And if I hadn't come, I would have been forced into a life of marital drudgery and unhappiness.

No. I had made the right decision, regardless of the unpleasantries and risks I would endure.

As long as they didn't discover I was a woman, I could suffer almost anything.

4

I had never seen anything like the festivity that accompanied us from Paris to Washington, DC, after Lindbergh landed. Father had received a telegram from President Calvin Coolidge, inviting us to attend the welcome home celebration for Lindbergh in our nation's capital. We extended our stay in Paris for a week and then set sail to Washington, instead of New York.

The following week, we had been on a ship making our way back to the States in 1927, while in 1727, I had been on a ship hugging the eastern shoreline of the southern colonies on our way to Florida and then on to the Bahamas. The two ships were vastly different in size, technology, speed, and comfort. In 1927, I was waited on by a maid and a steward. All three scrumptious meals were served in the stately dining room, and in between meals, I had the luxury to read, write letters, play shuffleboard, and listen to the endless notes Father was preparing for his radio sermons. In 1727, I was helping night and day in the ship's galley cooking bland meals that I would serve to the captain, his officers, and then the rest of the crew. In between meals, I scrubbed the deck, cleaned out the goat pen, picked eggs, milked cows, and hauled supplies.

But now, Washington, DC, beckoned. We'd been here for almost a week. It was the first time I'd been to the capital, and it had amazed me from the moment we arrived. Excitement hummed among those who sat on the temporary stage under the Washington Monument at quarter to one that sunny afternoon. Red and white bunting, floral garlands, and American flags decorated the white pillars of the stage. I sat to Father's left, while Mother sat to his right, and Irene was next to her. We had prominent positions near the front of the large stage to the right of the microphones. As the most popular preacher in America, it didn't surprise me that Father would be included in the celebration. He represented the religious values of our nation, something the president would be keen to convey to the world.

Thousands of people stood under the shadow of the monument—so many, I couldn't begin to guess the number. Maybe even a hundred thousand. Men's bowler caps, white straw boaters, and fedoras bobbed up and down next to women's colorful, wide-brimmed hats or tighter cloche caps.

Everyone who arrived on the stage stopped to greet Father. Genuine respect and admiration shined from their faces. Most knew him because of his passionate preaching, but some remembered his years as a playboy baseball star. It was hard to imagine Father living a loose and wild life as a ballplayer. After he'd found salvation, he'd given up his baseball career to attend seminary at Moody Bible College in Chicago. There, he met my mother, and for thirty-five years, they had built their lives upon their shared faith in the gospel.

"Reverend Baldwin," a military man with a French accent said as he stopped in front of Father. "It's a pleasure to meet you in person. My wife, Grace, and I had the honor of attending one of your tent revivals in Virginia last year."

The gentleman was bedecked in US military whites with several pins and ribbons on his chest. The beautiful woman next to him, presumably, Grace, was in an elegant blue dress with a cloche cap covering most of her blond hair. At their side were two young girls who looked to be somewhere between eleven and thirteen. The older one had blonde hair like their mother, but the younger girl's hair was a deep red.

"I'm Brigadier General Lucas Voland," the man continued as Father shook his hand. "This is my wife, Grace, and these are our daughters, Lydia and Kathryn."

"It's a pleasure to meet you," Father said. "I'm very aware of your service to our country." He made introductions and then said to Mother, "The general was an important flying instructor during the war and helped to create the United States Army Air Corps. If I'm not mistaken, Mrs. Voland was also an aviator and was the first woman to make a transcontinental flight."

"Your memory serves you well," Mrs. Voland said.

"Won't you sit with us?" Mother asked.

As Father and the general continued to speak, Mrs. Voland and her daughters took the empty seats next to me. After they were settled, Mrs. Voland said, "I've heard you recently came from France, Miss Baldwin. My husband is from Paris, and my sister, Hope, was the first woman to fly from England to France over the English Channel in 1912. We've visited several times, and I never tire of the beauty of the country."

"It was my first time," I told her, amazed at the daring feats she and her sister had undertaken for aviation. No wonder she was standing on the stage with us. "I thought it was lovely."

"My daughters haven't been there yet," she said as she looked at Lydia and Kathryn. "But I long to take them to their father's home country."

"I've been there, Mama," the younger daughter, Kathryn, said as she stared up at her mother. "With Austen's family."

Mrs. Voland nodded and then put her hand on her daughter's shoulder before saying, "Of course. How could I forget?"

Kathryn smiled, revealing identical dimples in each cheek. She was a beautiful little girl with a charming twinkle in her brown eyes.

How could Mrs. Voland forget that her daughter had been to

France? I turned to the older daughter, assuming she had been there, as well. "And what about you?" I asked Lydia. "What is your favorite thing to see in France?"

"I haven't been there," she said, an equally delightful smile on her face.

"Oh, I'm sorry. I just assumed."

Mrs. Voland only smiled.

The United States Marine Band began to play "Hail to the Chief" as a cavalcade of dark vehicles arrived with President and Mrs. Coolidge.

Everyone stood and cheered at their arrival, and Mrs. Voland looked relieved to end our conversation.

The president and his wife stepped out of their vehicle with Secret Service men positioned all around. They walked up the steps to the stage and joined the dozens of dignitaries and their guests who had been invited to attend.

Father stood a little straighter as the president walked up to him and shook his hand, thanking him for coming before moving on to the next dignitary and finally making his way to the front of the stage where General Voland stood.

The band finished playing "Hail to the Chief" and began another rousing song to keep everyone's attention occupied until Lindbergh arrived.

A brilliant blue sky stretched over Washington, DC, without a cloud in sight. It was warm, but not overly hot, and a gentle wind fluttered the hem of my dress. I took a deep breath, thinking about where I was standing—my place in history. How different this life was from the other one I led. How strange that tonight I would go to sleep, and tomorrow I would wake up on a British merchant ship, bound for Nassau, surrounded by rough sailors, squealing pigs, endless waves, and sunburn.

As much as I hated the expectations and pressure Father's position brought into my life, I couldn't deny some of the privileges it afforded. Even being in Paris and meeting Ernest Hemingway—though that was more of Irene's doing.

Thinking of that night made my pulse race. I prayed no one would ever know.

A commotion caught my eye as Lindbergh's parade of vehicles approached. Thousands of people followed from the naval yard where he had arrived with his airplane, *The Spirit of St. Louis*, on a battleship. They were on every available surface for as far as I could see. In trees, on the tops of cars and buildings, all of them trying to press closer.

Finally, Lindbergh and his mother exited their vehicle and approached the stage. The crowd went wild with cheers, applause, and shouting. A woman fainted near the front of the crowd, and several people bent down to help her up.

Lindbergh was a tall, handsome, shy fellow. His cheeks were pink with embarrassment as he shook people's hands. His popularity was due, in part, to the innocence he portrayed in a world fraught with gangsters, crime, and danger.

A world my father was trying to reform—and my brothers had embraced.

When Lindbergh came toward us, Father reached out his hand and said, "Hello, Mr. Lindbergh. I'm Reverend Daniel Baldwin."

Lindbergh shook Father's hand and nodded, a congenial smile on his face. "How do you do?"

"I'm from Minneapolis," Father continued quickly, no doubt conscious of all the others who wanted to speak to the aviator.

That caused Lindbergh to pause and take a closer look at Father. "It's nice to see someone from back home. I'm from Little Falls."

"Yes, I know," Father said. "I hope we can talk about you visiting Minneapolis in the near future."

"I would like that."

Father's face beamed. "I am hoping to hold a tent revival and would like for you to speak—"

"I am focusing on promoting aviation," Lindbergh said with a quick nod. "Nothing more. Thank you." He moved on, dismissing Father as he continued to shake hands.

I could see the surprise in Father's face. He was the one who usually dismissed people.

As we all took our seats and the ceremony to award Lindbergh the first ever Distinguished Flying Cross medal began, Father sat silently between Mother and me—his chin lowered in both disappointment and contemplation.

An hour later, we were on our way back to our hotel.

Father was quiet as he stared out the cab window.

Mother and I shared a glance, and Mother finally said, "Things will work out, Daniel. I don't know what you were hoping for when you spoke to Lindbergh, but God has a way of surprising us if it's His will. His plans are better than ours."

Father pulled his gaze back into the car and smiled at Mother. He reached out to her and, in a rare show of affection, patted her hand. "You're right, Marian. I won't lose sight of God's sovereignty. I never do."

His ability to control his emotions, yet keep his dogged determination, amazed me. How could he be so disciplined? So . . . perfect? Day after day, I saw his unwillingness to waver in his calling. It was inspiring—and intimidating. He wholeheartedly believed that every Christian should pursue their calling with the same intensity, and he pushed those around him to be as passionate as him.

Yet, I had no desire to follow in his footsteps. At least, not on such a large scale. Every time he pushed me to do more, be louder, fight harder, all I saw were my inadequacies. I feared I was a disappointment to him and to God. But I tried anyway, and would keep trying, even though the pressure intensified as his international audience grew.

"Lindbergh's wholesome appeal has captured the attention of the world," Father said. "If he were willing to come to Minneapolis and speak at one of my tent revivals, I believe we would see one of the greatest awakenings in our country's history, while strengthening our stance on the benefits of Prohibition. But how to get him to come?" He looked out the window again, and I knew that whatever obstacles stood in his way would not be there for long. Somehow, my father would find a way, and Mother and I would be beside him.

We arrived at the Willard Hotel and went to our separate rooms. Irene had decided to nap, but I couldn't sleep after all the excitement and had pulled a book out of my purse. It was my favorite story, *Gulliver's Travels*, one I'd read countless times and never tired of.

A few minutes after I settled into my book, a knock at our door startled me. When I opened it, I found a bellboy standing in the hallway with a silver tray. Atop it was an envelope.

"A letter for you, Miss Baldwin."

"Thank you." I accepted the letter and gave him a coin for his trouble, then closed the door and took a seat near the window for better light.

The envelope was addressed to me, but there was no return address. The only person who knew I would be in Washington, DC, was my sister-in-law, Ruth.

My heart started to pound hard as I slipped my finger under the envelope flap. Ruth lived in Minneapolis with my oldest brother, Andrew, and their three small children. What was so urgent that she couldn't wait to tell me until I returned home?

I pulled the single paper out of the envelope and scanned the contents, dread filling my chest.

My dearest Caroline,

I'm desperate and do not know where else to turn. You are aware of some of Andrew's choices since his return from the war, but you do not know them all. I have wanted to spare you from the worst of it, but I fear this will not keep. A woman by the name of Alice Pierce has contacted me, claiming she is carrying Andrew's illegitimate child. She is but one of many indiscretions Andrew has had over the course of our marriage, though many of them have been paid to disappear. You may wonder why I stay with Andrew, but I think you know the answer. A divorce would scandalize your father's name, and I love your parents too much to let that happen. This is my burden to bear, and I have taken up the call, though I do falter from time to time.

I don't know if Alice is truly pregnant, or if she is trying to blackmail us. Andrew says she means nothing to him. A dancer at a nightclub from Saint Paul. He is attempting to ignore the situation, but I fear that if we continue to disregard it, she will approach your parents.

I'm imploring you to keep your eye out for Alice, and if you see her, please deflect her. I will continue to work on Andrew to deal with this situation, but you know how stubborn he can be.

Please pray for Andrew. He is not the man I married, nor has our life been what I thought it would be. I naively believed Reverend Baldwin's son would be as God-fearing and honorable as his father. Perhaps he was at one time, but the war changed him. It changed us all.

I long to see you again, dear Caroline. Please know I only share this with you to ask for your help, not your pity.

> *Love,*
> *Ruth*

I crumpled the letter and lowered my head, lifting my feeble prayers to a God I hoped would listen.

Father's calling had not only impacted my life, but it had overflowed into my brothers' lives, as well, though it seemed only Ruth was suffering. She couldn't divorce Andrew for fear of a scandal, so she stayed and put up with the pain.

And for what? To pretend our family was different from all the others.

5

JUNE 12, 1727
FLORIDA COAST

Ruth's letter was still fresh in my mind as I woke up the next morning on the *Adventurer*. My hammock creaked as it swayed gently to the rhythm of the moving ship. My cabinmates came and went at all hours of the day and night, which suited me fine. I wasn't eager to get close to any of them. I kept my distance, did my work, and tried to stay as inconspicuous as possible.

I'd mastered rolling out of the hammock, making sure my binding was still tight and in place. The fabric had become stained with my sweat, and I longed for a bath, but there was none to be had. And now that I smelled like the rest of them, it was probably easier to believe I was a boy.

I had quickly learned when the head was being used and when it was free. Usually, right after a watch ended it was occupied, so I waited another twenty minutes and then used it in privacy. When I was done, I walked through the forecastle and onto the main deck. The chickens were squawking, and the squeal of a piglet told me that someone had misstepped. The cattle were silent but would soon need to be milked. We had been in St. Augustine for the past three days, and the captain had sold some of the livestock, so the goats were no longer bleating on the main deck.

We were now on our way south again with fresh supplies. Florida was a thin line on the starboard side of the ship and would soon be gone from sight.

Nassau was our next stop. I could feel the tension coiling in my belly. What would I say to my mother when I found her? Worse— what if she wasn't there? I tried not to think too far into the future because too many unknowns made me feel anxious.

I was about to open the latch to enter the galley when one of the lookouts from the crow's nest shouted to the captain standing on the quarterdeck, "Ship along the starboard!"

I turned in the direction the lookout pointed as Captain Frisk lifted his spyglass. It was hard to make out the ship, coming from the northwest, but I saw the speck in the distance.

We had passed many ships on the way from Charleston to St. Augustine, so it didn't give anyone alarm. The trade route was littered with hundreds of merchant ships. But they were always on the lookout for pirates. Pirating had been at its peak about ten years ago when Blackbeard was causing terror along the eastern coast in retribution for his pirate friends who were hanged in Boston. But King George had brought an end to the tyrannical pirates, killing Blackbeard and Charles Vane, two of the most notorious pirate captains. He had managed to shift the allegiance of hundreds of others by offering them the King's Pardon. And he had done it all with the help of his navy and a man named Woodes Rogers.

But that didn't mean they were all gone. Piracy was still a serious threat to the merchants traversing these waters, and they were diligent to watch for them.

Harry would be angry if I was late, so I went down the ladder and into the galley at six bells to begin my morning chores.

Breakfast was oatmeal with fresh milk, and since I was the one responsible for milking the cows, I grabbed two buckets and headed down another ladder into the dank hold.

I could smell it before I stepped foot into the chamber. It was the foulest smelling place I'd ever been. Must mingled with manure and the stench of rats.

One of the young sailors, Timothy, was already there with the cows. He tended to the animals, mucking out their stalls and refreshing them with clean hay. He wasn't more than sixteen or seventeen, and he had a pleasant, ruddy face. His blond hair was bleached from the sun, and his blue eyes were crystal clear.

"No fresh milk on the return trip," he said to me with a New England accent as he pitched some of the soiled hay out an opening in the side of the ship. The fresh air that came in through the opening was a godsend. "Enjoy it while we can."

I wasn't even sure I would be on the ship when it came back, so I only nodded. The less I interacted with the rest of the crew, the better.

After I removed the stool from the hook near the first cow, I took a seat and positioned the milk bucket under the cow's udders.

Timothy stopped mucking and rested on the handle of his pitchfork. "Why are you so quiet, Carl? Missing a sweetheart back home?"

Looking away from Timothy, I leaned into the cow and started to milk. "No."

"Something's eating at you," he said. "Every morning, you come down here, I try to make conversation, and all I get from you is a nod, a shrug, or nothing at all."

"I don't have much to say," I told him, though my response was muffled against the side of the cow.

"If you want a friend, here I am." He talked as we worked, sharing various facts about sailing, not needing me to answer.

I finished milking as quickly as I could and then carried the full buckets to the galley, trying not to spill along the way.

After I gave the milk to Harry, I had a few free minutes before it was time to serve breakfast, so I went up to the main deck to get some fresh air.

The activity on the topside had increased. Captain Frisk still had his spyglass trained toward the northwest.

The other ship was much closer.

"Hoist the topsail," he yelled at the sailors on the deck. "It looks like the galleon is trying to overtake us."

"Is she waving the death's-head flag?" one of the sailors asked.

"Not yet," Captain Frisk said, "but that doesn't mean she won't."

I shaded my eyes as I tried to get a better look at the oncoming ship. It was large—much bigger than the *Adventurer*.

My pulse increased as the topsails were unfurled, and the *Adventurer* picked up speed.

"All hands on deck," the captain yelled as he pulled the spyglass from his eye, his voice and face set in stone. "She just raised the black flag."

The activity increased as all the men, even Harry, went to work trying to outrun the pirate ship. I moved to a corner of the deck, trying to stay out of the way.

Captain Frisk called out orders as he kept his spyglass directed at the pirate ship. But it didn't take a spyglass to see that the ship was drawing closer, and there was no way we could outrun her.

After another hour, Captain Frisk came to the same conclusion.

"Drop the mainsail," he yelled to his crew, defeat in the slant of his shoulders. "She has us, boys. All we can do is surrender, or we risk an attack that could leave this ship at the bottom of the sea."

"Who is it?" Timothy asked as he appeared at the rail beside me.

Harry wasn't too far away, so he said, "Looks to be Captain Zale. That old cur has been sailing these waters for two decades, and he's yet to be caught. Either he's the most brilliant pirate in the Atlantic, or he's fearless and not afraid to face the gallows."

"Or he's a ghost," Timothy said. "I heard he disappeared after he got the King's Pardon."

"He did indeed," Harry continued. "Ten years ago, but it was a ploy. As soon as Woodes Rogers left Nassau, Zale was back on the hunt. They say he's still after the Queen's Dowry."

"Queen's Dowry?" Timothy asked. "I thought the pirates gave up on that years ago."

Whatever Harry was about to say was interrupted when the ship in question approached, looming almost twice as large as the *Adventurer*. An ominous black flag with the skull and crossbones flew proudly at the top of her main mast, whipping fiercely in the wind.

"What will happen to us?" I whispered to Harry as my eyes beheld the massive ship.

"Just keep to yourself," he whispered back. "They'll take what they want and then be done with us. As long as Captain Frisk complies, no blood should be shed."

I swallowed and nodded. I knew how to keep to myself.

At least a hundred pirates lined the railing on the other ship, hooting and hollering their victory as some of them began to swing on ropes, landing with a thud on the main deck of the *Adventurer* to tie the two ships together. They were a rowdy, colorful bunch, of different ethnicities and carrying various weapons. Most of them were white, but there were Asians, Black men, and Indians among them. Their clothing was bright and influenced by fabrics from all around the world. Some wore red sashes around their waists, others had red scarves over their heads, and still others were shirtless.

Two imposing men appeared at the rail, both wearing all black, with swords at their sides. They carried themselves differently, with authority and confidence.

"That's Captain Zale." Harry cursed under his breath. "The older one."

"And who's the younger one?" Timothy asked.

"His son, Marcus Zale, the quartermaster of the *Ocean Curse*. That ship has seen more battles than any other, I'd wager."

I had quickly learned that the quartermaster was the second in command and was treated with the same respect and authority—though the captain's say was final.

Both men had long dark hair, which was clubbed at the back and blew in the wind. Captain Zale had a dark beard, while his son was clean-shaven. They were both tall and broad, with focused vision as they surveyed the ship they had just taken without a fight.

I stared at both men, captivated by their presence. Even if I had not known they were pirates, I would have taken notice of them in any situation, at any time.

The son's intense gaze scanned the main deck of the *Adventurer* and landed on me.

I caught my breath and looked down, trying to be small and invisible. After a moment, I looked up again, but he was still staring at me. I tried to step closer to Harry, my heart hammering hard in my chest.

The pirates secured the ship and bound Captain Frisk's hands. Then the large Black man whistled, and Captain Zale and his son grabbed hold of two ropes and swung onto the *Adventurer*. Their long black coats fluttered in the wind, and they landed with a thud on the deck.

"Search the hold and the captain's quarters," Captain Zale ordered his men in a British accent. "Take anything of value."

As some of his men departed to search the ship, Captain Zale and his son climbed up to the quarterdeck where Captain Frisk was bound, his face red with anger.

"What are you transporting?" Captain Zale asked Captain Frisk.

"Nothing of value."

"You lie." Captain Zale sneered. "We can do this the easy way or the hard way."

"I assure you, I'm only transporting livestock and victuals."

"Where are you bound?"

"Nassau."

Captain Zale stepped close to Captain Frisk, towering over him, and said, "If you're lying, you'll rue the day you tried to fool me. My men will burn this ship to the waterline if need be."

For a heartbeat, Captain Frisk stared at the pirate, but then his shoulders stooped, and he said, "You'll find a chest of gold under the trapdoor beneath my bed."

Captain Zale's lip came up in a satisfied snarl. "That's more like it." He yelled to his men, "Get the gold and then let's be gone. Take anything you can carry."

While a handful of pirates stayed on the main deck to keep

the crew of the *Adventurer* in sight, others swarmed the ship and began to haul off anything they could find. Boxes, barrels, and bags of food were taken from the hold.

"I'm looking for crew members," Captain Zale said as he walked down from the quarterdeck, scanning Captain Frisk's sailors. "If you'd like to join my crew, step forward. I run my ship as a democracy, where every man has a vote and a share of the prizes we earn. You will eat like kings and not have to toil for another man's profit. Each of the men you see on my ship were once like you, living under the yoke of oppression. But now they are free."

The sailors I had worked with for the past three weeks said nothing, all of them staring down at the deck. No one was offering to join ranks with a pirate.

Captain Zale waited for a moment and then said, "If that's the way you want it, then I'll choose which of you are coming with us."

I tried desperately not to fidget as he walked among us.

"You," he said as he pulled one of the men forward by the front of his shirt. "And you," he said, pointing at another.

I held my breath as he walked past Timothy.

"You're young and strong and teachable," Captain Zale said as he put his finger against Timothy's chest. "You'll do."

He started to walk again and then stopped in front of me. I looked down at his boots, praying that he wouldn't force me to leave the *Adventurer*. I was so close to Nassau, I could feel the answers to my questions at my fingertips.

"You," he said, putting his fist under my chin and forcing me to look up at him.

I tried not to cower, but I couldn't help it. He was older than I first guessed, with sea-wizened wrinkles around his gray eyes and silver streaking his hair.

"How old are you, boy?" he asked me.

I swallowed and tried to find my voice, but it came out in a strange squeak. "Fourteen."

"We could use another cabin boy," Captain Zale said. "You're coming with me."

I shook my head hard. "Please." I tried desperately to remember the voice I'd been using as Carl Baldwin. "I need to go to Nassau."

Captain Zale growled. "Get on board my ship! I won't tolerate any back talk from you, either."

One of Captain Zale's men grabbed me by the arm. I tried to break free, but there was nowhere to run.

"Don't put up a fight," Harry said to me. "Just begone. Don't give them reason to beat ye."

My eyes widened. Would these men beat me? And what if they found out I was a woman? What else might they do to me?

The binding around my chest felt dangerously close to coming loose, so I stopped struggling and allowed the man to haul me across the deck.

My gaze caught on Marcus Zale. His face was a mask of indifference, though his dark eyes showed a hint of displeasure. He stood by the gangplank that had been pulled out, connecting the two ships. When his father approached, he said something quietly to the older man, but Captain Zale shook his head once and Marcus stood straight, emotionless.

I was dragged past both men and forced to walk the precarious plank into the belly of the pirate's ship.

I wanted to weep but forced myself to steady my emotions.

My mother was farther away than ever.

We entered the ship on the gun deck, just below the main deck. Timothy was ahead of me, and though I hadn't been friendly toward him, I was thankful he was there. At least there was one friendly face among hundreds of untrustworthy pirates.

"Don't be afraid," Timothy said as we were prodded out of the way by pirates loading the plunder they had taken from the *Adventurer*. "If we do what they say, we'll be treated fairly, and we can escape at the first port of call we make."

I swallowed the panic that raced up my throat, wondering why

I had ever thought this was a good idea. No one knew where I was, and there would be no one coming to rescue me. I was at the mercy of a pirate captain.

"Up to the main deck," one of our captors said, pushing us to take the ladder.

When I reached the top deck, I had a view of the *Adventurer* below. Captain Zale and his son were speaking to Captain Frisk, who was still bound. Captain Frisk did not look pleased, and Captain Zale was speaking close to his face, no doubt an intimidation tactic.

"Captain Zale is trying to get information out of Captain Frisk," Timothy said quietly beside me. "He'll be asking if there are any British or Spanish naval ships upon these waters and what merchants we've seen along the way."

I nodded, unable to find my voice.

"The *Ocean Curse* is a galleon," Timothy continued. "It's not the largest ship at sea, but it's one of the fastest of its size. There are two other ships that are larger, but the Spanish and British Royal Navies use those. They're really the only threat against Captain Zale."

"Does that mean he is unstoppable?"

"Nay." Timothy shook his head. "But almost. And from what I can see"—he looked around the main deck where a dozen cannons were positioned, six on either side, ready to fight—"he's modified the *Ocean Curse* and added more cannons. There are at least fifty on board this ship."

"Is that a lot?"

"More than a ship like this usually has."

For another hour, we watched as the pirates moved barrels and boxes of food from the *Adventurer* to the pirate ship. They left the livestock, which meant no more fresh milk and eggs but also no more manure. And when Captain Zale seemed satisfied, he and his son left the *Adventurer* and boarded their ship, allowing his men to pull the gangplank back. The ropes holding the vessels together were cut with long knives and swords, and then the

Adventurer started to float away, my hopes and dreams of seeing my mother going with it.

I swallowed my fears and said to Timothy, "Do you think the pirate ship will go to Nassau?"

He shrugged. "Since the Royal Navy took hold of Nassau again, a lot of pirates stay away."

"But there is a chance?"

"I suppose."

I had to hold on to that chance.

Captain Zale and Marcus climbed the ladder and came to the main deck and were soon joined by all the pirates. There had to be at least two hundred of them, and they were all looking to their captain and quartermaster.

"Good work, men," Captain Zale said. "There'll be an extra dram of rum for each of you tonight."

The men cheered.

"And that goes for the new recruits," he said with a hearty laugh. "Whether you wanted to be here or not, you're one of us now. I think you'll like what you find aboard the *Ocean Curse*. Soon, you'll wonder why you didn't volunteer."

Redness crept into Timothy's already ruddy complexion, and I suspected that he wanted to disagree.

"Once word gets out that we overtook a British merchant ship," Captain Zale continued, "they'll be on the lookout for us. We'll head to Barataria and lay low for a couple of weeks to sell some of our plunder before we return to Florida."

"Barataria?" I whispered to Timothy.

"Near New Orleans," he whispered back.

"Everyone to work." Captain Zale turned away, but then said, "I want the new boy sent to my cabin."

Someone pushed me from behind, and I moved cautiously among the other men. The *Ocean Curse* had a three-story stern with a set of stairs on either side up to the quarterdeck and the captain's cabin.

Captain Zale and Marcus walked up the steps ahead of me, disappearing through a door.

I rubbed my sweating palms on my trousers and tried to still my pounding heart. I just needed to be obedient and not let on that I was a woman. I could make an escape at the first possible opportunity and find another job as a cabin boy on a ship heading to Nassau. I might not get there as soon as I had hoped, but I would get there.

One of the largest of the pirates stood next to the captain's cabin. He was the one who had whistled for the captain and his son to board the *Adventurer* once it was secure. His black eyes followed me as I climbed the steps, and when I was about to open the door, he put his large palm out in front of my face. His black skin glistened with sweat. I looked up at him, trying to hide my fear, but knew I was failing.

"Don't get any brave ideas while you're serving the captain and quartermaster. Do you understand?"

I nodded, though I didn't understand. Did he think I would try to hurt them? What could I do?

"If you don't give me any trouble, I won't give you any trouble," he continued. "Do I make myself clear?"

"Aye, sir."

His seriousness disappeared, and he grinned. "I'm Hawk."

Once again, I nodded, but my nerves were so tight, I couldn't have given a verbal response if I had tried.

Hawk pushed open the captain's door and motioned me through.

I entered a long, narrow room with more cannons. At the end was another door, so I walked to it and tapped lightly.

"Come," said a loud male voice.

With trembling hands, I turned the doorknob.

The captain's cabin was impressive, with whitewashed walls, a large table for meals, and a desk. There were two cushioned chairs and an alcove bed with a red curtain.

Captain Zale sat at the desk while Marcus stood at the diamond-paned window, watching the *Adventurer* as we sailed away from her.

"What's your name, boy?" Captain Zale asked me.

Marcus turned from the window, his penetrating gaze upon me. This close, he looked younger than I had first suspected. Perhaps in his midtwenties. And besides the dark hair and the similar build, the father and son didn't look anything alike. Captain Zale's small eyes were grayish blue, but Marcus had dark brown eyes, filled with both sadness and fire.

"Speak up!" the captain said impatiently.

I jumped, pulled from the quartermaster's intense gaze. "Carl Baldwin."

"Carl Baldwin, you'll be sharing responsibilities with the other cabin boy, Ned. He's been with me for the past two years and knows my preferences. I'm assigning you to assist Marcus."

"I don't need—" Marcus began to protest, but the captain held up his hand and he quieted.

Did Marcus speak with a Scottish brogue?

I frowned, surprised because the captain was clearly British by origin.

"There's enough help in the galley, so you will be at our beck and call." Captain Zale stood, his full height dwarfing the room. "It's high time we acted like the gentlemen we are."

Gentlemen? Were the captain and Marcus truly gentlemen? What had brought them to their pirating ways? Hopefully Timothy knew more. He'd been a well of knowledge I hadn't expected. Perhaps befriending him was a good idea.

"We'll follow the tip around Florida to the Gulf and lay low in Louisiana for a time," Captain Zale explained to me. "In a week or two, we'll head back to the eastern coast to continue our search for the Queen's Dowry. I chose you to serve Marcus, but I also chose you for your size to help with the treasure's recovery. Until then, you'll need to learn our habits, our preferences, and our schedules to best serve us. Do you understand?"

I nodded, trying to remember everything he was saying. All I wanted was to escape with Timothy in Louisiana.

"You will sleep in Marcus's cabin," he continued, "so you can be available at all hours of the night, should you be needed."

"It isn't necessary," Marcus tried to protest again.

Captain Zale took a deep breath and then fixed his hard gaze on his son. "I will not be questioned."

Marcus's jaw tightened, and he turned to the window once again.

"You will find Marcus's cabin directly above mine," Captain Zale continued. "It needs to be scrubbed and his bedding washed."

I nodded, thankful for a job that would keep me busy, though the thought of sleeping in the same cabin as the quartermaster made me tremble all over again.

The day passed quickly as I scrubbed Marcus's cabin. It was smaller than the captain's, but no less comfortable or impressive. The walls were not white, but natural wood, darkened with time. An alcove bed was built into one of the walls, with a red curtain for privacy. A smaller table with four chairs was in the center of the room, and two cushioned chairs, much like the captain's, were in the corner. I would have a cot in the opposite corner of the room, farthest from Marcus's bed.

But what surprised me the most was his bookshelf filled with books. There were books on every subject, including science, philosophy, theology, and more. Not to mention fictional books, as well. I perused some of the titles as I dusted and saw several of my favorites. *Don Quixote*, *Paradise Lost*, *The Pilgrim's Progress*, and even *Romeo and Juliet*. I also found *Gulliver's Travels*, which had only been published the year before.

Either Marcus Zale was a reader, or this ship had been stolen and the books belonged to someone else.

I had taken two short breaks to serve dinner and supper in the captain's cabin with the other cabin boy, Ned, at noon and six. After the men had been served, Ned and I were allowed a break to eat our own meals. Ned was quiet and aloof, but I didn't give him much attention.

The sun had fallen, and I was back in Marcus's cabin putting his clean bedding on his bed. The sheet and blankets had dried in the Caribbean sun and smelled fresh.

I had lit a lantern, but it was cloudy from soot and cast shadows across the room, not providing much light. Tomorrow I would need to remember to clean the chimney.

All day long, I had been thinking about ways Timothy and I could escape, but until we were on land again, I would have to cooperate and bide my time.

As I was spreading the blanket over the bed, the door opened, causing me to jump.

It was the first time Marcus had entered his room since I arrived. I quickly finished and climbed out of his bed, my cheeks warming at being caught in his intimate space.

He was standing near the door, watching me, that same brooding expression in his dark eyes. It made me aware of everything. My clothing, my hair, my stench.

"Are you finished?" he asked.

I nodded and then stepped farther away from his bed. "Just now. Is it to your liking?"

His gaze took in the room. The cobwebs and dust were gone, and the floor had been scrubbed. "Aye. It doesn't look like it did this morning. Well done."

"Thank you." My voice was small.

He nodded at the cot in the corner and asked, "Will it do?"

"Aye."

"Good."

We both stood for an awkward moment, and then I said, "Is there anything else I can do for you?"

He sighed deeply. "My father expects you to wait on me like a valet."

A valet? I didn't even know what a valet did.

"But I won't ask it of you," he said, his Scottish brogue puzzling me again. It was rich and deep. "You can turn in, if you'd like. You worked hard today."

A rush of relief washed over me. All day long I had been fretting that I would be required to do more than clean and serve, but Marcus Zale surprised me. His dark, foreboding persona had made me assume he was unkind and harsh. But in the little time we'd spent together, he had been neither.

I sat on the cot and slowly took off my buckled shoes, but that was all I would remove.

Slowly, I pulled back the top cover and crawled under it.

Marcus began to disrobe, taking off his sword first, then his long black coat and his cravat. His clothing was well made, if a little worn.

I quickly turned to face the wall, my cheeks growing warm. I'd never seen a man in any state of undress until I saw the pirates without shirts on today.

And I'd never been alone in a room with a half-dressed man.

"You won't disrobe?" he asked me.

"Nay," I said quickly, my voice higher than I intended. I cleared my throat and said more calmly, "I prefer to sleep in my clothes."

There was a gentle chuckle, and then the light went out.

I could hear him climb into his bed and settle under his covers. There was a sigh and then silence.

I closed my eyes and went to sleep, thankful I would have one day in 1927 before I had to come back to the pirate ship and look into the fiery eyes of Marcus Zale again.

A thought that both terrified and intrigued me.

6

JUNE 28, 1927
MINNEAPOLIS, MINNESOTA

Everything looked lush and green as we walked up to our home
on Dupont Avenue in the Lowry Hill neighborhood of Minneapolis. Our three-story Victorian home was nestled among other
beautiful houses on the tree-lined street. It sat on a little rise from
the sidewalk and was painted a cheerful yellow with white trim.

A welcome respite after months of travel.

"It feels good to be home," Mother said as Father slipped the
key into the front door, and they shared a smile.

We'd been gone for almost three months and had made a quick
stop in Des Moines to return Irene to her mother before continu-
ing to Minneapolis.

Some of the neighborhood children had left their afternoon play
to see what all the fuss was about as the taxicab driver hauled our
luggage into the house. I waved at several of my piano students,
and they giggled as they ran away. I couldn't wait to welcome them
back into the house and hear their sweet attempts at making music.
Before singing in the Dingo Bar, it was the one pleasure that music
brought into my life.

The sounds of the neighborhood drowned out the echoes of

my own concerns, making me forget, for a moment, my troubles in both 1727 and 1927. I'd been on the *Ocean Curse* for over two weeks already, and we had yet to stop at a single port of call. For sixteen days, I had served Marcus Zale and his father, scrubbed every square inch of their cabins, and washed all their bedding and clothing. I'd always assumed pirates were unclean, but Captain Zale had a penchant for finery and etiquette that surprised me. He ran his ship with precision, and he expected perfection from his crew. He appeared to have the money for good food and drinks and was happy to share it with his men—including me. To my surprise, when everyone lined up for their weekly pay, I had been given a share, which I had quickly stored away under the mattress of my cot.

But it was my close proximity to Marcus, both day and night, that consumed my thoughts when I was on the *Ocean Curse* and when I was away. The men respected and admired him because he was calm and levelheaded, in stark contrast to his father. When Marcus spoke, the men listened—and I listened. He was well-educated and intelligent, and I often saw him with a book in hand when he had spare time. He was currently reading a book by Aristotle, and it made me wonder about his past. At what age had he joined his father on the *Ocean Curse*? I had so many questions, and the more time I spent with him, the more I wondered.

But now was not the time to ponder Marcus Zale. Today I needed to focus on the tasks ahead of me in 1927, and all I wanted to do was speak to Ruth. To find out if Alice Pierce had disappeared, or if she was still a threat to my family.

The air inside our house was stale, but it was still good to be back. Dark woodwork graced the wainscoting, doors, windows, stairway, and fireplaces. Wood pillars flanked the entrance into the parlor to the left and the grand stairway ahead of us. To the back of the house, the kitchen was the only truly modern room, though the two bathrooms had been updated recently.

This was the house I had grown up in, and it was like an anchor for my weary soul. In this home, my life felt normal. No one was

watching, judging, or expecting perfection. My home on Dupont
Avenue represented what I wanted most—to live a quiet, meaning-
ful life with those I loved. No arranged marriages, microphones,
or critical audiences.

"I will be in my study if you need me," Father said as he left us
in the foyer and walked into his study adjacent to the main hall.

Mother sighed as she took off her hat and set it on the hall table
with her purse. "There is much to be done before we can rest." She
lifted a stack of mail that had been collected by a neighbor boy
and sifted through it. "This is for you." She handed me an envelope
that was on the top. "It's postmarked from France."

I frowned. Who could be writing to me from France?

"I'll phone Ruth and tell her we're back," I said to Mother as
I turned the envelope over to inspect it.

"Thank you, dear. Tell her that she should bring the grandchildren by tomorrow."

"I will."

The house was warm as I walked through the parlor and into
the dining room where the telephone hung on the wall. With a
frown, I opened the envelope, surprised at the bold, slanted script
I found within. But it was the brief message, dated May 22, 1927,
that shocked me to my core.

*Dear Miss Reed . . . or should I say, Miss Baldwin? I like
finding new talent. It's a gift that should be shared with the
world. A war buddy of mine owns the Coliseum Ballroom
in Saint Paul, and he's always looking for good singers. I'm
sending him a letter of introduction on your behalf. When
you get this letter, take my advice and see him. The sooner
the better. Prove to him I'm not a liar and I met the most
talented young woman he'll ever hear. I've included his name
and address at the bottom of this page.*

Your ardent admirer,
Ernest Hemingway

My lips parted as I stared at Mr. Hemingway's letter. He'd known who I was after all, and he'd taken the time to write to me!

"Be sure to let Ruth know that she and Andrew are invited to Father's first live broadcast on Sunday night," Mother said as she entered the dining room with the stack of mail.

I quickly lowered Mr. Hemingway's letter to my side, hoping she couldn't see his writing.

Mother paused and glanced at the letter. "I hope it's not bad news," she said. "You're white as a sheet."

My heart was pounding so hard, I was afraid she'd hear it. "No—not bad news."

Mother stared at me for a second and then continued through the dining room toward the kitchen. She was never one to pry into her children's personal affairs. Sometimes, I wondered if she didn't pry because she was afraid of what she might find.

"As soon as you're through with your call to Ruth," she said from the kitchen, "I'll need you to run to the grocer's. We have nothing in the house for supper."

I refolded Mr. Hemingway's letter and slipped it back into the envelope. I should destroy it, but I didn't want to. I was trying to think of where I'd keep it when the front doorbell rang.

Mother poked her head out of the kitchen. "Will you get that, please? I'm making the shopping list for the grocer."

Nodding, I slipped Mr. Hemingway's letter into my pocket. His suggestion to sing at the Coliseum Ballroom was ridiculous. It was a notorious speakeasy, so notorious that even I knew about it. I wouldn't sing for his friend, but I'd keep his letter as a reminder of meeting him.

The foyer door opened into a little vestibule, which was handy in the winter months to trap the cold air. Since the front door had a long glass window in it, I was able to see a young woman standing on the porch. She was attractive and stylish, with a burgundy dress and a black cloche cap over her blonde bob. But it was the small suitcase she held that made me the most curious.

Her emotions were hard to read as I offered her a smile and opened the door. "May I help you?"

She looked beyond me into the foyer and then met my gaze. "Is this the residence of Reverend Daniel Baldwin?"

My instincts immediately came to life as I gripped the doorknob. Very few young women came looking for my father. "Yes. May I help you?" I asked again.

She blinked several times, and a single tear slid down her cheek. "I need to speak to Reverend Baldwin. It's urgent."

The hair on the back of my neck stood on end as I realized who this might be. "And who may I ask is calling?"

"I'd prefer to meet with the reverend, if I may." She wiped the single tear aside with her white-gloved hand. Her behavior would have been believable enough to convince me if I hadn't been prepared for her.

I didn't want to alienate this woman if she wasn't Alice Pierce— but I needed to hold my ground if she was. "I don't let anyone speak to my father unless I have a name."

"Caroline?" Mother asked as she entered the foyer with a gentle smile.

The young lady took an eager step forward when she saw Mother. "Mrs. Baldwin?"

"Yes," Mother said. "How may I help you, dear?"

More tears fell down the young lady's cheeks as she bit her trembling bottom lip. "I'm in the worst sort of trouble, and I've heard that you and Reverend Baldwin are the kindest souls on earth. You're my last hope. May I speak with you?"

Panic robbed me of speech for a second as I took a step between my mother and the woman. "I'm sorry," I said, anxious for her to leave. "I don't believe we can help you."

The young woman's expression changed from desperation to determination in the blink of an eye—yet it was almost indiscernible. There for a moment and then gone the next.

"Caroline," Mother said as she put her hand on my arm to move me to the side. "The Lord says in the book of Matthew,

'Verily I say unto you, Inasmuch as ye did it not to one of the least of these, ye did it not to me.' It is our Christian duty to help those in need. I'm surprised at you." Mother tenderly pushed me to the side and held her hand out to the young lady. "Come inside, dear. We'll get a nice cup of tea and see what we can do to help you."

"May I speak to the reverend?" she asked. "I would like spiritual guidance as well as practical advice."

Mother patted her hand. "Of course, my dear."

Desperation squeezed the air from my lungs. I hadn't even been home for thirty minutes, and I had already failed Ruth. Had this woman been watching our house? Waiting for us to return?

Soon, Mother and Father would know the truth about Andrew, and it would destroy them. What would Father do? He prided himself on always being honest, but how could he be honest with his congregants about his children when one of them was an adulterer, among other things?

I didn't know what to do. I couldn't kick this woman out of the house without raising suspicions. I couldn't confront her with the truth in front of my parents.

Mother stopped at Father's office door, poked her head inside to ask him to join them, and then took the woman to the parlor and offered her a seat.

I followed, and my father entered a few moments later.

"Reverend Baldwin," the woman said, swallowing as she rose to greet him. "It's an honor to meet you."

"Please." He motioned to the sofa where she'd been sitting with Mother. "Have a seat."

"Caroline," Mother asked, "will you start the tea?"

I didn't want to leave them, but Mother would think I was rude not to help.

With a quick nod, I left the parlor and walked toward the kitchen, keeping an ear on the conversation.

"Now," Father said, "tell us your name and why you've come."

"My name is Alice Pierce," she said.

It was Alice! I stayed near the door to listen, not caring about the tea.

"And why have you come, Miss Pierce?" Mother asked.

"Please, call me Alice. I—" She paused and then started over. "I'm in a desperate situation."

"You mentioned that," Mother said. "What kind of situation?"

"I'm with child." Alice began to sob—I could hear it all the way in the kitchen.

As Mother tried to calm the young woman, I quickly filled a teakettle with water, lit the gas stove, set it to boil, and then returned to the parlor to find Mother's arm around Alice.

Father had a very stern look upon his face—the kind of look he had when he was processing something weighty.

"And why did you come to us?" Father asked. "Why not your own parents?"

Alice lifted her face and dabbed at the tears on her cheeks with a handkerchief. "My parents are both dead. I live on my own and work for a living."

"And what of the father?"

I held my breath. Would she blame Andrew?

Alice glanced at me, standing in the doorway, then looked at my father. "He's married, but I didn't know he was married when I met him. He led me to believe he loved me and was going to marry me." She buried her face in her hands. "I'm so ashamed."

"There, there," Mother said, patting her back. "That's how they all do it, dear. It's like leading a lamb to slaughter."

Father continued to frown in contemplation.

"I didn't mean to lose my virtue," Alice added. "But he was so charming. When I told him I was pregnant, he admitted he was married and said he had his own children to look after."

Mother studied Father with deep concern. "How awful, Daniel. Can you even imagine a person like that?"

"Do you have a home?" Father asked her.

"No." She shook her head as she indicated her suitcase. "I was renting an apartment in Saint Paul and working at—at a diner. But when my boss heard that I was going to have a child, I was fired, and I didn't have enough money to make my rent. I was forced out of my home today, and that's why I came here, out of desperation."

"Well, don't worry," Mother said, squeezing Alice's shoulder. "We'll let you stay here for the time being until we can get you back on your feet. Isn't that right, Daniel? It's the least we can do."

I stepped forward, ready to stop this nonsense, but Father was nodding—and whenever he made a decision, he stuck to it. "I think that's the best course of action for now. Miss Pierce may use the guest room until we can find employment for her and a place to live."

"Oh, thank you," Alice cried in appreciation. She hugged Mother and looked like she might stand to give Father a hug, but he crossed his arms and made it plain that he wouldn't allow her to touch him.

"You're very welcome, dear," Mother said. "Now, let's see about that tea, and then we'll show you to your room."

Alice wiped her cheeks as Mother rose from the sofa and helped her to her feet. She kept her arm around Alice's shoulders as they walked past me.

"Father," I said, taking a step forward.

"Judge not, lest ye be judged," Father said as he, too, rose from his seat. "We'll find the man responsible for this situation and force him to make it right."

As he walked out of the parlor to return to his study, one question kept replaying in my head.

Why hadn't Alice told my parents that Andrew was responsible for her pregnancy?

That evening, I sat in the parlor with my parents listening to the nightly news on the radio. Alice had gone to bed right after supper, claiming to have a headache. Until then, I had been watching her closely, expecting her to tell my parents the truth, but she kept the information to herself. I wanted to tell her that I knew her secret, but she hadn't given me the opportunity. She stuck close to Mother all day.

The soft glow from the floor lamps above Father's and Mother's heads made the room feel safe, cocooned. Closed off from the outside world, except for the radio against the wall. I had been longing for this moment for months—but with Alice upstairs, I couldn't relax or enjoy being home.

Father had his Bible open on his lap but was staring at the floor as he listened to the news. Mother had her knitting needles in hand, and they were clacking a steady rhythm as she, too, listened.

I had been trying to read *Gulliver's Travels*, but I was too restless, wondering when it would be appropriate for me to go upstairs and confront Alice. Even my favorite book couldn't distract me from her presence.

"In other news," the broadcaster said on the radio, "today the Guggenheim Fund for the Promotion of Aeronautics announced that Charles A. Lindbergh will undertake a Goodwill Tour of the United States. The tour will commence on July 20th in New York where Lindbergh left on his historic trans-Atlantic flight in May."

Father sat upright, his Bible nearly falling out of his lap. He'd been trying to contact Lindbergh since we'd met him in Washington, DC, but hadn't heard back from the aviator.

"Over the course of ninety-five days," the broadcaster continued, "Lindbergh will visit eighty-two cities and twenty-three state capitals. At each stop, he will give a brief speech and participate in a parade. One of his stops will hold special significance when he visits his hometown in Little Falls, Minnesota. It's said that the town of just five thousand people will host the greatest celebration in its history, with their hometown hero as the guest of honor."

The broadcaster continued with the next news story, but Father turned down the radio and looked at Mother. "If Lindbergh is going to Little Falls, he could easily stop here first."

"They'll probably want him to go to Saint Paul," Mother said with a scathing look—something she only reserved for Minneapolis's twin city and greatest rival.

"But that's why we must attract him to Minneapolis." I could see the wheels of Father's mind working already. "I will call the mayor tomorrow, and we will host an emergency meeting of the community leaders. We'll make an offer to the Guggenheim Fund that they can't refuse."

Mother set down her knitting needles. "Do you think it will work?"

His smile was wide as he said, "It's almost too good to be true, Marian. The people will come to see the flier, and then we'll encourage them to stay and attend the largest tent revival meeting this country has ever seen."

"But Lindbergh said he wouldn't speak at your revival," Mother reminded him.

Father waved away her concern. "I don't need him to speak. I just need him to come to Minneapolis."

The front doorbell rang, making me jump. "I'll get it," I said, hoping it wasn't another one of Andrew's conquests.

But when I opened the door, I was surprised to find an old family friend. "Lewis."

He was dressed in a fine suit and holding his fedora in his hands. I hadn't seen him since Christmas. Somehow, he looked more dapper and confident than ever before.

"Hello, Curly Carrie."

And apparently still fond of the nickname I had despised as a teen, received once he found out my synthetic curls were the result of magic wave curlers.

"You know I hate that name."

He grinned and winked at me. "That's why I use it."

With a sigh I said, "Won't you come in?" I moved aside and opened the door wider, knowing I couldn't shut it in his face. "My parents will be happy to see you."

He paused for a moment, his face growing serious, as if he was going to speak, but then he nodded and stepped into the foyer.

I had known Lewis most of my life. He was my brother Thomas's best friend and had grown up down the block. They had both wanted to be policemen since they were young and were now employed with the Saint Paul Police Department.

But that begged the question, had Lewis become as corrupt as my brother Thomas? I had heard rumors about Thomas's work with the Saint Paul Police from Ruth, though I didn't know if any of them were true. I hoped and prayed they weren't.

"Lewis!" Mother said as soon as we walked into the parlor. "What a wonderful surprise."

"Hello, Mrs. Baldwin. Reverend Baldwin."

"Come in," Father said to Lewis, just as eager as Mother. We didn't see him as often as we had when he and Thomas were younger, but he still came by on occasion.

"I can't stay long," he said as he glanced at me. He was tall and muscular, nothing like the skinny kid he had been in high school. "I was in the neighborhood and thought I'd see if you folks made it home safe from your trip."

"Just this afternoon," Mother said as she patted the sofa. "Have a seat."

He moved across the room and sat next to Mother, offering her a smile. She took his hand in her own and squeezed it as she looked at him.

For years, he had been a fixture around our house, almost like another brother. Teasing me incessantly and bothering me to no end. At the age of twenty-four, I hoped his teasing days were behind him, but I wasn't holding my breath.

"How did you like Europe?" Lewis asked, though he looked in my direction again.

"It was grand," Mother said, letting go of his hand. "And did you hear that Reverend Baldwin will be giving a weekly international broadcast?"

"I did," Lewis said. "I hope to listen in each Sunday night, sir."

Father nodded his approval. "It would honor me if you attended the broadcast, Lewis."

Lewis's face lit up, and he nodded. "I will indeed."

They spoke for some time about our trip, and Lewis told us what he had been doing since we saw him last winter.

"Do you have a special girl yet?" Mother asked, her eyes shining.

Lewis, who had never been shy one day in his life, suddenly looked a little uncomfortable as he played with his fedora. He glanced up and met my gaze and then said, "Not yet."

"Well, she'll be one fortunate young lady when you find her," Mother said.

After a few more minutes, Lewis stood and said he needed to head home.

"I'll walk you out," I told him as I also stood to leave the room.

His smile was so sweet, it surprised me. Where was my childhood bully?

We walked into the foyer, and Lewis held the door open for me to step out onto the front porch.

The sun had set, and the stars were sparkling above the trees. Lights were on in the homes on our street, and the yards were quiet as all the children had been tucked in for the night.

"Thank you for stopping in," I told Lewis. "This has been a surprisingly pleasant evening."

He laughed, but there was a little hurt in his gaze. "What's that supposed to mean?"

"You know what it means. I used to dread when you came over. You teased me incessantly."

"I didn't tease you incessantly."

"You did!"

He shook his head, his infectious smile making his face light up. "If I teased you, it was only to get your attention."

"My attention?" I frowned. "By making my life miserable?"

He turned his fedora uncomfortably in his hands. "Did I really make your life miserable?"

"Yes," I said, but I laughed. "It's okay, Lewis. I've forgiven you and moved on. I'm sure I was a pesky younger sister and you and Thomas were just trying to get rid of me."

"No." He shook his head, and then he took a deep breath, his hat becoming still. "I teased you because I liked you, Carrie."

I stared at him for a moment, confused. "What do you mean?"

"I had a crush on you," he said, his voice growing gentle.

"A crush?" I pressed my lips together, trying not to giggle, knowing he was still teasing me. "If you did, that was a funny way of showing it. I despised you, Lewis."

Something painful crossed his face, but he quickly covered it with a chuckle of his own as he put his hat on his head. He started to walk away. "I guess I don't blame you. I'd probably feel the same way if someone treated me so poorly."

I felt bad for giggling, even if he was teasing, so I reached out and put my hand on his arm. "Please don't be upset at me."

He stopped and looked down at my hand before laying his over mine. "I could never be upset at you, Curly Carrie." He winked. "Goodnight."

I pulled my hand away, feeling horrible, though I wasn't sure why. "Goodnight, Lewis."

As I stood on the porch, I watched him walk down the steps and toward his waiting car. He started it and then waved at me before he pulled away into the night.

7

JUNE 29, 1727
GULF OF MEXICO

The setting sun was hotter than ever as I tossed the dirty water over the side of the ship, still thinking about Lewis's visit from the night before. There was something different about him, something I couldn't put my finger on. A change, though it was subtle. I'd spent the morning thinking about it as I scrubbed the floor in the captain's cabin, and then the afternoon as I'd scrubbed Marcus's cabin floor. I should have been strategizing my plan to get Alice to leave, or looking for a way to escape the *Ocean Curse*, but all I could think about was Lewis.

"The crew is starting to whisper," Timothy said as he came up next to me at the railing and leaned against it.

The Gulf of Mexico spread out before us in an endless sea of blue water. Nothing broke the monotony of it except the passing clouds overhead. And today, there wasn't one in sight. The air was thick with humidity, making my skin sticky and wet, and my patience thin.

Timothy had been a good friend since we'd joined the *Ocean Curse*, finding me in moments like this, usually to talk about our escape. Though sometimes he just wanted to gossip.

I'd discovered a lot about the captain and his crew through Timothy. Most of the men were rough and frightening. The less I interacted with them, the better, so Timothy's insights were helpful.

"What are they whispering about?" I asked as I returned the empty wash bucket to my side, glancing out of the corner of my eye to make sure no was watching or listening.

Sweat dripped down my back, making my binding itch more than ever. Not for the first time since running away from Middleburg Plantation, I wanted a bath in the worst sort of way. I didn't care if I fit in better being filthy. My hair itched, my body smelled, and I could hardly rest at night from the layer of grime on my skin. It only added to my irritation.

"Some are starting to think there's a Jonah on board."

"A Jonah?" I frowned, staring at my friend. I'd discovered that his father had been a mariner and he had learned most of his seafaring knowledge at his father's knee. "What is that?"

"It's when someone on board is making the entire ship unlucky. Like Jonah, from the Bible, who was running away from God. A great storm came upon the ship he was on, and the sailors threw Jonah off the ship to stop the storm. Soon, Jonah was swallowed by a big fish."

"I know the story of Jonah," I said, familiar with the biblical account. "But why do they think there is someone like that on board?"

"Since we haven't come across any merchant ships in days and the wind has been stagnant and we're not making any progress to Barataria, they're suspecting there is a Jonah aboard."

"Who can be a Jonah?"

"It's usually a clergyman, who is from the line of Jonah the prophet." Timothy shrugged, saying nonchalantly, "It could also be a woman or a witch."

My mouth parted at the last two options, and my irritation fled, replaced by fear.

"They're saying if a Jonah is on board, it'll only get worse until they can uncover him and throw him into the ocean."

Panic tightened my chest as I stared at him. Was he serious?

He began to laugh and shook his head. "It's just superstition, Carl. No need to look so stricken. There's no witch or woman on this ship—though, I suspect there might be a clergyman in hiding." He turned to look at the ragtag crew of pirates with a suspicious, if teasing, eye.

"I need to get supper served," I told him as I swallowed and moved away from the rail. I hadn't once suspected that Timothy knew I was a woman, but I didn't want him to look any closer than necessary.

"Be on the lookout for a Jonah," he said with a chuckle. "You never know who might be a secret clergyman."

I tried to give him a smile, but it fell flat. Now more than ever, I wanted answers from my mother, but those answers were farther and farther away as we floated listlessly in the Gulf of Mexico in the hot, stagnant air.

The supper bell chimed, so I set down the bucket and went to the galley. It was bigger and cleaner than the one on the *Adventurer*. The cook was French and didn't speak much English. Timothy said that he had been taken captive, too, because the captain wanted only the best. But the cook seemed happy enough, and I couldn't ask him if it was true or not.

Ned was already in the galley, eager to prove himself to the captain. Ever since I had arrived, he had seemed jealous of my presence and tried to outdo me every chance he could get.

The cook handed over the platters of roasted beef, stewed peas, boiled turtle, and fresh bread. We carried them across the main deck and up the flight of stairs where Hawk was waiting to open the door. Though he was one of the biggest men I'd ever met, I'd soon learned he was also the jolliest—when not in battle. And since we hadn't come across another ship since the *Adventurer*, I hadn't seen him wield his strength or height since then.

Hawk followed us into the outer room as he opened the captain's door.

Captain Zale was sitting at the table, a glass of wine in hand as he listened to his navigator. The boatswain, who was the supervisor of the deck crew, was also at the table. The surgeon was there, as well, though I had gathered he was also here against his will. He'd been abducted in Charleston three years ago, and every time he tried to escape, he was hauled back to the ship at the captain's command. Dr. Hartville was irreplaceable, or so Timothy told me. The only person who could treat whatever ailed the captain, though I saw no physical signs of disease.

Marcus was also at the table and looked up at our arrival. My pulse quickened, and my palms grew clammy. I couldn't account for my nervousness around him. I saw other crew members stand a little straighter in his presence, and Timothy was so afraid of him, he went in the opposite direction when he saw Marcus approach. But Marcus had not been demanding or threatening to me. On the contrary, he'd been polite and kind.

Perhaps it was his contemplative silence that set me on edge. He often spoke, but when he was silent, people steered clear of him. There was something stormy and ominous about his silence. He often stood at the window or the rail and stared at the ocean as if he was searching for answers.

And that was how he looked at me.

I had never wondered what another person was thinking as much as I wondered about Marcus Zale. Ever since the *Ocean Curse* had pulled up alongside the *Adventurer* and his gaze had caught mine, he had been aware of me. He was watching me, seeking answers.

Did he suspect I was a woman?

Ned and I silently served the evening meal as the men continued to talk around the table.

"I don't think it's necessary to go all the way to Barataria," the navigator, Jack Tanner, said to the captain. Jack was a younger man, perhaps in his early thirties, with a thick British accent. He had a refined air about him that suggested he'd been raised with money and privilege. How had he ended up on a pirate ship? "'Tis already been two and a half weeks since we overtook the

Adventurer. If we head back now, it'll be another two weeks, at least—provided this blasted weather improves. By then, the authorities will have given up the chase. That is, if they were looking for us in the first place."

Captain Zale leaned forward, his gaze intent on Jack's face.

I set the platter of beef in front of him and the turtle next to it. Ned put down the stewed peas and the fresh bread. The aroma made my stomach growl.

Marcus was the only one who glanced up at me when I set the food on the table. He nodded his thanks.

"I've heard the *Atlantis* has also been looking for the Queen's Dowry," Jack continued. "We can't waste a minute."

I'd quickly realized the Queen's Dowry was Captain Zale's greatest goal. Timothy told me that in 1715, two Spanish treasure fleets had left Cuba later than planned and been caught in a hurricane off the coast of Florida. Eleven of the twelve ships were sunk, and over fifteen hundred men had lost their lives. The resulting treasure hunt had brought ex-privateers from all parts of the world to the Florida coast. They'd uncovered coins, jewels, gold, and silver. But after the initial recovery, most people had lost interest.

Not Captain Zale—or the pirate ship the *Atlantis*, apparently. Captain Zale, like many others, still believed the greatest treasure of all was the dowry that was being brought to Elisabeth Farnese, the Duchess of Parma, who was King Philip V's second wife. The dowry reportedly included more than twelve hundred pieces of jewelry, a gold heart made of over one hundred pearls, fourteen-carat pearl earrings, and an emerald ring weighing seventy-four carats. It was supposedly on the flagship, the *Capitana*, which had never been found.

"You're advising we turn around?" Captain Zale asked.

I watched Marcus as the men discussed their plans. He listened quietly, as if weighing their options.

If we turned around, I couldn't escape in Barataria—but I'd be much closer to Nassau. If we met another ship, perhaps I could sneak away. Or, if we visited a port along the eastern shores of

Florida, I could escape and wait for a ship that was heading farther south.

Marcus's gaze lifted to mine, as if he knew what I was thinking.

The meal continued as the men discussed their options. Dr. Hartville was a silent observer, much like Marcus, but, unlike Marcus, he
seemed more intent on filling his belly with the fine food and drink.

When the men were satisfied, Ned and I took the leftovers. I
went to the cabin I shared with Marcus, and Ned went to his cot
in the outer room where he and Hawk bedded down.

I loved the privacy and solitude that Marcus's cabin provided.
Not only that, but the captain and quartermaster shared their own
privy, which none of the other crew members had access to, and I
was allowed to use it. I no longer had to worry about being caught,
or to hide my female necessities. Being abducted off the *Adventurer*
hadn't been my desire, but at least there were advantages.

Marcus's cabin was dimly lit, though I had cleaned the chimney
on the lantern. A soft glow warmed the room as the evening stars
started to shine outside the windows. It was hot and humid in the
room, but at least I was alone and could enjoy a bit of solitude. I
also had a perfect view of the water and had seen dolphins playing
around the stern on many occasions.

Now, however, the water was still. The air was still. And there
was no evidence of life outside the windows.

I sat at the table with my supper, my thoughts turning to tomorrow and the confrontation I would have with Alice. I needed to get
her out of the house before Ruth arrived with her children and she
learned I had let Alice sleep under my parents' roof.

The door creaked open, and I turned quickly.

Marcus stood in the open doorway.

I swallowed the cold bit of beef, though I hadn't chewed it properly. It hurt as it slid down my throat, causing my eyes to water.

Marcus walked into his cabin and slowly closed the door behind
him. His black breeches, black cotton shirt, black boots, and the
cutlass at his side were imposing, but his height and the breadth
of his shoulders filled the cabin until it felt like I couldn't breathe.

He usually didn't come in until a little later, closer to bedtime. Had he come to retrieve something? Perhaps one of the many books he kept on the shelf?

I stood from the table, my hands a little shaky. "Do you need something?"

"Continue your meal," he instructed.

Swallowing my nerves, I resumed my seat, but my appetite had vanished.

I stared down at my plate, trying to force myself to take a bite of my food, but I just pushed it around with my fork.

He went to the shelf and stood, looking at his books, but made no move to retrieve one. The tension in my stomach tightened like a rope, and the silence turned deafening.

"I heard you tell the captain that you need to go to Nassau," he said, his voice low, as he kept his back toward me. "When you were still on the *Adventurer*."

"Aye." I swallowed, hating that my pulse was galloping. "To find my mother."

He turned to me then, his dark eyes studying me in the dim light. He was handsome, though not classically so like some men. It was his countenance—the way he held himself, the intelligent and probing look in his eyes—his very presence that was attractive. It demanded attention. There was no other way to say it. I couldn't look away, even if I wanted to. He was both frightening and intriguing.

"Where did you come from?" he asked.

"Charleston."

"Why is your mother in Nassau?"

Something compelled me to tell him the truth. I couldn't hold it back, even if I had wanted to—and I didn't. "She ran away with a merchant sailor when she was just thirteen. Less than a year later, she took me to my grandfather in South Carolina and then disappeared again. I need to find her."

"If she left, mayhap she doesn't want to be found."

"Even by her d—" My heart pounded. I'd almost said daughter. "Her child?"

"Mayhap you're the one she wants to hide from."

His words sliced right to my heart, stealing the air from my lungs. It was my greatest fear, one I'd never voiced, and it had been spoken from the lips of a pirate. I stared down at my unappetizing food, forcing the tears to stay in place. I couldn't cry, not in front of Marcus Zale or anyone else.

"I didn't mean to hurt you." His voice was low, apologetic, his brogue deepening. When I didn't respond, he asked, "Why do you think she's in Nassau?"

I swallowed my emotions and lifted my chin. "She left me a letter. Why would she leave me a letter if she didn't want me to know where she was?"

"Did you just find the letter?"

Nodding, I said, "It was hidden in a wall in her room."

It was his turn not to respond. Did the knowledge that she'd hidden the letter from me confirm that she didn't want me to know where she was—or had she simply hoped I wouldn't know until I was old enough to go to her?

A brush of wind rocked the *Ocean Curse* for the first time in days.

Marcus walked to the window near my cot.

In the distance, on the southwestern horizon, a wall of clouds darkened the evening sky. Lightning jumped inside the oncoming storm as another gust of wind pushed at the ship.

"Will we be safe?" I asked.

"Aye. Safe enough."

Even though we were floating on the open water and an ominous wall of clouds was pushing its way toward us, something in his voice was soothing. Reassuring. He'd probably seen countless storms from this very window.

"Did you run away from home, like your mam?" he asked, his back toward me again.

There was no space in this room for guile or pretense. Something about Marcus made me want to be honest. "Aye."

"Is your grandfather still alive?"

"Aye."

He finally turned to me, leaning against the window ledge, his arms crossed.

We were closer now. I could see the lamplight flicker in his brown eyes. His gaze seemed to penetrate mine as he said, "And he doesn't know where you are?"

Shame made my cheeks burn. "No."

"And you have no one to search for you."

It wasn't a question, but a statement.

We stared at each other, and though I should have lowered my gaze, something compelled me to watch him. I felt like I was being put to a test—though I didn't know the stakes—and I was afraid I might fail.

"Do you want to stay on the *Ocean Curse*?"

I should have immediately shaken my head, but my traitorous heart seemed to have a mind of its own. Just because Marcus Zale intrigued me, it wasn't a good reason to stay captive on a pirate ship.

"No," I said. "I want to find my mother."

The storm clouds were moving quickly toward us, and the wind had picked up. The ship began to move again.

"No one should be held against their will."

My heart twisted with hope, and my mouth parted. Would he allow me to leave?

"When the opportunity arises," he said, "I'll help you escape. But I don't want you to go from one bad situation to another. I'll keep my eyes open for the right time."

Tears threatened again, and I had to look away from him as I said, in a quiet, broken voice, "Truly?"

"Aye. The captain is willful and stubborn. He has no care for other people's freedom and only has one thing in mind."

"The Queen's Dowry?"

"Aye," he said again, this time with irritation tinging his Scottish brogue. "For twelve long years, every decision he's made has been with the treasure in mind. He hopes to leave pirating and become a gentleman one day, but he can't do it unless he has the treasure. That's why he chose you. You're small and can fit into a diving bell to look for the treasure at the bottom of the ocean. But 'tis a dangerous job, and I don't want you to do it. You cannot let him know I'm helping you escape."

I was a lowly cabin boy, and Marcus Zale was the quartermaster of a massive pirate ship. He didn't owe me an explanation or a promise to help me, but he was offering both.

Could I trust him?

My life experience in both timelines had taught me that almost everyone had an ulterior motive—even if it was a selfless one. Why did he want to help me?

He left the window and took a seat across from me at the table.

The glass panes rattled under the force of the wind, matching the sudden trembling of my nerves as I sat up straighter. It was one thing when he was at a distance or I was serving him, but now, with him staring at me across the table, just a few feet separating us, I felt vulnerable and exposed under his scrutiny.

He had clearly come into his cabin with a purpose tonight.

"How old are you?" he asked.

My nerves were so upended, I couldn't remember—not even my real age.

The ship creaked as it moved through the water, and he waited for my answer.

"Fourteen," I whispered.

For the first time, I saw a glint of humor in his gaze. It changed his entire demeanor, softening him and making him feel like my equal. "I'd wager you're older than fourteen."

Sweat beaded on my forehead. I wanted to run out of the room—away from his probing eyes and undivided attention. His handsome gaze and demanding presence. But there was nowhere to run on a ship, and it would only cause more questions.

I stilled my nerves and decided not to answer him directly, but with my own question. "Why would I lie about my age?"

"Mayhap to hide the fact that you're not a boy at all."

His sentence hung between us like a cannon suspended in air. He stared at me, waiting for me to respond. But I couldn't. I was speechless with both surprise and fear.

"How old are you, lass?" he asked, his voice low and gentle.

I swallowed, knowing it was pointless to deny it. I had always been at his mercy, but I felt especially so now. "Twenty."

"Does anyone else know that you're a woman?" he asked me. I shook my head slowly. "How do *you* know?"

The humor returned to his gaze, and his mouth relaxed. "Your movements caught my eye on that first day from up above the *Adventurer*. I couldn't be certain, but I've been watching you closely ever since. You don't undress in front of anyone, you wait for the head when no one else is occupying it, and you serve a table like a woman trained in etiquette and deportment."

"I was on the *Adventurer* for weeks and no one said anything."

"You do a good job hiding the truth," he said. "I knew I was taking a risk in asking you, because I wasn't completely sure—but now that I know, 'tis impossible not to see."

"What will you do about it?"

A slight frown tilted his brow, as if it was obvious. "I'll protect you."

Warmth burst through my chest at that simple statement, and heat climbed up my cheeks. I hadn't felt protected since I'd left the security of Middelburg Plantation—and even then, Grandfather would rather marry me off to the highest bidder than guard my heart.

"What's your real name?" he asked next.

"Caroline," I whispered.

My name seemed to soften him further, and the first gentle smile tilted his lips. "Caroline." He said my name like it was poetry or a song, something beautiful to reflect upon and admire. "And your last name?"

"Reed."

"Caroline Reed." He studied me in the flickering lamplight, as if he were trying to imagine me in finery and not the soiled and smelly clothes of a cabin boy.

I felt self-conscious about my appearance, especially under his scrutiny, and began to fidget. I longed for a bath, sweet-smelling soap, clean undergarments, and a dress. Though I loved the freedom in trousers, I missed feeling feminine and attractive. Especially now, with his intense eyes upon me.

I lowered my gaze, my cheeks warming further.

"And you did all of this to meet your mam?" he asked.

I nodded.

"I admire your dedication and courage, Caroline Reed." His brogue deepened with sincerity. "I will help you find her."

"Why?"

He lifted his chin. "Because despite what you may think of me, I'm an honorable man."

I stopped fidgeting as shame coursed through me—yet, why would I assume he was honorable? I'd met him when I was taken captive by his father. I had every right to assume the worst. Unless he proved himself different, which was what he was trying to do.

He stood and went back to the window, staring at the oncoming storm. When he turned to me, he said, "You can't tell anyone else that you are a woman."

"I won't."

"They're a superstitious lot and would send you overboard, but not before—" He paused.

My cheeks burned with the implication of his silence.

He swallowed and looked out the window again. "'Tis best that you stick close to my cabin until I can find a way to get you free. Do your duties, when required, so as not to draw unwanted attention, but don't interact with the others if it isn't necessary."

"I won't."

Silence filled the cabin again as I waited for him to continue. When he finally moved away from the window, he said, "I'll be needed on the main deck for this storm, but you should stay here."

There was nothing left for me to say, so I remained quiet.

He reached for the knob on his cabin door but turned back to me. "Is there anything you need?"

I thought of a whole list of things I needed—like a bath and a comb and a fresh change of clothes—but I shook my head instead.

"You're doing a fine job, lass. Living at sea is one of the hardest jobs there is." He didn't give me time to respond before he left his cabin.

I stared at the closed door for several minutes after he was gone, wondering if my secret was safe with Marcus Zale.

And realizing I had no choice but to trust him.

8

JUNE 29, 1927
MINNEAPOLIS, MINNESOTA

I had gone to sleep with the storm blowing the ship over rolling waves, and I woke up to a storm slashing against the windows of our house on Dupont Avenue. Lightning filled the dark sky, and thunder shook the earth.

My room was cheerful despite the storm, with soft white curtains, floral wallpaper, and white trim. A white canopy bed offered more delicate fabric to the room, and a plush rug softened the hardwood floors. For a moment, I savored the comfortable bed and my clean skin and hair.

But thoughts of Marcus filled my mind. Now that I knew he was aware of my identity, everything was different.

I pushed aside my covers, not wanting to think too deeply about the captain's son. I wanted to trust him, to believe that he would help me escape, but I couldn't be certain. Was he just trying to get me to trust him so he could sabotage me? I wasn't sure what he would gain from it, but there might be something in it for him.

Only time would tell—and I had a lot of that.

As soon as I forced thoughts of Marcus from my mind, he was replaced with thoughts of Alice. I needed to get her out of our house before Ruth and her children arrived.

I quickly changed into a green dress with a dropped waistline, a pleated skirt, and a scooped neckline. Since I wore a hairnet to sleep at night, my marcel waves were still intact and I only had to touch them up a bit to make them presentable.

My hair reminded me of Lewis's visit the night before and the dreaded nickname he'd given me when I was fourteen. I wouldn't believe him when he said he teased me because he had a crush on me. He had liked to make me look foolish when we were younger, and if I started to believe him now, it would only increase my foolishness.

I finished my toilette and left my room, pushing Lewis out of my mind, too.

The guest bedroom door was slightly ajar, so I peeked inside and found that Alice was gone. Alarm filled me as I rushed down the stairs. I didn't want Alice to have access to my parents without my presence.

Since the storm had passed, the sun was now peeking from behind the clouds. Water dripped from the eaves, and the birds chirped outside. As I came to the bottom of the steps, the doorbell rang.

Ruth stood on the porch with her three small children—a big grin on her face—and my heart fell. I hadn't realized she'd be here so soon. I glanced toward the dining room where Alice was probably waiting for breakfast.

How was I going to tell Ruth that Alice was staying with us?

My nephews saw me, and they also grinned as I opened the vestibule door. Peter was five and John was just three. Little Sarah was in her mother's arms. She'd had her first birthday while we were away and had grown so much since I'd last seen her.

I forced a smile and opened the front door.

"Auntie Carrie!" the boys said as they ran toward me.

"Hello, sweethearts," I told them, giving each a big hug.

Ruth looked exhausted. She was only twenty-nine, but she looked much older. Her skirt was wrinkled, no doubt from holding Sarah on her lap in the streetcar, her hair was disheveled, and she had dark circles under her eyes. Yet—she smiled at me and offered me a hug with her free arm. "Welcome home. I hope we're not too early. The children couldn't wait to see their grandparents and aunt."

I returned her hug, whispering in her ear, "Alice is here."

Ruth's arm tightened, and she held me longer than necessary. When she pulled back, I saw panic in her gaze. Panic and questions.

I didn't want the children to hear or repeat something they shouldn't, so I simply said, "She arrived soon after we got home yesterday, and I couldn't stop her. Mother and Father offered her a place to stay."

Ruth's face paled, and she whispered, "Do they know who she is? How she claims to be connected to Andrew?"

I shook my head as I heard Mother approach.

"Are those my grandchildren?" Mother crouched in the foyer and put out her arms for Peter and John. They raced toward her, giggling with glee.

Alice appeared in the parlor doorway. She looked rested and refreshed in a floral-patterned dress, her hair in place, her porcelain skin without a flaw. She was a beautiful woman, a little younger than Ruth—but she didn't carry the same burdens my sister-in-law carried.

"You've grown so much," Mother said to the children, oohing and aahing over their suits and their haircuts.

Ruth stared at Alice, and Alice stared back. She clearly knew who Ruth was, and she looked just as pleased with herself as she had before. Perhaps even more so now.

But what was she after? Money? Attention? Fame? Or did she simply want to destroy our family?

"And Sarah," Mother said, oblivious to the tension that had entered with Ruth and the children. She reached for the baby, but Sarah seemed shy and scared. It had been a few months since we saw her last, and she buried her face in her mother's shoulder.

"That's alright," Mother said as she placed her hand on Sarah's back. "She'll warm up to me soon. Won't you all come in for breakfast?"

"Oh no." Ruth quickly shook her head. "We—we can't stay."

"But, Mama," Peter said. "You told us we could play at Grandmother's."

Ruth put her protective hand on Peter's shoulder, clutching Sarah on her hip. She swallowed and said, "I'm sorry, Petey. I forgot we have an appointment this morning."

"Must you go?" Mother asked Ruth. "I haven't seen the children in months. And Father hasn't had a chance to see them yet, either."

"I'm sorry, Mother Baldwin," Ruth said, starting to back away. "We can't stay."

"Oh, but you haven't met our guest yet," Mother said in an attempt to stall her. "Ruth, this is Miss Pierce. And Miss Pierce, this is our daughter-in-law, Mrs. Andrew Baldwin."

"How do you do?" Alice asked Ruth, showing no sign of discomfort.

Ruth nodded but couldn't speak or meet Alice's unwavering gaze.

Mother frowned. Ruth had always been unfailingly kind and thoughtful.

Right now, she looked like she might faint.

"I'm sorry, but I really must go. We'll return soon," Ruth promised, though I knew she wouldn't come back if Alice was in the house.

"Goodbye," Mother said, a bit forlorn.

"Come, John," Ruth said to her son, who was standing by his grandmother's side.

John frowned and shook his head. "I want to stay at Grandmother's."

For the first time, I saw Ruth lose her temper. "Obey me this instant," she said to her son in a sharp voice.

John's brown eyes grew wide, and he scurried across the foyer to his mother's side.

Ruth didn't apologize to us, and she didn't say goodbye as she turned and fled the house.

Mother stood at the door, staring at Ruth's retreating form, her brow troubled. "I wonder what could be bothering her?"

I felt sick to my stomach as I turned toward Alice.

She simply looked away.

I tried calling Ruth several times that morning, but she didn't answer her phone. No doubt she felt betrayed by me, and perhaps even my parents, though they didn't know Alice's identity.

Before lunch, Alice went up to her room for a nap, and I followed her a few minutes later. Father had left the house to meet with the mayor regarding Lindbergh's visit, and my mother was in the kitchen with our hired girl, Ingrid, planning the week's menu.

I tapped on Alice's bedroom door and waited, trying to steady my nerves. Anger had radiated through me since Ruth left. My dear, sweet sister-in-law didn't deserve this. Not from Andrew, not from Alice, and not from me.

Alice opened the door, only partway, and said, "Yes?"

"I know who you are."

"Of course you do. I knew that from the moment I met you. No doubt the mousy little Ruth warned you about me."

"Don't speak about my sister-in-law that way." I was trying to keep my voice low, but it rose with anger. "I want you to leave this house immediately."

"How will you make me?" Alice asked, putting her hands on her hips. "By telling your parents who I am? It'll only hurt them to know the truth."

"I don't even know what the truth is. You're probably not even pregnant."

A glimmer of fear or unease filled Alice's eyes, and she said, "I am pregnant."

I paused. It was the first time I had seen anything real or authentic in her. She was afraid of being single and pregnant. But who did she have to blame? Surely my brother hadn't tricked her into this. They were both at fault. Unless . . . "Is my brother even the father?"

Alice's chin lifted as she glowered at me. "If I say he is, then he is. Now beat it, Miss High and Mighty. I'm sure you have a few skeletons in your closet that you don't want aired. It wouldn't take me long to find them, either. So, you stay on your side of the house, and I'll stay on mine, and we'll get along just fine."

"I don't know what you want from my parents, but I'm begging you not to hurt them." I didn't care if I had to grovel in front of her. "And don't hurt Ruth, either. She's the sweetest person in the world. Andrew doesn't deserve her. It's not her fault that her husband—"

"You just leave my affairs to me, you understand?" Her gaze was filled with ice. "Then I can leave yours to you, and we all get what we want."

I wasn't even going to pretend like I wasn't hiding anything. It would be a lie to defend myself. "What do you want?"

Again her defenses slipped, and I saw behind her mask, if only for a moment. "I want, for once in my life, to not be the victim. To have control of my own destiny."

And with that, she closed the door in my face.

I stared at the wood panel for a heartbeat, wondering at her comment.

The rest of the afternoon dragged on as I tried getting ahold of Ruth. I called a few of my music students to let them know I was resuming lessons, and then I spent an hour practicing on the piano in our parlor. It had been months since I'd played, and my fingers ached, but my heart was strengthened. When I played for myself, music was a healing balm.

My mind returned to Mr. Hemingway's letter, tucked safely away in my correspondence box, and the joy I had felt singing in the Dingo Bar in Paris. His idea was ludicrous. I couldn't sing at a speakeasy in Saint Paul. But I couldn't bring myself to destroy the name and address of the proprietor, either.

"Caroline?" Father asked, interrupting me as I played Chopin.

I stopped abruptly, my heart pounding from the music and the intensity of my thoughts.

"Yes?"

"It's almost four."

Nodding, I closed the cover over the keyboard and turned on the stool. Father had organized an emergency meeting with the mayor of Minneapolis and several other leaders to petition Lindbergh to stop in the city on his tour. They would arrive at four.

"I'm wondering if you'll sing a hymn at the start of my broadcast on Sunday evening."

I blinked several times. The weight of his request felt like a boulder in my gut. "Your international broadcast?"

"Yes."

I couldn't say no. He wouldn't understand if I didn't want to perform for so many people. In his mind, the bigger the audience, the better. More people to reach for the gospel of Christ. Of course he was right—but it also meant the bigger the audience, the more opportunity to disappoint.

"If you'd like me to sing, I will," I told him, trying not to show my nerves. I wanted him to believe I was as confident as him.

"Good." He smiled. "I thought we'd start with 'Amazing Grace,' since that seems to be a universal favorite. If it goes well and the station director is pleased, we'll discuss what you'll sing next week." He started to turn away and then said, "See that Alice doesn't come downstairs while we're meeting. I'd hate to have to explain her presence in our house. You understand?"

I understood, but I wasn't sure that Father did. If he really knew who Alice was, he'd be more concerned.

"It's not that I'm embarrassed," he said quickly, "or ashamed that we're helping her. I just want to focus on the meeting about Lindbergh."

"I understand."

He left me in the parlor by myself, still a little stunned that I would be singing on the radio.

The doorbell rang, and I rose from my stool to welcome Father's guests.

As I opened the vestibule door, I was surprised to find Lewis standing on the porch in his police uniform. A blue coat, buckled at the waist over blue trousers, and a military-style hat with his badge number at the front. I had never seen him in uniform.

It made me pause as I realized how much he had matured.

Yet, when he grinned, he was the same old Lewis.

"What are you doing back here?" I asked as I opened the front door.

"What kind of a welcome is that, Miss Baldwin?"

I lifted an eyebrow. "As long as you call me Miss Baldwin—or even Caroline—I'll be very welcoming."

His blue eyes twinkled with mischief. "Then I'll refrain from calling you—"

"Don't," I protested.

His smile was wide. "Can't I even finish?"

"No. But I am curious why you're here."

"Your father invited me to the meeting."

I frowned. "But he's trying to keep Saint Paul out of it."

With a nonchalant shrug, Lewis entered our foyer. "Something about keeping your friends close and your enemies closer."

"You're not an enemy."

"According to you," he said, getting a little closer than usual, "I haven't been much of a friend, either."

My pulse sped at his nearness, and my breath stilled—but then he tapped the tip of my nose like he used to when we were children, and I realized he was still teasing me.

I lowered my eyelids and scowled at him, which only made him laugh.

But something else caught his attention.

Alice stood at the top of the steps, her smile wide. She walked down the stairs, letting her hand trail gently on the railing.

Lewis didn't let his gaze wander from Alice but said to me, "Are you going to introduce me to your friend, Carrie?"

"She's not my friend," I said, irritated for reasons I couldn't identify. I needed to get Alice upstairs or out of the house before someone else saw her and asked questions.

"Then who is she?" he asked, even though Alice could hear him.

"I'm Miss Alice Pierce," she said, extending her hand dramatically, like an actress in a movie. "And who are you, Mr. Police Officer?"

He grinned, smitten, as he took her hand. "Lieutenant Lewis Cager, at your service."

"Alice and I were just leaving," I said to Lewis as I grabbed my purse from the hall table. "Father is in his office."

"We were leaving?" Alice asked.

I moved between them and took Alice's arm, drawing her out of the foyer.

"Goodbye, Lewis," I called.

His laughter filled the foyer behind me as I led Alice into the kitchen, toward the back door.

"That was rude," Alice said as she pulled away from me.

"We have to go to the baker and the butcher for Mama."

Alice walked beside me, but her stiff posture changed, and she began to laugh. "You're jealous! Is Lewis your sweetheart?"

"No."

"Maybe not yet, but deep down inside, you want him to be."

Her accusation was ridiculous.

Lewis Cager was my childhood tormentor. Nothing more.

Or so I used to think.

9

JUNE 30, 1727
KEY WEST, FLORIDA

I woke up to an empty cabin and a bright blue sky the next morning. Thoughts of Lewis's visit and Alice's assumption turned in my mind. When the breakfast bell rang, I left the cabin and headed toward the galley. Throughout the stormy night, the ship had trekked toward the east, and now we were near the island of Key West. Captain Zale had ordered the anchor to be lowered and a launch to be sent to the island for fresh water. Timothy had told me, upon passing the Florida Keys the first time, that a well had been dug there by pirates and was open to one and all to use, though no one occupied the island.

"Oatmeal, bacon, and fresh bread," Ned said as I entered the galley. He had already picked up all three platters, and they were resting precariously in his hands and on his left arm.

"Let me help," I told him.

"I have them." He moved past me, irritation in his voice.

I sighed and grabbed the pitcher of ale. Since fresh water was scarce and unsafe to drink, rum, ale, and wine were necessary evils. The rum and wine were diluted by clean water at the start of a voyage, and the alcohol kept them free from spoiling. Each man was rationed a gallon a day, which meant that some of them were drunk from sunup to sundown. That was one of the many reasons that milk was such a treat at sea.

I raced to keep up with Ned. "You don't have to prove anything to me."

He lifted his chin. "I'm proving to the captain that you were unnecessary. I can manage on my own."

I wanted to roll my eyes at his stubbornness.

Hawk opened the door for us, as usual, and followed us in.

When Captain Zale looked up and saw Ned trying to balance three platters, while I only held the pitcher of ale, he squinted at me. "Why aren't you helping Ned?"

"He was late," Ned said as he set the bread down. "I couldn't wait for him any longer."

"I wasn't—"

"Avoiding your chores, are you?" the captain asked me with a scowl.

"I wasn't late—" I tried again, but Marcus shook his head to indicate that I should stop protesting.

"See that you're not late again," Captain Zale said. "Or you'll have me to answer to."

I dutifully filled each man's cup, starting with the captain and moving around the table past Hawk, Dr. Hartville, Jack, and then Marcus, trying not to serve like a woman. When I neared Marcus, I was conscious of my smell, but even more so of his presence and what he knew about me.

My hand shook as I poured his drink, and he glanced up at me, a hint of a smile in the depths of his eyes.

"Have we decided on our course?" Marcus asked as he looked away from me and back to his father.

I finished pouring his drink and then stood back, waiting to assist.

Ned stood next to me, his shoulders stiff and his chin high. He couldn't be more than seventeen or eighteen and was a pleasant-looking young man with strawberry-blond hair and bright blue eyes. But when he scowled, his entire demeanor changed.

"I think we should head back to eastern Florida," Jack inter-jected before Captain Zale could respond.

"I think it's too soon," Captain Zale said. "After we get the fresh water, we can stay out to sea for several more weeks, if needs be."

"What about going to Barataria?" Dr. Hartville asked, almost too eager.

"The storm pushed us so far east, it doesn't pay to head back in that direction," Captain Zale said as he took a bite of his thick oatmeal. "There are other places to sell our goods."

"What about Nassau?" Marcus asked casually.

I startled, and my attention shifted to the captain.

"Nassau?" Captain Zale asked, giving his son a strange look. "We haven't been to Nassau in years. The Royal Navy has it too heavily guarded."

"There are still ways to get in," Marcus said, eating his oatmeal as if it didn't matter either way to him—though I knew he was doing this for me, and it did matter. "The people there are hungry for the goods we have in our hold, and they'll pay a high price for them. We can lay anchor in one of the outer islands and send two or three men into town to let our old contacts know we're there to do business."

Captain Zale frowned as he thought about the prospect, then he finally shook his head. "I don't like the idea. The Royal Navy patrols those waters closely. 'Tis not worth the risk when we can sell our goods in other places." He kept shaking his head. "I'd rather try Havana."

I didn't want to show my disappointment. There had to be a way to get to Nassau, and if Marcus was really on my side, I would find a way sooner than later.

After breakfast, Marcus rose from the table and approached Ned and me. "I'd like warm water brought up to my cabin for a bath."

"Right away, sir," Ned said, though he would complain later and tell me he wasn't Marcus's cabin boy to be ordered about.

"No need to rush," Marcus said. "After your breakfast is fine."

He left the captain's cabin, following the other men. The captain and Marcus took regular baths, a luxury that had surprised me when I first boarded the ship. It meant more work for Ned and me, but I didn't begrudge their luxury, and it passed the time.

Ned and I took a seat at the table, and we began our breakfast with their leftovers. I didn't bother to take my food to Marcus's cabin after breakfast or lunch, since I had chores to do. It was only the evening meal that I ate there.

"A bath he wants," Ned scoffed as he shoveled oatmeal into his mouth with a chunk of bread. "Someday I'll be the captain or the quartermaster and I'll get me own bath, whenever I want. And I won't be toting the water, either."

I didn't care about Ned's plans. All I wanted was to speak to Marcus and see if he had any other ideas for getting me to Nassau.

As soon as we finished our breakfast, we brought the empty platters and pitcher to the galley where we cleaned them. The cook could understand enough English to get by, so when Ned told him we needed hot water for the quartermaster's bath, he went to work.

As I washed the breakfast dishes, Ned hauled the bathtub from the captain's outer room up to Marcus's cabin. By the time he returned, the water was hot enough to start hauling it, two buckets at a time, from the galley to the cabin on the third floor.

The sun was hot on my shoulders as I moved under the weight of the buckets. Sweat ran down my back and into my binding. It trickled past my temples and made my scalp itch.

Marcus was on the quarterdeck with Jack, looking over a map, while Captain Zale was speaking to Hawk. The launch team had not returned with fresh water, so we remained anchored. But it appeared that the men were still trying to decide which way to go next. I hoped Marcus was advocating for Nassau.

For thirty minutes, Ned and I carried water back and forth until the tub was finally full.

Marcus was in his cabin when we brought the last buckets in.

Ned and I poured first one bucket and then the next. Steam rose in a tantalizing swirl from the tub as we finished.

"Take the buckets," Marcus said to Ned as he removed them from my hand. "I require Carl's assistance."

Ned grabbed the two extra buckets and was about to leave when Marcus said, "And have the cook warm more water to clean my clothes. Set it outside my door for Carl when he's done helping me."

With a nod, Ned exited the cabin without a backward glance, closing the door behind him.

My heart pounded hard as my defenses rose. What kind of assistance could I give him? Unless . . .

Panic made me move toward the door as Marcus went to the chest where he kept his clothing and other personal items.

"You needn't fear, lass," he said quietly, evenly, without looking at me. "The bath isn't for me."

My hand paused on the doorknob.

"You can borrow some of my older clothes while you wash and dry yours, and you can stay close to the cabin today, so no one sees you." He turned from his chest with a bar of soap, a comb, and a pile of clean clothes, his Scottish brogue rolling off his tongue like velvet to my ears. "You're a wee thing, and I fear you'll drown in my clothes, but 'tis the best we can do for now."

I swallowed the rush of emotions that clogged my throat. "Why are you being so kind to me?"

He stood on the opposite side of the tub, tall, broad, and strong—though his hands were full of a sweet offering. He slowly set the things down on the nearby table. And when he faced me again, he said, "I can't free you like I want, not yet. But you don't need to feel like a captive—at least, not with me. I'd treat you like a guest, if I could, but I can't draw attention to you. 'Tis a risk to let you bathe and clean your clothes, since the others will notice, but I know how it feels to be dirty, and no one should have to feel that way if they don't want to."

My throat felt tight, and tears came to my eyes. I couldn't help it. I blinked hard to keep them at bay, but one escaped and rolled down my grimy cheek.

It was the first tear I'd shed since I was very young.

"Don't cry, Caroline." His voice was almost pleading. "'Tis just a bath."

I shook my head and wiped away my stubborn tear. "'Tis not just a bath. 'Tis a gift."

My tear seemed to undo something within him. He swallowed and looked around at the items he'd gathered, as if he didn't quite know what to do with himself. He moved the comb and fidgeted with the soap, and I wondered if he was trying to find the right words to express his own emotions. Finally, he cleared his throat and said, "Don't let the water get cold. I'll watch the door to make sure you're not bothered. Take your time."

With that, he was gone, and I let myself cry. My tears were almost as cleansing as the bath.

But I heeded his warning, and I didn't let a moment pass before I started to undress, tears and all.

I stripped down until all I was wearing was the binding around my chest. I loosened it and took a deep breath for the first time in over a month, feeling freedom as it slipped to the floor. But I didn't linger. I untied the ribbon holding back my hair and then grabbed the bar of soap and climbed into the tub.

With a moan, I submerged my body, relishing the sensation as the hot salt water eased my sore muscles. Though I bathed frequently in 1927, a full body bath was a luxury here, and I enjoyed every blissful moment, always aware that Marcus was just outside the door.

As much as I wanted to savor the bath, I cleaned my body as quickly as I could, lathering and rinsing my shoulder-length hair twice, not knowing when I might have another opportunity.

When I stepped out of the water, my skin was pink from the heat and smelled of the gentle fragrance of the soap.

I smelled like Marcus.

After squeezing all the excess water out of my hair, I dried off with the towel Marcus had provided and started to dress.

It was strange to step inside his clothing, intimate in a way that nothing had ever been before. The breeches and shirt were twice my size, which made me smile. I found a section of rope to secure them, but instead of stopping at my calves, where they settled on Marcus, the hems rested on my ankles. The shirt was impossible to tuck in, since it went down to my knees, but I did my best. I had known he was much bigger than me, but until now, I hadn't realized how much.

My bare feet were poking out from the bottom of the breeches, but he hadn't thought to give me stockings. I didn't want to put on my buckled shoes without them, knowing how dirty they were, as well, so I kept my feet bare as I tried to comb out my hair.

Despite the silky soap, the salt water was not kind to my thick hair, and it took some work to get the comb through it. I wanted to dry it fully before I put it in the ribbon again, so I left it loose around my shoulder. Then I picked up my dirty clothes and the bath items.

A knock at the door startled me.

"Are you dressed?" Marcus asked in a voice just above a whisper. "I'll bring in the clean water to rinse your clothing."

I wasn't prepared to see him like this, yet I had little choice. "I'm dressed."

But only barely.

He slowly opened the door, and then paused before entering.

I clutched my dirty clothes to my chest, trying in vain to not look so vulnerable.

His dark eyes took in my bare feet, the large trousers cinched at my waist, the oversized shirt—his shirt—and my unbound hair before his gaze found mine.

Not for the first time, Marcus Zale took my breath away. It was the look in his eyes—stormy and tender, yet defenseless and powerful all at the same time.

I sensed danger, but not from him—from myself.

My attraction for Marcus was intensifying, and I hadn't realized how much until this moment as I stood before him in his clothes, after he'd given me a priceless gift.

"Your hair is bonny."

"Thank you." I lowered my gaze, afraid my flaming cheeks would give away my growing feelings for him.

He left the cabin and returned with the smaller tub of water before closing the door. "You can wash your clothes in the bathwater and then rinse them in the clean water." He set down the tub and went to his chest and pulled out a section of rope. "I'll string this up in here so you can dry your clothes without anyone the wiser."

"What if someone asks for me?"

"I'll tell them you're not feeling well. No one likes to be sick, so they'll leave you be."

I had no time to lose, so I dropped my clothes into the bathtub and rolled up my shirtsleeves, then I began to scrub the binding with the soap I had used to bathe.

It felt good to be clean and to have someone who cared enough to look after my comfort. As I scrubbed my clothing, I began to hum. I couldn't help it.

"'Tis a bonnie sound," Marcus said after a moment.

I paused, my cheeks warming at his praise. I hadn't realized I was humming loud enough for him to notice.

"Please don't stop," he said. "'Tis the nicest thing I've heard in a long while."

I felt self-conscious, but if it pleased him, I would continue.

As we both worked, I glanced in his direction and saw a gentle smile on his face while he secured the rope to a nail on the wall.

My own smile tilted my lips.

When he finished, he seemed reluctant to leave and busied himself by returning his comb to his chest and hanging the towel I'd used to dry off. I rinsed the binding and the shirt I had just finished washing. As I hung the binding, I was self-conscious again, hoping he didn't guess what it was for.

"Do you also sing?" he asked.

I turned and found him watching me.

"Aye."

"'Tis a shame you can't sing here on the ship."

"Even if I could, I'm not sure I would sing for the others. I don't like to sing for a large audience."

He nodded, as if he understood. "Even if you only sing for an Audience of One, 'tis a joy for God to hear what He's created."

My hands stilled as his words struck something deep within me. Not only because he mentioned God, but because I'd never thought of singing for an Audience of One. Did it please God to hear me sing? I had only ever thought that I was somehow disappointing Him. I'd never considered that He might take joy in my voice simply because He created it. And wasn't His opinion all that mattered?

I was still pondering this when Marcus walked to the bookshelf and asked, "Do you enjoy reading?"

"Aye." I couldn't hide the pleasure in my simple answer, nor the knowledge that he didn't seem to want to leave. "'Tis a luxury."

Marcus smiled at my response. "Read whichever books you'd like."

My pulse sped up at the thought. "You wouldn't mind?"

"Nay. I like knowing that someone else is enjoying them."

"Have you read all of them?"

"Aye. Two or three times over."

"Which is your favorite?"

He examined the shelf and shook his head. "'Tis too hard to pick a favorite. Some are weighty tomes on religion and politics, some are scientific or philosophical." He pulled one from the shelf and set it on the table near me. "And some are just for pleasure. Start with this one."

It was *Gulliver's Travels*.

My lips parted in surprise as I looked up at him.

"You've read it?" he asked.

"Aye, many times over, but I'd love to read it again."

"Mayhap we can discuss it later."

I nodded, unable to find the words.

He finally left his cabin since he was needed on the quarterdeck.

As the morning passed, and I waited for my clothes to dry, I sat on my cot and picked up where I'd left off in *Gulliver's Travels*, unaware of the passing time.

The storm had brought with it cooler air and carried some of the humidity away. I relished my clean body and the softness of Marcus's cotton shirt against my bare skin. It was a rare day of idleness, which was good for both my body and soul. At lunchtime, there was a knock at the door, and when I opened it, I found Marcus holding a plate of food for me.

I took it with a glad heart.

"Are you enjoying the adventure again?" he asked me as he nodded at the book lying open on the table.

"Aye." I grinned. "I'll be done before nightfall."

His smile was so sweet and eager, I felt almost giddy thinking about him joining me that evening to discuss the book.

When my clothes were dry, I slipped out of the borrowed ones I was wearing and refastened the tight binding, then put on the clothes that fit me properly, buttoning up the vest to cover any vestiges of my femininity. My hair was dry, so I secured it with a ribbon and then put on my stockings and shoes.

The supper bell was soon ringing, though I dared not leave the cabin unless Marcus felt it was safe to do so. Would he bring me a meal again? I waited, but there was no sign of him.

I had finished *Gulliver's Travels*, so I put it back on the shelf and lit the lamp before perusing the other titles. I was surprised to find a Holy Bible among them.

I pulled the book from the shelf, curious to discover it was well worn. Marcus's mention of God had stayed with me, creating more questions about him and his past.

As I thumbed through the Bible, I thought about the countless sermons I'd heard my father preach. I believed the things he taught, believed the Bible was the Holy Word of God. I just didn't know whether God wanted anything to do with me. No matter how good I was, or how many times I asked forgiveness for the sins I committed, I was still bound to two lives. I prayed daily that God would release me from the curse—because it was the only thing I knew to call it—yet, He had not taken the burden from me.

My heart felt heavy as I flipped to the front cover where someone had listed births, deaths, and baptismal records with dates that went back to the mid-1600s. But who were these people? The surname at the top of the list was MacDougal. Scottish.

Was this Marcus's family Bible?

The final name entered was Maxwell MacDougal, December 27, 1700.

There was a light knock, and then the door opened before I could put the Bible back on the shelf.

Marcus stood in the doorway, balancing two plates in one hand and two mugs in the other. His gaze slipped over me again, though this time I looked as I had before my bath, only cleaner.

"I hope you don't mind," I said as I quickly closed the Bible and put it back on the shelf.

He entered the cabin and closed the door with his foot before setting the plates on the table. "Nay. I said to read whichever you prefer. Come and eat."

I joined him at the table, realizing this would be the first time we ate together.

"Did your father think it strange that you didn't eat with him?" I asked.

"If so, he didn't seem to care."

There was beef, stewed peas, fresh bread, and ale. The same as usual, but it was tasty and filling, so I didn't mind.

We began to eat and discuss *Gulliver's Travels*.

Our conversation was lively and enjoyable. Marcus asked me what I thought was the deeper meaning of Jonathan Swift's novel and the four adventures of Gulliver. Our discussion shifted between politics, religion, and philosophy, both agreeing and disagreeing with some of Gulliver's conclusions. However, we agreed that the book should have had a different ending and that Gulliver had not truly learned his lessons.

When the conversation came to its natural end, I finally asked

Marcus the question that had been burning in the back of my mind all evening. "Was the Bible your mother's?"

"Aye." He continued to eat, though I noticed a shift in his countenance as he moved his food around the plate with his fork. "You've told me about your past," he said, as if considering his words carefully. "Mayhap I should tell you about mine."

I waited, silent, not wanting to give him any reason to keep this information to himself. I longed to understand this pirate before me. He was a study in contrasts, both light and darkness, good and bad, stormy and calm—and I needed to know why.

"I was born in Scotland, as you might have guessed," he began. "My father was a hard man, angry and bitter because he was the third-born son of the laird. My mam had delivered two stillborn sons before I was born, and no others after me, so my father had high expectations for my life. His family members were Jacobites and supported the Stuart king, but my father supported King George and the House of Hanover. It became increasingly dangerous for Father to stay in Scotland, so he left for the Americas when I was only ten years old."

I watched him as he spoke and could see that retelling his story filled him with anguish.

"My father was a mean, cold, unfeeling man," Marcus continued, "and those two years that he left my mam and me with his clan were the happiest of my life. When he sent for us to go to America, I was afraid and unhappy. I didn't want to rejoin him and suffer at his angry hands."

My heart constricted for Marcus, yet I sat perfectly still as I listened.

He finally looked up at me, sadness and regret in the depths of his eyes. "When we were on our way to Massachusetts, our ship was overtaken by pirates. As I watched them seize the plunder and force several of the sailors into service, I knew this was my one and only chance to change my future. To take hold of my own life. As my mam watched, I offered myself up for service to the pirate captain."

My lips parted as I shook my head in confusion. "I don't understand."

"Edward Zale is not my father, Caroline. He's the pirate I gave my life to fifteen years ago, when I was only twelve years old. Before I understood what I was doing." He lowered his voice, as if afraid someone might hear. "I didn't want anyone to ever find me again, so I changed my name from Maxwell MacDougal to Marcus Zale. In those days, we were active and busy, and our crew changed many times over the years. Eventually, people began to think I was Captain Zale's son. I didn't correct them—and neither did he."

I was speechless as I stared at him, my mind spinning with questions, though there was only one pressing for an answer. "You said the Bible was your mother's."

He ran his hands over his face as I waited. When he was finally ready to talk, he said, "I'll never forget the way she cried out in horror as I left her side to join Edward Zale. She wept and begged, but I turned a cold heart to her, despising my father more than I loved my mam."

"That can't be true."

"How else do I explain betraying her?" He shook his head again. "She knew she was defeated, so she took our family Bible—her most prized possession—and extended it to me, saying, 'Dinna forget where you came from, son. Dinna forget your Maker.' I took the Bible and didn't look back, but stepped forward into a new life."

Silence filled the cabin as his words settled into my heart.

"Have you been happy?" I asked.

"Nay. And her haunted eyes visit me in my nightmares almost every night. If I could go back and make a different choice, I wouldn't hesitate. I would choose her, even if it meant living with my father." His voice was heavy as he said, "At least then I would be a free man by now, and I wouldn't have a lifetime of regret to mock my every move."

I didn't know if he would turn me away, but I didn't care. I lifted my hand and placed it over his.

His breath stilled as he met my gaze.

"We can't change our past," I said, "but we can change our future."

"I wish it were that simple." He slowly removed his hand from mine and began to eat.

I wished it was, too.

The past I wanted to change was the one my mother had chosen—but to change the future, I needed to know why we had two lives. I was trying my hardest to get the answers, though I wasn't any closer to Nassau.

10

JULY 3, 1927
MINNEAPOLIS, MINNESOTA

It had been a few days since I had learned the truth about Marcus's childhood and we'd discovered our shared love of reading. Something had shifted between us. There were no pretenses, no hidden agendas, nothing hindering us from knowing each other. I felt vulnerable—yet I knew he did, too. I trusted Marcus with my past, and he had trusted me with his. Even though I was a captive in his cabin, I had never felt safer.

The only thing I truly feared was that someone might notice my growing feelings for him.

It had also been a few days since Ruth had discovered Alice was living in our home. Ruth refused to speak to me but had agreed to come to my father's first live broadcast.

That Sunday evening, Father drove our family's green Chevrolet touring car while Mother sat in the front and I was in the back. Though it was past six, the sun was still bright and hot, but Father insisted upon keeping the top of the car up, in case of rain.

Sweat dripped down my back, and I tried to fan myself.

I hadn't admitted it to my parents, but I'd never been more nervous to sing. There would be a small audience at the studio, though that didn't bother me. It was the possibility of thousands of others listening by radio that made me the most uncomfortable. I didn't want to disappoint Father or his producers or anyone who tuned in to the show.

What I longed for was the quiet of our home—or the unexpected refuge of the little cabin on the *Ocean Curse* where there were no expectations beyond my ability to serve Marcus and Captain Zale.

We took Lyndale Avenue to Hennepin and pulled up at the new Nicollet Hotel less than ten minutes after leaving our house. The redbrick building was massive and covered an entire city block. It was a plain structure, with most of the expenses reserved for the inside.

Father parked, and the three of us got out of the Chevy. I watched Father for signs of nervousness as I tried to still my own. I fidgeted with my dress and my hat, but my mother's calm hand made me stop.

We entered the lavish lobby and were greeted by two representatives from the WCCO radio staff who escorted us up the elevator to the thirteenth floor. Everything about the hotel was fresh and new, and the radio station was modern and impressive.

"We'll be in here this evening, Reverend Baldwin," the station manager said as he led us down a hallway and through a door with a black-and-white sign above that said *On Air*, though it wasn't lit up.

The room was probably twenty by twenty and had checkered tan and white tiles on the floor. Cream-colored soundproof panels lined the walls, and two large windows had heavy white drapes. About a dozen wooden chairs were lined up against one wall in two rows, and I was surprised to discover that both of my brothers had already arrived along with several other guests, including Ruth and Lewis.

Lewis caught my eye and winked at me, while Ruth wouldn't look up from her clasped hands.

My brothers, Andrew and Thomas, both rose when we entered

the room. They were younger versions of Father in their well-tailored suits, both tall and handsome with strong features, light-colored hair, and muscular frames. Thomas carried himself with the confidence of a police officer, while Andrew played the part of a banker—though Ruth told me that he had left his job at the bank a year ago to bootleg illegal alcohol from Canada, something my parents would be appalled to know. Father's staunch support of Prohibition had been the catalyst to his international fame. It was Andrew's need to do his work in secrecy that kept the public from learning the truth—but how long until he was caught by the feds? If and when that day came, Father's reputation would be ruined along with Andrew's.

"Boys," Mother said, her face lighting up at the sight of her grown sons.

They each gave her a kiss on the cheek and shook Father's hand, then they turned to me. I had missed them while in Europe and accepted their brotherly hugs, one at a time.

"Look at you," Andrew said as he pulled back and shook his head. "Paris was good to you, Carrie. Put some color in your cheeks."

The color in my cheeks had nothing to do with my experience in Paris—but it had everything to do with my nerves about singing tonight and what might happen when Andrew and Ruth came to our house and saw Alice.

Mother took a seat with our family while Father and I were led to the microphone hanging from the ceiling in the middle of the room.

"Reverend Baldwin," the station manager said, "as soon as we give you the cue, you'll speak right into this microphone. There's no need to shout since it will pick up even a whisper."

Good-natured chuckles came from the audience, since everyone knew how fired up Father became when he preached. His voice often shook the chandeliers in our old church when he was in the middle of a good sermon.

Father offered a smile at his own expense, and then the manager turned to me. "Miss Baldwin, we have a piano player ready and waiting, and she'll accompany you while you sing."

I nodded at the manager and the pianist who was sitting at a grand piano in the corner of the room.

We had a few minutes before the show started, so I made my way across the room to where Ruth was sitting in the front row, between my brother and my mother.

"Hello, Ruth," I said.

"Hello." Her voice was small, and she didn't look up at me.

Lewis was on the other side of Andrew, and he was watching our interaction.

"Mother said that you and Andrew are coming over for a late supper."

"That's what Andrew has told me," she said, playing with the handle of her purse. "We couldn't turn down your mother's invitation."

"I am eager to speak to you." I tried not to sound too upset. Thankfully, Mother was engaged in conversation with the person on her other side.

"There is nothing you can say to me," Ruth said.

I met Andrew's gaze and gave him my most disappointed look. He just shrugged, which made me angrier than before. He was ten years older than me and had been twenty-one when he went off to war. He and Ruth had just been married at the time. They'd known each other since high school and had been so in love and eager to start their lives. When Andrew returned, he'd taken a job at the bank, and things had appeared good on the surface for a few years. But then, everything began to fall apart.

Ruth often commented that the war had changed him. The truth was, the war had changed everyone. Some more than others. The thing that the Lost Generation, the flappers, the gangsters, the bootleggers, and even the Prohibitionists and moral reformers had in common was a glimpse of their own mortality. The difference was that one group of people was focused on how short their lives were and wanted to live it up while they could, while the other was thinking of how long eternity was and how best to get everyone there together. The Spanish flu had heightened the problem, and the strict regulations of Prohibition had sealed the fate of America's current problems.

Lewis watched the entire interaction between Ruth and me carefully, questions in the furrow of his brow. But when I met his gaze, his expression softened and he said, "You look lovely tonight, Carrie. It's been a long time since I've heard you sing. I've been looking forward to it all week."

It didn't seem possible, but my nerves increased, and I felt sick to my stomach. I just wanted it to be over.

"It's time, Miss Baldwin," the station manager said. "After the station pauses for identification, our host will introduce this new weekly show, and then he'll introduce you and you'll begin to sing. Will that suit you?"

"Yes, of course."

I followed him to the microphone, my hands sweating and my legs shaking. I was wearing a pretty blue dress and a white cloche hat, which I touched now to make sure it was on straight.

The clock chimed seven, and the manager indicated for the audience to be silent; then the *On Air* sign lit up inside the room. After the station identification was done, the manager pointed to the host of the show, who was sitting at a table in the corner with his own microphone, and he began to speak.

Father was sitting near the piano, his head bowed and his hands clasped.

I hoped he was praying for my nerves, since I wasn't sure if God listened to my prayers.

When the host was done with the introduction, the manager pointed at the pianist, and she began to play the achingly familiar chords to "Amazing Grace."

I stepped up to the microphone, took a deep breath, and then began to sing.

All I could imagine were the tens of thousands of people listening and panic began to choke me. Father continued to pray, and

Mother watched with her eyebrows raised as if holding her breath, hoping I wouldn't make a mistake.

But then the words from a pirate, two hundred years and thousands of miles away, filled my mind and heart unexpectedly. What if I was only singing for an Audience of One? What if I focused on the One who had given me my voice in the first place?

And in that moment, my perspective shifted.

It no longer mattered what everyone else might think. My nerves disappeared as my voice and heart filled with courage.

Thoughts of Marcus made me smile, and thinking that God was taking pleasure in my humble offering gave me joy.

As I finished the last verse, I lowered my gaze from the back of the room to the faces of the audience. Everyone was watching me, but it was Lewis whose gaze held something more than appreciation for my song.

As soon as I thought I saw something deeper, though, he winked at me again and the moment faded. I could just imagine him pulling on one of my braids and telling me I needed more practice.

The song ended, and the studio audience clapped politely; then I went to the only open seat in the front row, which happened to be next to Lewis.

The row of chairs was snug, and I didn't know the person on the other side, so I sat a bit closer to Lewis. Our legs brushed, and he grinned at me with a teasing smile.

Father approached the microphone and offered a prayer before he began his sermon.

Though I'd been listening to him all my life, I never tired of his voice. It was deep and rich and engaging. He spoke about sin and unrighteousness, but he never left it there. He always gave hope for the path forward. And just like the song, he promised there was grace for everyone. He didn't seem a bit nervous, and for the first time, I wondered if perhaps he was preaching for an Audience of One, as well.

"I'm joined in the studio tonight by my loving wife, Marian, and our three children, Andrew, Thomas, and Caroline." Father glanced at us, a rare light of pride in his face. "One of my mentors once told me that a preacher's teaching is only as good as the fruit it bears in his own life. If you have no influence on the lives of your spouse and children, then you have no business influencing anyone else."

There were murmurs of approval around us, but my chest tightened at his words. I glanced at my brothers, but neither one showed any sign of discomfort or shame.

"The Bible tells us that pride cometh before the fall," he continued, "so I speak not with pride, but with humility when I say that I am blessed with the best wife and children a man can have. My wife serves sacrificially alongside me. My oldest son, Andrew, is an upstanding husband, father, and decorated war hero. My second son, Thomas, is a respected lieutenant in the Saint Paul Police Department, and my daughter, Caroline, who you just heard sing, is a godly young woman who joyfully uses her gifts to bless others."

I couldn't breathe as he spoke those words. Guilt washed over me as I thought about all the dishonesty in my life—in our family's life. I secretly chastised my brothers, yet I was just as blameworthy as them in different ways. I *didn't* serve joyfully—at least, I hadn't until tonight. And it wasn't because of Father's teaching, but because of a pirate's simple faith.

Father's sermon was all about moral character and righteous living, things my brothers and I lacked. How had we not heeded our father's words? I wasn't sure why my brothers rebelled against his teaching, but I knew why I did. I cared too much about what people thought of me, and I feared that the sins of Anne Reed and my grandmother in Salem had stained my soul. Was I destined to follow in their footsteps, whether I wanted to or not?

The thought of falling for a handsome pirate told me I wasn't too far from their path.

A small caravan of cars left the parking lot of the Nicollet Hotel an hour later and moved toward our home on Dupont Avenue where Ingrid was preparing a late supper.

Father pulled into the driveway and let Mother and me out of the Chevy before he brought it to the garage in back. Andrew and Ruth's car pulled up to the curb seconds later, followed by Thomas's and then Lewis's.

Another car I didn't recognize stopped on the opposite side of the street. There were two men inside, both wearing their hats low on their foreheads. When the driver nodded at Andrew, my brother got out of his car and strolled across the street to talk to them.

Ruth didn't move.

Thomas got out of his car and bounded up the sidewalk past me to the porch where he opened the door for Mother and then distracted her as he ushered her inside.

She didn't seem to notice Andrew or the strangers in the other car, which was probably Thomas's intention.

Lewis was the next to exit his vehicle. He glanced toward the meeting across the street, but he, too, ignored the situation.

I waited for him with a frown. "Who are those men Andrew is speaking to?"

With a shrug he said, "I don't know."

I tried getting a better look, but Lewis stepped into my line of sight and said, "It's Andrew's business. He's a big boy."

"You won't tell me—even if you know."

"Andrew's making his own decisions, Carrie."

"You're a police officer, and if those are gangsters, you—"

"I'm off duty."

I shook my head in frustration, but Lewis changed the subject as he started to coax me up the sidewalk toward the house. "I missed you more than I realized I would when you were in Paris."

The sun was low on the western horizon, creating a soft glow on the yard, making his blue eyes sparkle.

"You missed me?" I asked, though he was only trying to distract me. I had my eye on Andrew, who was still across the road.

Ruth wiped her cheeks as if she was crying but made no move to leave her vehicle.

"Would that surprise you?" Lewis asked, drawing my attention to him.

"A little."

He shrugged. "It surprised me, too. Maybe that childhood crush is still alive and well."

I rolled my eyes and started for the porch. "I wish you could be serious for once, Lewis."

He reached out and took my hand to stop me. "Is that what you really want, Carrie?"

Something about the way his voice had shifted, and the tenderness in his touch, filled me with apprehension. Lewis had never been serious.

Pulling my hand away, I tried to laugh it off. "I don't know what I would do if you were serious."

"We can find out."

I chuckled outwardly, though inside I was not laughing. I knew how to handle the easygoing, lighthearted Lewis Cager.

This man was entirely different.

"Come inside," I said as I wrapped my arm through his like I would an old chum, while glancing over my shoulder at Andrew. "Last one in has to help Ingrid with the dishes."

I tried to pass off his words and actions with nonchalance, but he was stiff beside me as we walked into the house.

It didn't take him long to relax, though, and he was soon teasing poor Ingrid, whose cheeks were aflame with embarrassment.

A few minutes later, I moved the curtain aside and saw that the men were gone, and Andrew was standing beside the open passenger door of his car speaking to Ruth.

She hadn't moved and was still staring forward, her body rigid.

"Where are Andrew and Ruth?" Mother asked as she came down the stairs.

I stepped away from the window and said, "In their vehicle. And where is Alice?"

"In her room. She said she didn't feel well and didn't want to intrude on our family time."

I closed my eyes briefly, thankful for the reprieve.

The front door opened a moment later, and Andrew and Ruth entered. Andrew bypassed me in the foyer and joined Thomas and Lewis in the parlor.

"Are you feeling alright, Ruth?" Mother frowned at her pale daughter-in-law.

"I'm fine," Ruth said, though she wasn't doing a good job convincing anyone.

"If you need anything, you know to ask." Mother glanced into the parlor and said, "Now, Thomas, put that down. It was a gift from the French ambassador!"

She hurried off, leaving Ruth and me alone in the foyer.

"I'm so sorry, Ruth," I said the moment Mother was out of earshot. "I wanted to get Alice to leave, but she tricked Mother and Father into letting her stay. They don't know who she—"

"Don't." Ruth put up her hand. "I don't want to know any more. I've determined to make the best of this and try to be a grown-up about it. It's not your fault or your parents' fault. I will take the blame."

I frowned. "You? There is no one to blame but Alice and Andre—"

"No." Her voice was firm. "If I was a better wife—"

"Ruth, that's ridiculous and you know it."

"If I was a better wife," she continued, "my husband would not stray. I often allow my exhaustion to get the better of me, and I don't honor my husband as I should."

I stared at her, shocked and horrified. "You are an amazing wife and mother, Ruth. It's your husband—"

"I won't hear it, Carrie. If you can't speak nicely about my husband, then I don't want you speaking about him at all." She swallowed and took a deep breath. "Now, I'm going to join the family and make sure that everyone has a splendid time together. Your parents deserve nothing less."

Anger vibrated through my body as she walked away—not anger at her, but at my brother and at the woman in the guest room upstairs.

"Andrew?" I said as I came to the parlor door. "May I have a word with you?"

Ruth shook her head at me, but I couldn't bear her nonsense. If she wouldn't talk some sense into her husband, I would.

Andrew sighed and then rose from the sofa.

I turned on my heels and strode out the front door to the porch. Thankfully, he followed without a fight.

"I know what you're going to say, Carrie. And frankly, it's none of your business."

"That *woman* is upstairs, in our *parents'* house," I seethed. "It is my business. Do you have no regard for anyone but yourself? Father's livelihood and reputation is teetering on the edge, and you're going to tell me to mind my own business?" My voice was rising to a dangerous level, so I forced myself to calm down. "What about your wife and children? Your own reputation?"

He shrugged. "What is a reputation, anyway? Who cares?"

"I do—all of us do. Why are you being so selfish?"

"You're so naïve, Carrie." He reached for the pack of cigarettes in his pocket but returned them, apparently remembering where he was. At least he had some respect for our parents' home.

"How am I naïve?"

"There's a big world out there, and it's ripe for picking. Father's views are so narrow and old-fashioned. The 1920s are a rebirth, and the rest of the world is moving on, but he's stuck in one place. I have no desire to stay there with him."

"His ideas are not old-fashioned. They're timeless. God's Word is eternal. He doesn't change just because society changes." Even if I wasn't sure God cared about me, I was certain about His character. "You're giving in to the desires of your flesh, and you're hurting everyone you love in the process."

"You're starting to sound like the old man," he scoffed and then patted me on the head as if I were a child. "Naïve and in your own little bubble. It'll pop one day, and you'll realize I'm right."

I pulled my head away from his hand and clenched my teeth. "If it's old-fashioned to see to the happiness and well-being of your family, then I don't care if I am naïve. There is right and wrong, Andrew, whether you want to accept it or not. What you're doing to Ruth and our parents is wrong. What you're doing to Alice is wrong, too." I didn't have any fond regard for her, but the truth was the truth. "You need to deal with her before she becomes a bigger problem."

Andrew rolled his eyes and leaned against the pillar. "Fine. I'll see what I can do."

I wanted a concrete plan, but at least he seemed receptive to my plea.

"And stay home with your wife and children, where you belong," I said, pushing a little further. "Ruth loves you, and when you come to the end of your life, she's all you'll have left—if you're lucky. Treat her like the rare treasure she is and stop hurting her."

"Stay out of my business." Anger glinted in his eyes as he pushed away from the pillar. "Ruth's fine."

I wasn't afraid of my brother, so I pressed on. "And who were those men across the street?"

He shrugged. "That's none of your business, either."

"Are they . . . ?" I paused and lowered my voice even further. "Gangsters?"

Andrew's chuckle was sardonic. "Let's just call them business associates, shall we?"

"Why would you tell them where our parents live?"

"They were in the neighborhood, and we had a transaction to make." He patted his pocket. "I gotta feed my kids, don't I?"

He walked back into the house, leaving the front door open.

I stayed on the porch, taking several deep breaths, wanting to calm down before I joined the others. The last thing I needed to worry about was gangsters hanging around my parents' house.

"Everything okay?" Lewis asked as he stepped onto the porch, the screen door creaking with his arrival.

I tried to steady my nerves as I said, "I'll be fine."

"Does your beef with Andrew have something to do with Alice?"

"Is it that obvious?"

"I'm a police detective, Carrie. It doesn't take much to notice the tension in this house."

"I'm happy my parents haven't figured it out."

He shrugged and leaned against the pillar that Andrew had just occupied. "You might be surprised."

I stared at him. "You think Mother and Father know?"

"It might explain why they've allowed a complete stranger to live with them."

Nibbling my bottom lip, I contemplated his words.

"Come on," he said with a smile, putting his arm around my shoulder. "Let's go inside before your mother starts to worry. Ingrid's roast smells delicious, and I already saved the seat next to you at the table."

"So you can tease me?"

He laughed. "So I can flirt with you."

I rolled my eyes—but deep down, I knew he wasn't teasing, and I wasn't sure what to do with that information.

Because the only man who had made my heart race with attraction was on a pirate ship, two centuries away. And he hadn't teased me once.

11

JULY 4, 1727
MATANZAS, CUBA

I stayed on the ship the next day as Captain Zale, Marcus, and Hawk went ashore to Matanzas to sell some of the plunder they'd taken from the *Adventurer*. The bay where we were anchored was beautiful, and from where I stood at the ship's rail, I saw several wooden homes, churches, and businesses in the small Cuban city. Heavy clouds hovered above us, threatening more rain, and the wind had caused whitecaps to form in the dark water. It blew the palm trees this way and that, until they looked like they might snap.

My mind wandered to the night before around the supper table with my family—and Lewis. He had sat next to me, and he had teased me like old times. I used to despise it, but now I appreciated the familiarity of his playfulness. At least it was something I understood and could predict. His seriousness caught me off guard and made me feel strange.

"We haven't seen you around much this past week," Timothy said as he came up next to me at the railing. "The quartermaster said you've been feeling ill. I'm happy to see you're looking better than ever."

It had been four days since my bath, and I was still appreciating my relatively clean skin and hair. I'm sure the others noticed, though Timothy was the first to mention it. Ned had only scowled at me when I resumed my serving duties, probably realizing the bathwater he and I had carried to Marcus's cabin had been for me.

"I'm feeling better," I said, though I kept my gaze on the bay.

Timothy leaned against the railing. "The sky doesn't look good. Some are convinced that our Jonah is bringing all this bad weather."

I didn't respond.

"They're also saying that's why we haven't had much luck selling off the plunder. Hopefully the captain can get a good price for some of it today."

We'd stopped in Havana the day before, but the local government had run us out of the city. Havana was larger than New York and Boston, and it should have been a good place to sell their loot, but the large forts guarding the city, and the wall that was almost completed around it, meant that they had control over who entered and exited.

So Captain Zale had chosen to stop at the smaller city of Matanzas to the east of Havana, though his reception was yet to be seen.

"'Tis just superstition," I said to Timothy about the Jonah on board.

"Some of them are taking sick, too," he continued. "Fever, stomach troubles, and the like. They're trying to figure out when all their bad luck started." His voice was low. "Some have said it was the day they attacked the *Adventurer*. They already questioned me and one of the other men who came aboard that day. They told me to talk to you about it, since the captain and quartermaster don't let you out of their sight too often."

My palms began to sweat, and I ran them down my trousers. "I have work to do."

"I'm only telling you because they're watching us, Carl. But I'll tell them you're not a threat. You have my word."

With a quick nod to acknowledge his comment, I moved across the deck to the stairs leading to the captain's cabin, trying not to catch the eye of the other pirates. There was little else to occupy my time until supper, so I went into the outer room but paused when I saw Ned lying on his cot.

He had looked pale at breakfast, but I hadn't thought to ask if he was sick.

"What do you want?" he asked me when I approached.

"Are you feeling poorly?"

"Why do you care? You probably made me sick."

"Do you need Dr. Hartville?"

Ned moaned and turned his back to me. "Just leave me be."

Was Ned sick with whatever was ailing the other crew members? Would they blame it on me and assume I was the Jonah? If so, Ned would be the first to call me out.

"I'll take your chores until you're better," I told him.

"Sure you will," he said. "You've been waiting for the perfect time to throw me over and move in on the captain."

"Don't be—" I paused. No matter how much I protested, Ned would believe what he wanted. "Let me know if you need anything," I said instead.

A commotion outside the room made me step out onto the main deck. The captain was returning on the launch with Marcus and Hawk—and their boat was still full of the goods they'd brought to sell.

I went to the galley for their lunch and returned as they were just entering the outer room.

Captain Zale stopped near Ned's cot and frowned down at the young man. "What ails you?"

Ned glared at me. "Carl has made all of us sick. Some of the others are complaining, too."

All eyes turned to me, and my mouth slipped open to protest, but again, Marcus shook his head to keep me quiet.

"At least Carl recovered quickly," Captain Zale said, but then he turned back to me. "You'll take on Ned's chores until he's able to do them again."

I nodded as Ned laid his head back on the pillow, clearly too ill to protest.

Captain Zale, Marcus, and Hawk entered the captain's cabin, and I followed with their meal.

The captain tore off his black gloves and threw them onto the table as I set down the platters of pork and bread. I had to return to the galley for their stewed peas and ale, but when I returned, Jack and Dr. Hartville had joined the small party.

"We've been blacklisted in Cuba," Captain Zale said to his men as I placed the peas and ale on the table. "I need to get rid of the plunder before we head back to Florida."

"Mayhap Marcus's idea to go to Nassau is wise after all," Hawk said as he took the mug of ale I poured for him. "We haven't been there in a long time."

I quickly glanced at Marcus, my hope rising, but he had his gaze on the captain.

Ever since I'd learned that Captain Zale wasn't his father, it had changed everything I thought about them. Their strained and complicated relationship made more sense. I'd noticed the lack of warmth and affection between them and wondered about it, but not anymore. It also explained their different accents. They weren't blood related, so the differences in their looks were more obvious than before. It made me wonder how I hadn't seen it, but the mind was a powerful thing, and when it believed something, it was hard to see something different. Perhaps that's why so many people accepted that I was a boy.

I handed Marcus his mug and our fingers brushed, causing his gaze to flicker to mine for a heartbeat.

My pulse pounded hard, though I wasn't sure if it was from Captain Zale's decision about Nassau or the feel of Marcus's skin against mine. I tried not to let my feelings show on my face—afraid that the men in the room might notice, but even more afraid that Marcus might.

"Mayhap you're right," the captain finally said. "I'm willing to risk the navy at Nassau to get rid of the plunder. 'Tis been in the hold too long."

It took everything within me not to cry out with excitement.

I handed the captain his ale, my hands shaking with anticipation.

In just a few days, I would get the answers I wanted from my mother.

A hint of a smile tilted Marcus's lips before he took another bite of his dinner.

The rain started as soon as we were out of Matanzas Bay. It blew hard, and the ship rose and dipped precariously, causing those who were sick to feel worse.

Ned's moans could be heard every time I was near him, and when I caught his attention, he scowled at me. As soon as my chores were done, I went to Marcus's cabin to be free of Ned. Since I hadn't been sick, I couldn't have gotten him sick—though he didn't know that.

Clouds darkened the sky, so I lit the lamp and went to the bookshelf. Marcus had suggested I read Daniel Defoe's *Robinson Crusoe* next, but it was the Bible that caught my eye tonight.

The front page was full of Marcus's family names, and I couldn't help but wonder who they were. Each name was a different story of heartache, love, loss, and hope. I let my finger trail the names. Donal, Fiona, Alastair, Alish, Liam . . . and Maxwell.

Maxwell MacDougal. Did Marcus even remember what it was like to be Maxwell MacDougal? Did he want to become him again someday? Or did he plan to die as a pirate? I wanted to tell him he had a choice in the matter, but I wasn't one to counsel him. For so long, I hadn't felt like I had freedom of choice in my lives. Perhaps Marcus and I had more in common than I first realized. We both had two names, two different lives, and uncertainty about the future. Maybe that was why I was so drawn to him. We were kindred spirits.

Something outside the window caught my attention.

The *Ocean Curse* was approaching a small frigate on the portside.

Apprehension tightened my chest, and I quickly replaced the Bible before I ran out of Marcus's cabin.

Rain pelted my face as I looked up at the mainmast, my heart falling at the sight.

The black death's head flag whipped in the wind, the skull and crossbones taunting the frigate and all who were aboard her. The only time the ship flew the pirate flag was when they were overtaking another vessel.

As a crew member, I was now a pirate, whether I wanted to be or not. If Grandfather saw me now, he'd realize his worst fear had come true.

I was no better than my mother.

A cheer arose from the pirates as every able-bodied man stood on the main deck of the *Ocean Curse*, their hands raised in victory as several of them boarded the frigate.

Wave after wave caused the ship to rise and fall. I hadn't noticed the chase because the ship had been careening wildly for hours.

As the pirates overtook the frigate, Marcus and Captain Zale stood at the rail, the wind whipping their coats and hair about them just as it did the pirate flag. They were a formidable pair, their swords at their sides, and though Marcus had been kind and thoughtful toward me, watching him now, capturing the frigate, my body trembled with fear.

Yet, it wasn't the terror of being captured or tortured or abused that scared me. It was knowing that my traitorous heart didn't care that he was a pirate, while my mind screamed at me to retreat. To put up my defenses and push Marcus Zale from my life.

I wanted to cry, or yell, or demand that he let the frigate go. Not only because the people aboard it didn't deserve to be robbed, but because I didn't want it to be Marcus who did the plundering.

Why did men like him and Andrew think their own desires were more important than anyone else's? Their choices hurt the people around them, yet they somehow rationalized their behavior.

The injustice in the world was maddening, no matter what

century I occupied. I hated how defenseless I felt, how weak and insignificant. It would be easier to give in and join the madness, to satisfy my own desires. It didn't matter if I was in 1727 or 1927; the struggle to do the right thing was eternal.

Yet, my conscience cried out to me. The words I'd spoken to Andrew just last night reverberated in my mind. There was right and wrong. There was truth and justice—no matter how much they wanted to deny it. They sought to change the truth when it didn't serve them.

Marcus grabbed a rope and stepped onto the railing to board the frigate, but he turned and his stormy gaze caught mine.

I stared at him defiantly. The rain continued to slash against me, soaking my clothing and mingling with my tears, but I didn't care.

Marcus's chest rose and fell as a war waged within his eyes. He didn't tear his gaze from mine. Would he board the frigate? Rob her of her cargo and her dignity? I held my breath, wanting him to make the right choice.

Captain Zale said something to him and then, holding a rope, leapt from the railing and disappeared.

Marcus set his jaw and followed.

I was huddled on my cot in the dim cabin, swimming in the shirt and trousers Marcus had lent to me earlier that week after I bathed. My wet clothes were strung on the ropes that were still hanging in the room, and my hair was unbound, drying around my shoulders.

I stared out the window toward the starboard side of the ship at the rolling sea. Rain still pounded the windows, and the wind blew hard. Darkness had fallen, and the storm marred the sky, so there was no light from stars or moon. If I were prone to seasickness, this would have been the night I suffered the most. I was thankful the malady had not bothered me.

But something else made me feel sick—sick at heart, if not in body.

Hours had passed since the *Ocean Curse* had captured the frigate. The supper hour had come and gone, but I hadn't been to the galley to see if the cook had food for me. I didn't care if Captain Zale returned and was angry that his meal wasn't on his table. And I had no appetite to feed myself.

It was close enough to midnight that I could have gone to sleep and not had to face Marcus until I woke up here again, but I couldn't bring myself to return to 1927. Not yet.

There were too many emotions filling my heart and soul tonight. I was so overcome by them I'd almost forgotten we were on our way to Nassau and to my mother.

The cabin door opened, but I didn't bother to look in that direction. I knew who had come.

Marcus paused, perhaps surprised to see that I was still awake. Though I was wearing his clothes, I had my blanket pulled around my shoulders for heat and for modesty.

He slowly closed the door, and I finally turned my face toward him.

Marcus was soaked from head to foot. Water dripped from the ends of his dark hair and pooled around his boots on the floor. Our gazes met as they had on the main deck, but this time I couldn't read his emotions. Was he angry at me for being upset? Was he ashamed? Or was he feeling victorious?

He looked from me to my clothes on the line and then back to me, and I suddenly realized I was wearing his only other suit of dry clothes.

I got up, keeping the blanket around my shoulders, and went to the clothesline to see if my things were dry. They were still damp, but not as wet as his.

"I'll change," I told him as I dropped the blanket and started to pull my shirt from the line.

He took a few steps into the room and put his hand on mine to stop me.

My breath stilled as I felt the heat of his body behind me and his skin against mine. My mind warned me to move—my heart begged me to stay.

He lifted the blanket from the floor and settled it over my shoulders.

"What will you wear?" I whispered.

"I'll make do." His voice was low and deep.

I closed my eyes as I lowered my hand. I couldn't move, nor did I want to.

His hands were still on my shoulders as he said, "I know you're angry with me, lass."

I had no defenses when he stood this close to me. My mind was a muddled mess and incapable of counseling me, while my heart was crying out for love, for affection, for something that it had never felt before. I needed reassurance, especially on a night such as this.

I desired to be loved, and I longed to be wanted.

He lifted my unbound hair from beneath the blanket before gently placing his hands on my arms. Heat radiated from his touch.

"I'm sorry," he said.

My eyes were still closed, and his words felt like a sweet embrace. Remorse filled his voice, and I knew he meant what he said. But he'd still done it.

I was aware of my breathing, of feeling like I couldn't get enough air into my lungs.

"Will you always be a pirate, Marcus?"

His hands slowly lowered from my arms, and he stepped away from me.

He hadn't answered my question audibly—but he'd answered it.

And there was no room in my life for a man who would hurt me the way Andrew hurt Ruth.

12

❧

JULY 8, 1927
SAINT PAUL, MINNESOTA

For four days, I had gone back and forth between my lives in a quiet fog of anger and disappointment. After the frigate capture, I had hardly spoken to Marcus. I performed my duties on board the *Ocean Curse* but did little else. Whenever he entered the cabin, I found reason to leave it. I made sure I was asleep before he came in at night and lay in the cot with my back to the room until he was gone if I woke up before him. Every time our gazes met, I saw the pain in his eyes—yet I battled the compassion I felt for him, knowing he chose this lifestyle.

We would arrive in Nassau tomorrow. I was so anxious to meet my mother, I could think of little else in both 1727 and 1927. I didn't even want to consider what might happen if she wasn't there. Surely, someone would know where she had gone. Seeing her was all I wanted to focus on, since everything else in both my lives filled me with despair.

Alice still lived with us, despite my conversation with Andrew. She'd started to meet with my parents to discuss her skills and possible job opportunities, but it was taking longer than I would

136

like. The sooner she moved out of our house, the better. Every day she remained was a threat. But that only begged more questions. It didn't make sense that she hadn't revealed the truth to my parents.

Which was why I was on my way to the Saint Paul Police Department on that sweltering July day. If Andrew wouldn't do something about Alice, then perhaps Thomas would. Alice had lived in Saint Paul before coming to our house. Maybe Thomas was privy to her situation and could help me persuade her to leave.

The Saint Paul Police Department had recently been moved to the Ramsey County Courthouse on Fourth and Wabasha Street. I left home after lunch and boarded the Hennepin Avenue electric streetcar. The open-air conveyance was sweltering, and the press of people made it worse. At Marshall Avenue I changed cars. This line ran from Minneapolis, across the Mississippi River, and into downtown Saint Paul where I made one more change at Selby Avenue.

The Ramsey County Courthouse was large and outdated, though it was still beautiful with a massive nine-story bell tower, steep roof, and detailed brickwork. The streetcar stopped right in front of the building, and I was happy to get off.

It took me a few minutes to find the police station inside the courthouse. I'd never visited Thomas at work and wasn't sure how he would feel about me showing up unannounced, but this couldn't wait until I saw him again. It could be weeks or months, and Alice needed to leave now.

The hallway outside the police station echoed with the tapping of my heels. A receptionist greeted me with a tired smile, and the busy office behind her was loud and chaotic. Dozens of police officers sat at desks doing paperwork, answering phone calls, or visiting over cups of coffee. There were people in plain clothing throughout the room, though it was hard to tell which ones might be criminals and which ones were there to make complaints or give testimonies.

"May I help you?" the receptionist asked me.

"Is Lieutenant Baldwin available?"

The woman looked me up and down with a critical eye. I was wearing a simple black-and-white-striped dress with a white wide-brimmed hat to keep the sun off my face. I had put a little rouge on my cheeks and lips before I left, not even enough for Father to complain.

"He left for the day," a man said behind me.

Turning, I found Lewis entering the police station in uniform. For some reason, my heart started to hammer.

"Hello, Lewis."

"What are you doing here?" He didn't seem happy to see me, which was strange.

"I need to speak to Thomas. It's rather urgent."

He nodded his head toward the hall and opened the door for me to follow him.

We entered the hallway, and he walked several yards away from the station's front door before addressing me. "Thomas isn't here."

"Do you know where he is?"

"I have a good guess."

"Is he at his apartment?"

Lewis paused as he contemplated answering my question. Finally, he sighed and said, "I don't think so. It would be a waste of your time to look for him there."

"Where is he, Lewis?"

He frowned and crossed his arms. "What do you need from him? Can I help you?"

I clasped my purse in both hands and decided to trust him. "I need to speak to him about Alice Pierce. Andrew has done nothing to get her out of our parents' house, and I'm starting to get worried that he won't."

"And you think Thomas can help?"

Shame warmed my cheeks. "I was hoping that he might have some dirt on her."

Lewis's mouth parted, and he lowered his arms, a teasing yet incredulous look on his face. "Caroline Baldwin. Would you stoop so low?"

I couldn't meet his eyes, so I shrugged. "If it means protecting Father and Mother, then yes."

"Well, you don't want to go where Thomas is right now."

I looked up quickly, frowning. "Why not?"

He shook his head and turned slightly away in frustration, as if he'd said too much.

"Where is he, Lewis?" I took a step closer to him. "I'm his sister. I should know where he's at."

"Oh, really?" He looked down at me, a playful gleam in his eyes. "We're not kids anymore, Carrie. He's a grown man, and he has a right to his privacy."

"I need to talk to him, and I don't know when I can get away next." I tried to convey how serious I was. "Please, Lewis. This might not be important to you, but it's very important to me. If Alice does something to hurt Mother or Father, I couldn't live with myself."

I knew using Mother and Father would weaken his defenses. He sighed again. "It's not that I can't tell you. It's that you don't want to know."

"I don't think there's much you can tell me that I don't know about my brother." I whispered, "I—I know he's a crooked cop."

"Almost every cop in Saint Paul is crooked." Lewis's voice was filled with disgust.

"Are you crooked?"

He studied me for a second. "What if I said I was?"

I lifted my chin, anger and pain thumping in my chest. Thoughts of my brothers and Marcus coming to the forefront. "I'd tell you that I'm tired of deceitful, disrespectful, selfish men."

A half smile tilted up his lips, and I realized he was teasing me again. "Then I won't say it."

Frustration made me walk away from Lewis. I was tired of playing games, of being told I wasn't capable of taking my life into my own hands. In 1727, I had finally left my grandfather's expectations behind and done something for myself. In 1927, I was ready to do the same.

I didn't want Lewis to determine what I should and shouldn't know about my brother.

"Carrie," he said as he jogged to catch up to me before I exited the courthouse. He put his hand on my arm. "I'm sorry."

"I need to speak to my brother." I ignored his apology, my voice betraying the depth of my irritation. "I didn't come all the way down here for you to tell me I'm too innocent or naïve or weak to deal with reality."

"I didn't say any of those things about you. I think you're one of the strongest women I know." He shrugged. "You might be naïve and innocent, but that's what I like most about you. It's hard to come by nowadays, especially in my profession."

I pulled away from his hold, tired of him mocking me, and pushed open the front door.

The heat was unbearable as I stepped outside, like opening an oven door.

"I'm not going to keep chasing you," he said as he caught up to me again.

"And I'm not going to put up with you treating me like a child."

He put both his hands on my arms to still me. "I'm not trying to treat you like a child. I'm trying to protect you."

"I should be the judge about whether or not I need protection." I disentangled my arms.

"Fine." He crossed his arms again, almost angry. "He's at Nina Clifford's brothel."

I paused, horrified. "Are you teasing me again?"

"I wouldn't tease about something like this."

"Is he there as a police officer? Is there a raid?"

"Nina's house is the most protected business in Saint Paul." He stared at me, as if challenging me. "She pays a steep fee to keep the police out of her place—unless they are paying customers."

Disgust rolled over me, and heat climbed up my neck, burning my cheeks. "Thomas is—" I couldn't finish the statement.

"Every Friday afternoon when he gets off work."

"How can you be so flippant?"

He frowned. "You asked me not to coddle you, so here's the truth: Thomas frequents the most notorious brothel in Saint Paul at least once a week, and that's probably where he's at right now."

I lifted my chin, trying not to be as innocent or naïve as he claimed I was. I had to deal with this reality, whether I liked it or not. I knew Thomas was crooked. Ruth had told me about the bribes he took and bragged about to Andrew. But I didn't realize he had lowered himself to such depravity.

Lewis took my hand and guided me to a bench under a large maple tree.

We took a seat, and I was thankful to be off my wobbly legs in the shade.

"I shouldn't have been so abrupt," he said.

"I asked you to tell me the truth."

"I know, but I should have eased into it."

I was happy I didn't have to look at him anymore. Sitting on the bench, I could focus on my hands or the sidewalk in front of us. I didn't want him to see the depths of my disillusionment.

"Your brother's a good guy," he said. "He's just trying to find his way."

"At a brothel?" I said it louder than I intended.

An older couple passing on the sidewalk looked up at me, startled.

Lewis chuckled. He was still holding my hand, and I was suddenly very aware of him. Of his cologne, his gentleness, his concern.

I removed my hand from his, needing space to think.

"I can tell him you stopped by," Lewis offered. "Maybe he'll swing by your parents', and you can talk to him then. From what I understand, he was kind of fond of Alice before she hooked up with Andrew."

"Thomas was fond of her?" The realization was startling.

"From what I heard."

It didn't matter; what mattered was getting Alice out of the house. "I can't risk my parents hearing us talk, and I don't want to wait any longer."

I stood, ready to face my next challenge.

"Where are you going?"

"To Nina Clifford's brothel. Can you tell me where it is, please?"

Lewis's mouth parted in surprise again, but he couldn't stop me. If he didn't tell me, someone else would.

And I was determined to talk to my brother, so I started to walk toward the east.

"Don't be ridiculous," Lewis said as he caught up to me.

"I thought you said you weren't going to chase me anymore."

"If you'd ever let me catch you, maybe I could stop."

I pushed his strange comment away and kept walking. "Am I going in the right direction?"

"No."

"You're lying. I'll find out where this brothel is, whether you tell me or not."

He growled. "You're the most stubborn person I know." He put his hands on my shoulders and turned me toward the west. "Walk for about five minutes this way, take a left onto Washington Street, go two doors down on the left, and you'll be at her front door."

I turned to him. "You're joking with me."

"I'm dead serious." And he looked it, too.

"Her brothel is practically right outside the police station?"

"Until last year, it was literally outside our front door. Nina built her brothel across the street from the old Central Police Station."

"On purpose?"

He started to walk west along Kellogg Boulevard with me. The street sat high above the Mississippi River, and the traffic was thick. Exhaust made the heat feel more suffocating as I waited for him to continue.

"Yes, on purpose."

"Why is the Saint Paul Police Department so corrupt?" I walked fast to keep up with him.

"Because of the O'Connor System."

When I didn't respond, he continued.

"The system started as a way to discourage criminal activity, but it has backfired since Prohibition. And with a new police chief, more corrupt than the last, it's worse than ever."

"What is the O'Connor System?"

"When a criminal comes into Saint Paul, they check in with Dapper Dan Hogan at the Green Lantern saloon on Wabasha Street, pay him a fee, and promise not to commit a crime while they're in the city. Some of the most notorious criminals in the country have had asylum here over the past seven years."

"What if they're being chased by federal agents? Don't the feds have jurisdiction over the local police?"

He shrugged. "The police tip off the criminals. It's part of the fee they pay for protection."

"They have time to get away?"

"That's how it works."

"And the police are getting rich off this system?"

"Exactly. It makes Saint Paul one of the safest cities in America, but Minneapolis has become one of the most dangerous places. The criminals can commit a crime there and then come into Saint Paul for asylum."

I glanced at him and saw he was serious. Of course I heard about all the crime in Minneapolis, but I'd never wondered why I didn't hear about as much in Saint Paul.

"And what about Nina?" I asked. "Or the other brothels and speakeasies?"

"We're told to turn a blind eye to them."

I paused. "How can you sleep at night?"

"Because—" He paused, as if he'd said too much. "Don't worry about it, Carrie. I find a way."

It was a strange answer, but I wasn't sure I wanted to know more. I'd already learned my brother was more corrupt than I'd realized. I didn't want to discover that Lewis was, too. Maybe that's why Mother didn't ask questions. She didn't want to know.

Perhaps I liked being naïve and innocent. Maybe my parents had been kind to shelter me from the harsh reality around me. Grandfather, too, had protected me from the worst of the world. Had it been so bad to be unaware?

We took a left onto Washington Street, and I was surprised to find it was pleasant and respectable. Many of the houses were made of dark stone exteriors with pretty embellishments and manicured lawns.

"One of these is a brothel?" I asked, incredulous.

He only shook his head. "I hope you know what you're getting yourself into. What if someone recognizes you and tells your father?"

I hadn't thought about that, which was strange, since it was usually all I thought about.

Pausing, I put my hand on his arm. "Will you go in and ask Thomas to come out?"

He pulled back, surprised. "You think I want people to see *me* entering this place?"

"Please, Lewis."

"You are the most incorrigible person I know, Caroline Baldwin."

"Tenacity is a gift."

He rolled his eyes. "Stay here. I'll see what I can do."

I waited at the corner while he walked to the second house and up the stairs to the front door. He looked right and left, clearly uncomfortable, especially in his police uniform. But if the department was as corrupt as he claimed, who was going to get upset at him?

The door opened, and Lewis entered the house.

Sunshine beat down on me, and my skin was slick with sweat. I found shade under a tree, but it felt like hours as I waited for Lewis to emerge.

People passed on Kellogg and Washington, some even walking

into the brothel, but no one seemed to pay me any attention. When someone looked my way, I turned my face, hoping to hide under the brim of my large hat.

Finally, the door opened, and Lewis stepped out with Thomas. I was both relieved and disappointed. I had hoped that Lewis was wrong, and Thomas wasn't at the brothel.

Anger radiated off my brother like heat waves as he approached. His face was red, whether from rage or embarrassment, I wasn't sure, but it was frightening.

Perhaps I should have waited to talk to him at another time.

Without a word, he took me by the upper arm and almost dragged me back toward Kellogg Boulevard.

"What in the world do you think you're doing?" he asked through clenched teeth. "Are you insane, Carrie?"

"You're hurting me."

"Good. Maybe it'll knock some sense into you."

"Let her go, Thomas," Lewis said, coming up alongside me.

Thomas finally let me go but didn't stop walking.

"I need to talk to you," I said, trying to keep up with my brother.

He stopped abruptly. "Do you know—do you have any idea? What if someone saw you?"

"What if someone saw you?" I countered, my anger returning.

"It's not the same thing and you know it."

"It's exactly the same. We represent Father, just like he said during his sermon the other day."

"Don't be so naïve, Carrie."

I clenched my hands. "I'm so tired of people saying that to me. I'm not stupid, Thomas. I know what you're doing is wrong, il-legal, immoral, and just plain foolish! Whether you like it or not, we have a responsibility—"

"I've heard enough." He ran his hand through his hair. "You got my attention, what do you want?"

Lewis stood nearby, but he tried to look inconspicuous as we talked.

I took several deep breaths, trying to remember why I'd come.

"I need you to get rid of Andrew's . . . paramour." I didn't know what else to call her. "She will hurt our parents if we don't do something about it, and Andrew doesn't seem to care."

Something caught in Thomas's gaze at the mention of Alice, but he said, "What makes you think I do?"

"Please, Thomas. For Ruth, if for no other reason."

"What do you want me to do?"

"I don't know. You can think of something. I've asked her to leave, but she refuses. I can't tell our parents who she is or what we know about her without hurting them. Lewis said you might know her. Is that true?"

Again that same look. "I met her before Andrew did, while she was working at the Wabasha Street Caves. I was the idiot that introduced them."

"So it's true? Were you in love with her?"

He glanced toward the river, and his lack of a response was all I needed to know.

I had never heard of the caves, or that Thomas had been interested in Alice, and I didn't want to hear any more. "Please get her to leave. That's all I'm asking."

He let out a long breath. "Fine. I'll see what I can do."

"Thank you."

"Now go home. You don't belong here."

"Come on," Lewis said. "I'll walk you back to the streetcar stop."

Thomas didn't bother saying goodbye and strode back toward Washington Street.

Lewis was silent for several minutes, and I had nothing left to say. I knew my brothers were living dishonorable lives, but I'd had no idea how debauched they'd become.

When we arrived at the courthouse, I tried to keep my chin up. Even though Lewis was aware of our family's secrets, I didn't know until today how much he knew. It was hard to look at him.

The streetcar bell rang as it drew closer. I turned to Lewis to say thank you, not sure how I would find my voice.

But he surprised me by taking my hand. "I'm sorry, Carrie. I wish I could give you a better world."

Then he lifted my hand to his lips, pressed a kiss, and headed back into the courthouse.

13

Nothing else mattered the next day as I walked along Bay Street in Nassau with Marcus and Hawk. Captain Zale had stayed on the *Ocean Curse*, since his face would be unwelcome in the old pirate capital. Marcus and Hawk were taking a risk to be seen, but they weren't as notorious as their captain.

Thatch-roofed homes and businesses were interspersed among the palm trees and sand. On the top of the hill, Fort Nassau dominated the town with views of the surrounding harbors. The smells of roasting meat, smoldering fires, and animal pens assailed my nose. The only reprieve came from the breeze, which rustled the palm leaves above my head and carried the scents away for a moment or two.

I searched the faces of everyone we passed, looking for a sign of familiarity. Would I even recognize my mother if I saw her? No one had ever told me what she looked like. I'd assumed I resembled her in some way, but I couldn't be sure.

"Remind me of her name," Marcus said, for my ears alone.

"Anne Reed."

Tension still reverberated between us, though he had made no attempt to speak of the captured frigate after the night of the storm. We'd returned to our normal routines, but things were strained between us. I wanted him to tell me that what he did was wrong and he wouldn't do it again, but just like I had to deal with the reality of my brother's choices—I had to deal with the reality of Marcus's. He was a pirate. He belonged in this place of coarse men and women, drinking, carousing, and conducting business that made my cheeks fill with heat. Was this the kind of life Marcus wanted? He said he regretted leaving his mother fifteen years ago, so why didn't he change his life now?

"Keep to yourself," Marcus said to me as he nodded at Hawk to start inquiring about selling the plunder. "I'll see if I can find someone who knows your mother."

Hawk walked in one direction and Marcus in the other, though I kept my eye on Marcus. I didn't want to lose him in the crowd. I stayed on the sandy street, trying not to fidget as I waited. People approached, trying to sell their wares to me. I inspected some of the fine jewelry and cloth, but kept shaking my head no. The money I had been earning on the *Ocean Curse* was tucked safely under my mattress, but even if I had brought it with me, I wouldn't be tempted to purchase anything. I had nowhere to wear fine jewelry or pretty clothing.

Besides, all I could think about was finding my mother.

The morning wore on, and my stomach began to growl as I followed Marcus and Hawk's progress along Bay Street. Each time Marcus left a business, I looked to him with anticipation, but a quick shake of his head would fill me with disappointment.

Perhaps my mother wasn't here after all.

At midday, Marcus met me on the street, his countenance heavy. "I'm sorry, lass. No one has heard of Anne Reed."

"How is that possible?" I asked. "She said she lived here."

"Mayhap she used a different name."

I hadn't thought of that possibility.

"Let's get something to eat, and we'll keep trying." Marcus put his hand at the small of my back.

I inhaled at his gentle touch. It was filled with both understanding and protectiveness, communicating his concern for me.

He led me to an open-air restaurant under a thatch roof. It sat on a point facing the harbor and Hog Island. Dozens of ships had been abandoned on the beach, left to rot in the sun. Others were at anchor in the harbor, waiting for their crews to set sail again.

"Where is Hawk?" I asked.

"He is visiting an old . . . friend." Marcus said the word *friend* in such a way that I suspected Hawk was at a brothel. Thoughts of Thomas at Nina Clifford's brothel made a shiver run up my spine, but I pushed the memory away. Today I would think about my mother.

We sat across from each other at the end of a long, rough-hewn table. There were others dining at the establishment, but they were far enough away, I felt some semblance of privacy.

The wind blew off the harbor, offering a cool breeze to temper the heat. It ruffled Marcus's dark hair, while the sun brightened his deep brown eyes. His commanding presence had brought attention throughout the day, and even now as we sat in the restaurant, several of the young women were watching him, trying to draw his attention. I didn't want to contemplate whether or not he would have joined Hawk at the brothel if I wasn't with him, but the thought wouldn't leave.

A flicker of amusement warmed his gaze. "The answer is nay."

My cheeks burned at his perception. "How do you know what I was thinking?"

"Your eyes give away everything." He clasped his hands on the table. "I know the moment I look at you whether you are suspicious of me, angry with me—" He paused, and I knew he was thinking about the night he'd plundered the frigate. "Or pleased with me, though you haven't looked happy with me in a long time."

I thought about the many times he had pleased me, and I couldn't help but smile.

He returned the smile and shook his head. "'Tis that look that goes right to my heart. I would do anything to make you happy."

A middle-aged woman approached with two tankards of ale and two plates of stew, interrupting our conversation. Wrinkles threaded across her face, and streaks of gray lined her dark hair. Her skin was tanned from the sun, and her clothes were threadbare. The only thing truly remarkable about her were her light blue eyes that almost looked translucent.

She set the food down and said, "'Aven't seen the likes of you before. Where do you hail from?"

Marcus glanced at her, but didn't seem eager for her to stay. "Scotland."

"And what 'bout you?" she asked me.

I wasn't sure what Marcus would want me to say, so I simply said, "South Carolina."

She lowered her hands to her hips. "You look familiar."

My instinct was to cower, to hide my identity—but what if I looked familiar because I looked like my mother?

"Mayhap you knew my mother," I said tentatively, aware of the young women who were paying attention to our end of the table.

"Aye? And who might that be?"

"Anne Reed."

The woman slowly dropped her hands to her side. Her surprise turned to concern, and then she bent forward and said quietly, "Did you say Anne Reed?"

"Yes, ma'am."

"She was your mother?"

My pulse escalated, and I sat up straighter. "Did you know her?"

"Aye." She stared at me hard. "But most who knew her are long gone—most but me."

This woman knew my mother! I leaned forward. "Is she here?"

She set her hand on my shoulder. "Anne Reed died fourteen years ago, come October."

I shook my head, not willing to accept what she was saying. "She can't be dead."

"I'm afraid she is."

Marcus was silent as he sat across from me, disappointment in the slope of his shoulders.

My chest became heavy with despair. I'd come so far, risking my life, only to discover that my mother was dead. How was I going to find the answers I needed? How would I know why we carried this burden? Or how I could get rid of it?

"What is your name?" Marcus asked the woman.

"Mary Jones," she said. "I—I knew Anne well."

"Mayhap you'd like to speak to Mary alone," Marcus said to me. "I'm sure you have questions for her."

"Come with me, love," Mary said.

Without another word, I stood from the table and followed Mary out of the building, toward the beach. The sun was blinding as it reflected off the white sand.

"I 'ave questions of me own," she said as soon as we stopped near the bones of a forgotten ship. Her gaze penetrated mine. "Anne had a daughter—not a son."

Nodding, I said, "My name is Caroline Reed. I dressed as a boy to find passage to Nassau."

"You've done a convincing job, but I can see you beneath the costume. You look like your mum."

"Do I?" I searched her face, seeking answers. Something to hold, to take with me. "I'm desperate to know all I can about her. My grandfather told me very little."

Mary sighed. "I'm not proud of me past, but my friendship with Anne was something I can hold me head up about. Never did I 'ave a more loyal friend than her."

"How did you meet? How long did you know her? Did she tell you anything about me or my father? Was she—"

"Hold on, love," she said as she held up a hand and then motioned to a large piece of driftwood that looked like it had once belonged to a ship. "Let's 'ave a seat. I think your man will wait."

"He's not my man."

"No?" She smiled. "Now that I know you're a woman, it makes sense why he looks at you the way he does. He cares for you, love."

My heart sped at her words, and I glanced back at the restaurant where I'd left him. He had stood and was now leaning against the doorframe, his arms crossed, watching from a distance. His attentive care for me had brought me to this woman who had known my mother, and he was still vigilant to ensure my safety.

Perhaps he did care for me, more than I realized. It was a revelation I had to push to the back of my mind as I sat on the driftwood and faced Mary. I couldn't contemplate Marcus's feelings for me when I needed to focus on learning about my mother. "What can you tell me about Anne Reed?"

Mary gazed at the ocean, squinting, as if trying to see into the past. "She was young, much younger than me, but she had an old soul. She came to Nassau with her husband in '06, I believe. He was a quiet seaman of no consequence—and no match for Anne's fiery ways. I don't like to speak ill o' the dead, but I think he was your mum's passage out of South Carolina. As soon as she arrived, mayhap the first day, she met and fell in love with a young, reckless pirate of the worst sort named Sam Delaney. He was her match in every way. They were both passionate and stubborn. But he did right by her and purchased a divorce from her husband, then he married her at sea.

"That's when I met her. I was living much like you, dressed as a man, working as a pirate. There were several women out there living like us, but they hid it well. Still do. Your mum saw through my disguise, though, and we became friends, fighting alongside the men. Plundering ships was our business." Her pride was evident as she spoke those words. "Back in the day, there was respect for pirates. The colonists saw us attacking their oppressors and taking back what was ours. Being a privateer was legal—if you had permission from the king. You could plunder an enemy's ship and take what you wanted. But if you didn't have permission, you were an outlaw. I ask you, what is the difference? Approval from the king? That makes it right or wrong?"

I listened quietly, soaking up all the information. The lives of the pirates weren't too unlike those of the gangsters in 1927. When alcohol was legal, there had been problems with the law, but nothing like the trouble that had started once the government decided alcohol was illegal. Organized crime had skyrocketed and then become so overwhelming, it was paralyzing America. Just as pirating had begun to paralyze Great Britain when the king deemed privateering—the capture of enemy ships—illegal.

I had expected this kind of story about my mother, but it still hurt to know she had left her first husband to take up with a pirate. Yet . . .

"Which man was my father?" I asked, almost breathless.

"Anne was pregnant when I met her," she explained. "Thirteen was young, but I knew other girls her age facing the same circumstances. She was desperate to keep it a secret. She told me she had to get away, to take you far from Sam. I never knew if that was because you were conceived from her first marriage, and she didn't want Sam to know—or if you were Sam's child, and she didn't want Sam to know."

"You never learned?"

She shook her head. "Sorry, love. I don't even know if your mum knew who your father was."

"What about when she came back?" I asked. "Was Sam angry she left?"

"Angry doesn't begin to describe his mood. He recklessly stormed the Caribbean for months while she was gone, but when she returned, it was as if she'd never left. And they picked up where they'd left off. For five years, they moved about the Caribbean, the American colonies, and even crossed the Atlantic to Africa now and again. I never saw two people so much in love, but they seemed to fuel each other's wildness. Eventually, Sam met his fate at the end of a noose, and your mum was heartbroken. We returned to Nassau, but she was never the same."

"How did she die?"

Mary's blue eyes were sad as she said, "She went to sleep one night and never woke up."

I frowned. "What do you mean? What killed her?"

154

"I don't know, love. Some think she died of a broken heart." Mary toyed with a loose thread on her skirt. "It was her twenty-first birthday. She died young, but she lived more life than some who die at a hundred."

"She died on her twenty-first birthday? How awful." My twenty-first birthday was quickly approaching on September 2. It was far too young to die.

Neither one of us spoke for a few moments, but there was still one pressing question. A question I wasn't sure Mary could answer, but I had to ask.

"Did she—" I paused. How would I ask this question without sounding insane? "Did she ever talk about her strange life?"

Mary frowned, but she searched my face. "What strange life?"

I briefly closed my eyes, not knowing how to even voice this question without stating it outright. But this was my last chance—the last link I had to possibly find the answers. Who cared what Mary thought of me?

"Did she ever mention anything about a second life?" I whispered, though no one was close enough to hear. "Not here, but in a different time and place?"

The silence grew between us, until Mary said, "You mean, when she went to sleep here and woke up somewhere else?"

I grabbed Mary's hand and nodded. "Yes. Did she ever speak of it to you?"

"How did you know?" she asked me in a stunned hush.

I swallowed my trepidation and said, "Because *I* live two lives, and I found a letter she wrote saying that she did, as well."

Mary shook her head, pulling her hand back. "I hardly believe it. Sometimes I thought Anne was addlebrained, or she'd had too much to drink when she spoke of it. I was the only person she confided in, and I humored her, but she was so convincing."

"It was true," I assured her. "Can you tell me where else my mother lived? What year did she say?"

Mary frowned and took her time, as if she was thinking hard to remember. "She said she lived in Texas."

"Texas? Do you know when?"

Again, Mary frowned.

"Please tell me," I begged.

"Before she died, she said she was living in 1913, I think it was."

My eyes widened. "She lived in Texas in 1913? That's only fourteen years before my time now." I thought through the possibilities. "My mother might be alive in my other life in 1927."

Mary didn't speak, but she looked troubled, as if she couldn't quite believe what I was saying.

"Do you know her name there?"

"She said her first name was Anne there, too, but they called her Annie. Her last name was—" She paused in thought. "Barker, I think. Annie Barker."

My breath stilled as the familiar name pierced my heart. I knew the name Annie Barker. Everyone in America knew the name.

"It can't be true," I told her, shaking my head. "She must have had a different name."

"That was the name she told me," Mary said with more confidence. "She was called Annie Barker in Texas in 1913. I haven't thought about it in years, but it's not something a person forgets."

I stood, dread filling me with the knowledge of who my mother might be in 1927.

Annie Barker was a wanted bank robber, bootlegger, and kidnapper.

She couldn't be my mother.

Marcus didn't press me for answers when I returned to him, but thanked Mary for the meal, paid for our food, and then gently placed his hand on the small of my back again to lead me out of the stifling restaurant.

I leaned into his strength, thankful for this one person who stood by my side. Mary's words about Marcus returned, and I studied his face to search for the answer.

As he looked back at me, unguarded, I saw the truth. Marcus Zale cared deeply for me.

My heart pounded with awareness as his hand slipped around my waist and tightened.

"I'm sorry about your mother, lass. I wish things were different for you."

I nodded, wishing they were, too.

He sighed. "We need to find Hawk and return to the *Ocean Curse*. We've done all we can here."

I didn't want to return to the pirate ship or face life in 1927 tomorrow. I wanted to stay with Marcus, to feel his arms around me, to forget about everything that was hindering me from what I wanted.

But I had no choice. Instead, I blindly followed him through the market until we saw Hawk. Marcus removed his hand from my waist before Hawk could see, and I missed his touch instantly.

The large man told us he had located a buyer for the goods on the *Ocean Curse*, so after Marcus led us back to the ship, he ordered some of his men to take the goods to the buyer and make the transaction.

I went to Marcus's cabin, feeling truly sick to my stomach about my mother. I sat on my cot for what felt like hours, hugging my knees to my chest and trying to make sense of what Mary had told me. The hidden harbor we occupied was calm and tranquil, contrary to my tumultuous mind and heart.

As the sun fell behind the horizon and the stars appeared in the sky, my thoughts began to darken, as well.

My mother had been a pirate in this life and possibly a gangster in her other life. In all my imaginings, I hadn't thought we occupied both lives together—or that my mother could be a villain in both times. Surely, she'd be just as surprised as me to learn the truth. I prayed, even though God felt so far away. I hoped there was more than one Annie Barker in Texas, and that my mother wasn't the notorious criminal reigning terror across the Midwest.

If she *was* the Annie Barker I feared, then both her lives would be filled with crime—which led me to wonder if she had a choice. Was she predestined for evil? Was that part of the curse that my grandmother had placed on her in 1692?

The door to Marcus's cabin opened, and he appeared. His countenance was heavy as he entered the room and closed the door behind him.

Relief filled my heart, knowing I wasn't alone anymore.

Despite my anger at him earlier in the week, I rose from my cot as he opened his arms to me, and I entered his embrace.

He wrapped one arm around my waist as his other came up, and he cradled the back of my head in his hand.

I pressed my cheek to his chest, listening to the steady rhythm of his heart. It beat fast and strong, matching the tempo of my own. This was the first time he'd embraced me, but it felt as if I belonged here, as if my heart and body had finally found a home.

"Do you want to talk about it?" he whispered.

I had no one to share this burden with, and it was too much for me to bear alone. He might never believe me, but I had to tell someone. I couldn't say anything to Ruth or my brothers, and my parents had already chastised me. I thought about Nanny and how I'd tried to tell her, but she had rejected the truth, as well.

Marcus understood what it was like to lose a mother and to be an outcast—which is how I felt. My entire existence was lived as an outsider, and the one person I thought might understand, my mother, was probably a dangerous criminal. And because he had trusted me with his past, I could trust him with mine. I felt it, deep within. Even if he was a pirate, even if he made choices I didn't understand, Marcus was honorable and trustworthy.

And more than that, he cared about me.

"Aye," I said as I moved out of his embrace. My legs felt unsteady, so I took a seat on the cot as he pulled a Windsor chair away from the table and brought it to my bedside. He sat facing me, his elbows on his knees, and waited for me to speak.

The cabin had never felt so intimate as it did in this moment.

Light from the single lantern barely reached us, and the stars outside the ship sparkled with brilliance.

"I fear you won't believe what I have to say," I told him, searching his face.

"You've given me no reason to doubt you before, lass."

Perhaps it was the fear of never finding my mother, or the pain in knowing she was no longer here. Whatever it was, I was not worried about what Marcus would think. His concern for me prompted me to share the deepest pain with him. "My mother came to Nassau with her husband, but then she took up with another man before returning to South Carolina to leave me with Grandfather. She lived as a pirate for five years, before her second husband was hanged. Shortly after, she died in her sleep on her twenty-first birthday." It was still hard to believe, and my voice choked with emotion.

Marcus leaned forward and took my hand into his. "I'm sorry, Caroline."

His hand was so much bigger than mine, so coarse from pulling ropes, moving cargo, and brandishing his sword. Yet it was achingly tender and soothing. He'd not only become my protector, but also my confidant and my source of strength. Other men in his position might have taken advantage of me, but he had only shown me kindness. Had God provided a protector in my foolish, headstrong pursuit? I had not thought to thank God, but I did now.

Perhaps He did hear my prayers, even ones I had been afraid to whisper.

"What will you do?" he asked as he ran his thumb against my skin, turning it to fire, making it hard to concentrate.

I swallowed and said, "There is more to the story."

"There usually is," he said with an affectionate smile.

"This is the part I'm not sure you'll believe." I gently pulled my hand away, needing to focus as I told him the rest. I'd only ever tried to tell Nanny and Mother the truth. Would Marcus look at me the way they had? I wasn't sure I could bear it. But I needed to tell someone.

If Anne hadn't been brave—or foolish—enough to tell Mary, I would never know that she might be alive in 1927.

Marcus sat back and waited.

I had to stand to tell him this part, to give myself space. I paced to the other side of the cabin and decided to dive in without preamble. "I have two lives. This one and another in 1927. When I go to sleep here, my consciousness travels to my other body in 1927. There, my name is Caroline Baldwin. I'm the same age, I look the same, and I have all the same memories and thoughts. When I go to sleep there, I wake up back here, and no time has passed while I'm away."

A slight frown tilted his eyebrows, but he didn't speak.

"My mother, Anne Reed, had the same ability. She told me in her letter, and then Mary confirmed it for me today. Anne lived here until she was twenty-one, but she was also alive in Texas in 1913 at the time." I felt like I was rambling, but I needed to get it all out. "I believe that Anne's mother, my grandmother, was killed as a witch in Salem in 1692. And I'm afraid she placed a curse on us. It's the only thing that makes sense. I need to find Anne to know if it's true. And, if it is, how to be rid of the curse."

Silence filled the room until I felt like it would suffocate me. I slowly walked back to my cot and took a seat, facing Marcus.

"I told you it was unbelievable." My voice was quiet, but I had come this far. I would tell him the rest. "The worst part is that Mary told me my mother's name in 1913 was Annie Barker, and the only Annie Barker I've ever heard of is a notorious criminal, wanted in several states for theft, bootlegging, and kidnapping." Saying the words out loud made them feel real. Horrible.

His frown deepened, and my disappointment became so keen, it felt like a physical twist in my gut. I looked down at my hands, feeling the weight of Nanny's displeasure and Mother and Father's punishment all over again.

"Your claims seem impossible," he said as he took my hands into his again and I looked up at him. "But your eyes speak the truth. And if I've learned anything, 'tis that the eyes cannot lie."

The weight began to lift as breath escaped my mouth in a quiet exhale.

Marcus believed me. He looked into my soul, and he recognized the truth. No one, not even those I knew and loved the most in the world, had looked beyond the impossible. Something profound shifted within me, and I felt a connection to Marcus that I'd never felt with anyone.

He understood me.

"I don't know how or why, but 'tis true," I said, swallowing my emotions. "And I hate it. I want to be like everyone else and only live in one place."

"And which one would you choose?"

There was more to his simple question—it was in the way his voice dipped with the need to know my response.

I shook my head. "I don't know."

He studied me, not with disbelief but curiosity. "This is a fantastical story."

I nodded.

"What will you do?"

"I'm going to look for Annie Barker in 1927." And I knew someone who might have the connections to help me. Lewis.

But how would I tell him I needed to find Annie Barker without telling him why?

"I wish I could help you there," he said, pulling my thoughts back to the pirate ship, where Marcus was still holding my hands, his brogue deep. "What can I do for you here?"

His handsome face was so close to mine, and my traitorous heart beat a rhythm that was frightening. I wanted him, even if it wasn't wise or realistic. I wanted him to pull me into his arms again, to shelter me, love me, protect me. But to do that, he'd have to give up pirating. Because I couldn't love a man who took wealth and dignity from others.

When I didn't answer, he rubbed my hands with his thumbs and said, "Do you want to return to South Carolina? To your grandfather?"

"No." That much I knew. "If I return there, he'll force me to marry a man I do not love."

Something flickered through Marcus's eyes, and his grasp tightened.

Hope clawed to life in my heart. I wanted him to know how I felt, and wanted to believe he felt the same for me, but it scared me to be so vulnerable since there was no future with Marcus. I would be forced to watch him go the same way as Sam Delaney—on the end of a noose.

Marcus stood and walked to the other side of the room. "If you don't want to go to South Carolina, then where do you want to go? You don't belong here."

"I don't have anywhere else."

"You said your grandmother lived in Salem. Mayhap you have family there."

"I cannot go to Salem. If my grandmother was killed as a witch, I cannot imagine they'd look kindly upon my arrival."

"Witchcraft is no longer a hanging offense," he said.

"It doesn't matter. I don't know her name, only my grandfather's, and he had no family in Salem. He came from England, and then after my grandmother's death, he moved to South Carolina. I wouldn't even know how to look for her relatives, and I doubt they'd want me."

His gaze was so raw, so tender, my heart beat hard when he said, "I can't imagine anyone not wanting you."

I swallowed the rush of emotions and said, "I don't have anyone to turn to."

He continued to pace, setting his hand at the back of his neck. "I don't have anyone, either—anyone I know who might take you in." He paused near the bookcase and touched the family Bible. "Unless." He took a deep breath. "Mayhap I could find my mother if she's alive. She was the kindest soul on earth. She'd take you in."

My lips parted as he turned back to me.

"You'd look for your mother—for me?"

"I'd do anything for you, Caroline."

Tears filled my eyes, but I forced them away.

I was all alone in 1727—yet for the first time in this life, I didn't feel lonely.

Because I had Marcus.

14

JULY 9, 1927
SAINT PAUL, MINNESOTA

For the second time in two days, I found myself on the electric streetcar, traveling from Minneapolis to Saint Paul. It was Saturday, which meant that Lewis was likely off duty. I had never been to his home but had found his address in Mother's address book. He lived on Grand Avenue in the Summit Hill neighborhood, which was a fashionable part of Saint Paul full of expensive shopping and beautiful homes. Which begged the question, How did Lewis afford to live in such a nice neighborhood on a policeman's salary?

I didn't want to think of what he told me about the crooked policemen in Saint Paul, or where he might be getting some extra cash.

It was still early, but I could not wait to speak to him. Ever since I'd learned the news that my mother in 1727 could also be alive in 1927, I had thought of little else—except, perhaps, Marcus.

I switched cars at Snelling Avenue and rode for a short distance until I reached Grand. The street was filled with people shopping, strolling along the tree-lined sidewalks, and breakfasting in cafes. Though it was early, it was already hot and humid.

When the streetcar stopped at the corner of Grand Avenue and Dale Street, I exited, happy to leave the cramped quarters behind. I had to backtrack a couple of blocks to reach 581 Grand Avenue, but when I did, I was pleased to find an attractive two-story apartment building made of brown brick with white cornices and trim work. I hoped Lewis was home and that I could find a way to convince him to help me look for Annie Barker.

More than anything, I wanted to prove the criminal wasn't my mother and that I would find another Annie Barker from Texas. But I needed help, and Lewis would have access to that information. I could have asked Thomas, but he would still be angry with me.

I crossed Grand Avenue and walked up the concrete steps to the front door, looking over my shoulder before letting myself into the building. If someone learned that I had visited a single man at his home, the gossip could hurt Father's reputation as much as it could hurt mine. But this couldn't wait.

It was only a little cooler inside as I walked down the hallway to apartment number three.

Even though I'd known Lewis most of my life, it still felt odd to visit him at his home. Alone. But after yesterday and going to Nina Clifford's brothel with him, this wouldn't be the most shocking thing I'd ever done.

With a firm rap, I knocked on his door and then stepped back to wait, hoping no one would find me in the hallway.

It took a few moments, but I could hear the sliding of a lock, and then the door opened.

Lewis stood on the other side holding a bowl of cornflakes, his face unshaven and his hair mussed, as if he'd recently woken up. He was wearing a pair of trousers, a simple white undershirt, and suspenders. His feet and arms were bare.

He looked surprisingly handsome.

"Carrie!" he said with both shock and pleasure. "What are you doing here?"

I had never seen him in such a state of undress—at least, not since we were young and had gone swimming at a lake near our home. But he'd only been a boy then, and not the man standing before me.

"I—" My cheeks were flaming, and I was more flustered than I anticipated. "May I come in?"

"Let me put on a shirt." He set his bowl on a nearby table and left the door open, disappearing into the back room.

I cautiously entered his home, closing the door behind me in case someone would come along and see me there.

His apartment wasn't very large, which was why he could probably afford it on his salary. But it was tidy and comfortable. To the left of the main room was a kitchen, and to the right were two doors. Lewis had gone into one, which I presumed was the bedroom, and the other was open, revealing a small bathroom.

I stood in the parlor, clutching my purse, though I didn't regret coming. I needed to find Annie Barker, and I didn't care what it would take.

A few minutes later, Lewis reappeared wearing a white button-down shirt, which he had tucked into his trousers. His suspenders were now over the shirt, and he was wearing socks and shoes. His brown hair had also been combed—but he hadn't taken the time to shave.

"Have a seat," he said as he picked up his cereal bowl and a stack of newspapers and brought them to the kitchen. "Would you like something to drink or eat?"

"No, thank you." I sat on the edge of the sofa, trying not to fidget with my purse. Instead, I set it on the coffee table and clasped my hands on my lap.

When Lewis returned to the parlor, he seemed uncertain about where to sit—next to me on the sofa or on the nearby chair? Finally, he sat on the chair and asked, "What are you doing here, Caroline?"

"I need a favor."

"Oh." He leaned back in his chair, obviously disappointed. "Do you need help getting rid of Alice?"

"No—yes—but that's not why I'm here." I licked my dry lips,

wishing I had taken his offer for something to drink. How would I explain this request? "I need help finding someone."

His frown deepened. "Who?"

I nibbled my bottom lip and then blurted out, "Annie Barker."

A dozen questions crossed his face before he asked, "Annie Barker, the criminal?"

"Yes." I shook my head. "No."

"What do you mean?"

"I need to know if there is more than one Annie Barker from Texas."

"Why?"

"I'm looking for someone with that name, but I'm hoping the one I'm looking for isn't the criminal."

He was quiet for another moment, and then his serious expression softened. He joined me on the sofa and began to laugh. "If you wanted to come and see me, you could have come up with a better excuse."

My lips parted in surprise, and I backed away from him. "You think I'm teasing?"

"You must be. What in the world would you need with Annie Barker? She's one of the most wanted women in America. Even if you were serious, and we needed to find her, it would be almost impossible. No one can find her. That's why she's wanted."

"I'm hoping that the Annie Barker I need *isn't* the criminal," I reminded him. "That's why I want your help. I've never been more serious in my life, Lewis."

His face sobered, and he frowned. "Why do you need to speak to someone named Annie Barker?"

I could no longer sit, so I stood and walked to the window. The apartment had a view of the side lawn and the apartment building next door. "I can't tell you. But I promise I have a good reason."

He joined me near the window. "If you truly want my help, I need to know why you want to talk to her."

"You wouldn't believe me, even if I told you."

He crossed his arms and said, "Try me."

Unlike Marcus, I had known Lewis for years, but I still didn't know if he'd believe me.

"Please don't laugh," I said.

Lewis took a step closer to me, his voice lowered. He put his hand on my shoulder. "What's wrong? I've never seen you like this before."

"I'm desperate, Lewis, and you're the only person who might help."

He took my hand, much like he had yesterday, and drew me to the sofa where he sat beside me. And like yesterday, he didn't let it go. "What is it, Carrie?"

I had to tell him the truth or there was no way he'd help me. Before yesterday, I wasn't sure I could have told Lewis about my second life, but telling Marcus had made it easier.

"You're going to think I'm insane, but I promise this is true." I took a deep breath. "I have two lives, Lewis. This one—and one in 1727." I explained to him how it worked and how I woke up each day in a different life. I told him about my mother and what I had learned from Mary about her name in 1927.

I told him everything—but I didn't tell him about Marcus, or how much I had come to care for a pirate.

Lewis never looked away from me as I spoke. I could see confusion and even doubt in his gaze, but he listened intently, probably like he did when he was questioning a witness. He didn't laugh or chastise or scoff.

"If it's true," he said slowly, "how is it possible?"

"I'm not sure. It's always been this way, ever since I can remember."

"You're telling me that the entire time we were growing up, you were living two lives at the same time?"

"Yes."

"What do your parents say?"

Until then, I hadn't realized he was still holding my hand. I drew it away and began to fiddle with the fold in my skirt. "I tried telling them when I was little, but they accused me of lying, and I was told to keep quiet."

"I'm sorry to hear that. But do you truly think you were cursed by a grandmother in Salem?"

"I don't know. That's why I need to find the right Annie Barker. She is the only person who might answer my questions."

"What if you were able to find her—which would be almost impossible if she *is* the criminal—and she has no more information than you?"

I didn't even want to think about that possibility. "It's a risk I must take. I need to know who I am—or what I am." I was quiet for a moment and then said, "Do you believe me, Lewis?"

He took a deep breath and then let it out. "I've never known you to lie, and I don't know why you would make up such a strange story, so I have no choice but to believe you."

Something broke inside me, and I leaned into him. He paused for only a heartbeat and then put his arms around me, drawing me into his embrace.

"Thank you," I whispered. But I quickly realized I was far too vulnerable to remain in his arms—alone—in his apartment, so I gently pulled away.

He tentatively reached for my hand again, and this time I was conscious of his skin against mine. The moment had become too serious, and I didn't like it when Lewis was serious.

"Carr—"

"Will you help me?" I asked as I pulled my hand away. I didn't want him to say something to make either of us uncomfortable. "Will you investigate and find out if there is more than one Annie Barker?"

He clasped his hands together and nodded, defeat in the slope of his shoulders. "Of course."

"Thank you." I tried to smile. "And promise me you won't tell anyone what I've said about—about why I need to find Annie. I don't think anyone will understand or believe me, and I wouldn't want to bring shame or embarrassment upon my family."

"I won't."

Neither one of us spoke for a moment, but when Lewis tried to reach for my hand again, I quickly stood and said, "Thank you. I'm sorry for showing up unannounced. I suppose I'll always be the annoying little sister at heart."

The look he gave me made me regret my choice of words immediately.

Lewis Cager did not see me as an annoying little sister, not anymore—perhaps he never had.

15

JULY 10, 1727
ATLANTIC OCEAN

I slowly blinked my eyes open to the brilliant sunshine streaming through the thick, wavy glass windows on the *Ocean Curse*. We were back at sea, which meant the rhythmic creaking and swaying of the ship would be constant companions again.

"Good morning," Marcus said from across the cabin.

I turned and found Marcus sitting in one of the chairs near the shelves, a book in hand.

"What are you doing?" I asked as I sat, pulling my blanket up to my chin.

He slowly closed his book and set it on the table beside him. "I wanted to see what happened when you sleep."

"You were watching me sleep?" I wasn't sure why that made me feel so vulnerable—we slept in the same room every night—but it did—and I didn't mind.

"For a wee bit. I haven't been up for long."

I put my bare feet on the ground and pulled the covers around my shoulders, clasping them tightly next to my chest. "And?"

A gentle smile tilted his lips. "Nothing remarkable, I'm afraid."

For the first time in a long time, I wanted to laugh. "What did you think would happen?"

"I don't know." He shrugged. "I was hoping you would talk in your sleep, but that didn't happen."

I wrinkled my nose. "Did I do anything?"

"Nay." There was still humor in his voice. "You slept like a wee bairn. Peaceful and content."

Warmth infused my cheeks, and I smiled, though it soon dimmed. "I didn't feel peaceful while I was away. I asked a friend to help me find Annie Barker, and—" How did I tell him that I felt uncomfortable with the affection Lewis was starting to show me? I didn't want to encourage Lewis, yet I needed his help. Could I maintain a friendship with him without leading him on? "'Tis hard to gain someone's trust and help when you have to tell them you live two lives."

"Aye." He leaned forward, resting his elbows on his knees. "You said it was two hundred years in the future. What is it like?"

I clutched the edges of my blanket as I, too, leaned forward, excited by his enthusiasm to learn about my lives. There was something freeing about telling him and Lewis the truth about my existence. I had always known it was a burden too difficult to bear alone, but until now, I hadn't realized how much it helped to talk about it.

"It's so different than here," I said, slipping into my accent and turn of phrase I used in 1927. All my life, I'd been careful to speak properly in whatever time I occupied. People looked at me strangely when I misspoke, and I didn't like drawing unwanted attention or answering questions that would make people suspicious. But now that Marcus knew the truth, I could be myself around him. That, in itself, was the most freeing thing of all. "There are horseless carriages that are powered by motors, and airplanes that fly through the sky, carrying passengers. There are radios and telephones that transmit people's voices over hundreds or even thousands of miles. And there is no more need for candles and lanterns because we have electric lighting. We also have running water indoors, with warm baths and showers, just by turning the handle of a faucet."

Marcus's face went from curious to disbelieving in a heartbeat, and I realized I probably sounded more insane than before. The differences in my lifestyles from one time to the next were shocking. The advancements that humans had made, even in the past two decades of my life in the 1920s, were astounding.

"People fly in 1927?" he asked me.

I nodded, my voice lowering with disappointment that he had become skeptical. "In machines called airplanes. A man just flew over the Atlantic Ocean, from New York to Paris in thirty-three and a half hours."

He thought about that for a moment and then said, "And where do you live?"

"Minnesota."

A frown formed between his eyebrows. "I don't know Minnesota."

"It's at the headwaters of the Mississippi River, in the middle of the North American continent." In 1727, the land was mostly inhabited by fur traders and Indians, and it had no official name. I wasn't sure how much I should tell him about America, but what would it matter if he knew it all? "In 1776, the American colonies will declare independence from England and there will be a war, which will result in America becoming its own country. Many people will migrate to America and will begin to move west, across the Mississippi River, and fill up the vast land. Eventually, it will be divided into forty-eight states."

His skepticism increased while his frown deepened. "The colonies will gain independence? England is the strongest nation on Earth. How will that happen?"

"Some say it's a miracle." Would Marcus or I live long enough to see it happen? "The world is constantly changing, and history is full of surprises," I said. "We are all part of God's story. And He can do what He wills."

"Aye." Marcus nodded, his skepticism fading. "That I know. Do you think 'tis His will that you live like this?"

It was my turn to frown. I'd never considered such a thing.

"Mayhap it isn't a curse after all," he continued before I could respond, "but a gift from God that only a few are privileged to experience."

"A gift?" I shook my head, wanting to scoff. "Nay, 'tis not a gift."

"I would love to see another time and place." He stood and walked to the window, leaning his forearm against the top of the frame. "To be free of this ship, this life, if only for a day."

"Why don't you leave?" I asked, my pulse ticking higher. "Start over?"

"Where would I go?" he asked. "What would I do? I'm a wanted man."

I broached my suggestion with caution, not knowing how he might respond. "Mayhap if you find your mother, you could rejoin her. Take back your old name."

He didn't move as he continued to look out the window at the vast, empty ocean.

"I've thought of it on a thousand sleepless nights," he said, his voice low. "But I can't face her after what I did. She probably despises me."

Six bells rang. I would be missed if I didn't leave now to get the captain's breakfast. Marcus, too, was expected in the cabin below. But I rose from my cot, still holding the blanket close, and joined him at the window.

"If it was me," I said, slowly, cautiously—but with certainty, "I would not care what separated us, whether you had left against your will or of your own choosing. I would want to see you again, to know that you were alive and well." My voice dipped, though I tried to steady it. "To lay my eyes upon you, if only one more time."

Marcus slowly turned away from the window, his intense gaze searching mine. He was so much taller than me, but it was not his height nor his breadth that made me feel defenseless in his presence.

It was the fire I saw behind his eyes, the intelligence and desire for something more than what he had. It was the same desire I held, both here and in 1927. To live a life of my own choosing—not the ones chosen for me.

I wanted to return to his embrace, but I backed up, feeling like I had laid bare my heart, though unintentionally. "I must get breakfast."

I quickly turned away from him and lowered the blanket onto the cot, then put on my vest, shoes, and hat before escaping from his cabin.

If I wasn't careful, I would reveal my heart to Marcus and then I would be powerless.

But it wasn't the fear of revelation that scared me the most. It was the fear that even if he did return my affection, I couldn't accept it.

I hurried to the galley and found that breakfast was still waiting for me.

"Where is Ned?" I asked the cook, but he only scowled at me, then began to spew French words I didn't understand.

I took the pot of oatmeal, the pitcher of ale, and the platter of bread and made my way to the captain's cabin. As always, Hawk was waiting for me to open the outer room door.

"You're late," he said.

"Where is Ned? He wasn't in the galley."

"Sick again." Hawk tilted his head toward the outer room. "Can't leave his cot."

I entered the room, my hands full, and found Ned still asleep. I didn't bother to wake him, knowing he'd probably hurl more angry words at me. He had seemed to rally for a few days, only to be down again. Perhaps it was more than a passing illness that afflicted him.

When I walked into the captain's cabin, all the men were present and seated at the table—Marcus included.

"You're late," Captain Zale said with a snarl.

"'Twas my fault," Marcus said quickly.

I set the food and drink on the table, my cheeks warming at the memory of what I'd told him about my two lives and of him watching me slumber.

"I kept him this morning," Marcus said to the captain.

There was nothing the captain could say to that since I was tasked with serving Marcus.

I had never spoken without being spoken to first, but as I filled Dr. Hartville's mug with ale, I asked quietly, "Is anything to be done about Ned?"

"Mind your own business," Captain Zale said, his harsh words full of anger.

Embarrassment and fear silenced my tongue as I continued to serve the men.

"Are you certain you want to head back to the Florida coast?" Marcus asked the captain as they began to eat their meal.

"Aye." Captain Zale took a long drink and dropped the cup to the table with a thud. "The sooner, the better. Hawk said that there was talk in Nassau that the *Atlantis* is already there. I'll move heaven and earth to get to the Queen's Dowry before someone else."

I'd heard about the *Atlantis* several times around this table and gathered that the captain of the other pirate ship had once served on the *Ocean Curse* before abandoning the crew to start his own. Captain Zale not only wanted to find the Queen's Dowry first, but he also wanted to beat his nemesis.

"The Spanish Armada has increased their patrol of the Florida coast," Marcus told him. "Is it worth the risk? Mayhap we avoid staying close to Florida and go north for a wee bit."

"North?" Captain Zale frowned.

"Merchant ships should be plentiful at this time of year," Hawk said with a shrug, supporting Marcus's suggestion. "'Tis been a while since we've overtaken a cargo of tobacco off the coast of Virginia."

A pirate ship was a democracy, and each man had his vote, but the captain's vote carried the greatest weight unless the prevailing opinions differed from his own. If Marcus could get enough men on his side, perhaps we could head north to his mother.

"We can have all the tobacco we want if we get the Queen's Dowry," Captain Zale said, tearing a chunk of bread from the loaf. "Now that we have the diving bell, we'll have no trouble locating the treasure."

"That diving bell is a health hazard," Dr. Hartville said. "It'll be the death of whoever is forced to use it. 'Tis hardly big enough for a grown man."

The captain's gaze lifted to mine, and a half smile tilted his lips. "Carl is small and healthy. We'll send him down. 'Tis the reason I chose him."

My hand froze as I poured the ale into Hawk's cup. I'd recalled the captain making mention of his desire for me to help with the search before, but I'd been so preoccupied with thoughts of my mother that I hadn't considered the possibility.

Marcus's spoon stopped midway to his mouth, and he slowly lowered his hand. Perhaps he, too, had forgotten the captain's plans. "You can't send the lad to the bottom of the ocean. He has no experience."

"We'll teach him," the captain said, shoveling oatmeal into his mouth.

"'Tis not wise," Marcus tried again. "We don't even know if he swims."

"Do you swim?" Captain Zale asked me.

I stood straight, holding the pitcher of ale in both my trembling hands. I couldn't lie. I had grown up swimming in the lakes near my home in Minneapolis and the Cooper River on Grandfather's plantation. I loved to swim, but I had no wish to enter a diving bell and go to the bottom of the ocean. I wasn't even sure what a diving bell was, though I could easily imagine.

And how could I hide the fact that I was a woman if I was forced to dive? Most men would swim without their shirts on—

something I couldn't do. If the others believed I was modest and I was allowed to dive in a shirt, it would become wet and could do little to hide the evidence of my femininity, even with binding.

I had no choice but to tell the truth, though I wondered what Anne Reed would have done in my place. Would she lie to protect herself at all costs? I didn't want to be anything like her—not to mention that my father, Reverend Baldwin, had preached about standing before God with a clean conscience.

Marcus watched for my response.

"I can swim," I finally said.

"Even if you couldn't," the captain said with a laugh, "I'd make you dive."

"I won't let him go," Marcus said, steel in his voice.

Silence filled the cabin as the captain stared at Marcus, a hint of surprise in his gaze. In the several weeks I'd been on the *Ocean Curse*, I'd rarely seen Marcus stand up to the captain.

"He's my cabin boy," Marcus said, taking ownership of me for the first time, "and I've found him to be indispensable."

No one spoke or ate as they looked between the captain and Marcus.

The captain's astonishment was soon replaced with anger. His jaw clenched as he narrowed his eyes. "I gave him to you, and I can take him away whenever I like. I'm in charge of the crew of the *Ocean Curse*, and if you don't like that, you can desert the ship. But I warn you—if you try, I'll personally hunt you down and shoot you like a traitor. No cabin boy is worth that trouble."

After another tense moment, the men returned to their meal, but Marcus left the cabin.

"Hawk will show you the diving bell and explain how it works," Captain Zale said to me. "Be prepared to dive when we reach the site of the Queen's Dowry."

I didn't know how long that might be, or how I would be prepared to face the bottom of the ocean.

But I would have no choice.

16

JULY 11, 1927
MINNEAPOLIS, MINNESOTA

It had been two days since I visited Lewis in his home and three days since I'd called Thomas out of Nina Clifford's brothel to ask him to help with Alice. But I had not heard from either one again. I also hadn't heard anyone whispering rumors about me visiting either place, for which I was thankful.

I sat in the parlor with my parents and Alice on that sultry July night. The humidity was so high my skin felt slick, and my temper was short. Captain Zale's threat to send me to the bottom of the ocean in a diving bell increased my angst. What would happen if I died in 1727? Would I die in 1927, as well? And what of Marcus? Now that he showed an interest in seeking out his mother—even if he was doing it for me—I didn't want him to stop. Perhaps I could convince him to give up pirating, though I wasn't certain he could ever be free. He'd said himself that he was a wanted man. Even if he took his old name, there were some, like Captain Zale, who might reveal his identity for revenge. And the king had no tolerance for pirates.

Alice sat on the sofa across from me, fanning herself with a copy of *Photoplay*, a popular magazine celebrating motion pictures and the actors and actresses who starred in them. She'd picked it up last time we went to the grocers. Father had frowned when he saw it, but she had insisted the copy was for her Christian enlightenment, because there was an article about Cecil B. DeMille's new film, *King of Kings*, about the life of Christ.

"It has to storm soon," Mother said as she readjusted the electric fan closest to her. She wasn't prone to complaining, but her voice held a hint of a whine. "This weather cannot hold out much longer."

As if she'd summoned it, a flash of lightning lit up the dark sky beyond the parlor windows. I set aside *Robinson Crusoe* and left the sofa to inspect the oncoming storm.

Father was waiting for the nightly news. His petition to get Charles Lindbergh to visit Minneapolis had been successful—though Saint Paul would host the majority of Lindbergh's visit—and tonight WCCO news would share details about the tent revival starting the same day.

I moved the curtain aside to look at the dark yard as another flash of lightning lit up the sky.

Alice kept her eyes on me. She'd been living with us for almost two weeks, and she acted just as leery of me as I was of her. I still wasn't certain about her intentions and was left to wonder if she had truly come because of desperation and not to cause trouble, as I had assumed.

"Mrs. Baldwin and I would like to speak to you about your future, Alice," Father said. "We have waited, hoping to find a position for you in the Twin Cities, but we've exhausted most of our resources."

I let the curtain fall back into place as I waited for his decision. Mother and Father had been making inquiries about getting her a job, but there were few people willing to hire a single, pregnant woman.

Alice set aside her magazine and sat up a little straighter. "Yes?"

Father was calm as always as he clasped his hands in his lap. "Mrs. Baldwin has spoken to our sister-in-law in Des Moines, and she has located a home for unwed mothers in Sioux City, Iowa.

We've decided this is the best course of action for you and will see that you have the train fare and all the proper funds to get there and then return to the Twin Cities once the child is born and placed with an adoptive family."

Alice's lips parted as she leaned forward. Father's pronouncement was so unemotional, so final. "A home for unwed mothers?"

"We think it's best," Mother said, offering a gentle smile. "As soon as possible."

"No." Alice shook her head as she put her hand over her stomach. "I won't let them take my baby away from me."

"We're at a loss, then," Father said. "As much as we'd like to help, you cannot continue to live here."

"But." Alice looked between them, desperation on her face. "You'd turn me away?"

I stepped forward, afraid Alice would share the truth and weeks of trying to keep it a secret would be for nothing.

The front door opened, drawing our attention to the foyer. Thomas strode in, as if he'd only just gone out for a quick errand and had returned.

"Hello," he said as he took off his hat and tossed it onto a nearby table.

"Thomas!" Mother rose from the sofa, her face lighting up with joy. "We weren't expecting you."

My shoulders stiffened at the sight of my brother. I couldn't put his recent visit to the brothel out of my mind. Was he finally here to take Alice away?

"Hello, son," Father said as he, too, rose. He shook Thomas's hand. "It's good to see you again."

Alice was still seated, her face pale, but I saw the recognition in her eyes. If what Thomas said was true, he'd once cared for Alice before Andrew came along. But had Alice cared for him?

"Who is your guest?" Thomas asked, though I knew it was only for our parents' benefit.

"This is Miss Alice Pierce," Mother explained, appearing a little uneasy. "Haven't we mentioned her?"

"No." Thomas made a show of crossing the room to offer his hand to Alice. Even though he was playacting, I saw through the ruse. There was pain and intensity in his gaze. "It's a pleasure to meet you, Miss Pierce. You're the reason I'm here."

She stood, a question tilting her brow.

"Whatever do you mean?" Mother asked him.

Thomas glanced in my direction but made no move to greet me.

I didn't greet him, either.

"You can imagine my surprise when I was asked to summon Miss Pierce from this address," Thomas said to my parents.

"You were asked to summon her?" Father frowned. "By whom?"

"Her aunt," Thomas said.

"My aunt?" Alice blinked in confusion, and I wondered if she even had an aunt.

With a brief but withering look in my direction that the others might not have noticed, Thomas continued, "Your aunt Gladys visited the Saint Paul Police Department looking for you. She heard about your plight and would like for you to live with her."

"My aunt Gladys?" Alice looked more bewildered than ever.

"How wonderful," Mother said. "It's an answer to prayer. You won't need to go to Iowa after all."

"I would like to speak to you in private, if I may," Thomas said to Alice.

Nodding, Alice followed Thomas out of the parlor and onto the front porch.

"This couldn't have worked out better," Mother said. "I wonder why Alice didn't reach out to her aunt sooner."

I suspected I knew. There was no Aunt Gladys, but Thomas was making good on his promise to get Alice out of our parents' house. I wasn't sure how he would convince her to leave, but now that she knew my parents had plans to send her to an unwed mothers' home in Iowa, it might not be so hard.

A rumble of thunder shook the house, and the lightning continued.

Father resumed his seat, glancing at the clock. "The evening news should be starting soon."

Mother paced as she clutched her white embroidered handkerchief. "I hope Thomas can convince her to go to her aunt. She'd be much better off there than with strangers in Iowa."

"Don't fret, Mother," Father said as he picked up a newspaper, unconcerned. "God has a plan."

She nodded and then took a seat on the edge of the sofa.

Finally, the front door opened, and Thomas and Alice reappeared.

"Thank you so much for your hospitality," Alice said to them, her voice stiff. "I've decided to go to my aunt's home, tonight."

"Oh, how wonderful." Mother rose to give Alice a hug. "We're so happy for you, dear."

Thomas glanced at me and lifted an eyebrow, as if to say, *I did what you wanted. Are you happy?*

I smiled.

"Come in while Alice gathers her things," Mother said to Thomas. "Visit awhile."

Thomas glanced at the clock and said, "I suppose I have a minute."

I was still standing by the window, unable to sit until now. But with the threat of Alice gone, I finally felt like I could relax.

As soon as I took a seat, however, the doorbell rang.

"Oh dear," Mother said. "Who could that be? Caroline? Will you?"

Nodding, I got up and went into the foyer. The porch lights were on, so I could see Lewis standing on the other side of the door.

My pulse sped at the sight of him. Had he come with news of Annie?

He was wearing what appeared to be a new suit and hat, and when he saw me, he smiled.

"Hello," I said as I opened the door. "Did you come with news?"

"May I come in?"

I was hoping that what he had to tell me could be easily shared here and now, but it was rude not to invite him inside. And my parents would wonder who had come.

"Of course."

"I see Thomas is here." He pointed his thumb over his shoulder at Thomas's car.

"He came to collect Alice," I whispered as I took Lewis's hat and hung it on the coat-tree.

"I'm sure that makes you happy."

"You have no idea. Although," I said, quietly, "I can't figure her out. Why did she come here if she didn't intend to tell my parents about Andrew? Or blackmail them in some way?"

"Maybe she had a change of heart once she got to know them. Your parents are pretty great. Or, maybe she just needed their help, like she said. Not everyone has an ulterior motive, Carrie."

Could that be the case? Had I misjudged Alice?

"Look who came to visit," I said as I led Lewis into the parlor.

"Oh, how marvelous." Mother rose from her seat once again and greeted Lewis with a hug. She looked at me, quiet expectation in her gaze. "I'm sure Caroline is happy to see you again."

I hoped she didn't think Lewis was here to court me. He had been stopping by a lot more often, but it was only to help me. At least, that's what I wanted to believe.

We made small talk for a few minutes before Alice appeared, her suitcase in hand. Her face was still pale, and her eyes were red, as if she'd been crying.

"My dear," Mother said as she reached for Alice's hand. "Don't be afraid. God has gone before you, and He will take care of all your needs. He has a plan, I promise."

Alice lowered her suitcase and placed her free hand over Mother's. "Thank you so much for everything." She looked down at their hands. "I confess, these tears are not from fear, but because I'll miss you. When I came here—" She swallowed, and I held my breath. When she lifted her gaze, there was something soft and tender in her sad expression. "You've been so kind. I don't know what I would have done without you. You've shown me the meaning of real Christianity, and it's impacted me deeply."

"You're so very welcome." Mother gave her a kiss on the cheek. "Write to us, dear, and let us know how you're getting along with your aunt."

Alice wiped the tears from her cheeks. "You're the closest thing I've ever had to a mother. Thank you. I hope I can be as kind and loving as you to my own child one day."

My lips parted in surprise at Alice's genuine affection for my mother.

Lewis gave me an *I told you so* look.

Father also stood and said his goodbyes before Alice turned to me.

"Thank you," she said.

I nodded, though she had nothing to thank me for—except, perhaps, that I hadn't told my parents her real identity. If it had been up to me, I wouldn't have let her move in with us for the past two weeks. But my parents' generosity toward Alice had also impacted me. Maybe I had been wrong about Alice and all she needed was a little help to pick herself back up.

Thomas said goodbye to everyone, and then he escorted Alice out of the house.

Mother, Father, Lewis, and I looked at one another and then Lewis said, "Do you mind if I stay?"

"Of course not." Mother grinned. "Have a seat. I'll get some refreshments." She left the room, humming contentedly as Father turned up the sound on the radio to listen to the news.

I lowered myself onto the sofa, and Lewis joined me.

"You don't mind if I stay, do you?" he asked.

I slowly shook my head, but a new worry began to grow.

Perhaps Lewis hadn't come to tell me about Annie, but to court me after all.

The evening wore on, and Lewis made no attempt to leave. Outside, a storm blew with intensity, bringing more lightning and thunder. Wind rattled the windowpanes, and the rain slashed against the siding.

After the news ended, Father went on and on about the plans he was making for the tent revival that would coincide with Lindbergh's visit. Lewis listened with polite attention.

Mother's smile was fixed as she watched Lewis and me together. I didn't have the heart to tell her that I wasn't interested in Lewis romantically, but perhaps things wouldn't come to that. If Lewis was interested in courting me, and he made any hint in that direction, I would tell him how I felt.

At nine o'clock, I could see both of my parents fighting fatigue. My mother lifted her handkerchief to hide a yawn, and Father's eyes kept drooping closed before he blinked a few times and nodded.

They were usually in bed by now, but Lewis didn't seem ready to leave.

"Well," Father finally said as he set his hands on his thighs. "I suppose Mother and I will retire for the night. Caroline, you'll show Lewis out?"

"Yes, of course."

"Goodnight," Lewis said as he rose to shake Father's hand and nod at Mother. "Thank you for your hospitality." But he didn't move toward the door to leave. Instead, he remained next to the sofa.

"Goodnight," my parents said.

For the first time that evening, Mother looked more concerned than happy. They'd never left me alone with a young man in the parlor. I couldn't imagine what they'd think if they knew I'd visited Lewis in his home.

Or that I was a captive on a pirate ship in 1727, sharing a cabin with a handsome quartermaster.

As soon as my parents were out of the parlor, Lewis resumed his spot next to me. He picked up *Robinson Crusoe*, which had fallen in the cushion crack, and shook his head. "Still wasting your time and filling your head with fantasies?"

I took the book from him, recalling all the times he'd teased me about reading when we were younger. I'd always felt embarrassed and somehow ashamed—something Marcus had never made me feel.

"Why did you come?" I asked him as I set the book on the end table, out of his reach. I wouldn't let him make me feel bad about something I loved. "Do you have news about Annie?"

His lips came up in a teasing smile. "What if I don't have news about Annie? What if I came just because I wanted to see you again?"

I would normally assume he was teasing me, but now I wasn't so sure.

His laughter filled the parlor, but I could tell it was laced with discomfort. "I can see from the expression on your face how that would be received."

"I'm sorry, Lewis." I didn't want to assume he was courting me, so I wasn't sure how to word my response. "You've always been—"

"The annoying older brother type. I know. You've told me."

I shook my head, feeling both frustrated and annoyed. "I can't tell if you're teasing me or if you're serious."

"Because I can't tell how you'd react if I was honest with you."

I fidgeted with the pleats in my skirt, trying to make sense of this change in him. "Why can't things stay as they were?"

He was quiet for a moment, but then he said, "You want me to continue teasing you relentlessly?"

Lewis was trying to hold on to his pride. I didn't want to reject him outright, but I couldn't pretend to have feelings for him when I didn't. I'd never thought of Lewis that way. "Well," I said with a smile I didn't feel, "perhaps not relentlessly, but I would like to be friends."

He wasn't looking at me, but he gave a half smile. "I guess I can make that work."

My heart was breaking, though I couldn't understand why. Even though I didn't have romantic feelings for Lewis, I did love him. I didn't want him to be disappointed or hurt, and I didn't want to lose him from my life completely.

"You're in luck," he said as he sat up straighter. "I did come to tell you about Annie Barker."

"You did?" My focus shifted with a renewed sense of hope.

He stood and walked to the window to look out at the storm before answering me. "I inquired about her and her gang, including the man she's romantically entangled with, the gangster Lloyd Rogers. They work with the gang on some jobs and alone on others. They've held up a couple of banks, but they mostly rob smaller stores and funeral homes in the least likely of Midwestern towns."

"Funeral homes?" I couldn't believe that my mother—if this was her—would rob funeral homes, too.

"It looks like they're on the move north again," he continued. "I've mapped out the last few reports that have been linked to them, and they were in southern Missouri, central Missouri, and then northwestern Missouri last week. If I'm not mistaken, they're working their way into Iowa and will more than likely end up in Saint Paul at some point to lie low."

I sat up straighter. "They'll be in Saint Paul?"

"That's my best guess, but don't get your hopes up, Carrie. I could be wrong."

"But you could be right."

He shrugged.

"And did you have a chance to investigate whether or not there are other Annie Barkers from Texas?" I held my breath, hoping I wouldn't have to worry about the criminal.

He nodded, but his face was grim. "I found one other Annie Barker from Texas, but she's five years old. There was one in Oregon and two on the East Coast, but they are either too young or too old to be the right Annie."

My heart fell as I stared at him. "That means . . . ?" I couldn't finish the sentence.

"I'm afraid so, Carrie. I'm sorry."

The grandfather clock in the foyer chimed the half hour, and Lewis said, "I should be heading home. I've overstayed my welcome."

"You didn't overstay your welcome."

The look he gave me was so heartrending, I held my breath. He wanted more from me, but I couldn't give it.

"I'll let you know if I hear anything else," he said. "Goodnight, Carrie."

"Goodnight, Lewis." He walked out of the parlor, and I was tempted to call him back, but there was no point. It wouldn't work.

I couldn't promise Lewis something I didn't have to give, no matter how much I loved him.

17

JULY 24, 1727
FLORIDA COAST

The *Ocean Curse* was anchored in the Indian River on the coast of Florida, beside a long, narrow barrier island. I stood on board as the pirate crew prepared to launch the boats that would take us through the Indian River inlet and then up the shore to where they believed the flagship of the 1715 Spanish Treasure Fleet, the *Capitana*, was rumored to have sunk.

It had been almost two weeks since Lewis had come to my parents' home—and that was the last time I'd seen him. No more news about Annie Barker. No more visits from our old family friend.

Just silence.

I hoped his silence meant he was busy looking for her, but I had a feeling he was also staying away to protect his heart. My own broke every time I thought about our conversation.

Timothy appeared beside me as he leaned on the rail and watched the pirates move the diving bell onto the launch boat. The diving bell was made of wood, like an oversized barrel sawed in half and sitting upside down. It was about five feet tall and four feet wide with two small windows near the top. A long hose connected the bell to a manual pump sitting on the launch, which would be used to push air into the structure as I was underwater. A valve near the top of the bell would release used air, allowing me to remain below the surface for hours, if necessary.

"Are you scared?" Timothy asked me.

"Petrified."

Marcus stood on the quarterdeck, his feet planted and his arms crossed. He'd tried, in vain, for the past two weeks to convince Captain Zale not to make me dive. He'd offered to go down in my place, but the captain refused to listen. And, seeing the diving bell, I knew why. It was tiny, and I was the smallest person on board the ship.

Hawk had tried to put Marcus's worries to rest by assuring him that there would be no complications. As long as the pump worked and I had access to the recovery rope to signal those on the launch to bring me up, I would be fine.

I only wished I was confident in the limited training Hawk had given me. Not only had he instructed me about the bell, but he had given me clues to look for in identifying the *Capitana*, which had once been a British vessel named the *Hampton Court*. He said there were several shipwrecks on this coastline, and I needed to be sure I was looking for the right one.

"Is there any treasure even left out there?" I asked Timothy.

"Eleven ships went down with the Spanish Treasure Fleet that year," he said. "And only a few of them were found. But not the flagship, and that one had the biggest treasure of all."

"The Queen's Dowry," I said. "But why was there so much treasure being moved at one time?"

"Because Spain and France had been at war with England and Scotland for over ten years and Spain didn't want the treasure ships to cross the ocean from Cuba, afraid they'd be taken by their enemies. By 1715, the war had ended, and the king of Spain needed the treasure to pay his debts."

"And then a hurricane came up and destroyed all but one of the ships, sinking millions of pounds' worth of gold, silver, and gemstones," I finished.

"Over a thousand people perished, too."

"How do you know so much about this?" I asked him as I took my gaze off the bell.

Timothy shrugged. "My father told me. At first, it was just the Spaniards and the survivors of the hurricane who were salvaging the fortune. They camped out on the beach and lived here for months. But when word got out, people came from all over the world to take the treasure. Hundreds of sailors had been working as privateers for the king of England to aid the British during the war. They would overtake Spanish and French ships for England and steal their cargo, seize their vessels, and take their men. But since the war ended, the privateers were out of work. They came to Florida to see what they could take from their former enemies. Sometimes they scavenged the ocean floor; other times, they stole treasure that had already been recovered, right from the Spaniards. It was the birth of the Pirate Republic. Many of the men who came set up bases in Nassau or Port Royal, Jamaica, after that."

"Is that how Captain Zale got his start?" I whispered.

"No. He'd been pirating for a while before that, but my father told me that Captain Zale came here with all the others."

"How did your father know so much about this?"

Timothy's ruddy face was redder than normal as he said, "He was one of the pirates. But he accepted the King's Pardon and went home." He paused as he shook his head in dismay. "I wonder what he would think if he knew I was on a pirate ship, in the very same waters where his piracy began twelve years ago?"

I could imagine the activity on this stretch of coastline at that time. The desperation of the Spaniards, the excitement of the privateers turned pirates, and the uncertainty of the natives who stood nearby watching.

The wind tugged at the ship, though the sails were down, and the anchor held it in place. The bright sunshine was blinding and had tanned my skin to a deep brown.

I couldn't stop thinking about what was waiting beneath the water for me. The thought of treasure was darkened by the threat of sharks—and death. I wasn't afraid of swimming, but I didn't like tight spaces or not getting enough air. The worst thought, though, was not finding the treasure. The Spaniards and the pirates had looked for it for several years after the hurricane. What made Captain Zale think we'd find it now?

Heavy footsteps sounded behind me, and I turned to find Marcus approaching, which caused Timothy to leave.

"You don't need to do this," Marcus said for my ears alone, his brogue thick.

"And how would I get out of it now?"

"I'll dive."

Shaking my head, I leaned on the railing that Timothy had just vacated. "People have been diving for centuries. Mayhap I'll be good at it."

I was trying to lessen the tension that seemed to coil around Marcus, but I could see it wasn't working. He took a step closer to me. "As soon as we're able, I'll get you away from this ship, lass. I promise. I'd have tried already if I thought it was safe."

"I know." I straightened to face him.

The concern was etched so deeply into his brows that I wanted to reach out and smooth it away.

"I'll be watching the recovery rope closely, every moment you're underwater. If you have any trouble, don't hesitate to pull it."

I nodded, feeling sober and terrified again. I wanted to change the course of the conversation, so I said, "Why does Captain Zale think this is the spot? Hasn't it been searched before?"

"We've searched this entire coast," Marcus said, crossing his arms. "But we couldn't go deeper until we acquired the diving bell. You'll be searching new depths."

Hawk's approach brought our conversation to an end. "We're ready for you."

Without another word, Marcus and I followed Hawk to the launch boat, and I climbed aboard. There were only a handful of men who would leave the ship. Hawk, Marcus, me, and three others that Marcus had chosen. He trusted each of these men with his life—and with mine. The rest would stay on the *Ocean Curse* to watch for navy patrols or the elusive *Atlantis*, which we had not yet encountered, though the ship was rumored to be in the area.

The launch boat rocked in the gentle river. I stood next to the diving bell as the men rowed downriver and then through the inlet and out into the ocean.

"How deep will I go?" I asked Hawk.

"About thirty meters."

I blinked several times. Thirty meters was almost a hundred feet. "Will I be able to see anything at that depth?"

"You should have no trouble."

"Some of the ships sunk in such shallow waters," Marcus said to me, "that their masts were visible for several years after the hurricane. Others, like the *Capitana*, were so mangled by the reefs and the pounding waves that much of the wreckage sank to the bottom of the ocean, making it difficult to locate."

It took almost an hour to row to the location the captain wanted me to search. My nerves were so frayed, I could hardly concentrate on what Hawk was telling me as he offered last-minute instructions.

The crew lowered the large anchor and then waited for me. I would get into the water first and then position myself so they could move the heavy diving bell over me. There were bags of sand tied to the bottom to make it sink, and I needed to be inside it before its descent, or I wouldn't get a chance once it was on the bottom of the ocean. I could never hold my breath long enough to swim one hundred feet down to the bell.

Turning my back to the crew, I removed my shoes, socks, and hat, then I unbuttoned the vest and set it aside. The thought of what creatures might be under the water terrified me, but I wouldn't show my fear to Marcus. He was already watching me closely. If I gave any indication that I was afraid, he'd do something foolish to stop this from happening.

"Ready?" Hawk asked.

I nodded and then jumped into the ocean without a second thought.

The water was cool against my skin, but a welcome relief from the heat. Panic threatened to choke me as I positioned myself next to the launch and they pushed the heavy diving bell to the edge of the boat.

With one fleeting glance at Marcus, I dipped underneath and was surrounded by the musty smell of wood.

The diving bell scratched the floor of the launch as they pushed it off the rest of the way.

It immediately began to sink, so I climbed onto the small bench built into the side of the bell.

The pressure of the air inside kept the water level around my feet, and within seconds the windows of the bell sank beneath the ocean, disrupting my view of the bright blue sky.

I tried to breathe normally as the diving bell lowered farther and farther down. I watched my feet to look for sharks or other dangerous creatures but saw nothing except for the occasional colorful fish. I prayed I wasn't directly over the sunken ship. If the bell fell onto a mast, I would be impaled, or at the very least, it would ruin the diving bell, so the water would begin to leak in and drown me.

A hundred different thoughts filled my head as I tried not to panic.

It became darker and darker the lower I descended, but there was still enough light to see the ocean floor when the bell finally came to a stop. I was breathing so heavily, I felt like I might suffocate. I put my hand to the hole at the top where the air came through the hose and felt a steady stream, offering only a little reassurance.

Outside the windows, the bubbles from the descent began to clear, and I had a view of my surroundings. Remains from a ship were evident, though it had been torn apart, as Hawk had said about the *Capitana*. Several cannons littered the sandy floor of the ocean, resting on old coral, rocks, and debris. A bit of coral had begun to form on the metal, and small, colorful fish were swimming around it.

This could be the site of the *Capitana*'s demise, but it could also be another ship.

I tried to survey the wreckage from my vantage point before I would take a deep breath and leave the bell to investigate further. If this was the *Capitana*, I needed to be sure.

Even if it was, there was no way to know where the treasure might be sitting.

Part of the hull of a ship was just visible to my left, sticking out of the sand at an odd angle. It was as good as any place to start my search.

Taking a deep breath, I slipped off the narrow bench, and my bare feet hit the sandy bottom. Bits of dead coral poked into my flesh, but I didn't mind. What I was more afraid of was losing my way on the ocean floor, getting disoriented, and not finding my way back to the bell to get air. If the bell wasn't so heavy, I might move it toward the wreckage, but it had taken several men to move it on the launch. I would be no match for its weight.

It was time to start my search.

I took another deep breath, filling my lungs as much as possible. The sandbags created a space about eighteen inches wide between the ocean floor and the bottom of the bell. I dove under the edge of the bell and into the ocean.

My eyes burned from the salt water, and it was hard to keep them open, but I didn't have much time before I'd need to go back for air.

Panic tried to overwhelm me as I scoured the wreckage for signs of identifying the ship and, ultimately, finding the treasure.

When my lungs felt like they would burst, I made my way back to the bell and took several deep breaths before I went back out.

It was almost impossible to identify the ship. It was spread out over the ocean floor and in so many pieces, I couldn't make out the masthead, the shape of the hull, or any other definitive features. Repeatedly, for what felt like hours, I combed the bottom of the Atlantic Ocean, staying close enough to the bell to return for air when my lungs wanted to give out.

Finally, after dozens of trips, my gaze landed on something that sparkled like gold.

Thirty minutes later, I pulled on the recovery rope, my heart pounding hard as I cradled the pieces of eight in my hands. I'd never felt so exhausted, yet the elation at my discovery gave me a surge of energy.

I sat on the bench inside the bell, breathing hard. On the last few excursions to the wreckage, I had pushed myself to the point of recklessness as I recovered the gold coins.

The bell began to rise through the water at a slower pace than it had fallen. But I was on my way up again, and I had something to show for my efforts.

When the windows of the bell revealed that I had come to the surface, the first person I saw was Marcus. The fear and concern on his face filled my heart with joy. The delight at discovering the treasure from the *Capitana* was nothing compared to the exhilaration I felt seeing the apprehension in his eyes and knowing it was for my welfare.

My white cotton shirt was sticking to my binding, showing every curve that I had been trying to hide for weeks. I probably looked like a wet dog, with clumps of hair hanging around my face. My burning eyes were probably red and swollen from being open in the salt water. Even now, they were blurry and felt like they were on fire. As soon as I could, I'd need to rinse them with fresh water.

Holding the coins close, I dove into the water and then came up outside of the bell, my head bobbing on the surface of the ocean. I couldn't help but grin as they all looked to me for an answer.

"I found gold!" I yelled. "There is treasure just nine meters or so in that direction." I nodded with my head since my hands were full. "Here. Take these pieces of eight." I set my hands on the launch and opened them to let the coins spill out.

An uproarious cheer came from the pirates as they rushed to the edge to look at the gold.

All but Marcus, who reached for me.

I took his hands and allowed him to help me from the water. He looked so relieved, as if he wanted to pull me into his arms for reassurance, but his gaze took in my form, and he quickly looked away.

I pulled at the clinging shirt and grabbed my vest to put it on with trembling hands, though it would soon be soaked. It would at least give me some semblance of modesty. Thankfully, the others were so busy examining the coins, they didn't pay attention to me.

When I turned back to Marcus, he shook his head, his lips turning up in a smile. "That was the longest three hours of my life," he said quietly, as the others celebrated the discovery of gold.

"Three hours?" I had no idea I'd been down there so long.

"Aye." He took a deep breath, as if he'd been holding it the entire time.

The temperature was colder than I remembered—or perhaps my body felt cool from the water—and I began to shiver.

"Are you alright?" Marcus asked as the crew began to pull the diving bell out of the water and onto the launch.

I nodded. "Just a little cold and dizzy."

I sat on the floor of the boat and wrapped my arms around my knees, setting my forehead on top of them. I couldn't seem to stop shaking, and soon my stomach began to turn with nausea.

Without warning, I needed to vomit, so I leaned over the side of the boat and let the contents of my stomach release. But I didn't feel any better when I was done. The world was spinning faster and faster.

Marcus knelt beside me, calling orders to his men to make haste to the ship.

And then my world went black.

The next thing I knew, my eyes fluttered open, and I was in Marcus's alcove bed on board the *Ocean Curse*. My head pounded, and my stomach was still nauseous, but not nearly as bad. Everything hurt. My muscles, my joints, and my chest as I tried to take a deep breath.

He sat on one of his chairs, leaning forward with his elbows on his knees and his head bent, as if in prayer. Outside, it was dark, but in his cabin, the soft glow of the lantern gave me the opportunity to see the anguished lines of his body.

"What happened?" I whispered, finding my voice didn't want to work.

He looked up quickly. His face was just as ravaged by fear as the rest of him. He took my hand in his and brought it to his lips. "I didn't know if you'd live. Dr. Hartville was here to see you. He bled you and told me that if you didn't wake up by morning, you wouldn't ever wake up again."

I felt the bandage around my left arm where he'd likely bled me. It was a practice rarely used in 1927 and for good reason. But I'd woken up. Perhaps it had been useful.

"How long have I been unconscious?"

"Only a few hours."

"What happened?" I asked again.

"Dr. Hartville called it diving sickness. Some people get ill minutes or even hours after they come to the surface. He doesn't know why it happens to some and not others, but 'tis more common the longer you stay beneath the water. And if you have it once, you're more likely to get it a second time. He said you can't dive again, or it would kill you."

I tried to absorb all he was telling me, but I couldn't stop thinking about the pressure of his hand, or how thankful I was that he had stayed by my side. I felt too weak to fight the emotions that were welling up inside me, afraid I would say something I shouldn't.

Instead, I pulled my hand from his and placed it on my clammy brow. "Did Dr. Hartville discover—"

"Aye. He knows you're a woman now. It was impossible to keep it from him as he examined you. But you needn't worry. Your secret is safe with him. He won't tell the captain, though he gave me a stern lecture."

"A lecture?" I frowned.

Marcus slowly lifted his hand to my brow and moved aside a tendril of my hair. When his gaze met mine, I lost my breath, and this time, it scared me more than being beneath the ocean waves.

"He said I'm to take care of you, to not mistreat you, or—" He paused as embarrassment colored his voice. "Let's just say he has nothing to worry about."

A noise outside Marcus's cabin made him pull away from me. A second later, the door opened, and Captain Zale appeared. He wore his black, formidable clothing and his sword at his side.

My pulse pounded hard, and I wondered if Dr. Hartville had told the captain after all.

Marcus stood as the captain walked in, uninvited.

"Is he awake?" the captain demanded.

"Aye. Just now." There was venom in Marcus's voice, directed at the captain.

"Good. I need to know everything I can about the *Capitana*."

"Did Dr. Hartville tell you that Carl can never dive again?"

"Bah," the captain said as he approached me. "What does Hartville know? He still hasn't cured what ails me. I've thought of tossing him overboard many times."

I had wondered myself about the captain's ailment. From all appearances, he seemed hearty and hale, yet he kept the doctor close at hand.

"He knows about this," Marcus said, not backing down. "If Carl dives again, it will kill him. We'll need to send someone else."

"That doesn't concern me now. What I want is to know what the boy saw down there." He stopped near Marcus's bed and stared at me. Though I was covered under the blankets, I shivered again. "Tell me what you saw, boy."

I needed to obey his commands, or I would face the consequences. So I told him everything from the moment I landed on the bottom of the ocean floor until I came up again.

Perhaps it would be enough. I had done the thing for which he'd taken me captive. Maybe he would let me leave the ship now.

But that meant leaving Marcus.

18

AUGUST 5, 1927
MINNEAPOLIS, MINNESOTA

As I stood in the living room of my parents' house on Dupont Avenue, I stared out the front window watching for Lewis to arrive. He'd called and said he had information to share with me and had asked if he could take me to Como Park to see the new sunken garden. He wanted to speak freely and didn't want my parents overhearing. Almost a month had passed since I had heard from him, and I was anxious to know what he had to say about Annie.

But as much as I wanted to find Annie, my mind was on a pirate ship anchored in a hidden cove on the coast of Florida. It had been almost two weeks since I'd found the treasure, and I was still recovering from diving sickness. Dr. Hartville had told me it could take several weeks, so Marcus was true to his word and took care of me. He insisted I sleep in his bed, and he used the less comfortable cot in the corner. When I was awake and he could be with me, we played cards and dice and spoke of our lives before the *Ocean Curse*. When I was alone, I read several of the books from his shelf, devouring the words that had caught his attention. And in the evenings, after he brought me supper, we spent hours discussing them. When I thought about Lewis's disdain for books, I was more thankful for Marcus.

The salvage team had been working to recover as much treasure as they could, but after twelve days and more gold than I had first imagined, they still hadn't found the Queen's Dowry—that special treasure chest of jewels that had been designed for the queen of Spain upon her marriage to Philip V. They'd come to the conclusion that the ship I discovered wasn't the *Capitana*, but another of the treasure fleet.

And Captain Zale was getting more and more impatient.

"Caroline?"

I was startled at the sound of my mother's voice.

"Is everything okay?" she asked.

I nodded and smiled. "I'm just waiting for Lewis."

Her curious look turned into one of concern. "He hasn't been here in over a month. I hope you didn't scare him away."

"It would take a lot to scare Lewis Cager away." I tried to make my voice sound light, when the truth was, I had missed Lewis. But it was for the best. I had let him know I wanted our relationship to stay platonic, and he had honored that wish.

"Well," Mother said in her gentle and unobtrusive way, "I like Lewis, and I think he could make you very happy." She joined me near the window. "I know that you modern women aren't putting as much emphasis on marrying young and starting families, but perhaps you can give Lewis a chance to prove himself. I suspected he was in love with you when you were teenagers. I used to want to shake him and tell him the way to your heart wasn't through teasing and provoking. But I've seen him become more serious and mature. I was hopeful that something was blossoming between you, but when he didn't call or stop by for weeks, I knew something must have happened." Her hopeful eyes sought mine. "But perhaps you've mended the rift?"

"Lewis and I are just friends. I told him I didn't want things to change, so that's why he stayed away."

Her face fell with disappointment, but she mustered a smile. "I just want you to be as happy as I've been."

"Have you been happy, Mother?" I asked, searching her face.

"Why, Caroline!" She blinked several times. "What a strange thing to ask me. I couldn't possibly be happier."

"But your life with Father—it hasn't been easy. His job demands so much of you—of us."

"No life is easy, child. If it was, it wouldn't be worth having. All the important things in life are hard. Marriage, parenting, building a worthwhile career, friendships, faith. It's the difficult things that mold us and shape us, challenging us to become better versions of ourselves. If it was easy, we would never strive to become better." She straightened the lapel of my shirt and said, "Don't dismiss Lewis just yet. Open your heart to the possibility and see what God might be saying about him."

The doorbell rang, and I said, almost too quickly, "It sounds like he's here."

I glanced in the foyer mirror as I put on the navy-blue cloche cap that matched the neckline and hem of my pleated skirt and shirt. Mother's conversation only added more guilt and pressure on my shoulders. I had disappointed Lewis. I didn't want to disappoint her, too.

I grabbed my purse as Mother came up behind me to open the door and greet Lewis.

"Hello, Mrs. Baldwin," he said.

"Hello, Lewis. It's so nice to see you again. Won't you come in?"

His blue-eyed gaze landed on me, and when he smiled, I realized I'd missed him more than I thought. It had been a month in 1927, but to me, it had felt twice as long because of my time in my other life.

"If it's okay with Caroline," he said, "I'd like to head to the conservatory before it gets too late."

"Of course." Mother put her hand on my back and gave me a gentle push. "Go. Have fun. Don't stay out too late."

"Goodbye," I told her as she closed the door behind me. I stood on the porch, a little closer to Lewis than I intended, and said, "Hello."

"Hi, Carrie." His appreciative gaze slipped over my appearance. "You look nice."

My cheeks warmed under his praise, and I smiled. "I think I like it more when you tease me instead of compliment me."

"Why?" he asked as he got a little closer. "Does it make you uncomfortable?"

I laughed, knowing he *was* teasing me now.

He grinned. "If you told me I looked nice, I'd be very pleased."

"Is that another new suit?"

He tugged at his lapels and affected an air of sophistication, then he tapped his straw boater and said, "Why yes, it is."

"I liked your old one better."

His mouth slipped open, and I laughed again, but he knew I was teasing him.

"You look very handsome, Lewis Cager."

"Thanks." He motioned to his Chevy with the tip of his head. "Ready?"

I nodded and accepted his arm as he led me down the porch steps toward his waiting vehicle.

It was less than ten miles to the Como Park Conservatory in Saint Paul. I'd been there a few times before, but it had been a while, and I was eager to see the sunken garden. The nearby zoo was just as entertaining.

As the vehicle made its way east toward Saint Paul, the lighthearted banter faded and neither of us spoke. The awkwardness was mounting, so I said the first thing that came to mind.

"Is this supposed to be a date, Lewis?" I blurted.

There was a heavy pause before his laughter filled the vehicle.

I crossed my arms. "Why is my question so funny?"

"It's not your question," he said as he brought his laughter under control. "It's your delivery."

"My delivery?"

"Some people beat around the bush, but not you. That's one of the things I've always liked about you." He shrugged as he turned onto Lyndale Avenue. "There are no pretenses with you, Carrie."

We continued down Lyndale toward Hennepin Avenue, and I said, "Why didn't you answer my question?"

He looked out the side window and sighed. "I guess it's because I was hoping that the question would answer itself by the end of the evening."

Mother's request returned to me. She'd asked me to open my heart to Lewis and give him a chance to prove himself.

So when he looked at me, I smiled.

His grin lit up his face. "It takes the pressure off things, doesn't it?"

We drove through Minneapolis and into Saint Paul before I said, "Have you heard anything about Alice?" I'd thought about her many times in the past month, but I hadn't seen Thomas or Andrew to inquire. My relationship with Ruth had been strained, and I was trying to build back her trust, but she was the last person I would ask. "Do you know where Thomas brought her?"

Lewis nodded slowly and then glanced at me, as if to judge my reaction. "He brought her to a hotel. She was living there until a couple of days ago."

"Where is she now?"

He paused for a second and then said, "With Thomas."

My mouth slipped open. "She's *living* with my brother?"

"That's the way of it."

"As in, she's *living* with him?"

"Yes," he said, as if he was trying to make a child understand. "They're together now, Carrie. As in, a couple."

My eyes widened at that pronouncement, and I shook my head. "She can't be—they—this is awful, Lewis."

"You wanted her out of your parents' home. What did you think would happen? They were a couple before she met Andrew. While she was living at the hotel, Thomas went to visit her, and things picked up where they had left off."

"I didn't think Thomas would take advantage of Alice."

"He didn't take advantage of her. Thomas is a lot of things, but he's not a scoundrel. He's been in love with Alice for a long time. She finally realized the mistake she made with Andrew, and Thomas was willing to take her back."

I felt nauseous just thinking about the ramifications. "I thought we were rid of the Alice problem."

The look of disappointment he gave me cut me to the heart. "Alice is more than a problem to deal with, Carrie. She's a human being that was misused by Andrew, and when he learned she was pregnant, he told her he was married and cast her aside. Maybe she could have made different choices, but she loved Andrew and believed he loved her, too. She thought he was going to marry her. That's when she went to your parents, but then she realized they were good people and didn't deserve to be hurt because of their son's mistake."

"She told you this?"

"Yes. And Thomas didn't set out to convince Alice to fall for him again, but she did. And they seem happy. As happy as they can be, given the circumstances."

"Are they really in love?" I asked, hating how horrified I sounded. "So quickly?"

"It's been a month."

"A month! How could they know in a month?"

"Sometimes, it only takes a heartbeat to know."

His words were so soft, so gentle, they hit me like a gale-force wind. Hadn't I known in less than a month that my feelings for Marcus were deeper than they should be?

We drove in silence again. The assumptions I'd made about Alice weren't fair, and I felt ashamed.

"Do you think Thomas will marry her?" I finally asked Lewis.

"I don't know. I hope so, for both their sake and the baby's."

He pulled into the parking lot, and we got out of his vehicle. I'd almost forgotten about Annie, which was the whole reason he'd asked me to come with him. Or was it?

Como Park was a beautiful oasis in the Twin Cities, with walking paths, gardens, a glass-domed conservatory, and more.

Lewis bought a bag of breadcrumbs to feed the ducks and geese in Como Lake. We laughed as they squawked and quacked, fighting for the food. When we ran out, they began to crowd around us, pecking at our feet as we walked away.

After visiting the black bears and the deer, we went into the sunken garden inside the glass conservatory. The air was fragrant with the scent of flowers, though it was hotter and more humid inside than out. I walked peacefully among the exotic plants, stopping from time to time to admire each one.

When I glanced up, I found Lewis watching me.

He smiled and said, "I could watch you looking at flowers all day."

My heart filled with affection for Lewis, and in that moment, I wished I could give him what he wanted. But affection wasn't romance, and it wouldn't be fair to either one of us if I tried.

We continued to move through the maze of gardens inside the conservatory. It was a large structure with a beautiful man-made pond running down the middle of it. Lily pads sat atop the water, and a statue stood at the end.

Every time I exclaimed about a new flower, Lewis was there to appreciate it with me, though he seemed much more interested in me than the plants. And when our hands brushed together as we walked along the narrow path, he took my hand in his.

He led me to a bench near the pond, and said, "Do you want to sit? I have something to tell you."

My pulse ticked up a notch, hoping this was about Annie.

I took a seat, and he sat beside me, closer than necessary. I took my hand out of his, but our shoulders pressed against each other as we looked at the pond. Perhaps it was safer to touch him than to look into his gaze.

"There's been another report about Annie Barker," he said. "This time, she was in Dexter, Iowa, about thirty miles west of Des Moines. She and Lloyd robbed a bank there with the help of Lloyd's brother and sister-in-law."

"When?"

"This past Monday."

"So, they could be on their way to Saint Paul now?"

"They don't tend to move fast, if their history can be trusted. They usually camp out for a few days between robberies and lay low until the law isn't actively on the lookout for them—or unless they've been located. On some occasions, their campfire is still burning when the law enforcement agents arrive."

I was both excited and terrified to speak to Annie. If she was as ruthless and coldhearted as she sounded, could I even get close enough to let her know who I was before she opened fire?

"I'm sorry that I don't have more information," he said. "But it does appear that she's getting closer."

I nibbled my bottom lip, wishing I could go to her—but it would be impossible. I wouldn't know where to even look, and I could never leave my parents long enough to make a trip to Iowa. The best plan was to wait until she came to Saint Paul, where she'd have to check in with the police and let them know she was in town. Then Lewis would tell me.

"Thank you," I said, my heart warming for this man who had agreed to help me.

"Well," he asked after a few seconds of silence, "does this feel like a date to you?"

My heart and mind were so confused, I wasn't sure how to answer. What I felt for Lewis was warm and comforting and sincere—but it didn't feel romantic. It didn't feel exciting or daring or thrilling like my feelings for Marcus. I loved having Lewis's company, but I didn't tingle at his touch—not like I did at Marcus's.

Tears gathered in my eyes because I knew I would hurt him. "I'm sorry, Lewis."

There was silence between us again, and then he kissed the top of my head before he said, "Come on. I'll take you home."

19

AUGUST 13, 1727
FLORIDA COAST

I had a lot of time to think about Lewis and our visit to Como Park as I stayed in Marcus's cabin the next week. My energy had returned, though my joints were still stiff and painful first thing in the morning. As I moved around the cabin, stretching and cleaning, the pain began to ease. Dr. Hartville visited me daily and reassured me that my body would heal with time if I continued to rest when needed. I had already made so much progress, it was easy to believe him.

My days were pleasant as I sat near the windows and watched the dolphins play in the lagoon and birds flutter about the barrier island. This was what my heart longed for—the simplicity of life. No radio broadcasts, no pressure to sing and perform, and no unrealistic expectations. The only secret I had to keep here was my gender, and in the cabin, with no one watching, I didn't even have to worry about that. I could be myself completely.

The captain had ordered three of his smallest crew members to work on recovery efforts. These men were bringing up handfuls of coins on each dive, and none of them had suffered from diving sickness like I had.

As I sat in Marcus's cabin, the sun had already set, but the lamp offered enough light for me to see the book in my lap.

It was Marcus's Bible. I had pulled it off the shelf today, curious about his family. After reading through the names and the dates, I began to thumb through the thin pages and found myself lost in the book of John. I had always loved the way John saw his relationship with Jesus, as the one whom Jesus loved. Perhaps it was because I had not felt that same love, had instead felt that I could not draw close to God because of this burden I carried from birth. I longed to see myself as John saw himself.

Lyrics from "Amazing Grace" filled my mind and heart, and I began to hum the song. Here, in the quiet, simple cabin, the words were the same, but the meaning had more impact. I wasn't singing for a crowd of a thousand. I was singing for an Audience of One.

A noise at the door brought my head up. My heart sped when Marcus entered. His arms were laden with plates of food, and when he saw me, he smiled.

"I've missed the sound of your song," he said. "'Tis good to hear it again."

As always, my cheeks warmed under his praise.

"How do you fare today, lass?" he asked.

I rose and set the Bible aside to help him with the food. "I'm feeling much stronger."

And even more so now that he was home.

The thought caught me off guard. And I wondered when I had started to think of this small cabin on the *Ocean Curse* as home. Did the peace I felt here have something to do with it feeling like home, or was it Marcus, and him alone, that made me feel as if I belonged in this unlikely place?

He continued to examine me as he set the food on the table. "Your color is better today, and your eyes look clear and bonnie again."

My pulse sped at his compliment, and not for the first time, I wished I could wear a pretty dress to highlight my curves and style my hair to look more attractive. But even without all my feminine accoutrements, he still thought I was pretty.

We sat across from one another at the table, but Marcus's gaze fell on the Bible.

"I hope you don't mind," I said.

"Nay." He left the table and retrieved the Bible. "I don't mind at all."

When he sat down again, he ran his hand over the worn binding and said, "Do you believe in God, Caroline?"

I had shared a lot about my other life with him, but I had not told him much about my father or his profession. Perhaps I hadn't wanted him to expect me to be perfect. "My father in 1927 is a well-known minister. He preaches to people all over the world through the radio. I grew up reading the Bible, attending Sunday school, and sitting through hours of his sermons."

Marcus's brown eyes were probing as he said, "Just because you attend church and read the Bible doesn't mean you believe."

I sighed as I pushed my boiled beef around the plate with my fork. "My relationship with God is complicated."

"I can understand that."

"What about you?" I asked him. "Do you believe?"

"Aye, with all my heart. But my relationship with God is complicated, too."

"Mayhap 'tis complicated for most people."

"It didn't seem that way for my mam."

"I suppose it doesn't seem that way for my parents, either. If my grandmother hadn't cursed my mother and me, mayhap my relationship with God would be easier."

"But what if it wasn't a curse? What if God chose for you to be born with two lives?"

He had suggested that one other time. I'd wrestled with that idea, but I couldn't imagine how or why.

"Here." He opened the Bible to the book of John, not far from where I'd been reading, and found chapter nine. "When Jesus came upon the man born blind from birth, His disciples asked if the man was blind because of his sin, or because of his parents' sin. But Jesus said it was neither. That he had been born blind so that God could manifest His power and goodness through the man."

I stared at Marcus, frowning. "What does that mean?"

"Mayhap you were born this way so God can work through your life, Caroline. Not because your mother or grandmother sinned, but because God has a plan for you." He shook his head. "I chose to sin against my mother, and I choose to continue to live as a pirate. I know 'tis not what God wants, but I don't know how to stop. That's what complicates my relationship with Him. But you didn't choose to sin against God. Even if your mother and grandmother did, that is not your guilt or shame to bear. Boldly walk before God and believe He hears you and sees you. Look for His blessings and don't let the sins of your ancestors stop you from taking hold of God's goodness."

I stared at him, surprised at his passion and fervor. "You could be a preacher."

He slowly closed the Bible, but he let his hand rest upon it. "Aye, mayhap if I'd made different decisions, God would want me."

I laid my hand over his, wanting to minister to his heart and soul like he'd just done to mine. "God didn't send Jesus for the healthy, Marcus. He sent Him for the sinner. He sent Him for all of us. There is not a preacher alive who can stand blameless before God. We can't change the past, but we can change the future. No matter how long you're gone, you can always return home."

He had not lifted his gaze from our hands, but when he did, there was so much pain and heartache.

"I wish it was that easy." He turned his hand to clasp mine, running his thumb gently over my skin. Under the formidable exterior of Marcus Zale's pirate life, there was a tender, complex man.

Silver threads of pleasure tingled up my spine and wrapped around my heart. I couldn't hide my feelings from him, no matter how hard I tried.

"Caroline . . ." He said my name with such longing, hope flickered to life within my chest. For just a moment, he opened the door to his soul, and I could see the internal battle he was facing before he shuttered it again, gently pulling his hand away. "I don't want to hurt you the way I have everyone else I've ever cared for."

"You won't hurt me," I said, though I knew it wasn't true. Every time he robbed another ship, it would hurt me.

"The other day, when I watched you get lowered in that diving bell, I felt powerless to protect you, and it was the worst feeling in the world. And then, when you became sick, it felt like my heart was pulled from my chest. You don't belong here, lass, and the longer you stay, the more powerless I become." The emotions upon his face became so intense, he stood and walked to the window, where I couldn't see them. "I can't protect you like I want, and I can't watch you suffer, as I have the past two weeks. It would kill me."

"Then come away with me," I pleaded, leaving the table to join him. I stood just behind him—so close, yet it felt as if the ocean stood between us.

"I wish it was that simple," he said quietly. "My life is bound to Captain Zale's. I hold too many of his secrets for him to let me leave without a fight."

I slipped my hand into his, taking a step closer, and lifted my other hand to wrap around his arm, leaning into him.

He curled his fingers around mine and then turned, his eyes searching mine, before he lifted his free hand to my cheek.

My heart felt as if it stopped beating. Was this how my mother felt when she fell in love with Sam Delaney? Throwing all caution to the wind for the man she loved? Because in this moment, I was willing to sacrifice almost everything for the man who stood before me.

Marcus lowered his forehead to mine, and I closed my eyes, loving the feel of him being so close yet hating the things that were pulling us apart.

"I can't let you throw your life away." His words were so strained, I knew it took strength for him to speak them. "Every night I go to sleep, I wonder if tomorrow will be the day I die. 'Tis a miracle that I've lived this long. I can't bear to wonder if the same fate awaits you or what might happen if I died and you were left here without me. I want you to be happy and safe—I want you to have the life you desire."

He was the first person who had ever uttered those words to me. Grandfather wanted me to have the life that would benefit him. My mother and father in 1927 wanted me to have the life they deemed right for me. And Annie Barker didn't seem to care.

Marcus wanted me to have the life that I desired, yet I couldn't imagine what kind of life that would be without him.

He slowly pulled away, resolve in his face. "When you were unconscious, and I didn't know if you'd live, I thought a lot about your grandfather and your nanny. I imagined how hard it would be for them to learn that you had been taken captive on a pirate ship and then perished. I'm sure they're sick with worry and would like to know where you are. And I realized you were right. I need to find my mam and tell her I'm sorry. Just like your grandfather, she shouldn't live the rest of her life wondering about me."

"At least my illness brought about something good." I tried to smile.

"Your people need to know where you are, lass," he continued, his resolve stronger.

I took a step away from him. He didn't let my hand go.

"I can't return to South Carolina. My grandfather will force me to marry—"

"You needn't return home unless you want. But you should post a letter to him, at the very least." He took a deep breath and finally let my hand go. "And then I will take you to Massachusetts and find my mam and see if there is a place there for you."

My heart was too heavy to speak, but I finally asked, "And what will you do?"

He turned back to the window. "The only thing I know."

Marcus would stay the course as a pirate. Not because he wanted to, but because he believed he didn't have a choice.

215

AUGUST 14, 1727
FLORIDA COAST

I'd had time to think about Marcus's words as I gave piano lessons in 1927 and listened to my father's plans for his tent revival. The truth had settled in my heart, and I knew Marcus was right. I owed my grandfather a letter, at the very least, though I couldn't think of a way to explain why I'd left.

Marcus was gone when I woke up the next morning, but he'd left breakfast on the table for me. I was tired of being idle, so as soon as I finished eating, I decided it was time to return to my duties.

I was still a little stiff and sore as I exited Marcus's cabin that morning.

The sun was bright, and it blinded me as I stood on the poop deck and surveyed the ship. The tall masts, sails, ropes, and cannons had become familiar to me. At least a hundred pirates were going about their work or resting on the main deck under the hot Florida sun. Some were mending clothing, a few were playing cards, and still others were napping.

The nearby island was marshy and uninhabited, offering cover from passing naval vessels that would recognize the *Ocean Curse*. The birds that inhabited it were making a cacophony of sounds.

After I deposited the dirty dishes in the galley, I went back up to the main deck and Timothy spotted me as he came out of the forecastle. I hadn't spoken to him since the morning of the diving bell incident.

"'Tis good to see you up and about again," he said with a broad smile. "How are you feeling?"

"Much better. Still a little sore, but I'm restless lying about the cabin."

A few older pirates were sitting in a group nearby, mending a stained sail, and I noticed their interest in Timothy and me. The grizzliest of them scowled at me while the others spoke in hushed tones.

I moved toward the opposite rail as Timothy followed.

"Are the rumors still persisting about a Jonah on board?" I asked him.

"Aye, but the rumors have shifted a bit."

I frowned. "What are they saying now?"

"They're now certain the Jonah is a woman." He spoke quietly as he bent his head toward mine. "And they think they know who it might be."

My stomach felt queasy again, and I was suddenly weak. Marcus would be near the recovery site, over an hour away. If I was overtaken by a horde of superstitious pirates, it would be too late for him to help me. I was almost too afraid to ask, but I had to know. "Who?"

"Ned."

"Ned?" I spoke louder than I intended, so I lowered my voice and drew closer to Timothy. "The captain's cabin boy?"

"Aye. Just watch him—you'll see it, too. I don't know how I missed it before."

I scanned the deck, looking for a glimpse of Ned, but Timothy shook his head. "He's not here. He always stays close to the captain's cabin and doesn't speak to anyone other than the captain. That's why no one has confronted him yet. If you really look at him, you'll see that he has fine features and small hands."

Fine features? I turned my face away from Timothy, afraid he might look too closely at me and see that I had the delicate hands and face of a woman.

"I've worked alongside Ned," I told him. "I've never suspected he's a woman." Yet as the words left my mouth, I realized the benefit of others turning their attention to Ned—and away from me. "But I'll keep my eyes on him."

"My father warned me about the dangers of having a woman on a ship, so if you suspect 'tis true, you'll need to alert the captain."

I nodded, wanting to change the subject. "How did your father feel about you going to sea? If he was a pirate, was he afraid you might become one, too?"

Timothy shook his head. "He thought I was too smart to become a pirate, but the more time I spend on the *Ocean Curse*, the more I can see the allure."

"You aren't thinking of staying with them, are you?"

He lifted his shoulder and stared at the lagoon where the shimmering water was reflecting the bright sun. "Merchant ships don't pay well, and they treat their sailors abominably. The abuse I suffered on the *Adventurer* was hard to endure. Here, I have a vote, and I know I'll share in the treasure that's recovered from the shipwreck."

"The treasure is one thing," I said, feeling anxious to convince him that the pirate's life wasn't for him. "What about when you're called upon to rob and loot another ship? You don't want to be a criminal, do you?"

"It suited my father for a time."

"But the king isn't offering pardons anymore. There's only one way to leave pirating—death." It was the bitter reality Marcus also faced.

"Are you still planning to escape, Carl?" he asked, looking closely at me again.

It was a hard question to answer. If Timothy turned on me, and Marcus tried to help me escape, would Timothy tell someone?

"I don't want to be a pirate," I said, trying to be evasive. "But, if the captain finds the treasure he's looking for, mayhap he'll stop plundering other vessels and let some of his crew go."

"Captain Zale will never stop pirating. 'Tis in his blood, same as Marcus. They'll go down with this ship. Besides, they haven't found the Queen's Dowry, and they're not likely to, if my father's tale is true."

Frowning, I asked, "What tale?"

He moved closer to me, until our shoulders were brushing, and cast a look behind him before saying, quietly, "My father was a privateer for the British during the War of Spanish Succession, but after the war, he worked for different merchantmen while trying to support my mother and three children. He wanted to be

218

in command of his own ship but knew the only way he might do that was to become a pirate. In 1717, he found himself in Savannah, Georgia, without a farthing to his name, tired of the abuses he'd suffered as a merchant sailor. He met two Spaniards who claimed to have been on the 1715 treasure fleet and had survived the hurricane.

"The Spaniards were drinking heavily, so it didn't take much to get them to talk, and they told him they knew the location of the Queen's Dowry. But it's not where most people think. They'd been waiting until the initial search had died down and were planning to go back and get it themselves. My father convinced them to tell him where the treasure was located." Timothy shook his head. "He was desperate and destitute, which makes for a dangerous combination. When he left the tavern that night, he alerted two naval officers about the Spaniards. They were so drunk, they were easily overtaken and pressed into service for His Majesty's Navy."

My eyes widened as I listened intently to Timothy's story.

"My father planned to go after the Queen's Dowry himself, but he needed a ship. So, he started small, overtaking first a fishing vessel, then a small sloop. He found other desperate men who joined his crew, and soon, they had a frigate at their command. They were bold and reckless, but my father hated every minute of it. He hated seeing fear in the eyes of the men he robbed. His conscience was eating him alive, so when he got word that my mother had died in childbirth with their fourth child, he knew we needed him. He turned himself in to Governor Eden in South Carolina and received the King's Pardon before making his way home to Boston."

"He gave up on the Queen's Dowry?" I whispered.

Timothy nodded. "He said no treasure in the world was worth his sons growing up as orphans."

"'Tis an admirable tale, Timothy."

"My father is a good man."

I pressed closer to Timothy, so no one would hear. "Did he ever tell you where the treasure is hiding?"

"Nay. He said that no man should live with the temptation he has. It's been a constant battle to not go after it. But he remarried and has another passel of children and won't leave them or his wife to chase after gold."

"You must be feeling better," a deep, male voice said from behind us.

I spun, my heart racing as Timothy jumped.

Marcus stood on the main deck, his feet planted and his arms crossed.

Something stormy swirled in his gaze—something I'd never seen before. Jealousy?

Timothy was gone by the time I turned back to the railing.

"Should you be up and about?" Marcus asked me, a challenge in his voice.

I was feeling tired again, but I lifted my chin, not willing to let on that I was exhausted. "You're back early."

"I never left. The captain has called off the recovery efforts. We'll meet tonight to discuss our next move."

"Will we head north?"

"Aye." His arms were still crossed, and his gaze followed Timothy before he looked back at me. "But I don't think you'll like where the captain's heading next."

I leaned against the railing, suddenly feeling weaker still. There was only one place I didn't want to go.

"Charleston?"

With his brief nod, my heart fell.

20

I thought of little else but Marcus's announcement the next morning. It was Sunday, so I ate an early breakfast with Father and Mother and walked the five minutes to the church where Father had pastored most of my life until he'd begun to travel and gain notoriety. The new pastor was young and eager and liked the attention that Father's presence brought each Sunday we could attend. We sat through the service, and then returned home. The last thing I wanted to do was visit South Carolina, but I would have no choice. The only benefit would be to post a letter to Grandfather and Nanny, but I would have to do it right before we left the city, so Grandfather wouldn't have time to look for me.

"You are quiet today," Mother said as she walked beside me up the steps and into the house, just behind Father. "You haven't told me how your time with Lewis went the other night."

"It was pleasant," I said with a smile. "The sunken garden at Como Park is beautiful."

"Did he . . . declare himself?"

Father turned sharply at that question. "What is this?" he asked, standing in the foyer. "Who is declaring themselves for Caroline?"

221

"Lewis," Mother said.

"No." I shook my head. "He isn't declaring himself—didn't declare himself."

"Well," Father said, his voice gruffer than usual, "if he intends to, he must speak to me first. No man will declare himself to my daughter without my permission."

I wanted to roll my eyes, but I refrained, knowing it would disrespect him. Though I valued his beliefs, a lot of young people were starting to make their own choices about love and marriage, without their parents' permission. If Lewis was serious about me, and if I'd given him any hint of encouragement, he would honor my father and speak to him—but not before he told me.

The smell of roasted chicken filled the air as we stepped into the house. Ingrid had lunch on the table for us, so we washed up and took our places.

After Father said grace, he lifted one of the newspapers off the corner of the table where Ingrid had placed it. He rarely read the newspaper in the morning before church, but almost always looked at it as soon as we sat down for Sunday lunch. He didn't even read the front page as he opened it.

My attention immediately caught on the large headline: *Rogers and Barker Suspected in Grocery Store Heist, Lakeville.*

"What is that?" I asked my father. "On the front page."

He closed the newspaper and looked at the headline, frowning. "It's only rubbish. If they didn't give gangsters like Rogers and Barker so much attention, they'd go away. They're only doing it for the fame."

"They held up a grocery store? In Lakeville, Minnesota?"

"It appears so."

"When?"

Father looked closely at the article. "Last evening."

My heart began to hammer. Annie Barker was in Minnesota—and if she'd been in Lakeville, just twenty miles south of the Twin Cities, it might mean she was on her way to Saint Paul. But Lewis had told me that Annie and Lloyd often camped out for days after a burglary. What if she was camping somewhere between here and Lakeville? Could I find her? Would there be enough clues to track her down? Surely if the police couldn't do it, I probably couldn't, either. But I had to try.

My appetite was gone, though I forced down the food and tried to remain calm as we finished our meal. Mother and Father often napped on Sunday afternoons, so Father was fresh for his evening radio broadcast. If I took the family car to Lakeville, I could speak to the grocery store owners about Annie and see if there was anything I could discover about her and where she might be staying. I would have to get back to Minneapolis by six, when Father would need the car to get to the broadcast—and because I was supposed to sing the opening hymn. But that would give me four or five hours, enough time to learn something.

We were just finishing our meal when the doorbell rang.

Ingrid volunteered to answer it as I wiped my mouth, and a few seconds later, I heard Lewis's voice.

Mother tried to hide a pleased smile, while Father attempted to look stern.

"They're just finishing lunch," Ingrid said. "Won't you come in?"

The three of us left the table, since we were done eating, and met Lewis in the parlor.

"It's nice to see you again so soon," Mother said. "Won't you have a seat?"

"I'm not here to visit," Lewis said, his gaze landing on me. "I'm here to see if Caroline would like to go for an afternoon drive."

I studied him, trying to determine his motivation. Was it romantic? Or was he there to tell me about Annie?

"Do you mind?" I asked my parents.

"Of course not," Mother said.

"Just have her home in time for the broadcast," Father admonished.

"I will," Lewis promised.

I found my hat and purse on the hall table where I'd left them and said goodbye to my parents before following Lewis outside.

"Is something wrong?" I asked as we made our way down the porch steps and to his vehicle.

"Did you read the headlines this morning?"

"I just saw them when we sat down to lunch. Is that why you came for me? Do you know where Annie is?"

"No, I don't know where she's at, but I suspected that you'd head to Lakeville the first chance you got. And since I don't want you going alone, I decided I might as well take you."

I grinned and took hold of his arm. "Thank you, Lewis."

He looked down at me, his blue eyes shining as he winked. "Anything to spend time with you."

I playfully rolled my eyes, but inwardly, I wasn't laughing. It had taken me a long time to realize that almost every time Lewis teased me, he was sharing his real feelings. He probably thought it wouldn't hurt as much to be rejected if he could pretend it had all been a joke. But it wasn't a joke—not to him or to me.

We got into his Chevy and pulled away from the house.

The day was picture-perfect, with a bright blue sky, no humidity, and a gentle breeze. The temperatures had been in the upper seventies, and the landscape was lush with summer blossoms. Wildflowers grew along the sides of the road, and cultivated gardens dotted the yards in our neighborhood.

"Have you heard anything about Annie?" I asked. "Beyond what you read in the paper?"

"I wasn't on duty yesterday or today, so I haven't heard anything else," he said. "If they pulled off the robbery last night, they might still be in the Lakeville area."

"Do you think they'll head to Saint Paul?"

"Probably. But they might be planning other small robberies before they get there." He glanced at me as he said, "I was able to do a little research about Annie's life in Texas."

I turned to him, eager to hear what he had to say. "And?"

"Are you sure you want to know?"

The automobile rumbled as we turned onto Lyndale Avenue and headed south. I was quiet for a moment, wondering what had caused my time-crossing mother to lead a criminal life in both paths. Was it something she could control?

"I want to know."

"She was born in a small town in Texas in 1892," he began. "Her father died when she was a few years old, so she and a couple siblings were raised by her single mother. It was a tough childhood, from all accounts. She wasn't a great student and dropped out to get married when she was fifteen."

I frowned. "She ran away with her merchant husband in South Carolina when she was thirteen. She was so young in both lives."

Lewis readjusted himself in the driver's seat, as if he was uncomfortable with what I'd told him about my second life. I thought of Marcus, who was always eager to hear about it. Nothing I told him made him act uncomfortable. It intrigued him to know more, which allowed me to share freely.

"Apparently," Lewis continued, "Annie's marriage wasn't great. She stuck it out until she was twenty-one, but then left him, though there's no record of divorce."

"She died when she was twenty-one in her other life. I wonder if that affected her relationship with her husband here?"

Lewis didn't respond as he glanced out the driver's side window, not inviting more information from me.

"Does it make you uncomfortable when I talk about my other life?" I asked him.

"Honestly? I don't know how it makes me feel. I'm still struggling to understand it."

"I've been living this way for twenty years, and I don't understand it, either." I nibbled my bottom lip, not wanting him to stop telling me about Annie, but wondering if it was worth his discomfort.

"Anyway," he continued. "She worked as a waitress for several years until she met Lloyd Rogers, and from what people have said, it was love at first sight for them. Lloyd was raised rough and had already spent time in jail for auto theft, safecracking, and burglary. Apparently, Annie took up with him right away, and they've not only robbed banks, stores, and funeral homes, but they're also ac-cused of kidnapping a police officer and holding him for ransom."

As he spoke, my despair grew deeper and deeper. "So, if she's caught, she's facing prison time."

"That's the way of it." He let out a sigh. "I'm sorry, Carrie."

We were driving down Lyndale Avenue toward Bloomington, not far from Wold-Chamberlain Field, where Charles Lindbergh would land in his *Spirit of St. Louis* when he visited Minneapolis in just nine days. A lake appeared on the right, drawing my atten-tion as a crane lifted from the water, spreading its massive wings in flight. Sunshine sparkled off the surface of the lake, shimmering like a thousand diamonds. The earth was so full of beauty, yet riddled with heartbreaking ugliness, too. Why had Annie chosen such difficult and destructive paths? Both of her lives had fol-lowed similar patterns. An early marriage to a man she didn't seem to love, then passionate second relationships with men who had shared in her lawlessness.

"What will you do if you find her?" I asked him, almost afraid of the answer.

He was quiet for a few moments, and then he said, "I'll have to do the right thing."

As a Saint Paul police officer under the O'Connor System, I wasn't sure what his definition of the right thing would be.

"I need to talk to her, Lewis. That's what all of this is about. No matter what happens, you'll let me talk to her, won't you?"

"I know why you're doing this, Carrie. My priority is to get the answers you're looking for." He took my hand in his.

I offered him a smile and squeezed his hand before pulling away. "Thank you."

He returned my smile, but it didn't reach his eyes.

Lakeville was swarming with curiosity seekers. The city's wel-come sign boasted a population of seven hundred people, with dozens of wooden and brick buildings downtown. The grocery store that Annie and Lloyd had robbed sat at the north end of Main Street.

Several deputy sheriffs were trying to create a barricade from the tourists taking pictures of the little grocery store, while the owners were cleaning up the mess that Annie and Lloyd had left in their wake. Both large, plate-glass windows at the front of the building had been shattered, and a nearby fence had been broken, presumably by the getaway car, since the ground around it was torn up with tire tracks.

"They made a mess of things," Lewis said as we approached the crowd.

"How are we going to speak to the owners or the law enforcement?" I asked him. "It doesn't look like they're letting anyone get close."

"I'll show them my badge."

Lewis took charge as he gently nudged people out of our way and stopped by the first deputy he found.

"I'm Detective Lewis Cager from the Saint Paul Police Department." He showed the deputy his silver badge, and though he was wearing street clothes, the deputy nodded and let us pass.

An older woman was sweeping broken glass as a man nailed boards over the window. Both looked tired and careworn, with deep wrinkles around their eyes. The woman appeared to have been crying, and when she looked up at our arrival, her eyes grew wide.

"You," she said as she stopped sweeping and pointed at me. "Who are you, and what do you want?"

My mouth parted at her strange and unwelcome greeting.

Lewis glanced at me, curious, and said, "You must look like Annie."

The woman narrowed her eyes. "You know Annie Barker?"

I shook my head, not able to explain my connection to her. "No," I said honestly. "I don't know her."

"You look just like her—only younger." The woman put one hand on her hip. "Are you sure you don't know her?"

"What's this about?" the man finally asked as he approached. "Are you more curiosity seekers?"

"No." Lewis showed the couple his badge. "I'm a detective with the Saint Paul Police Department, and we're here to ask some questions."

The woman continued to eye me with distrust, but Lewis didn't let it stop him.

"We're looking for Annie Barker and want to know what you can tell us about her."

"I already told the sheriff everything I have to say." The woman went back to sweeping. "I got a business to run, and I don't have time for nonsense."

"What do you want to know?" the man asked, casting a disparaging look at the woman.

"What way did they leave town?" Lewis asked.

The man nodded to the north. "They headed out that way."

"Toward the Twin Cities?" I asked, though it was obvious.

"As far as I can tell."

"And were they working alone?" Lewis asked. "Or were there more than two of them?"

"I only saw the two of them. The woman came in first, browsing the shelves. After she had a basket full of food, the man came in with a gun and demanded all the money in our register. After I gave it to them, they ran out of here with the food and the money, but he decided to turn and shoot the windows out for the pure fun of it. Me and the missus had to duck, or we might have been killed. I heard them squeal out of here, and they must have hit the fence because it made a ruckus. As soon as I knew they were in their car, I ran out after them and saw them speeding out of town."

The woman scowled at me, as if I was the one responsible for this mess.

"Did you hear them say anything helpful?" Lewis continued. "Anything about where they might be heading?"

"Sure." The man nodded. "When Lloyd walked in, before he showed his gun, he said, 'What's taking so long, Annie? I want to get to Saint Paul before dark.' And she said, 'I'm ready when you are.' Then he showed his gun, demanded our money, and they left."

My gaze caught on Lewis's, and he nodded, letting me know he understood the significance of the man's statement.

"Thank you for your time," Lewis said to them. "You've been very helpful."

"I don't want to see you around here again," the woman said to me. "No one who looks like that Annie Barker is welcome in these parts."

Her words hurt more than they should. In 1727, I was carrying the shame of being Anne Reed's daughter. Now, in 1927, I was being judged because of her, too. She cast a shadow over both my lives, and I'd never even met her.

Lewis put his hand at the small of my back and led me to his vehicle. "Don't let her get to you," he said.

We got into his Chevy, and he pulled away from the store, heading back toward the Twin Cities.

"What will we do now?" I asked.

"I'm taking you home."

"I'm not going home until I talk to Annie."

"How are we supposed to find her this afternoon, before your father's broadcast? I'll need some time to ask around."

"Let's go to the Green Lantern. Isn't that where criminals check in?"

"I'm not taking you there, Carrie. Besides, even if she did check in, it doesn't mean she told them where she's staying."

"Please, Lew—"

"End of discussion. It's far too dangerous, and what would people say if they saw you there?"

I clenched my hands, frustration mounting. "I'm so tired of being told what I can and cannot do. I'm an adult. If I want to go to the Green Lantern bar, then I should be able to go."

"It's reckless." He shook his head. "I won't be responsible for putting you in danger."

"You won't. I'm choosing to go. Why must I rely on you and my father and Marcus to make all the decisions for me?"

He frowned. "Who is Marcus?"

My bluster faded as I realized I'd misspoken. I had never intended to tell Lewis about Marcus. What would he think if he knew I was a captive on a pirate ship and that I'd foolishly fallen in love with a pirate? But I had to say something.

"He—he's someone from my other life." I looked out the window, not wanting him to see my face, afraid I might give away my feelings. We were driving north toward the Twin Cities again, passing sprawling farmlands on either side of the road.

Lewis was silent for a moment, then he asked, quietly, "Are you in love with this Marcus?"

Marcus was two hundred years away, on a pirate ship in Florida. Yet he was just as real as Lewis. I didn't want to hurt my friend, but perhaps it would be best if I told Lewis, so he knew where my heart belonged.

With a deep breath, I said, "Yes. I am in love with Marcus."

His hands gripped the steering wheel so hard, his knuckles turned white, but he kept his face neutral as he nodded. "How long have you been in love?"

"Not long."

"Does he love you?"

Did Marcus love me? I knew he cared for me. His words the other night had revealed a depth of longing he couldn't hide. And he was scared to hurt me, but did he love me?

I clasped my hands on my lap, feeling defeated and scared. How would I face my life once Marcus was gone? Even if he did love me, there was no future for us. "I don't know if he loves me."

Lewis let out a breath and shook his head. "He loves you."

I looked up at him quickly. "How do you know?"

The gaze he turned to me was filled with such longing and tenderness, it broke my heart. "I can see it in your eyes. He loves you as much as you love him, even if he hasn't told you."

My heart beat hard. I wanted to believe Lewis, but it hurt too much to think that Marcus loved me as much as I loved him and neither of us could have what we wanted.

"What's keeping him from telling you?" he asked me.

I swallowed, trying not to let my emotions take over. "It's complicated."

"We have another twenty minutes until we reach Minneapolis."

"You're not going to like what I have to say."

"Try me."

And so I told Lewis all about Marcus Zale—and I was right. He didn't like it one bit.

After I told him everything, he was silent for a long time.

"You fell in love with your captor?" he asked, almost accusatory.

"Marcus isn't my captor," I said softly. "Captain Zale is my captor. Marcus has been nothing but kind. He encouraged me to tell my grandfather where I am, and he's going to help me find a place to live."

Lewis gave me such a scathing look, I knew he was both angry and afraid for me. "I don't trust him, Carrie."

"You don't know him."

"He's a pirate. He's no better than Annie and Lloyd."

"Or my brothers, or anyone else that's making poor choices." I crossed my arms. "You don't understand. Marcus wants to change."

He scoffed. "People don't change."

I stared at Lewis, surprised at his attitude. "Why would you become a police officer if you didn't believe people could change? Isn't that what you hope? That the criminals you apprehend will turn their lives around, given the opportunity?"

"No, Carrie. This is more proof that you're naïve. I am a police officer to save innocent people like you from scoundrels who want to hurt you. End of story. And Marcus Zale sounds like the biggest scoundrel of all."

"I knew I shouldn't have told you."

"Because you knew I would recognize a villain when I heard one." He pressed his lips together. "Why is love wasted on fools?"

My temper flared to life. "Are you calling me a fool, Lewis?"

He pulled over to the side of the road and leveled a challenging glare at me. "Yes! You have an honorable, hardworking, and dependable man right in front of you, offering you a happy life. And yet you have given your heart to a pirate who refuses to declare his love for you. I think that's the height of foolishness."

My body temperature had risen, and I was so angry, I chose to overlook the declaration he'd just made. "Take me home, Lewis."

"With pleasure. Because that's the most reasonable thing you've said all day."

Neither of us said another word on the way back to my house. When Lewis parked on the street, I got out of his vehicle and headed up the sidewalk.

I heard Lewis's door open, and a moment later, his gentle voice stopped me. "Carrie. Wait."

I stood for a heartbeat, now more sad than angry. When I turned, I found him just a few feet from me. I'm not sure if I went into his arms, or if he drew me in, but I found myself embracing him.

"I'm sorry," he whispered, close to my ear.

"I'm sorry, too."

"You have to know how I feel about you."

I simply nodded, unable to find my voice.

"I know your feelings don't match mine," he continued. "And maybe that's my fault for being—"

"It's not your fault—or my fault. It's just the way things are." I slowly pulled back. "I know I'm a fool for caring about Marcus the way I do, but my heart belongs to him, Lewis. I'm sorry."

"You don't need to be sorry." He tried to smile. "Because you're right. It's not your fault that you've fallen in love with a—" He couldn't seem to say the word.

"Pirate?" I asked, half smiling.

He shook his head, but I could see he was trying to make light of the situation. "One of the reasons I've always admired you is because you're intelligent and thoughtful. If you've found a reason to fall in love with him, then he must be a good man. I shouldn't have tried to belittle him in your eyes."

I returned to Lewis's embrace and whispered, "Thank you."

He held me tight, as if he didn't want to let me go, but he finally did. "I'm heading to the Green Lantern. I'll tell you if I learn anything helpful."

I nodded, trying to pull my emotions together.

"Please promise me you won't look for Annie without me," he said. "I couldn't bear if you got hurt."

"I won't."

"Good." He tried to smile again. "Goodbye, Carrie."

As Lewis pulled away, I knew why I was so upset.

There was some truth to what he'd said about Marcus.

21

AUGUST 15, 1727
FLORIDA COAST

The ship was underway the next morning as I woke up. It was still dark outside as I opened my eyes to face a new day—one that was taking me closer to my old life at Middleburg Plantation. Marcus had insisted I continue to use his alcove bed, while he was sound asleep on the cot in the corner. I lay for a few moments, watching him sleep.

He was on his back, with one hand on his chest and the other above his head.

My conversation with Lewis the day before still echoed through my mind and heart. If I couldn't make a life with Marcus, then what was I doing holding on to this hope? Would it be better if I cast aside my heart's desire and gave myself fully to Lewis? I didn't love him the way I loved Marcus, but I did care for him deeply. Was that enough to make a marriage work? Could I find the same passion and desire I felt for Marcus?

Would I need it?

The truth was that I *wanted* passion and desire. My heart ached just thinking about it. But Lewis was right. Marcus had no plans on changing his ways. Not for himself, not for his mother, and not for me.

That pained me more than anything else.

Perhaps I should return to Grandfather. There was no guarantee that Marcus's mother was still alive or that she'd want to take in a stranger. The journey to Massachusetts was fraught with risk. If I went back to Middleburg Plantation, I could tell Grandfather that I wanted to make decisions about my life. I had stood up to him once by running away. Perhaps he wouldn't be so quick to force my hand if he believed I would leave again. I didn't miss my life on the plantation or living by his strict rules, but I missed Nanny and some of the other servants who had been with us for years.

Yet, even as I considered what I would do next, the thought of saying goodbye to Marcus made my heart ache with an intensity that took my breath away.

It would be easier to forget about him if I didn't have to see him night and day. Sleeping in the same room. Sharing the same meals. Discussing books, philosophy, and religion. Being so close, I could reach out and touch him, feel his skin against mine, or get lost in the depths of his eyes.

It would be best to return home before it was too late. Face whatever the future held on the plantation instead of the uncertainty of living on a pirate ship.

I had no desire to go back to sleep or lie in bed and feel miserable about Marcus, so I rose as quietly as possible and got dressed.

The sky was starting to lighten as I stepped out of Marcus's cabin to use the head. There was a watch on duty in the crow's nest, but they wouldn't think anything of me going about my business, no matter the hour. I made my way to the stern, behind the captain's cabin, thankful for a bit of privacy.

But before I entered the head, I heard a soft, painful moan, followed by a whimper.

A very feminine whimper.

Whoever was in the head was suffering.

The only people who used the private toilet in this part of the ship were the captain, Marcus, Hawk, Ned, and me. I frowned, trying to make sense of what I was hearing, and then Timothy's conversation filtered through my mind.

Ned.

Another whimper met my ears, and I knew I needed to offer my help, even if it was unwanted. If nothing else, I could summon Dr. Hartville.

I tapped lightly on the door, and the whimpering stopped.

"Ned?" I asked as I slowly opened the door.

"Don't come in here!"

"Are you ill? Do you need help?"

"Stay awa—" But the words were cut off by a cry of pain.

I opened the door all the way and wasn't prepared for what I saw.

Ned was sitting on the floor, in front of the toilet, a pool of blood on the ground. He was in a nightshirt, clutching his abdomen—but it was clear he wasn't a man, after all. Ned was a woman, in the middle of losing a pregnancy.

My mouth parted in surprise as I rushed into the small space and knelt on the ground beside her.

Her face was pinched in pain and sorrow. "You weren't supposed to know." Tears streamed down her face. "No one was supposed to know."

"I'll get Dr. Hartville—"

"No." She grabbed my arm.

"But you're clearly in trouble. All this blood, it can't be good."

"I'm losing the baby," she said as more tears trailed down her cheek. "I didn't want it—was so angry I was pregnant. I waited two months to tell him. He was forcing me to go back to my family in Charleston." She let out a moan as she dropped her chin to her chest, breathing hard. "But I won't need to go home now."

My heart was heavy as I asked, "Captain Zale?"

She sobbed and nodded. "He'll kill you if he learns that you know the truth."

"I won't tell him," I promised.

"He'll know. He knows everything."

"Are you sure I can't summon Dr. Hartville?"

She shook her head. "Edward made me promise that if I stayed on the ship with him, I wouldn't tell anyone I was a woman. They're all superstitious. I've heard them whispering about me. They'll overthrow Edward if they know he allowed me on the ship, and then they'll cast me into the ocean." She wiped her running nose with the back of her arm. "He warned me that this wasn't a good place for me, but I didn't want to live without him. And it's no place for a child, either. He was right. I don't belong here. No one does."

"I'll help you, Ned." I put my hand on her shoulder. "I'll do whatever you need."

Her glossy, miserable eyes met mine. "My name isn't Ned. It's Nadine."

Part of me wanted to tell her that I was also a woman, but I couldn't take that risk. Nadine had always disliked me, and I had no guarantee that if she survived, she would keep the information to herself. Mary's words came back to me from my time in Nassau. How many women were dressed as men, living as pirates on the open water? Surely more than people realized.

Nadine was at the end of the miscarriage, and I assisted her as best as I could, fetching several buckets of water to help her clean herself and the room before the sun crested the horizon and the captain or Marcus woke up. Her nightshirt was ruined, so I went into the corner, out of her sight, and removed my vest and then my shirt. I put my vest on over my binding and helped her into the new shirt, which went down to her knees. After she tossed her ruined shirt over the side of the ship, I offered to help her back to the captain's cabin, but she insisted she return alone. She was pale and weak and could hardly stand, but I couldn't force her to accept my assistance.

I told her I'd see to everyone's breakfast, and for once, she didn't protest.

As I exited the head after Nadine had left, I found Marcus standing outside his cabin door. He frowned when he saw me without my undershirt, and a dozen emotions played across his face in a heartbeat. Surprise, confusion, anger, jealousy, and more.

Had he seen Nadine—who he thought was Ned—leave the head before me?

Without a word, he reentered his cabin, and I followed. I trusted Marcus to know the truth. I wanted him to know the truth. It was too much to keep to myself. Nadine could still be in danger. She needed medical help, preferably from a midwife. I knew of one in Charleston, but I wasn't sure if Captain Zale would allow it.

I closed the door behind me and faced Marcus.

"I was surprised to find you out of your bed before me," he said, confusion on his brow, "and then even more surprised to see Ned leave the head, half-dressed—only to have you follow, without your shirt."

"I know." I nodded, not wanting him to have any more reason to be upset. I quickly explained what had happened, sparing the gruesome details of the miscarriage but sharing the truth.

His mouth parted in shock and his eyes had widened. "Ned is—"

"The captain's mistress."

He blinked a few times and then slipped his hand behind his neck as he paced across the room. "I had no idea. All this time . . ."

"The mind really does see what it wants," I said.

"There was a wee bairn?"

"She lost it less than thirty minutes ago. She's heartsick and scared."

"I can understand."

"But she'll need some medical attention, and I'm not sure how to approach Captain Zale about it, since we're not supposed to know. And I don't know if she'll be willing to get the help, either.

She wouldn't let me send for Dr. Hartville." I watched him, trying to gauge his thoughts. "It would be best to continue to Charleston and get her some treatment."

"Dr. Hartville can't help her?"

"I don't think so. And even if he could, Captain Zale doesn't want him to know she's a woman."

Marcus nodded, still in shock. "I had no idea."

"Neither did I, but I think some of the men were starting to suspect her. Timothy told me as much yesterday."

He rubbed his hand across his forehead. "If the captain learns she miscarried, and doesn't realize she needs medical help, he might return to Florida and keep looking for the Queen's Dowry."

"Then I need to impress upon her how important it is for her to get help. She needs to go to Charleston."

"Aye. We must make haste." He glanced at my bare arms and then went to his chest of clothes and pulled out the shirt I'd borrowed in the past.

He left his cabin, and I quickly put on the shirt, trying to make it work, though it was so large, it was almost impossible. I was able to tuck it in and get my vest back on before I joined him outside the entrance to the captain's outer room.

Nadine had not made it any farther than her cot. She was curled up in a ball on her side. She hadn't even pulled the covers up around her body and was shaking violently from shock.

Marcus and I helped her get under the covers. His gentleness warmed me as he fetched another blanket from Hawk's cot and tucked it around Nadine's body.

"We need to get you to Charleston to see a midwife who can make sure you are safe," I said to Nadine. "You lost a lot of blood."

She shook her head. "Just leave me be."

"Your health and safety are all that matter right now," I told her. "At least let Dr. Hartville help you."

"No one must know about the miscarriage," Nadine said through chattering teeth. "The captain can't find out I told you."

"I won't tell anyone," I promised. "But when we get to Charleston, I will take you to a midwife. I know of one who has been helping women for decades. She can be trusted."

Her wide-eyed gaze shifted to Marcus, as if noticing him for the first time.

"You have nothing to fear," Marcus said, his voice low and soothing. "I won't tell anyone, either."

She looked back at me, her pale face filled with pain and sorrow. "There's someone in Charleston who can help me?"

"Yes. But until we get there, you need to stay in bed and rest. I will see to all your chores. We should be in Charleston in four or five days, and we'll get you help."

Nadine looked too weak to fight, so she simply nodded and closed her eyes.

The day was long and arduous. I was still recovering from diving sickness, so Marcus encouraged me to take naps between meals, but there was too much to do. The captain hadn't seemed concerned about Ned being sick again, and Dr. Hartville hadn't even glanced in her direction as he passed by. She'd been sick on and off the past few weeks, and they must have assumed it was the same illness that had kept her in bed before. I now knew it was morning sickness that had been plaguing her.

I checked on her often, making sure she hadn't started to bleed again or run a fever. I brought her something to eat and drink, though she refused both. She was pale and weak—and so very tired.

After supper, I returned to Marcus's cabin, ready to go to bed early.

I'd been so preoccupied with Nadine's trouble that I hadn't thought much about my own resolve from earlier that morning.

When I returned to Charleston, I had decided to stay.

The sun was low on the horizon when Marcus entered the cabin.

I had contemplated going to bed before he came in for the night but had decided it would be best to tell him my plans.

I was sitting on my old cot, wanting him to have his bed again. But the look in his eyes when he saw me sitting there told me he wasn't happy with my decision.

"Why are you not in the other bed?" he asked.

"'Tis yours."

"I gave it to you."

"Until I felt better."

"Nay. 'Tis your bed now."

I didn't want to argue with him, but there was tension between us. It had been building for days, since I had asked him what he planned to do once he delivered me to his mother in Massachusetts. He hadn't responded, telling me all I needed to know. I remained on the cot as he stood by the closed door.

"There's something I need to tell you," I said.

His brown eyes were dark tonight, darker than usual. Whether he was angry about Ned, or about me speaking to Timothy yesterday, or about something else, I wasn't sure. But he carried the weight of whatever was bothering him with stiff shoulders and a slight scowl.

"Will I like what you have to say?" he asked.

"Nay."

He sighed and pulled a chair out from the table.

I rose from the cot and sat across from him, laying my hands in my lap. "I've made a decision."

He watched me without speaking.

My heart begged me to stop, but my mind urged me to continue. "I've decided 'tis best if I return to Middleburg Plantation when we arrive in South Carolina."

Marcus was expressionless as he sat across from me.

I wanted him to protest, to tell me that *he* had changed his mind. That he was ready to give up pirating and run away to a far-off land where he could change his name and we could live in privacy for the rest of our lives. Together.

But he didn't. Instead, he rose from the table and went to the window. A habit I'd learned meant he was contemplating. Searching.

It gave me hope—until he said, "Aye. 'Tis best."

Those few words broke my heart in two. Marcus wasn't fighting for me. For us. He was going to let me go.

And I would let him.

22

AUGUST 15, 1927
MINNEAPOLIS, MINNESOTA

I was thankful for a reprieve from the *Ocean Curse* and Marcus the next day as I helped Mother prepare for the arrival of a special guest. It was a strange reality to have a broken heart over a man who lived two hundred years ago. If Mother noticed my somber mood, she didn't comment. She probably assumed it had something to do with Lewis. Had she or Father noticed us embrace yesterday when he dropped me off at the house?

Pushing thoughts of Marcus aside, I focused on what Lewis might have learned when he went to the Green Lantern bar. Did he know if Annie was in Saint Paul? Where she might be staying? How long she'd be there?

Just after lunch, a knock at the front door told us that our guest had arrived.

"She's here," Mother said excitedly as she rushed into the foyer. Father was away from home today, working on the tent revival and Lindbergh's arrival, which were only eight days away.

"Irene!" Mother said as she opened the front door.

My beautiful cousin stood on the porch with a suitcase in hand. She was wearing a pretty summer dress, and her blond

243

hair was a bit longer than it had been in May, but it was still stylish under her blue cloche hat. "Aunt Marian!" She set down her suitcase and gave my mother a hug. "And Caroline," Irene said next as she left my mother and hugged me. "It's so good to see you again."

Despite the trouble Irene had given me in Paris, I was happy she had come to be part of the Lindbergh celebration and the revival.

"Are you excited to see Lindbergh again?" I asked her.

"You have no idea. All my friends are so envious." She glanced at my mother and offered an embarrassed laugh. "And, of course, I'm excited to hear Uncle Daniel preach again. I'm a bit of a celebrity in Des Moines because I'm related to him."

"How kind," Mother said with a gentle smile. "Now, you must get settled, and then we'll have a nice long visit."

Though Irene had stayed with us many times before, I showed her to the spare bedroom on the second floor. She chatted about the train ride from Des Moines, a new dress her mother had made for her to wear for the Lindbergh festivities, and the job she had started as a children's governess this summer.

"Mama didn't want me to get a job," she told me as she removed her hat and gloves and set them on the bureau in the spare room. "But I know how tight finances are since Papa's death, and I wanted to help."

"That's very kind of you," I said, noticing something different about Irene though I couldn't quite put my finger on it. There was a softness to her, a gentleness she hadn't exhibited in Paris.

"It's helped me so much," she confided as she took a seat on the bed and patted the spot next to her.

I sat, smiling. "I could tell something was different."

Irene looked down at her polished nails and nodded. "I was hurting so much in Paris, Caroline. Losing Papa was a blow I hadn't seen coming, and it turned my world upside down. But I think seeing Mama suffer was the worst part. She's still very sad, but I haven't seen her cry in weeks."

"And how has the job helped?"

She shrugged. "It took my mind off things and gave me something to look forward to." Her eyes shone as she met my gaze. "The children are darlings, and they seem to love me, no matter what I wear or how I act. I've never felt such unconditional acceptance. I guess it gave me hope that my life could be full of a family of my own one day. I don't know. I suppose that sounds silly."

"Not at all. I'm happy to hear that your grief is easing and that your work has helped."

"I also owe you and your parents my gratitude, and perhaps an apology. I know I was difficult in Paris—"

"You don't owe us an apology."

"But I want to make one. I'm especially sorry for the night you followed me to the Dingo Bar. I didn't think about the consequences at the time, but I understand the position I was putting you and your parents in."

"Please don't apologize to them for that. It would be better if they didn't know."

She smiled and nodded. "I understand."

I hadn't thought much about that night in a long time, but I did now. "When we returned home, there was a letter waiting for me from Ernest Hemingway."

Irene's blue eyes grew wide, and she grabbed my arms. "What? You didn't destroy it, did you? He's only the most famous writer in America. You saved it, right?"

"I saved it," I said, "though I shouldn't have. If Mother or Father ever found it, I'd have a lot of explaining to do."

She stood and pulled me off the bed. "Where is it? Can you show me?"

Laughing, I brought her into my room, and I took my box of correspondence off the desk. "I put it in here because Mother is less likely to look through my personal letters. She values privacy. If she found the letter tucked under my mattress or hidden in my bureau, she might be more suspicious."

I handed the letter to Irene, and she opened it with enthusiasm. Her eyes grew wider still as she came to the end.

"Did he write to his friend at the Coliseum Ballroom about you?"

"I don't know."

"You didn't inquire?" She lowered the letter and stared at me. "When Ernest Hemingway makes a point to write to you, you should at least follow up on his suggestion."

"You just told me a minute ago that you realized the consequences of going to the Dingo Bar could have been worse. And that was in Paris! Can you imagine if I went to a speakeasy in Saint Paul?"

Her face fell, and she sighed. "I suppose. But, gee, that would be fun, wouldn't it?"

"Irene." I lowered my chin. "Don't get any wild ideas."

She grinned. "I won't go sneaking out, if that's what you mean. But it would be fun, don't you think? It's just a ballroom and dancing. There can't be anything wrong with that."

"The Coliseum has a reputation for being a speakeasy. And even if it didn't, people would still frown upon Reverend Baldwin's daughter at a ballroom."

"That's a shame." She handed back the letter as the telephone rang downstairs.

I put the letter back in my correspondence box and buried it under a few other envelopes.

"Caroline," Mother called up the stairs. "The telephone is for you."

I left Irene to unpack and went down the stairs to the dining room where the telephone hung on the wall. Mother had left the receiver dangling, but I could hear her humming softly in the kitchen. I lifted it and said, "Hello, this is Caroline."

"Hi, Carrie." Lewis's voice was clear on the other end. It was good to hear him again, especially after parting on such difficult terms yesterday.

"Hi, Lewis." My pulse sped, and I cupped my hand around the mouthpiece so Mother wouldn't hear. "Did you learn anything about Annie?"

"I guess we can cut to the chase." He chuckled, but then his voice grew serious. "I went to the Green Lantern yesterday, and Annie and Lloyd did check in there on Saturday night."

Even though I had suspected as much, hearing it made me feel kind of sick to my stomach. Annie was closer to me than ever before and I wanted answers, but I was almost afraid to get them. What if she told me something I didn't want to hear? Yet, it was too late to worry about that now. "Do you know where they're staying or for how long?"

"No, but I spoke to a few guys at the police station this morning and someone said they saw her last night at the Wabasha Street Caves. Rumor has it that she and Lloyd are making the rounds while they're in town, connecting with some of their local cronies. I wouldn't be surprised if they went to the Coliseum tonight."

The mention of the ballroom that Irene and I were just discussing felt jarring, yet I knew what I needed to do. Despite telling Irene it was a bad idea to think about going to the ballroom, I had little choice. I couldn't pass up an opportunity to talk to my mother, even if it meant risking my reputation and my father's. "I want to talk to her, Lewis."

"I'll try to make that hap—"

"Tonight," I said, quietly. "At the Coliseum."

"Don't be ridiculous."

"I'm not. It might be my only opportunity, and I need to take it. If she leaves before I can speak to her, I could lose the chance forever."

"There are too many risks."

I knew the risks, but I had to try to convince him. "It's a ballroom. Hundreds of people go there every night to dance."

"Not Reverend Baldwin's daughter."

"You'll go with me, right? You'll protect me if something goes wrong?"

He was quiet for a few seconds, and then he said, "You'll go whether I'm there or not, won't you?"

"Yes."

He growled. "Fine. I'll pick you up at eight."

"I'll have Irene with me."

"Irene?"

"My cousin, from Iowa. You remember her, don't you?"

"Vaguely. But it doesn't matter. I'll pick both of you up at eight."

Nerves fluttered through my stomach as I thought about going to the Coliseum. I didn't want to hurt my father's reputation, but if Andrew and Thomas hadn't done it yet, maybe the kind of people who frequented ballrooms and nightclubs didn't care. The whole generation had a live-and-let-live attitude, so maybe I would be safe.

"Thank you, Lewis. We'll see you tonight."

As I hung up the phone, Mother entered the dining room. She carried a tea tray and wore a bright smile. "I couldn't help but overhear the last part of your conversation, dear." Her eyes were shining. "Is Lewis coming to call tonight?"

How much had she heard? If her pleasant demeanor was an indication, it hadn't been much. "He wanted to take me out tonight," I said, "but I told him Irene is here, so he agreed to take her along."

"Oh?" Her eyebrows dipped together. "I hope he's not taking you somewhere unpleasant."

"No. Of course not." I wasn't lying, but it still felt like I was being dishonest. I couldn't tell her where Lewis was taking us, and I hoped she wouldn't ask. "Shall I get Irene for tea?"

"Yes, please." She moved into the parlor as I went past her up the stairs to tell Irene where we were going tonight.

No doubt she'd be surprised—and excited.

I was so nervous that evening, I didn't eat a thing at supper. My palms were clammy, and my stomach was in knots. A headache had begun to form behind my eyes, and I just wanted to get the whole thing over with. I was afraid both that my life would change irrevocably after I spoke to Annie and that it wouldn't change at all. I'd never felt so torn between the past and the future.

My entire life, I'd been trying to protect my father and his ministry, but tonight, I was risking it all to speak to Annie. I just prayed I wouldn't be recognized.

"You two look lovely," Mother said as we came downstairs after changing into evening gowns. "I hope you'll have fun with Lewis."

Guilt ate at me as I tried to smile.

Father was in his office, writing sermon notes for the three evenings he planned to preach during his tent meetings. He'd been advertising it all over the state of Minnesota and into northern Iowa, western Wisconsin, and the eastern parts of the Dakotas. It would be the biggest tent revival of his career, if everything went as planned. But he never wavered, showed anxiety, or worried that people wouldn't show up. Maybe his unfailing faith in God—and in his calling—was the very thing that attracted people to him. If he didn't believe it would be a success, then he'd never attempt to hold such a large gathering.

Was that the answer to my own fears and distance from God? If I believed I was cursed by my ancestor, and that I didn't have a choice in the matter, I lived as if I was defeated. But perhaps, as Marcus had pointed out, I wasn't cursed. And if I believed that, then it would affect the decisions I made and the way I lived. I could have victory, instead of defeat. It brought to my mind a passage from the book of Deuteronomy that said God had set before the Israelites life and death, blessing and cursing, and He had instructed them to choose life, that they and their descendants would live.

It was a weighty thing to consider—and something I would tuck away to ponder later, when I wasn't concentrating on talking to Annie.

Outside, the daylight was dimming, and the late August night was fast approaching. I was wearing an evening gown we had purchased in Paris on one of our last days. Since we stayed longer than planned, we had the opportunity to do a little shopping.

Mother had splurged to purchase the gown for me, and this was my first opportunity to wear it. The cream-colored silk flowed from a dropped waist in many delicate layers to the hem. It had a multicolored floral design printed on it and a gold belt around the waist. What had surprised me the most was that it was sleeveless, something that Mother appeared to be overlooking tonight.

Lewis pulled up to the curb as I grabbed my purse and glanced in the hall mirror one last time. Irene looked stunning in a shimmering gold dress, made of tulle and silk, with an equally elaborate gold headdress. I had chosen a simple pearl headband, and Irene had styled my brown hair into a roll at the back. It felt nice to dress up, but I couldn't help wishing that Marcus could see me like this. Elegant. Beautiful. Feminine.

Even though I tried to push thoughts of him aside while I was focused on Annie and my life in 1927, the truth was that he was always on my mind. I only had a few more days with him before we'd part ways in Charleston, and I'd never see him again. As much as I didn't want to think about it, I could think of little else.

Lewis knocked on the front door, and I took a deep breath, turning away from the mirror—and my heartbreaking thoughts of Marcus—to face him.

Mother opened the door, giving me the chance to admire Lewis in his tuxedo. He looked handsome, with a black tie and white waistcoat, his hair smoothed back, and his face freshly shaved.

"How nice you look," Mother said to him. "The girls have been getting ready for hours."

Lewis glanced up and admiration shone in his blue-eyed gaze as he smiled at me. "You look lovely, Caroline."

"Thank you."

"And do you remember our niece, Miss Irene Baldwin?" Mother asked Lewis. "She visited here when all of you were younger."

Lewis stepped over the threshold and into the foyer as Irene moved out from behind me.

He seemed surprised at the sight of her and said, "It's nice to see you again, Miss Baldwin."

They shook hands, and Irene's cheeks blossomed with color, whether from excitement or the appearance of our handsome escort I wasn't sure. "Please, call me Irene. How kind of you to offer to take me along tonight."

Lewis only smiled and tossed me a side glance. He hadn't really offered to take us. I had insisted.

Father exited his office in time to greet Lewis and say, "Don't stay out too late."

"We won't," I promised as I tried to hurry Irene and Lewis out of the house. The less interaction we had with my parents, the better.

Lewis offered both of us an arm, and we walked down the sidewalk together.

"How many men can boast two pretty ladies on their arms?" he asked as he grinned from me to Irene. "I'll be the envy of every man at the Coliseum."

Irene smiled coyly, and I only shook my head at Lewis's flirtation.

It took us about fifteen minutes to get to the Coliseum on the corner of Lexington Parkway and University Avenue in Saint Paul. Irene and Lewis reminisced about the last time Irene had visited, each recounting stories the other had forgotten.

"How old were you at the time?" Lewis asked her.

Irene, who was sitting in the back seat, leaned forward to rest her arms on the front bench and said, "I was just fourteen."

"That's why you look so different." His charming smile shined brightly tonight. "You've done a lot of growing up since then."

Irene's pleasant laughter filled the car, but I was too anxious about my meeting with Annie to join in their banter.

The Coliseum Ballroom was enormous. The newspapers boasted that the 100-by-250-foot dance floor was the largest in the world. As we pulled into the massive parking lot, I was surprised to see so many vehicles on a Monday night. It was both nerve-racking and relieving. With so many people, I hoped I would just be another face in the crowd.

I was even more surprised when we stepped out of Lewis's Chevy and I recognized a couple waiting by the front door, presumably for us.

Thomas and Alice.

My brother leaned against the building, smoking a cigarette, with his arm around Alice.

"What took you so long?" he asked as he threw his cigarette butt onto the ground and smashed it with the toe of his boot.

I paused as Alice smiled at me. Her pregnancy was more evident under her loose evening gown. "Hello, Caroline."

My anxiety rose another notch as I turned to Lewis. "Why did you tell them we were coming?"

"We needed backup," Lewis said as he opened the door into the Coliseum. "If something goes wrong, I want a trusted friend here to help."

"I don't even understand why you're here," Thomas said to me, frustration in his voice. "Lewis won't tell me." He paused and waited for me to tell him, but when I didn't, he said, "After the stunt you pulled a few weeks ago at Nina's, I shouldn't be surprised. Apparently, we all have secrets we're keeping from Mother and Father."

"I'm not keeping secre—" I paused, because I *was* keeping secrets. "Thomas, you remember Irene."

"Of course I do." He nodded at our cousin. "Irene, this is my girlfriend, Alice Pierce."

"How do you do?" Irene asked as she shook Alice's hand, struggling to keep the surprise off her face as she dropped her gaze to Alice's midsection.

I would have a lot of explaining to do to Irene.

"Shall we?" Lewis asked as he held the door open.

The five of us entered the building, but as I passed Lewis, I asked, "Do you have any other surprises for me tonight?"

He shrugged and smiled. "I hope not."

After Lewis paid for our entrance, we passed through the vestibule and entered the dance floor. The rounded ceiling was impossibly high, with a stage at one end under a brick arch. Glimmering gold curtains at the back of the stage highlighted a big band, elaborate chandeliers, and two globe lamps on either side.

The room was full of people. Some were sitting at tables on the perimeter of the room, while others were dancing on the wood dance floor. Every imaginable color of gown was present, and most of the men were wearing tuxedos or evening suits. Waiters moved around the room with trays of ice, glasses, and what looked like ginger ale. As they were set on the tables, I saw more than one person pull a flask from their jacket pocket to mix with the ginger ale.

"Why don't the police do something about the alcohol?" I asked Lewis and Thomas.

Lewis shrugged. "The owner pays the police department to look the other way."

Thomas had his arm around Alice as we found a table, and the pair sat close. It was clear they were crazy about each other, but Alice still looked uncomfortable—probably because she thought this was the first time I was learning about their relationship.

"I love to dance," Irene said as she took a seat. "And this foxtrot is one of my favorites."

Lewis grinned, taking the hint. "Would you like to dance, Irene?"

She was out of her seat before he finished his sentence.

"How about you?" Thomas asked Alice, smiling at her. "Want to cut a rug, sweetheart?" Alice nodded, and as they left the table, Thomas said to me, "Don't do anything stupid."

I wanted to make a face at my older brother and remind him that *I* wasn't the one doing anything foolish. He was escorting our brother's ex-mistress onto the dance floor, several months pregnant.

Their departure gave me the opportunity to study the faces of the women in attendance. There were at least a hundred. Some were sitting in the shadows, and some were on the dance floor, crowded by others.

How was I supposed to find Annie here? The best vantage point would be from the stage at the front of the room, but the only way—

My thoughts stilled. If I could get on the stage, and perhaps sing with the band, I could study the faces of the women on the dance floor. It would give me the best opportunity to find Annie.

A man approached our table, and it was clear he was coming to ask me to dance, so I quickly stood and went in the opposite direction toward the bar, not allowing myself to contemplate what I was about to do.

It took me several minutes to get an audience with the owner, and when I asked him if Ernest Hemingway had sent him a letter of introduction, he didn't even hesitate.

"Sure did! Come on. I was in the war with Ernie. Any friend of his is a friend of mine. Let's get you on stage."

He didn't give me much time to regret my decision as he led me through the crowd toward the front of the ballroom. There, he chatted with the band director, and then he told me I was up next.

I continued to scan the crowd, not certain what Annie looked like, but searching for an older woman who had some of my features. If the owner of the grocery store in Lakeville was surprised by my appearance, I assumed Annie and I shared the same likeness.

"Miss Reed?" the owner said. "The band is ready for you."

Mr. Hemingway had apparently given him my alias, which I appreciated.

I was taking a chance that people could see and recognize me, but the room was dim, and I doubted they would pay close attention—especially when the band leader introduced me as Miss Reed.

Though I wasn't sure what Lewis, Thomas, or Irene would think.

"We have a special guest singer tonight," the band leader said into the microphone. "Direct from Paris, France, Miss Reed."

Paris, France? I wasn't going to correct him as I walked across the stage. Better to let people think I was from another country.

Several people looked my way, but many of them continued to visit around the room.

I caught Lewis's eye from the table where we'd been sitting. His shocked expression turned to irritation, so I simply shrugged.

And then I began my search for Annie in earnest. The vantage point I had was perfect, as I had suspected. The lights from the stage lit up the faces of those on the dance floor.

When the band began to play "It Had to Be You," I didn't feel nervous. The lyrics slipped out effortlessly. I had come a long way since the Dingo Bar in Paris. I no longer worried about what people thought about my singing and simply enjoyed the song.

As I scanned the dancers' faces, most of them paused to listen and watch.

A woman at the back of the dance floor shifted, allowing me to see her clearly. I almost tripped over my words as I continued to sing. She had dark hair and eyes, and she looked like an older version of me. She was standing next to a man, but I barely glanced at him, since I was so intent upon studying the woman.

She was looking back at me, but if she recognized me, she didn't show any indication. Though why would she? If it was Annie, she would have no idea that she had a time-crossing daughter occupying the same life as her.

My heart beat so hard, I struggled to breathe. The ballroom filled with applause as I finished, and when the band leader asked me for an encore, I had to refuse. I had completed the task, and I needed to speak to the woman I suspected was Annie.

As I stepped off the stage, Lewis was waiting for me.

"What are you doing?" he asked quietly. "Do you want everyone in here to recognize you?"

"I saw her," I said, trying to look over his shoulder. "She's at the back of the room." I started moving in that direction.

People tried to stop me and compliment my singing. I didn't want to be rude, so I thanked them and kept moving deeper into the crowd.

The band began another song, and people started to dance again.

When I got to the back of the dance floor, where I had seen Annie, she was gone.

Disappointment and despair gripped me as I frantically searched for her.

Lewis stayed close to me as we walked around the huge room. Some of the men sitting in dark corners looked dangerous, and I stayed clear of them. Smoke curled around several tables, choking me. I couldn't imagine what my parents would say if they smelled cigarette smoke on Irene and me.

Annie wasn't at any of the tables, at the bar, or even in line for the ladies' room.

Finally, Lewis grabbed my hand, causing me to stop.

"I think you lost her," he said.

"She couldn't have gone far." I tried pulling my hand away to keep looking, but he wouldn't let me go.

"I'll ask around," he said, drawing me closer to him. "Maybe someone talked to her and knows where she's staying."

Tears of disappointment threatened as I tried in vain to see her in the crowd. "I was so close."

He put his hand under my chin to draw my gaze to his face. "I'll find her, Carrie. I promise."

Bitterness took hold as I wiped impatiently at a tear that fell. "Why won't God let me talk to her?"

"Because it's obviously not the right time. Trust His plan."

"I want to, but I also know that He doesn't like when we sit back and do nothing."

He lowered his hand, his expression incredulous. "You're not sitting back and doing nothing. You escaped a domineering grandfather to join a ship to look for her in the Caribbean. Then, you were kidnapped by pirates before you made it to Nassau where you learned she had died. After that, you risked everything to tell me the truth before traipsing across the county to a grocery store to learn that she was in Saint Paul, and you came to a ballroom, and sang on a stage, to see her in a crowd. You are doing everything you can to find Annie Barker."

I let out a breath and shook my head. "If anyone heard you saying those things, they'd think you had lost your mind."

His grin was wide when he said, "Chasing you as you chase her has left me feeling like that from time to time."

I chuckled, trying not to feel so disappointed.

"Come on," he said. "It's been a long time since you danced with me."

"Have I ever danced with you?"

"Exactly."

He led me onto the dance floor and twirled me around to the new dance called the Lindy Hop, inspired by Lindbergh's hop over the Atlantic.

It felt good to laugh with him—but it didn't make me forget the pain of disappointment at losing Annie again, or that I would soon be returning to Charleston in my other life.

23

AUGUST 21, 1727
CHARLESTON, SOUTH CAROLINA

Several days had passed since I'd visited the Coliseum Ballroom
and spotted Annie. Lewis visited our house almost every night, giving me updates on his investigation. He assured me Annie hadn't
left Saint Paul. She'd been spotted on several occasions, and as
soon as he knew where she was staying or where she might go
next, he'd take me to her.

He, Irene, and I enjoyed his daily visits—Irene more so than
I expected. She primped and preened for him, and he seemed to
enjoy her attention. I'd started to wonder if he was coming for
her company more than mine, using the excuse of updating me
as his reason.

But today wasn't the day to think about Lewis and Irene. Nadine had continued to suffer after her miscarriage, though I had
started to suspect it was a sickness of the heart and soul, more so
than the body. The captain continued his course toward Charleston, and after catching him at Nadine's bedside one morning, his
hand laid tenderly on her forehead, I knew he cared about her.
I had overheard Nadine tell the captain that she'd lost the baby,
and since we were still heading to Charleston, I knew he wanted

her to get help. They hadn't seen me before I slipped away, but it was clear that Nadine had chosen to be his mistress, even though he'd cautioned her against it. Though I wondered if she was now regretting the life she'd chosen.

On that hot August morning as we anchored in a lagoon just north of Charleston Harbor, I stood alongside Hawk, Marcus, and Nadine. A small sloop would take us to shore. The captain would stay on the hidden ship, not wanting to be caught. He believed Nadine would go into the city, see a doctor about the pregnancy, and return the next day under Hawk and Marcus's watch. There was more plunder to be divested of, so Marcus and Hawk would enter the city under those pretenses. But Marcus and I knew what our real intentions were. We would take Nadine to the midwife, and then I would return to Middleburg Plantation.

I carried a small satchel of coins I'd earned on the *Ocean Curse*. It felt strange and wonderful to have my own money, though I wasn't sure what I would do with it. If Grandfather wouldn't allow me to have the life I wanted, perhaps I could use the money to forge my own path. I was eager to see Nanny again, but my longing to see her was overshadowed by the pain of leaving Marcus.

I didn't want to think of the future, so I focused on the familiar shoreline of South Carolina as we made our way toward Charleston.

It was strange to think that I would never stand on board the *Ocean Curse* again. In just a few hours, Marcus and I would say goodbye and I would start the next part of my life—come what may.

He said nothing as we traversed the waterways from the lagoon into the harbor. We had hardly spoken the past five days, and the more I longed for him to fight for me, the more it hurt that he didn't. My love had started to turn to anger, but I wasn't a fool. It was my heart's way of protecting itself from the inevitable parting, though the truth was it still hurt beyond measure. And every time I looked at him, I saw the longing in his eyes, which only made the pain increase.

The cicadas hummed, and the mosquitoes buzzed around us.

Nadine was pale and despondent. I wanted to console her but couldn't. Even if she knew I was a woman, Hawk didn't.

As we came into the busy harbor, I had a strange sense of comfort at the familiarity. The tobacco harvest was underway and shipments of it were being sent all over the world, creating more traffic than normal.

It took some time for the sloop to maneuver through the harbor and dock near the long wharf. Very few people paid attention to us as we got off the launch and made our way into the city.

"Carl and I will take Ned to the doctor," Marcus said to Hawk. "If you want to start making inquiries about our cargo, we can plan to meet back here tomorrow evening."

Hawk gave one nod, trusting Marcus to be good to his word. The two men were closer than I'd first realized. Marcus had told me that Hawk was one of the only crew members that had been with him since he'd joined Captain Zale's ship, and he knew Marcus's real identity.

The large man disappeared into the crowd without another word.

Nadine said nothing as Marcus spoke to me. "Where is this midwife?"

"On Chalmers Street," I said as I began to walk in the right direction. "I'll lead the way."

Marcus and Nadine were silent as they followed.

I was dressed as a man, but I still watched for someone who might recognize me. The chances were slim, since I rarely visited Charleston with Grandfather, and when I did, it wasn't to socialize but to conduct business.

When we came to Chalmers Street, I took a right, thankful that I knew of this midwife. She'd been called to Middleburg Plantation on many occasions to help with the births of the indentured servants' children. Grandfather spared no expense in the health of his employees and servants, and Mrs. Drywell's reputation in Charleston was excellent. Her knowledge about childbirth and stillbirth was unmatched in the colony. Upon one trip to town, I had gone with Grandfather to pay for her services and remembered where her home was located.

When we arrived at her house, I started up the steps, but Marcus held back.

"I'll wait out here," he said.

Nadine followed me up the steps to the front door. After knocking, a servant answered, and I told her we had need of Mrs. Drywell's assistance. No questions were asked as we were led inside.

Twenty minutes later, I left the house, knowing Nadine was in good hands.

Marcus paced along the sidewalk, deep in thought, as I approached.

My heart beat hard, knowing what would happen next.

"Nadine will be cared for," I assured him. "She'll sleep here tonight, and you can collect her tomorrow. Mrs. Drywell will give her some medicinal herbs to calm her nerves and to heal any lingering ailments the miscarriage might have created."

"Thank you," he said, his brown eyes filled with a myriad of emotions too tangled to unravel.

I took a deep breath, hoping—willing—for him to tell me that he was having second thoughts about letting me go.

"I suppose I will head toward Middleburg," I said, trying to push back the tears that wanted release. I couldn't even look at him. It hurt too much.

"I can't let you return to your grandfather in such a state, lass."

I had been dirty for so long, I hardly noticed anymore. "I can't walk back to Huger alone dressed as a woman. It would be too dangerous."

"I will escort you home, if you'll allow me."

I finally looked at him, though it felt as if my heart was tearing. The longing in his eyes was so keen, it took my breath away. I wanted to shake him and ask him why he was letting me go when he didn't need to.

"I'll see you safely home before I return to the *Ocean Curse*," he promised. "I'd go mad with worry if I didn't take you myself."

He touched the sleeve of my shirt—his shirt—and said, "But first, I'll take you to buy a gown, and then I'll get you a room at an inn where you can take a proper bath. We'll rent a carriage, and I'll return you home in the morning."

We could have one more day together. The thought was both a relief and more agony.

It took me so long to respond, he asked, "Will it please you, Caroline?"

I nodded, unable to find words to convey how much it would please me.

He took me to Broad Street, where we found a dressmaker's shop. If the woman was surprised to find two men enter to purchase a gown, she didn't show it. She seemed too interested in making a sale, and I didn't blame her.

There were three ready-made gowns on display that would fit me. One was yellow, one was blue, and the third was maroon. Each was exquisite, made of the finest silk or cotton, with stomachers, bodices, petticoats, skirts, panniers, and lace.

"Choose whichever you prefer," Marcus said quietly.

I didn't even want to touch the fabric for fear I would soil it. "They're too fine," I told him.

"Nay." His eyes were on me and only me. "They are not fine enough."

I turned from him, needing to protect my heart. "Which color do you prefer?" I asked him.

He approached the blue gown, which was the most stunning of the three and no doubt the most expensive. It had fine lace trailing from the sleeves and a stomacher with intricate needlework of darker blue flowers.

"Blue, like the waters of the Caribbean near Nassau." He turned to the shop owner, who was watching us with wide eyes, and said, "I'll take the dress and anything necessary that goes with it."

Her eyes grew wider, if possible, as she nodded and went to work gathering all the necessary undergarments, stockings, shoes, and more.

"I cannot ask you to spend so much," I told him, grabbing hold of his sleeve to stop him. "I'll use my own money."

"Please don't deny me this small pleasure."

His words made me ache, but I nodded.

He pulled several gold coins from his pocket, which caused the shop owner to increase her speed, calling on a girl in the back to come and assist her.

"Could you recommend an inn nearby?" Marcus asked her.

"Indeed, sir." She scurried out from behind her counter and went to the door. She pointed to the west, away from the harbor. "The most beautiful inn is just down the street. A fine establishment with a good reputation. Called the Lining Inn. Tell them I sent you."

Soon, we were walking out of the shop with the owner's young son, who was carrying all our packages.

I felt conspicuous, but Marcus seemed not to notice the attention we generated.

When we arrived at the inn, I was surprised at its grandeur. The clapboard siding was painted a pretty blue with black shutters at the white-trimmed windows. The third floor boasted half a dozen dormers and two tall chimneys.

Marcus entered the establishment without hesitation, and I followed with the dressmaker's son behind me.

The proprietor had two rooms available on the second floor and gave Marcus both keys, promising to have two baths brought up soon. He made no comment about the packages, nor did he ask more questions than necessary.

After the boy delivered the packages to my room, Marcus paid him and sent him on his way.

I stood in the room, admiring the canopied bed, the ornate bureau, and the matching washstand. It was luxurious and strange after living on the ship for months.

Marcus walked to the window and looked down at the street. We'd been alone countless times before, but it suddenly felt different. This was my room, and soon I would be transforming back into the woman I had been before I met him. I swallowed the fluttering nerves and tried not to think about donning a gown and facing him as myself, for the first time.

"Thank you," I said to him. "You didn't have to go to all this trouble."

"If I could—" He paused and then turned to me, his voice raw with emotion. "I would give you the world, Caroline."

A knock at my door signaled the arrival of the servants with a tub and buckets of hot water.

"When you're ready," he said, walking toward the door, "I'll be downstairs waiting."

For the second time that day, my voice was robbed of speech, so I simply nodded.

With one lingering glance, he left my room, allowing me to become Caroline Reed once again.

The warm bath and lavender-scented soap were so splendid, I wanted to stay in the bathtub for hours. Yet the longer it took, the less time I had with Marcus.

After washing my hair and body, I stepped out of the tub and began the task of dressing. Nanny had always helped me in the past, tying my stays, arranging my petticoats, and pinning my stomacher. It was possible to dress myself, but it took longer than I wanted, and I missed her gentle, gnarled hands as they worked while her tender voice regaled me with stories from her past. She was the only reason I was eager to return home.

When I was finished, I stood before the mirror in the rays of the afternoon sun and marveled at the transformation.

The gown fit my body as if it had been made for me. The delicate lace caressed my forearms, and the heavy skirt belled in a becoming fashion, accenting my waist and bosom, which was finally free of the binding. Marcus had purchased a pair of slippers for me, and they were so feminine and delicate compared to the buckled shoes I'd been wearing for weeks.

I left my other clothes in a pile on the chair. I planned to return them to the servant at Middleburg, though I would leave the binding behind.

After I was dressed, I brushed out my hair, allowing it to dry around my shoulders. Just like 1927, my hair here did not have a natural curl, so I had to be creative to style it. Thankfully, it was thick, which made it easier, and the soap had softened it. The dressmaker had packed some hairpins, which I used to turn up the tresses in a series of loops and braids.

My stomach was filled with nerves as I worked, wondering what Marcus would think when he saw me this way. I'd never been so worried or preoccupied with my appearance before. I wanted to please him, though it hardly mattered. This was the last evening we'd spend together, and I wasn't even sure how much time we would have. Perhaps he would leave in search of someone to purchase the plunder on the *Ocean Curse*, and I would be alone in my room.

The thought saddened me, so I chose to focus on whatever time we had left.

When I was ready, I took a deep breath and left my room in search of Marcus.

It felt strange to walk with such heavy skirts again, to feel the brush of the petticoats against my legs and hear the rustling of the silk.

Butterflies replaced the heaviness in my stomach the moment I saw him. He must have left the inn to find a tailor and a barber, because he was wearing a fine suit of clothes, his face was freshly shaved, and his hair had been trimmed. His coat was dark blue with a row of shining brass buttons down the front. His breeches were the same color as his coat, but his waistcoat beneath was cream with gold needlework. He wore cream-colored stockings to the knee and gold-buckled shoes. At his throat was a cream-colored stock, and his dark hair was still damp but clubbed at the back with a black ribbon.

His broad shoulders filled out the coat magnificently as he

leaned against the window frame, a tankard in hand, staring out at the street.

When his gaze shifted to me, he slowly straightened, and his face filled with wonder. His eyes traveled from my feet up to my coiffure, and they shined with approval.

I'd never felt so lovely in all my life.

"Caroline." He said my name in such a way, it sounded like he was trying to convince himself that it was truly me.

I stood on the bottom step, my hand on the newel post, holding me like an anchor.

Marcus set his tankard on a nearby table and walked across the room, his dark brown gaze never leaving mine. When he arrived at the foot of the stairs, he reached for my hand, and I placed it in his.

With elegance and tenderness, he brought my hand to his lips. "I always knew you were bonnie," he said for my ears only, "but you've taken my breath away, lass."

Even standing on the step, I still had to look up at him. My heart pounded so hard, I was afraid he could hear it. And I knew my hand was trembling in his. But I was able to muster some control as he slipped my hand through the crook of his arm and led me into a large dining room.

There were a handful of other patrons, but the servant brought us to a table in the corner, brightened with a single candle, offering us intimate privacy.

Marcus held out a chair for me and then took a seat across from me.

The servant left to get our drinks and meals.

Neither of us spoke as Marcus continued to study me by the glow of the candlelight.

"I almost feel as if I'm meeting you for the first time," he said. "I feel like a nervous, inexperienced lad."

"And what would you say to me, if this was our first meeting?"

His smile was sweet. "I don't think I'd get the courage to approach you."

My own smile felt foreign after days of sadness, but I reveled in it now, determined to forget that this wasn't our first meeting—but our last.

"I've never known a more confident or bold man," I told him. "I think you'd have the courage to approach me."

He shook his head and set his elbows on the table as he clasped his hands. "Nay. That's the pirate you know. The man beneath is not as sure of himself. He knows nothing but pirating."

It struck me with clarity why Marcus Zale—or, rather, Maxwell MacDougal—was still a pirate. "You're afraid to leave pirating because you wouldn't know what else to do with your life."

He held my gaze. "While other men were learning trades or skills, or being educated for teaching or preaching, I was being taught to intimidate, manipulate, and maraud. I don't know how to come by an honest income, and I wouldn't know how to provide for a wife." His gaze caressed my face. "I wish I was a different man, Caroline. I wish, with all my heart, that I had stayed by my mam's side fifteen years ago and I had become the man you could be proud of today."

His honesty was so raw, I felt my nerves melt away, replaced with compassion and understanding. I reached across the table and placed my hand over his. "If you had, then who would have been on the *Ocean Curse* to care for me? Mayhap, just as you suggested that God has chosen for me to have two lives, He allowed you to make the choice to join Edward Zale so that your life could reflect the goodness and glory of God. Whether by our actions or not, I must believe that all of us can be redeemed from the choices we've made. None are so far gone that they can't find their way back. 'Tis the beauty of grace and forgiveness. Neither would be necessary if we didn't need them."

"Do you really believe that?"

I stared at him for a heartbeat before saying, "I do."

"Even when 'tis you that needs it?"

All my life, I had struggled to believe I was worthy of God's love, believing instead that I had been marked by a curse. But if it was true for Marcus, then it must be true for me. God would not create me for evil, as I'd always feared. But for good. It was His very nature to create goodness.

My mouth quivered. "Aye. I believe I do."

His eyes softened, and he unclasped his hands to wrap them around mine. "You are the best of women, Caroline."

The servant returned with our meals, and we ate heartily, laughing as we shared stories from our past. For an hour, I forgot everything about both of my lives. Everything except Marcus.

I savored the baked chicken with boiled potatoes, gravy, fried artichokes, apple pie, and almond torte. But it was nothing compared to the delicacy of time with the man sitting across from me.

When we were finished, Marcus paid for our meal and asked if I would like to go for a walk.

The evening had fallen on Charleston, and torches had been lit on the cobbled thoroughfares. Broad Street cut across the tip of the peninsula where the city sat between the Ashley and Cooper Rivers.

Marcus reached for my hand and drew it up to slip into the crook of his elbow. I stepped closer to him, loving the feeling of his presence. It was easy to pretend that we were two regular people enjoying each other's company on a beautiful summer night, though neither of us led normal lives.

This was a stolen moment, and both of us knew it.

We walked along the cobbled street, past stores, homes, and open lots. The air was filled with the scents of the city, some pleasant and some foul. At the end of Broad Street, we came to the Ashley River where a large boulder sat near the shore. A few stars had started to twinkle in the gloaming, and there were no torches to light our path here.

A soft symphony of crickets and frogs croaked from the river and nearby marshes, but they were our only companions.

When I looked up at Marcus, I found his gaze upon me.

"Will you sing for me?" he asked.

"Here?"

"I've wanted to ask you a dozen times on the *Ocean Curse*, but I didn't think it was wise."

Every time I was asked to sing in 1927, I felt the weight of expectations.

This time, it was different. Marcus desired to hear me sing for the pleasure it would bring him and nothing more.

"What would you like me to sing?"

"Whatever pleases you."

Irving Berlin's popular song "Always" was the first that came to mind because it made me think of Marcus. It had been released in 1925, and though it was from a different time and place, I began to sing.

> "Everything went wrong,
> And the whole day long
> I'd feel so blue.
> For the longest while
> I'd forget to smile,
> Then I met you."

His handsome gaze was riveted to my face, and when I finished, his hand came up to my cheek. I leaned into it.

"'Tis the loveliest sound I've ever heard, lass." His thumb brushed the ridge of my cheekbone, sending a trail of fire across my skin, causing me to close my eyes.

"Marc—" I paused and opened my eyes. "Or should I call you Maxwell?"

Something profound shifted in his gaze, and he drew me into his embrace, holding me close. I felt small and helpless in his arms, yet also free and empowered.

"I want to tell you all the things you long to hear," he said as his brogue deepened. "And there is so much I want to say."

"Then say it." I was breathless as I looked up at him. I was done with pretenses and fear. "Tell me what's on your heart, Maxwell."

"I'm afraid if I say what is on my heart, it will make the parting impossible."

"Why must we part?" I grasped the lapels of his coat. "Why does this have to be goodbye?"

His chest rose and fell against mine, and I could feel the beat of his heart, matching my own.

"I can't give you the life you deserve."

"Then give me the life you are able." I needed him to know the depths of my feelings, and this would be my last chance. "I love you."

Joy and sadness filled his gaze as he lowered his forehead to mine, his arms tightening around me. There was desperation in his embrace. "I love you, too," he whispered a moment before his mouth captured mine.

His kiss was filled with passion and longing, searching for an answer to a question I prayed he would find. I returned his kiss, deepening it with the desire that had been building for weeks. I loved Maxwell MacDougal, the man behind the pirate's mask, the man I knew he could be if he had the courage to walk away from the only life he knew.

My hands left his lapels, and I slipped my fingers into the hair at the nape of his neck, drawing him closer, needing more. I'd never been kissed before, but nothing had ever felt so right, so perfect.

When he pulled back, he was breathing heavily.

I sought my own answers as I looked into his eyes. "I want nothing but you."

He kissed me again, as passionately as before, and when he drew back, he said, "You make me want to be a better man, Caroline." His brogue lilted with desire. "But I don't know how or where to even start."

"Right here," I said, as I took his hand into mine. It was so large, so capable, I knew it was possible for him to do anything. "With me. We'll find a way."

He lifted my hand to his lips. "What if I fail you?"

"What if I fail you?"

"'Tis impossible."

"Aye. 'Tis the same for you."

He kissed me again.

We stayed as long as possible, and then he took my hand and walked me back to the inn.

When we stopped outside my room, he held me for a long time. "I don't know what the future holds," he whispered, "but I want it to be with you. We'll find a way, Caroline. Do you trust me?"

I looked up and smiled, my heart singing a new song.

24

AUGUST 22, 1927
MINNEAPOLIS, MINNESOTA

Anything and everything made me happy the next day. The memory of Marcus's kisses and his love warmed me from head to toe and made me feel giddy. Irene was the first to notice, though I had no way of telling her what had made me so joyful. But my mood wore off on her, and by suppertime, she was just as cheerful as me.

As we ate and listened to Father tell us about tomorrow's long-awaited arrival of Charles Lindbergh, I tried not to think about returning to Charleston. Because as much as I longed to be with Marcus again, I wasn't sure what would happen. Captain Zale wasn't likely to let Marcus go without a fight, and there was the matter of Nadine, who needed to be returned to the *Ocean Curse*. Marcus and I couldn't simply disappear together and start a life somewhere else. There would need to be plans and sacrifices and confrontations.

And even though Marcus had told me he loved me and promised to find a way forward, he hadn't asked me to marry him. That had not escaped my attention, and it was the only thing that truly dampened my newfound happiness.

"Lindbergh will land at the Minneapolis airport at two o'clock," Father said, "and the parade will start directly from there."

The parade would begin in Minneapolis and end in Saint Paul, where Lindbergh would dedicate a new airport. Tomorrow evening, there would be a reception for him at the Saint Paul Hotel, with invited dignitaries in attendance. We would race from there to the tent meeting being held in Minneapolis, where Father would deliver the first of three evenings of sermons.

The phone rang as we were eating, and Father frowned his disapproval. "Who would be calling during the supper hour?"

"I'll answer," I said as I set my napkin aside.

"It must be an emergency." Mother set down her fork. "Oh, I do hate emergencies."

I lifted the receiver to my ear and spoke into the mouthpiece. "Hello?"

"Carrie, it's Lewis," he said quickly. "Annie will be at the Wabasha Street Caves tonight, and word is that she's leaving town tomorrow. Can you be ready in fifteen minutes?"

My pulse escalated as I turned to look at my parents.

"Who is it?" Father demanded.

"Lewis."

Irene turned in her seat, her eager gaze on my face.

"Tell the boy he shouldn't call during supper," Father said. "It's bad manners."

"Is it an emergency?" Mother asked.

"It's not an emergency," I assured her, wondering how I would get away. Father wanted all of us to get to bed early so we would be refreshed for tomorrow. "He's wondering if he can stop by and take—"

"I'll take you out for ice cream," Lewis said in my ear. "Use that as an excuse. I'll make sure we get some."

My heart was beating hard, and I tried not to sound nervous. "He's wondering if he can take me out for ice cream."

Mother beamed, but Father didn't look pleased.

"Fine," Father said, "but you'll need to be home early."

273

"Is the invitation for both of us?" Irene asked, her hands on the back of her chair as she waited.

I didn't want Irene at the Wabasha Caves when I met my time-crossing mother. After taking her to the Coliseum, I'd had enough trouble explaining Thomas and Alice's relationship. How would I explain knowing Annie?

"I'm sorry," I said. "The invitation is for me only."

Her shoulders fell, and she turned around in her chair to face away from me.

"I'll see you soon," I said to Lewis and then hung up the receiver.

I didn't bother to take my seat, since I was no longer hungry.

"I think I'll go up and get ready," I said to my parents. "Lewis will be here soon, since we'll need to be back early."

"Have fun, dear," Mother said. "We'll keep Irene entertained this evening."

I felt horrible about Irene as I rushed up the stairs, but I had other things to worry about tonight. It was one thing to visit the Coliseum Ballroom, which was rumored to be a speakeasy, and another to visit the caves on Wabasha Street, which did not pretend to be anything other than a speakeasy. I'd never been there, but Lewis had told me stories of secret caverns, dark corners, and dangerous meeting rooms.

If anyone saw me at the Coliseum, there would be whispers and speculations. If someone recognized me in the caves, there would be no question why I was there.

None of it mattered, though. If this was my last chance to speak to Annie, I would risk it all.

Lewis was quiet as we drove from Minneapolis to Saint Paul. He'd greeted my parents and Irene before whisking me away, apologizing to Irene that he couldn't take her along. I'm certain my cousin was confused, since it was the first time we'd failed to include her.

"I'll have to find a way to make it up to Irene," Lewis said as we drove over the Franklin Avenue bridge across the Mississippi River.

"I was just thinking about her, too. I would have invited her, but I would have no way to explain."

"I had the same thought." I could hear the regret in his voice. "I've enjoyed getting to know her the last few days."

I glanced at him in the dying light, trying to read his thoughts and wondering if he was falling for my pretty cousin.

"I want you to be careful, Carrie," Lewis said. "There will be some dangerous people there tonight, but I didn't ask Thomas to come this time. It's best if we try to blend in. I want you by my side at all times, even if that means you have to speak to Annie in front of me. Do you understand?"

"I do."

As we drove down Wabasha Avenue, my mind spun with possibilities. Lewis had told me that the caves were man-made, dug out of a large sandstone hill by Frenchmen fifty years ago for a mushroom farm. They'd been closed for a while and then recently reopened as the Castle Royal.

We pulled into the parking lot, and I was surprised to find that the entrance to the caves was covered by a brick façade that looked like a castle built into the hillside. It even had fake battlements, stained-glass windows, and a dormer.

"How do you know Annie will be here?" I asked Lewis as he parked the Chevy.

"She was at the Green Lantern today," he said. "My informant learned she was coming here tonight to meet with an old gang member who has moved to Saint Paul, and then she and Lloyd are planning to head out tomorrow. Are you ready to meet her?"

"I've crossed two centuries for this meeting," I said. "I'm ready."

We left the Chevy and walked toward the Castle Royal. I'd chosen to wear something simple so my parents wouldn't get suspicious. It was a plain yellow dress, with no frills or embellishments, though I had worn a string of pearls and a white cloche hat.

Lewis opened the door and allowed me to enter ahead of him.

The first room was small, and the sandstone ceiling was low. A coat-check girl took Lewis's hat and told us to head to the right where we would pay a cover charge.

Music drifted through the caves, and the sound of laughter and loud voices echoed in a haunting cadence.

Lewis offered his arm, and I clung to it. My entire body was shaking, and I couldn't seem to catch my breath. I fidgeted with my necklace.

"I'll take care of you," he whispered as he took my hand away from my necklace and lowered it. "Try not to look so nervous. It might draw attention."

After paying our entrance fee, we were directed into another room. This one was long and wide, with a rounded sandstone ceiling and a bar. Dozens of people sat at the bar and the high-top tables. To the left was another cavernous room, accessed by small sandstone archways. A band was playing, and people were dancing. A massive chandelier hung over the dance floor, and electric wall sconces offered a soft ambiance.

"How many caves are there?" I asked Lewis.

"Several," he said. "There are secret meeting rooms and a restaurant, besides the bar and dance hall."

It was impressive and frightening, all at the same time.

I continued to cling to Lewis as we meandered through the caverns, keeping our eyes open for Annie. When we entered a crowded dining room, complete with a fireplace, I paused.

"There she is," I whispered as my stomach tightened. "At the table."

The same woman I'd seen on the dance floor at the Coliseum was sitting at a table with a white linen cloth. There were five dozen other people sitting around it. The man at her side had his arm behind her on the back of the chair.

When she looked up, our gazes collided, and time seemed to stand still.

She rose slowly as the man at her side gave her a strange look. Without a word, she left the table and approached us.

My instinct told me to back away from this notorious criminal, but this was the moment I'd been waiting for my whole life. My heart told me that this *was* Anne Reed.

"Who are you?" she asked as she stopped a few feet away from me. "You were onstage at the Coliseum the other night, too."

I nodded, my voice not wanting to work.

"Are you following me?" She looked from me to Lewis, her suspicion growing.

"May I speak with you?" I asked, though my throat felt raw. "In private?"

Her eyes narrowed, as if this was a trap, but she finally nodded. "Follow me."

I was still clinging to Lewis, but Annie stopped and said, "Alone, or not at all."

Lewis's arm tightened, but I pulled away. "I have to."

Something in my voice must have convinced him not to argue because he let me go, though he didn't look happy.

I followed Annie into another cavern, this one smaller and dimmer. There were tables in there, too, but the room was empty. It was so cold, goose bumps rose on my skin.

When she turned, she crossed her arms and lifted her chin. "What is this about?"

This was it. I had nothing left to lose.

"Are you Annie Barker?"

"Yes."

I swallowed but forged ahead. "And were you also Anne Reed?"

Her mouth parted as her arms slowly lowered to her sides. She was a pretty woman, though up close, I saw the toll that life had wrought upon her features. Wrinkles creased the corners of her eyes, and gray hair streaked at her temples.

"Who are you?" she asked.

"I'm Caroline."

My name sparked a cascade of emotions that played across her face. Shock dominated them all. "Who?"

"Your daughter. Caroline Reed."

She took a step closer, examining me. "You can't be—it's impossible."

"I live here, but I also live in South Carolina in 1727. My grandfather is Josias Reed."

Her face grew pale, and she looked like she was going to faint. I reached for her, and she grasped my arms.

We stood for several seconds, just staring at each other.

"You have two lives, too?" she asked.

"Yes, and I've been looking for you for months." I didn't know how much time we'd have, so I quickly told her about the letter I'd found in the wall of the plantation house and my visit with Mary Jones in Nassau. "When I learned that you lived in 1927, as well, my friend began to look for you. I was in Lakeville the day after you."

She slowly let go of me and took a step back, humiliation creasing her brow. "So you know about me?"

"Yes." The word held the weight of all her transgressions.

Annie crossed her arms again and lifted her chin like she had before, almost defiant. "I suppose you're ashamed of me."

"I'm confused."

She pressed her lips together.

"I have so many questions," I continued.

"I'm sure you do."

"How? How is this possible? Why do we live two lives?"

Annie shook her head and said the one thing I feared the most. "I don't know."

"What?" I wanted to reach out to her again, to demand a better answer. "What do you mean?"

"I don't know." She shrugged and paced away from me. "Until this very moment, I thought I was the only person in the world who lived like this. I had no idea you would be the same."

"What about your mother? Did she live like this?"

"I don't know, Caroline. I never met her. She died in Salem, and my father raised me in South Carolina. He refused to speak about her. I know nothing except her name and that she died in jail during the witch trials."

"What was her name?"

She let out a breath. "Rachel Howlett."

"And you never thought to go to Salem to find out if she had family or to see if they're like us?"

"No one is like us." Anger filled her voice as she said, "My mother died as an accused witch. The last person her family would want to see is me. But it doesn't matter," she said. "I stopped waking up there in 1713."

"When you died."

She frowned. "I died?"

"Yes, on your twenty-first birthday. You died in your sleep. Mary told me."

"I suppose I never wondered what happened to my body there."

"You weren't sick before that?"

"No. On my twenty-first birthday, I woke up here and then never went back there. It was a crushing blow, but to be honest, it was also a relief."

A thought struck me like lightning, rocking me so violently, it took my breath away. "Will I die there on my twenty-first birthday?"

She studied me in the dim light and shrugged. "I don't know, but that's only eleven days from now."

Eleven days. Would I lose Marcus in eleven days, just after I'd started to hope we might have a future? I couldn't bear the thought. "How will I know?"

"You won't."

"There must be someone who knows. Maybe Rachel's family, or one of her old friends. Someone." I sounded desperate because I felt desperate.

"Can you even get to Massachusetts in eleven days?" she asked.

How long would it take to sail from Charleston to Salem? Could it be done in less than eleven days? Because I would also need time to look for Rachel's family, if she had any left. "I don't want to lose my life there."

"I don't know if you have a choice."

I still had so many questions for Annie, but all I could think about was getting to Salem. Though one question still burned deep in my chest. "Did you have a choice?"

"What do you mean?"

"Your lives." I swallowed the nerves bubbling up again. "Did you have a choice to be a pirate, and to be . . . whatever it is you are now? Could you control that?"

I waited, feeling like the fate of my soul hung on her response. Did I have a choice?

"Yes," she finally said, sadness lining her face. "Everyone always has a choice. I didn't have to run away when I was thirteen. I didn't have to leave John Sterling to follow Sam Delaney, and I didn't have to take up with Lloyd. But desperation makes you do unspeakable things."

"John Sterling, the merchant? Was he my father?"

Annie shook her head. "Sam was your father, Caroline. But I knew if he found out about you, he'd force me to do something drastic. A pirate ship is no place for a child. I couldn't let that happen—but I couldn't stay on the plantation with my father, so I had to make a choice. That's why I left you there."

"You chose Sam over me."

She dropped her gaze.

My father was Sam Delaney, another notorious pirate. How was it possible that one set of my parents were infamous criminals and the other were devout law-abiding citizens? It was as if my very existence was divided by good and evil—yet the line between them was fine.

"When Sam was hanged," she continued, "my reason for living was gone—until I met Lloyd."

"Why?" I shook my head. "If you had a choice, why did you become a criminal?"

She hugged herself and shrugged. "My soul is lost, Caroline. I know I'll die this way. I've accepted that God doesn't care. I might as well have some fun while there's time. I was born to be a pirate, whether on a ship at sea or in a stolen roadster on land."

Her words echoed my own fears, that God didn't care and that my soul was lost. But Marcus had shown me it wasn't true. God *did* care. Everything He created was good. Even this strange existence was good. The way we chose to deal with it was up to us. We could either choose good or evil.

"God cares, Annie. It's a lie to think He doesn't, and it leads us to live for ourselves and not Him." I thought of my father's preaching, and a hundred different things came to mind, but I suspected that Annie Barker had heard many of them, so I chose not to continue. Instead, I approached her and wrapped my arms around her in an embrace, knowing she needed proof. "And I care, too."

She was stiff, but she slowly softened until she enfolded me in her arms and hugged me back.

"I've always wanted to tell you I love you," I whispered.

She began to weep silently, though her body shook with emotion.

"Can you forgive me, Caroline?" she asked.

"Yes."

Her hug tightened, then she stiffened again.

"What's going on in here?" a man asked.

"Lloyd." Annie pulled away as she wiped her tears. "Nothing's going on. We're just talking."

"Who is this, Annie?" he asked.

She had her hand on my arm, but she surprised me with her answer. "My daughter."

"Your what?" He narrowed his eyes.

The door opened again, and Lewis appeared.

In a blink of an eye, Lloyd pulled a pistol out of a holster under his jacket and aimed it at Lewis.

I screamed, and Annie shouted at Lloyd to put it away.

Lewis was just as fast, and a pistol appeared in his hand.

Before I had time to react, Lloyd grabbed me by the arm and

pulled my back to his chest. His arm was like a vise around my waist, forcing the air from my lungs.

Lewis's face blanched, and his pistol dipped before he leveled it out again.

"Get out of here, Annie," Lloyd yelled at her. "Through the back entrance."

"Let her go," Annie demanded. "She's done nothing wrong."

"I'll let her go when I'm ready." He was pulling me backwards with him into the depths of the cave.

"I said let her go," Annie told Lloyd.

"Do as she says," Lewis said, "so no one gets hurt."

"I don't aim to get hurt." Lloyd continued to pull me as Annie and Lewis followed. "Stay there," he yelled at Lewis. "Annie, get out of here."

"Not until you let her go."

A small opening at the back of the cavern revealed another pitch-black cave. Lloyd nodded at Annie. "Get in there. It leads to an exit outside."

"I won't move until you let her go."

"I'll shoot her if you don't get moving," Lloyd yelled. "Now move, Annie!"

Annie hesitated, and Lloyd shoved the barrel of the pistol hard against my temple.

I tried not to whimper as I pleaded with my eyes for Lewis to do something. Fear hovered in his gaze. All his police training had not prepared him for this moment.

"Fine," Annie said. "But let her go the minute I'm in that cave."

She moved to the opening but turned to look at me one last time. "I'm sorry, Caroline." And then she was gone.

Lloyd continued to pull me to the opening, and Lewis stepped closer, both hands holding his gun pointed at Lloyd.

With a shove, Lloyd pushed me away and I stumbled to the ground, my knees hitting the hard sandstone with blinding pain.

I turned just in time to see Lloyd disappear into the inky darkness.

Lewis rushed to my side as he put his gun away. "I'm so sorry, Carrie. I shouldn't have let you be alone with her."

"It's not your fault." I stood, but my knees were aching, and my heart was sore.

"Come on," he said, "I need to get you home."

"Will you go after them?"

He shook his head. "As much as I want to, they'll be protected by the police. Even if I arrest them, the chief will let them go. If not, then the whole system will crumble, and chaos will break loose in Saint Paul. No one would let that happen. But I'll send a warning to the smaller towns south of us to be on the lookout for them, and maybe someone else will stop them."

I hated to cry, but as Lewis walked me out of the Wabasha Street Caves, I let the tears from a lifetime of abandonment, rejection, and uncertainty slip down my cheeks. I had finally met Anne Reed, but she couldn't answer my questions.

Desperation made me feel sick. Could anyone answer them?

Tomorrow, as soon as I woke up in 1727, I had to tell Marcus that we needed to return to the *Ocean Curse* and get to Salem before my twenty-first birthday.

And I knew of only one way Captain Zale would agree.

25

AUGUST 23, 1727
CHARLESTON, SOUTH CAROLINA

When I awoke at the Lining Inn the next morning, my heart was still heavy with the lack of answers from Annie. I didn't want to face Marcus and tell him that we had to get back on the *Ocean Curse*, but there was no other way. We could try to find passage on a merchant ship, but the likelihood that we could get there in time was slim. We needed the command of our own vessel to make haste.

For the first time in my life, I felt like my existence was a ticking clock, and when it struck midnight on my twenty-first birthday, everything might change forever. I needed to know—and the only chance I had was to find someone in Salem who could tell me.

I couldn't waste another minute.

The sun had not yet risen over Charleston, but I got out of bed and took off the beautiful undergarments Marcus had purchased for me yesterday, and I began to dress in the clothes I'd been wearing as a cabin boy. I lifted the dirty binding, wishing I had a clean piece of cloth to wear instead, but it would have to do. There was no time to get more.

At least I'd had a bath, and my skin and hair were clean.

Soon, I was dressed as Carl Baldwin again. And as I stood in front of the mirror, I wanted to weep. The beautiful gown I'd worn the night before was lying on the back of a chair, and all the accoutrements were stacked in a pile on the table. I wanted to take them with me, but how would I explain their presence on the ship should someone find them?

I felt more nervous to appear before Marcus like this than I did last night to show him what I looked like in a gown. But I had no choice, not if I wanted answers.

I left my room and walked down the hall to his. With all the courage I could muster, I knocked on his door and stepped back to wait.

He must not have been sleeping, because he opened his door a few seconds later. He was wearing the blue breeches from last night, with a white cotton shirt, untucked and hanging loose about his torso. His hair was unbound, and he had no socks or shoes on.

"Caroline." He frowned as he took in my appearance. "Why are you dressed like that?"

"May I come in?" I didn't want to discuss this in the hall.

He moved aside as I entered and then closed the door. When he turned to me, I went into his arms, needing the reassurance of his embrace to tell him what I had come to say.

He hugged me back, holding me as close as he had the night before.

"What's wrong?" he asked as he pulled back and put his hand on my cheek. "Why are you dressed like this again? You don't like the gown?"

"I love it."

He smiled as he caressed my cheek with his thumb. "I hardly slept last night, thinking of you. I was just lying here, wondering when I could wake you." His smile fell as he studied me. "What's wrong, Caroline?"

"Can we sit?"

His concern grew as he nodded and moved some of his clothes off a chair. As I took a seat, he sat on the bed across from me.

"I saw Annie in 1927."

He nodded for me to continue.

"I asked her about her double lives and if she knew why it happened to us. She didn't."

"I'm sorry you didn't get the answers you hoped for."

"But she did tell me my grandmother's name in Salem," I continued. "Her name was Rachel Howlett."

"Do you think her family is still there?"

"I don't know, but I need to find them." I took a deep breath. "I asked Annie about her death here—on her twenty-first birthday—and she didn't understand it, either. She wasn't sick. She just simply died and stopped returning to this life."

Marcus watched me, as if trying to put the pieces together.

"I'm afraid it might happen to me, too," I told him. "My twenty-first birthday is in ten days. What if I don't wake up here after that? What if my body dies?"

Realization dawned on his face, and he stood, drawing me to my feet, as if preparing for action. "We can't let that happen."

I nodded, swallowing the emotions choking me. "I don't want to leave here in ten days."

"What can we do?"

"I want to go to Salem and see if Rachel's family is still there. If this happened to me and my mother, mayhap it happened to Rachel and her mother or sisters or aunts. I must find someone who can tell me how to stop this."

Marcus began to pace as he rubbed the back of his neck.

"How long would it take to get to Salem from here?" I asked.

"If we push hard and the winds are favorable, we could reach there in a week's time." He nodded at my clothing. "Is that why you've worn this again?"

"Aye. We need to get to the *Ocean Curse* as soon as possible."

He continued to rub his neck. "The captain will never take us there. We'll have to find another way."

"But how? We can't charter a ship, and if we buy passage on one that's already going in that direction, we'll have to follow their schedule." I clasped my hands, knowing that I had another way. "I know how we can convince the captain to go to Boston."

He stopped pacing and lowered his hand. "How?"

"The sailor I was speaking to the other day—Timothy—his father claims that he knows the location of the Queen's Dowry. If we can convince Captain Zale that this man is telling the truth, mayhap he'll go to Boston to find the answer, and I can make my way to Salem."

"Timothy?" Marcus asked. "Is he the one who came on board with you from the *Adventurer*?"

"Aye."

"What's his father's name? How does he claim to have knowledge of something no one else does?"

I told Marcus Timothy's story, and he slowly nodded. "If he can convince the captain, then your plan might work. But do you want to get back on board the *Ocean Curse*, Caroline? You're free here—you won't be free if you go back. And we have no guarantee that the captain will go along with our plans."

"I have no choice. If I don't try, then I take the risk of losing this life."

"Even if you try," he said, drawing me back into his arms, "there is no guarantee that you can save it."

I wrapped my arms around his waist, feeling the cording of his muscles under my hands, and said, "I'd rather spend my last week on a pirate ship with you than be with my grandfather at Middleburg Plantation. But it can't be my last week, Marcus."

He tilted my chin up with his gentle hand. "What happened to calling me Maxwell?"

"Do you prefer it?"

"Aye." He smiled. "I love hearing my name on your lips."

I would have said it again, but he quieted me with another kiss.

We didn't tarry long at the inn. I insisted we return the gown and other things to the dressmaker, who was not pleased. The woman agreed to give back most of the money Marcus had spent, though he told her to keep some of it for her troubles. I hated to part with the gown, but there were more important things to worry about as we returned to Chalmers Street to retrieve Nadine.

"I hope Hawk found someone to purchase our goods," Marcus said as we turned onto the street. "I can't tell him why I was too distracted to look for a buyer." He winked at me, and my cheeks grew warm. It would be difficult to hide my feelings from the others when we returned to the *Ocean Curse*.

I knocked on the door to Mrs. Drywell's home, and a servant answered.

"May I help you?" she asked.

"I'm here to retrieve Nadine," I said.

"I'm sorry." The servant shook her head. "The young lady left during the night."

My mouth parted in surprise. "Nadine isn't here?"

"No, but she left a note for you."

I accepted the note and read it quickly.

I can't return to my life on the Ocean Curse. *Edward was right all along. 'Tis no place for a woman.*

"There's the matter of payment," the servant said.

I turned to Marcus, who was already on his way up the steps to join me.

"Ned is gone?" he asked.

"Aye." I handed him the note, feeling helpless. "She left during the night."

Marcus read it and then pulled a coin from his pocket, handing it to the servant, whose eyes opened wide at the sum. Then he took my hand, and we began to walk briskly down Chalmers Street toward East Bay.

"I hope she has somewhere safe to go," Marcus said as he let go of my hand, his face grim. "There's no telling how the captain will respond."

"He can't be surprised that she was unhappy. From what she told me, he tried to discourage her from joining him in the first place."

"She's been with him for three years," Marcus said. "He must love her. He'll be devastated that she left without warning."

When we reached the harbor, I was out of breath. Thankfully, Hawk was waiting for us. He was leaning against a piling, watching the activity on the wharf. But when he saw us, he stood.

"Where's Ned?" he asked.

"Left in the middle of the night," Marcus said.

"You don't know where he went?"

"Nay."

"The captain won't be pleased," Hawk said, but he didn't seem as concerned as Marcus and me. Hawk didn't know that Ned was the captain's mistress. "Did you have any luck finding a buyer?"

"Nay," Marcus said again. "You?"

He shook his head and sighed. "The captain will be in a rage when he learns that nothing good came of this visit."

"Come," Marcus said. "Let's be away."

The launch had been instructed to return midmorning, so they were waiting for us, as well. If Marcus had taken me to Middleburg as planned, Hawk and the others would have had to wait all day for his return. Thankfully, they were ready to take us back when we needed them.

It took over an hour to get to the *Ocean Curse*. I hadn't expected to be back on the ship, but I was so eager to get to Salem, I didn't care how I got there.

Captain Zale stood on the quarterdeck, his arms crossed and his sword at his side. He watched the three of us as we approached. Marcus led the way as Hawk and I walked behind him.

"Where is Ned?" the captain asked as we mounted the steps.

"Can we speak in your cabin?" Marcus asked.

The captain's jaw clenched, and his eyes were hard with anger. He spun on his heel and walked toward the outer room.

Hawk remained outside, as was his custom, but Marcus and I followed the captain into his cabin.

When the door was closed, the captain demanded an answer. "Where is Ned?"

"Left. In the middle of the night."

It took a second for the information to sink in, but when it did, the captain lowered himself into the chair and looked at the floor. I'd never seen him so defeated. If I hadn't known that Ned was his mistress, his behavior would have puzzled me.

But he didn't seem surprised. He almost seemed resigned to her parting.

Marcus waited a few moments and then said, "We have some good news for you. There is a sailor on board who claims his father knows where the Queen's Dowry is located."

The captain slowly lifted his face. "Who claims this?"

I stepped out from behind Marcus and said, "His name is Timothy. His father was a pirate—"

"What's his father's name?" the captain demanded.

"I don't know."

"Bring him to me."

Marcus nodded in my direction, and I left the captain's cabin to locate Timothy. I hoped I wasn't getting the young man in trouble.

It didn't take me long to find him. He was darning a pair of socks on the main deck, and when he saw me approach, he grinned.

"The captain wants to see you," I said, not returning his smile.

He frowned. "The captain has never wanted to see me before. What did I do wrong?"

I had to be honest with him. "I told him about your father, about how he knows where the Queen's Dowry is located."

Timothy's mouth slipped open, and he quickly put aside his darning needle and stood. "I gave you no leave to tell the captain!"

"I'm sorry, I—" How could I explain myself? "I need to get to Boston, and I knew it was the only way the captain would agree to go. We could both be done with the *Ocean Curse*. You could return home. You won't have to remain a captive any longer."

"I don't know if my father will tell him where the treasure is located. I don't even know if the story is true or if it was a fairy tale my father told me to get me to sleep."

"Wouldn't you like a reason to go home? Get off this pirate ship and have your life back?"

That seemed to appeal to Timothy, and he slowly nodded. "Aye. It would be good to see my little sisters again."

"You could start over," I told him. "Do something good with your life."

He sighed and said, "Come. Let's get this over with."

We returned to the captain's cabin. Marcus was by the window, and the captain was pacing near the table.

Timothy paused at the sight of the captain, his ruddy cheeks paling with uncertainty.

The captain stopped pacing and demanded, "Who are you, boy?"

"Timothy Ludlow, sir."

"Ludlow?" The captain's eyes widened with recognition. "Who is your father?"

"James Ludlow," Timothy said.

"Slim Jim Ludlow?" The captain peered at Timothy. "Aye, you look like him. I spent many an evening with Jim over a pint of ale. Are you telling me that Jim knew where the treasure was and never told me?"

Timothy swallowed and nodded. "Aye. That's what he claimed, anyway."

"And where is your father now?"

"In Boston, sir. On Treamount Street. He accepted the King's Pardon and went home to take care of his family."

Captain Zale began to pace again as the three of us waited.

My heart was in my throat. The captain might agree, and we'd set sail for Boston, or he'd call it all rubbish and want to return to Florida—or he might want to stay in Charleston and look for Nadine, though his earlier behavior suggested that he had accepted her decision to leave him.

If he didn't want to go to Boston, I would be desperate enough to jump ship and find another way, though it would be close to impossible.

"I think 'tis time to pay a visit to my old friend Slim Jim Ludlow," the captain said. "Mayhap Jim will agree to tell me where the Queen's Dowry is, if I agree to give him a share of my profits." He put his hand on Timothy's shoulder and said, "And a share for his son, too."

Timothy's grin relieved me of my guilt about telling the captain his tale.

But it was nothing like the relief I felt knowing we would head toward Boston.

Marcus smiled at me, but I saw the concern in his eyes.

Neither of us knew what we'd find when we got to Salem.

If we got there in time.

After serving the captain and his men supper—this time Timothy had been invited to join them—I took my meal to Marcus's cabin as I used to do before becoming ill with diving sickness. It had been strange not having Nadine at my side as I served the meal. My thoughts and prayers were with her, wherever she had gone. Part of me was happy that the captain was letting her go without a fight. She deserved something better than life on the *Ocean Curse*.

Perhaps now the rumors of a Jonah on board would fade away.

I was just finishing my boiled pork and stewed peas when the door opened, and Marcus appeared.

The ship had left Charleston Harbor and was out to sea again. The familiar creaking of the wood and the rhythmic rolling of the ocean were like old friends now. Darkness had fallen, and the single lamp hung on the wall, illuminating the cabin with scant light.

My pulse increased at his arrival as it always did, but this time was different. Everything had changed in Charleston.

He closed the door as I stood, our gazes on each other. Was he just as uncertain about how things would proceed? We hadn't been alone since leaving the inn earlier. The cabin felt too intimate and private. His bed and my cot reminded me that we would be sharing the same space again.

I felt like a moth to a flame whenever he was near, and when he opened his arms to me, I entered his embrace freely, inhaling the scent of the soap he'd used at the inn.

He was warmth and strength, an anchor in an uncertain storm.

"Things are different now, aren't they, lass?" he asked as his chin rested on the top of my head.

"Aye." It was all I could say with the butterflies filling my stomach.

When I pulled back, he smiled down at me, but there was a sadness in his countenance, as well. "There is much we need to discuss."

His hand rubbed the small of my back, sending heat and pleasure up my spine. I wasn't sure how I would focus on anything we had to say to each other.

"I don't know how I'll stay in the cabin with you this week and honor you, Caroline."

It was a bold, direct statement, causing me to pull away in surprise.

Yet if he was feeling what I was feeling, I understood.

He took my hand and placed it against his chest where his heart was beating hard. "I laid awake last night, my thoughts so full of you, I couldn't sleep. You've unmasked me and captured my heart, two things I didn't think were possible."

I stepped closer to him, laying my free hand on his cheek. "Your heart is safe with me."

"Aye. I know it to be true."

"You've captured my heart, too," I whispered. "Completely."

He kissed me deeply, holding me tight. When he pulled away, he said, "I want to protect you. Your body, your heart, and your honor. I don't know what will happen when we get to Salem, but I don't want any regrets, no matter how much time we have together. You are more precious to me than anything on earth, and I will protect you at all costs."

His words filled my heart with warmth and affection. I wanted to stay in this moment with him forever.

"It will be impossible to sleep in this room with you," he continued, tracing my chin with his thumb. "But I can't sleep anywhere else without raising suspicions from the captain or the rest of the crew. I thought about asking you to sleep in Ned's bed, but I don't want you outside the captain's cabin or in the same room as Hawk. I wouldn't be able to sleep if you weren't here, under my care."

"I understand."

He placed his hands on either side of my face and shook his head. "I don't think you do, lass." The desire in his eyes was so bright, I felt it all the way to my toes.

I put my hands over his and slowly removed them from my face, needing to know the truth about what the future would hold for us—if I had a future here. I held his hands in mine, putting some space between us. "Am I fooling myself, Marcus?"

He frowned. "What do you mean?"

"This," I said. "Do we have a future together? You've told me that you will always be a pirate. Is that true?"

He took a deep breath and let my hands go as he walked away from me to the window. "I want to believe that we have a future together. Part of me wants to just focus on finding your family first, and then try to answer all the other questions later. But you deserve to know my intentions."

I stood where he had left me, trying not to fidget as I waited.

"I want to marry you, Caroline," he said as he turned to meet my gaze. "To build a home and a family. But the truth is, I don't know if that is possible. I've spent most of my life taking from others and there will be penalties to pay. I don't want you to suffer for my mistakes. It wouldn't be fair, and I couldn't live with myself if I caused you pain."

"What does all of this mean?"

"I don't know. And that's why I haven't asked you to marry me. I can't offer myself to you as I am—as the pirate, Marcus Zale. I want to come to you as Maxwell MacDougal, but I need to make my life right before God and man to do that. Yet if I do, I'm afraid that the consequences of my sins will be severe."

Pain squeezed my heart at his words. I tried to take in a breath, but it suffocated me, because I realized that my life wasn't the only one hanging in the balance.

I could lose Marcus as easily as he could lose me.

I walked across the cabin and stood by his side as we looked out the window at the vast North Atlantic Ocean and the countless stars. I slipped my arm around his waist and laid my head on his chest as his arms embraced me.

"I long to make you mine right now," he said as he kissed the top of my head, "but I can't offer you the name of Zale. If God is willing, someday I will give you a name that is true and honorable and worthy of you."

"MacDougal?"

"Aye."

When I looked up at him, he kissed me again, but this time his kiss wasn't filled with desire or passion. It was tender and heartfelt.

Apologetic.

When it was time to go to bed, he insisted I take the alcove bed, while he slept on the cot.

26

AUGUST 23, 1927
MINNEAPOLIS, MINNESOTA

When I opened my eyes in my bedroom on Dupont Avenue the next morning, I immediately wanted to return to Marcus and not have to spend a day away from him. But it was also torture to be with him and not know what the future held.

The white canopied bed was bright with the rays of sunshine pouring in through the window. I turned on my side and looked at the vibrant green leaves outside, gently swaying in the late summer wind.

Would God listen if I prayed for a miracle? If I believed that He created me and loved me, then I also had to believe that He was for me, and I could go to Him in prayer. It didn't mean He would give me the miracle, but it did mean that He would listen to my plea and do what was best.

I wanted to be with Marcus, to find a way to live as man and wife without the past hovering over us for the rest of our lives. Marcus had led a life of crime—I had not even thought to ask him for a list of his transgressions—but he longed to make it right. And wasn't that what redemption was for? The reason God had sent His Son to offer forgiveness to those who repented?

It was the message my father preached time and time again, from Romans chapter ten. "For whosoever shall call upon the name of the Lord shall be saved." And in 1 John it said if we confess our sins, God is faithful and just to forgive us. It didn't mean Marcus wouldn't have to pay the consequences for his actions, but there would be peace knowing he was right with God.

Even if that meant we couldn't be together.

My heart ached thinking about a future without him, so I did the only thing I could. I laid my future in God's hands, where it had always belonged, and prayed for a miracle.

"Caroline," Mother called from the hallway as she opened my door and peeked her head inside. "There's no time to dawdle in bed. We have a very busy day ahead of us."

Lindbergh's homecoming and then Father's tent revival tonight. He had asked me to sing, and I had agreed. But this time, I knew who I was singing for, and I wasn't nearly as nervous.

I quickly got out of bed and dressed in a white summer dress with a pleated skirt, a lace top with long sleeves, and a thick black belt around my waist. It was different from many of the other dresses I wore and had recently been purchased for this occasion at Dayton's department store in downtown Minneapolis. I would wear my white cloche cap and a pair of black buckled heels.

After touching up my hair and putting a little rouge on my lips and cheeks, I left my room. With prayers for Marcus close to my heart, I was ready for the day ahead.

As I walked down the front steps, the house was strangely quiet. I had expected Father and Mother to be chatting excitedly about the day's upcoming activities, or to hear Irene's giggles about seeing Lindbergh again. But there was no noise except the ticking of the grandfather clock in the foyer.

A strange anxiety stole over me as I crossed into the parlor and rounded the corner into the dining room.

Father stood at the window, his hands clasped behind his back, while Mother was at the table, her handkerchief to her face as she silently cried. Irene was pale—a sickly color that portended shocking news. Her gaze lifted to mine, and her blue eyes were round and filled with tears.

My heart sank as I saw the scene before me. "What happened?"

Mother's eyes lifted to mine, but she let out a cry and buried her face in her handkerchief, shaking her head.

My heart galloped as I looked to my father, who slowly turned from the window. I had never seen his face so grave—so filled with disappointment and defeat. He silently walked to the table, his regal bearing bent forward, as if the weight of the very world was upon his shoulders. Slowly, he lifted the *Minneapolis Tribune* off the table.

It felt like he was in slow motion as he handed the paper to me. I expected to see Lindbergh's name on the headline. Perhaps the pilot had been killed in a plane crash.

Instead, there was a picture, front and center, of my father in the middle of a sermon, holding a Bible and passionately preaching the Word of God. Around the picture of my father were smaller images with captions underneath. Lewis and me at the Castle Royal, speaking to Annie Barker. Me singing at the Coliseum. A picture of Thomas and Alice dancing together that night—Alice's pregnancy evident. An older one of Andrew with his arm around Alice, sitting at a table, with bottles of alcohol in hand as they grinned at whoever was taking the photo. And another of Andrew and Ruth with their three beautiful children.

Above this collage was the bold headline: *The Hypocrisy of Reverend Baldwin's Family.*

I stared at the images in shock. My stomach turned as panic gripped my heart. Someone must have been following our family, spying on each of us until they had what they needed. And they'd waited until today—the day of my father's biggest tent revival—to share the story.

My worst fears had been realized.

I quickly skimmed the article, hoping that there was some redemption in this story, but it was worse than I could imagine. Whoever had written it knew about Thomas's weekly visits to

Nina Clifford's brothel and Andrew's work as a bootlegger, bringing alcohol into Minnesota from Canada. They outlined Andrew's affair with Alice and then her move into our home before taking up with Thomas. It was an exposé on the transgressions of the Baldwin children as their father, the biggest hypocrite of them all, was about to lead the largest tent revival meeting in the country.

I lowered the paper and found that my father had gone back to the window and my mother's face was still buried in her handkerchief.

Tears came to my eyes as I felt their pain. We'd hurt them—I'd hurt them—and they didn't deserve it. My parents were good and kind. They lived the things they preached. They weren't hypocrites or liars.

We were.

"I'm sorry." My apology was so feeble, so insignificant in light of their suffering. I sank into my chair, feeling weak and unsteady.

Irene stared at her clasped hands. No doubt she wished she was anywhere but here.

Father and Mother said nothing, which was almost worse than if they had yelled. I deserved their anger and resentment. Mother's silent weeping was the hardest to bear. Her heart was breaking, and it was my fault. I had tried for years to live a life that would make them proud. But in just a few days' time, I had thrown caution to the wind to find Annie, and it was now splashed upon the pages of the largest newspaper in Minneapolis. Whoever had taken the picture of Annie and me knew who she was, and the caption under that photo had read: "Caroline Baldwin at the Castle Royal with Annie Barker, the Most Wanted Woman in America."

How had I not noticed there was someone taking a picture of us? It must have been a hidden camera, and the paper must have hired people to spy on our family. There had to be multiple people working together to unmask the Baldwin family, waiting for the perfect moment.

And they had found it.

I had done nothing wrong, but the pictures said otherwise, and it wouldn't pay to defend myself. Not now. Not with my parents just learning the truth about their children's lives.

"Is Alice Pierce who I think she is?" Father asked, his back still toward me. "Andrew's mistress?"

"Yes."

"And did you know who she was when she entered this house?"

I didn't want to answer, but I couldn't lie or stay silent. "Yes. Ruth warned me about her."

"Ruth knew?"

"I'm afraid so."

Mother's cries intensified, and Irene reached out and laid a comforting hand on her shoulder.

The telephone rang, but no one made a move to answer it.

"No doubt there will be many calls today," Father said. "I don't want anyone to answer a single one. I will make a statement at the meeting tonight."

"You're going through with it?" Mother asked as she finally lifted her face from her handkerchief.

"Of course." Father turned to her. "Why wouldn't I?"

"Because our lives have just been torn apart, Daniel. Everyone will know by tonight, and we'll be the laughingstock of the country. All our enemies will gloat, and our friends will abandon us."

Father walked to Mother and offered her his hand.

She took it and rose to face him.

With tenderness, he placed his hands on either side of her face. "If our friends abandon us, then they aren't truly our friends. And if our enemies don't gloat, then they aren't truly our enemies. We will survive this crisis, like all the others, Marian. And we'll do it with God's help."

"I don't think I can muster the courage, Daniel."

"You don't need to. God will give you the strength." He took her handkerchief and gently wiped at her tears. "And if you don't think you have it in you today, then you can stay home, and I'll face this for both of us."

My parents were rarely affectionate in front of us, but Mother went into Father's arms and he hugged her, rubbing her back with a gentleness that spoke volumes about how much he loved her and cared about her. They were a team, both working toward their common goals, shouldering life's difficulties, celebrating their wins, mourning their losses, and trying to ease each other's burdens. When one was weak, the other was strong. It was a beautiful example of marriage—something I longed to have with Marcus. I felt stronger when I was with him, just as I could see my mother felt with my father's strength.

Mother pulled back and took a deep breath. "God will give me strength to face everyone today. I won't cower, even if my heart is breaking."

Father nodded encouragement and gave her the briefest kiss.

"Now," he said as he held out Mother's chair and helped her to sit. "I want to hear everything, Caroline. Even if it's difficult and painful and sordid. I don't want you to spare a detail. I need to know what I'm dealing with if I'm to handle it well. No more surprises."

"I think I'll go upstairs," Irene said as she rose from her spot at the table. "This sounds like a family issue."

No one stopped her as she left the room.

Father took his seat at the head of the table, and both my parents looked at me intently.

I folded my hands and laid them on my lap, knowing this would not be an easy thing to do. "If I'm to explain it all, then there's something you need to know about me."

My mother briefly closed her eyes, as if she couldn't handle one more shocking detail, but my father stared intently. And, just like everything else in his life, he would face it with steadfast courage and determination.

"I tried telling you when I was young, but neither of you would believe me," I said as I watched them for their reaction. "But if you want to understand why I was singing at the Coliseum, or why I was standing with Annie Barker in the Castle Royal, then you'll have to face the truth." I paused just long enough to take a deep breath. "I live two lives. One here—and the other in 1727."

I told them everything about my two lives and why I needed to find Annie. I explained that Lewis was helping me, and that my search had taken me places I would never have gone if I wasn't desperate.

When I was done, my parents stared at me with confusion and disbelief.

"I've wanted to talk about this so many times," I told them, "but neither one of you would believe me."

"I'm not sure how to believe you now," Father said. "It's—it's so strange. Did you concoct this tale to cover up your real reasons for being with Annie Barker?"

"This isn't the first time she's told us this, Daniel," Mother said as her confusion began to clear. "Don't you remember all the strange things she said to us when she was a little girl? She talked about her grandfather and her nanny and the servants who lived on the plantation, as if they were real people and not a figment of her imagination."

"I talked about them when I was little?" I asked.

"You were an early talker," Mother said with fondness. "You prattled on and on about all sorts of things that made no sense at the time. I thought you were being a fanciful child, playing make believe. But I do remember when I started to get concerned, and I brought it to your father's attention."

"And I never spoke of it again after that," I told her.

She turned to Father. "Why would she go to such lengths to make up a story like this, Daniel? I believe her."

I waited as my father studied me, hoping and praying he would believe me, too, because I desperately wanted to talk to him about matters of faith. He wasn't a perfect man, but his heart desired perfection before the Lord, and he was good at offering wisdom and advice.

Slowly, he began to nod. "I have no reason to doubt you, Caroline. Until I saw this newspaper today, I never mistrusted you or your intentions. If you say these things are true, then I will choose to believe you."

I rose from the table to embrace my father. He also stood and took me into his arms.

A dam broke inside of me, and all the tears that had been building up during my life unleashed, cascading down my face in a sort of baptism. I felt renewed, clean, at peace. I didn't have to hide anymore. I could be Caroline Reed Baldwin. A strange conglomeration of the two lives I lived, no longer needing to be one or the other.

It felt good to be seen by my father. It didn't fix the scandal that had just been unleashed upon our family, but it eased the broken pieces inside of me.

There was nothing better than being loved—and accepted—completely.

After Mother hugged me, we went upstairs to freshen up, and then it was time to face the outside world.

It would not be so understanding.

The day went as planned, though things felt off from the start. Everywhere we went, people stared at us, whispering behind their hands. Some mocked my father as he walked through the airport at Wold-Chamberlain Field to wait for Lindbergh's arrival, but he ignored their taunting and kept his chin up.

Lindbergh arrived in his airplane, the *Spirit of St. Louis,* just two minutes behind schedule, but the crowd of thousands broke the fence and rushed his airplane. The police were forced to get Lindbergh to safety until the crowd could be controlled, which meant the parade from Minneapolis into Saint Paul had been delayed. Both the Minneapolis and Saint Paul mayors were on hand to greet Lindbergh and then ride in the parade ahead of him as escorts.

Because there was a contract with Saint Paul, Lindbergh had

to be at the new Saint Paul airport on time. This meant that the parade through Minneapolis was rushed, and many people were visibly upset that they didn't get a better look at the Minnesota hero.

Father, Mother, Irene, and I were in a car at the rear of the parade, though we tried not to draw unwanted attention. Some people recognized Father, and the heckling continued as we made our way to the Saint Paul airport and then on to the reception at the Saint Paul Hotel.

Since Father was on the Minneapolis committee, we were introduced to Lindbergh again, but there were so many people, we only had a moment of his time.

As soon as our audience with Lindbergh was over, we left the hotel. We'd intended to stay for the meal, but the mayor of Minneapolis had asked Father to leave, given the unique circumstances of the newspaper headlines that morning.

My cheeks burned with shame and embarrassment as we drove away from the Saint Paul Hotel and headed back across the Mississippi River toward Minneapolis.

No one spoke, and the silence, after a day of excited crowds cheering Lindbergh's name, was deafening.

"I'm sorry, Daniel," Mother said as we drove to the Hennepin County fairgrounds. "I know this day is not what you had hoped."

"I won't lie," he said. "It's a blow that's hard to accept. But I won't let it deter me from delivering the message God has laid on my heart, even if the three of you are the only people who will hear me." Father had been expecting thousands of people to attend his tent meeting, but after this morning's news, none of us were sure how many would attend.

Irene had been quiet all day. She wasn't giving me the cold shoulder, but she wasn't being warm or friendly, either. Was she simply uncomfortable because of what was happening, or was she angry with me?

When we arrived at the fairgrounds and made our way into the red-and-white-striped circus tent, there were several men waiting for Father's arrival. All of them had grim faces, and they took my father aside to speak in hushed tones.

The tent was huge, and inside were rows and rows of benches that would allow thousands of people to sit. At the front was a stage with a microphone, a pulpit, a stand-up piano, and nothing else. My father liked simplicity.

Several dozen volunteers were setting up the benches for the evening. I recognized many of them, but none would even look at me. A lot of people had put many hours and thousands of dollars into this event. It wasn't simply my father who would suffer if no one attended.

"Come," Mother said as she took my hand. "Let's take our seats."

We would have over an hour to wait.

"Do you think Thomas and Andrew will come?" I asked her, finally voicing the question that had been humming in my mind all day.

"They said they would come, and I hope that they will."

"Do you?"

Mother turned her blue-eyed gaze on me, and I could see the devastation in their depths—but there was also hope. "With all my heart."

Lewis arrived soon after us, his face filled with worry.

"I tried calling you all day," he said as he approached us. "I even stopped by the house, but you weren't in."

"We've been busy with the Lindbergh celebration." I stood, eager to talk to him.

But he turned to Mother and shook his head. "I'm sorry, Mrs. Baldwin. I can't imagine what you've endured today. Please know that Caroline was never doing anything—"

"She explained everything to us, Lewis," Mother said. "And we understand. Though the reverend and I were upset to learn that you took her to those places without our knowledge, we are relieved to know that you were there with her to keep her safe."

Instead of looking relieved, Lewis's guilt seemed to mount.

"Would you like to sit with us?" Mother asked him.

"Do you think it's wise, since I'm in the photo with Caroline and Annie Barker?"

"I think it's imperative," she said.

Irene moved aside so Lewis could sit between us.

The smell of the musty tent, and sawdust laid over the dirt to muffle the sound of shuffling feet, mixed with the heat and began to give me a headache. As the clock ticked, I feared that people would not come to Father's meeting. He'd never had a problem drawing in crowds before, but today was different. Today, people had learned that the things Daniel Baldwin preached were not being lived out by his children. That level of hypocrisy could not be ignored. I just wished that they knew our father's life, and the things he preached, had nothing to do with the decisions we made as adults. He was good and honest and trustworthy, even if we were not.

Father joined us, his face set in a determined line as he scanned the large, almost empty tent.

"Don't worry, Daniel," Mother said as she reached for his hand. "God will sustain us."

He smiled at her and then greeted Lewis, echoing Mother's sentiments.

As they were talking, Thomas entered the tent, with Alice on his arm, his expression hard to read. They were dressed in their Sunday best, and I didn't miss the shiny gold bands on both of their left hands.

Mother stiffened beside me, and Father's face was serious.

Thomas acknowledged our parents as he said, "Father and Mother, I'd like you to meet my wife, Mrs. Alice Baldwin. We were married yesterday at the courthouse and were waiting to tell you in person this morning. Unfortunately, things didn't quite go as planned."

No one said anything for a moment, and then Mother rose from the bench and went to Alice. She stood in front of her for a heartbeat, and then she embraced the younger woman.

Alice closed her eyes, and her lips trembled as she returned my mother's hug.

"Welcome to the family, Alice." Mother pulled back and put a smile on her face. "As you know, this won't be easy. Especially for Ruth."

Nodding, Alice looked down at her swollen stomach. "I wish I would have done things the right way from the start. But I guess that's not part of our story, so we're trying to make the best of it."

"That's all any of us can do." Mother motioned to the bench. "Won't you sit with the family?"

As Alice was taking a seat on the other side of Irene, Thomas turned to our father and said, "I'm sorry for the pain I've caused you. I hope you'll forgive me."

"Of course I forgive you, son," Father said, though the weight of the pain he carried was etched deeply into the creases of his face. "There will be time to talk later. You should take a seat next to your wife."

Thomas did as Father instructed just as Ruth arrived, alone.

She was pale and thin. She looked as if she'd aged a decade in the past couple of months. When she saw Alice, she paused, and my heart broke for her. I couldn't imagine the anguish it would cause her to know that Alice was now part of our family, or that every time she saw the child Alice carried, she'd be reminded of Andrew's infidelity. It amazed me that Thomas could accept it. I wasn't naïve enough to believe that everything would be easy, or that it would all work out well. But I could pray for each of them, hoping that God would bring beauty from the ashes.

Ruth seemed to find some sort of strength from within, and she continued toward our parents. Out of all of us, she was the most innocent, yet she had suffered far more than the rest.

She offered a tremulous smile for my parents. "I'm sorry Andrew couldn't be here."

"I am, too," Father said. "But I'm very happy that you've come." His voice was low and gentle. "I'm saddened by what I learned about him today. I cannot sit back and watch him destroy your life. I want you to know that if you need anything, our door is always open to you and the children. I do not condone adultery, nor will I counsel you to stay in your marriage. Do not feel you need to continue in this hurtful situation because of Marian or me—or anyone else. You should not have to endure what's happened to you, Ruth, and had I known, I would have done something sooner to help. Please forgive me."

Ruth began to cry, and Father stepped forward to embrace her as Mother placed her hand on Ruth's back.

"If Andrew seeks forgiveness," Father said, "he will have it, but I will put you and the children's needs ahead of his." No one spoke for a moment, and then Father said to Ruth, "I'm so sorry you've had to endure today's humiliation."

She pulled away and wiped her tears. "Today was difficult," she admitted, "because now the whole world knows the secrets we've been keeping. But it did not come as a shock to me. I've had years to deal with Andrew's infidelity."

Father nodded. "It pains me to know you've been carrying this burden alone. Will you forgive me?"

"You have no reason to ask forgiveness," she said.

Mother put her arm around Ruth. "Are the children being cared for?"

"Yes, with my parents."

"We will see that you're brought to your parents after the meeting," Mother promised, "or to wherever you'd like to go."

Ruth smiled, and then said, "Thank you. I don't know what will happen with my marriage, but it's good to know that I have your support."

Mother took her hand and brought her to the bench, on the opposite end as Alice. Perhaps, one day, the two women might find a way forward, but today was not that day.

My father looked at each of us sitting in the front row, and he nodded. It hadn't been easy to face his children, but he had done the right thing. And he would do the right thing again as he stood on that stage tonight, knowing that many of the people who came would be judging him—if they came at all.

My fears were soon put to rest as people began to enter the tent. At first, they trickled in, but about thirty minutes before the meeting began, they came in droves. The benches were soon filled, and people were standing on the outer edges of the tent. The noise had increased as people were visiting, waiting for the meeting to start. Father stood behind the stage with several of the men who had helped him plan the event, praying for guidance.

Before long, I was summoned onto the stage to sing the opening hymn.

My legs were shaking, and my stomach was in knots as I climbed the steps. The pianist was seated behind the piano, and she smiled at me. The entire tent quieted. Most of them were aware I had stood with Annie Barker in the most notorious speakeasy in Saint Paul. Did that mean I was defiled? Beyond redemption? Had most of them come to gawk and see how this drama might unfold on the stage? I didn't care why they came, just that they had.

For the first time in my life, I was prepared for this moment. Had I been concerned about the crowd and what they thought about me like I had been in the past, I would have buckled under the pressure. But now I understood that the only One I needed to think about was my heavenly Father. And His love was enough. More than enough.

When the pianist began to play "Amazing Grace," I felt the lyrics deep within my soul. I allowed the grace of God to saturate my words. It was a message for me, as well as for everyone else in the room. I knew the history of the song, which was written by John Newton, a slave trader who had lived an abominable life before finding salvation in Christ. He'd denied his faith most of his life, but after several near-death experiences, he began to understand God's grace and mercy. He studied the Word of God and needed to know if his soul was redeemable.

The answer was a simple yes.

And instead of letting the sins of his past corrupt his future, he had given his life to serving God, and he'd written the most beloved and transformative hymn of all time.

My parents understood that same message and had made it their life's work to share it with as many people as possible.

A few minutes later, after I'd finished singing and was sitting with my family again, my father took the stage.

The audience was silent as his steps echoed across the wooden platform and he stood before the microphone. I held my breath, praying he would have the words, the courage, the forbearance to stand up under their scrutiny.

"I have often stood on a stage such as this one," he began, looking a little older and wearier than before, "and I have preached about the grace and forgiveness of our Lord and Savior, Jesus Christ. I did not teach from head knowledge only—or from simply reading the Bible and retelling it in my own words—but from a place of experience. You see, I am a sinner, saved by God's amazing grace. I once lived a debauched lifestyle. As a baseball player, I traveled from town to town, drinking, gambling, and making choices that hurt the people I loved. I denied the gospel of Christ, the very good news that had the power to save me, and I laughed at those who preached it.

"But one morning there was a newspaper outside my hotel room, and on the front page was a story about me. I had been so drunk the night before, I didn't even remember. A group of people had found me, naked, in the middle of a park, and I wasn't alone. The story destroyed my life as I had known it."

My mouth parted as he spoke. I'd never heard this story, and by the looks on the faces of everyone but my mother, I was certain no one else but her had, either.

"That day was not unlike today," he continued as he searched the faces of the people in the audience. "I won't pretend that everyone in the tent didn't read this morning's paper. And I won't pretend that my wife and I weren't devastated at what we saw. But can I tell you? It was nothing compared to seeing headlines about my own misdeeds on the front page, because at that time, I didn't understand the power of redemption. Of forgiveness. Of second chances. But today I do. I know it can change lives drastically—because it changed mine. And if I live to be one hundred, I will never tire of offering grace and forgiveness to anyone who asks it of me, because how could I deny it to someone when it's a gift that God gave freely to me?" He paused, and his countenance became heavier still. "I have put all my focus and energy on my ministry, at the expense of my family. I placed burdens upon their shoulders that were too great to bear, and I never asked them what they wanted. I need to apologize to each of them today and ask for their forgiveness."

His gaze met Mother's, then Thomas's, then mine, and finally Ruth's. "I'm sorry."

I let out the breath I hadn't realized I was holding, and I simply nodded. Of course he had my forgiveness. He had never set out to hurt any of us.

After he received responses from each of us, he said, "Shall we pray?"

My mother took mine and Ruth's hands, and she bowed her head.

I caught Ruth's tear-filled eyes, and I offered her a smile, which she returned.

Our family wasn't perfect, and there was a lot of healing that would need to happen, but if Father and Mother could extend grace and forgiveness to us, and we to them, then we would find a way to move forward.

As I bowed my head to listen to my father's words of redemption, I prayed that it would extend to Marcus—because he, more than anyone, needed to understand the healing power of forgiveness.

27

AUGUST 31, 1727
NORTH ATLANTIC

A storm had delayed the *Ocean Curse*'s journey to Massachusetts, but we were just hours from arriving in Boston as I gathered supper from the galley. Misting rain still hovered in the air, and the dark clouds were low in the immense sky as the ship lifted and fell on great waves.

I balanced the dishes, missing Ned's help, and slowly made my way across the slippery main deck. Thankfully, Hawk saw me coming and met me at the base of the stairs to take a few things out of my hands.

"How much longer until we reach Boston Harbor?" I asked him.

He glanced toward the shoreline, hardly visible in the mist. "Two, three hours at most."

I followed him up the stairs and into the outer room.

It had been just over a week since Lindbergh's arrival in Minneapolis and the news broke about our family. The tent revival meetings had been such a success, they'd been extended from three days to five, ending on Saturday night. Father's messages had been so personal and vulnerable, and they had touched a need within the community. Word had spread, and each night, the tent was more packed than the night before.

The busyness had kept all of us preoccupied, which made me grateful. Thomas and Alice had come over for Sunday luncheon, and things had been awkward and uncomfortable at first, but I admired my parents for extending their love to them. Ruth and her children had moved in with her parents, but she and Andrew were trying to reconcile. Again, Father and Mother offered their support to Ruth and agreed to meet with the couple, if they wanted.

But my other life was not the one occupying most of my attention. We were hours away from Boston, and after that I would be on my way to Salem, which was a little over twenty miles to the north, along the coast. There, I would inquire about Rachel's family—my family—and hopefully I would get some answers.

Hawk and I walked through the outer room and into the captain's cabin. Timothy had been a guest at each of the meals since Captain Zale learned that his father was Jim Ludlow. It had given Timothy a sense of importance, but I prayed it wouldn't encourage the young man to continue with this lifestyle.

Captain Zale had been a tyrant since we'd left Charleston, probably on account of Ned leaving, though he'd never admit it. His behavior had become erratic, and his moods had shifted, sometimes from one minute to the next. He kept Dr. Hartville close, but Marcus told me that there was nothing ailing the captain except the fear of illness.

As we entered the cabin now, the captain said to Hawk, "Why are you helping Carl?"

"He needed an extra hand," Hawk explained as he set the platters of food on the table.

"If you and Marcus hadn't lost Ned, you wouldn't have to serve." Captain Zale's gaze bored into me. "Though, I wonder if he had some encouragement to leave."

Marcus was already at the table, watching the captain with wary eyes. Dr. Hartville was there, as were Jack and Timothy. I set plates down in front of each of them, trying not to meet anyone's gaze.

It was hard not to focus on Marcus. The past eight days had been so bittersweet in his company. The stolen moments, especially at the end of the day, had been the most enjoyable of my life. We talked about our hopes and dreams for the future, always with the knowledge that everything could be taken away in a heartbeat.

Perhaps it was the fact that it could all end in days that made each moment feel so full and satisfying. Being in his arms, enjoying his kisses, and then parting ways to sleep was the hardest of all—yet the sweet possibility of someday helped me endure.

But moments like this, when he was close, the desire to touch him was so strong. I couldn't help but brush against him as I set his plate on the table, or when I served his ale. It felt like electricity, even if the touch was fleeting.

I stood by and waited while they ate, impatient to take my meal to Marcus's cabin and have him join me. It would be late when the ship was anchored in Boston Harbor, so we would wait until morning to disembark. As Timothy brought the captain to his father, Marcus promised to take me to Salem.

From there, the rest was a mystery.

Captain Zale's scowl found me several times throughout the meal, but I always lowered my gaze. Marcus seemed to notice, as he looked from me to the captain whenever it happened.

When they were finally done eating, and the men rose to leave, Captain Zale spoke. "Dr. Hartville, I need you to stay."

The kind doctor looked wary.

I began to clear the table as Timothy, Hawk, and Jack left, though Marcus lingered.

"You may leave," the captain said to Marcus.

"I can help Carl clear—"

"Leave!" the captain bellowed.

Marcus frowned and tossed me a concerned glance, but he nodded and then stepped out of the cabin.

I tried to clear the table as quickly as I could, wanting to stay small and inconspicuous. It wasn't uncommon for me to remain behind and finish my work, though the captain usually left with the other men.

"What seems to be the trouble this time?" Dr. Hartville asked the captain with a sigh.

The captain stood close to the table, his arms crossed, as he stared at me. "'Tis not me that needs assistance," he said. "'Tis Carl."

I paused, holding my breath.

"He has recovered nicely from the diving sickness," the doctor said. "I haven't heard him complain once about another ailment."

"'Tis not an ailment," the captain said. "'Tis a question that has been plaguing me this past week."

The doctor and I waited as my hands began to tremble. I set down the dirty dishes I had been holding, so they wouldn't rattle.

"What question is that, Captain?" Dr. Hartville asked.

"Whether Carl is a boy or a girl. I suppose I could have checked myself, but I thought a professional would be best suited to the task."

Sweat broke out on my brow as I started to back toward the door—but where would I go on a ship?

Dr. Hartville knew the answer to the question, though he said nothing as the captain continued to stare at me.

"Does the doctor need to examine you, Carl?" Captain Zale asked. "Or are you willing to tell the truth?"

I felt like a cornered animal with nowhere to run. I couldn't endure the humiliation of an examination, but I didn't want to admit the truth, either. Not this close to Boston and the answers I needed. If only Marcus had stayed. He could step in and save me from answering.

The captain and doctor watched me. Dr. Hartville lifted a shoulder, as if he was telling me to give in.

"Dr. Hartville," Captain Zale said, "it appears that Carl wants to be examined. Proceed."

"No!" I put out my hand, realizing I had no other choice but to tell him the truth. "I am a woman."

The captain's lips curled up in a satisfied smile. "As I thought. Dr. Hartville, you may leave us."

I shook my head. I didn't want the doctor to leave, but he didn't have a choice, either. He slipped out of the room without a moment's hesitation.

"I've been watching you closely since Ned left." He took a step closer to me, and I backed up. "I started to notice the secret looks you and Marcus gave each other. The subtle touches and the early nights when he went back to his cabin. It all started to make sense."

Where was Marcus now? Had Dr. Hartville alerted him?

"How long has Marcus known?" the captain asked.

I licked my dry lips, trying to decide what to say. Would Marcus be in trouble if I told the captain that Marcus had known almost from the start? I opened my mouth to respond when the door opened, and Marcus strode in.

The captain turned at the arrival, giving me the opportunity to move around him and get out of the corner.

Marcus reached for my hand, and I took it, relief flooding through me.

"I've known the truth for a long time," Marcus said.

"Ahh." The captain paced around us, a snarl on his lips. "I can't fault you for enjoying her company while I had Nadine's."

"'Tis not like that," Marcus said.

Captain Zale laughed derisively, then he became serious. "If you don't enjoy her company, then you won't mind if I take her off your hands."

Marcus's grip tightened, and I stepped closer to him.

"I do mind," he said. "I intend to make Caroline my wife."

"Caroline?" The captain's eyebrows rose, and then he laughed again. "Your wife? And how will you manage that? Your life belongs to me and to this ship and crew. 'Tis no place for a *wife*. Nadine didn't believe me, but she eventually came to her senses. I can't say I blame her, but she should have had the courage to tell me she was leaving."

I saw the struggle in Marcus's gaze, old lies warring with newfound hope. He wanted to believe we had a future together. We both did.

"As your captain," Captain Zale continued, "the crewmen are under my direction, and I am taking what is rightfully mine." He reached for my wrist and pulled me toward him.

I cried out in pain.

Marcus still held my other hand, but he saw my discomfort and let me go.

The captain pulled me closer, my back to his front, reminding me of being in Lloyd's grip.

"Leave us," Captain Zale said to Marcus as he ran his nose up the side of my face. "I will show Caroline her new duties."

In a flash, Marcus pulled his cutlass from its sheath and sliced it through the air, resting it against the captain's neck.

Captain Zale stiffened, his hold tightening around my chest.

"Let her go," Marcus said evenly through clenched teeth.

"You wouldn't dare," Captain Zale sneered.

"Without a moment's hesitation."

I felt as if I was living through the same scene from the Castle Royal, but this time it was Marcus who was defending me. I saw no hesitation, no fear, no uncertainty in his gaze. His hand didn't quiver, and his intentions were clear. He meant to free me and would not back down until he succeeded or died trying.

The captain pushed me away, and I fell just like I had in the caves, but he did not run, like Lloyd. He pulled his own cutlass from his sheath, and the sound of steel rang against steel.

"No!" I cried as the two men began to parry. I didn't want Marcus to get hurt because of me, yet at the same time I sensed that this fight wasn't just about me. It was for the years of abuse Marcus—and the others—had suffered at the hands of Captain Zale.

"Get out of here, Caroline," Marcus yelled as he moved his sword this way and that, hitting the captain's over and over.

They lunged around the cabin, the small blades of their cutlasses easy to maneuver in the tight space.

"You're not safe," he said to me as I lay on the floor where the captain had shoved me.

I should have obeyed his command, but I couldn't leave him.

They were equally matched in strength, height, and skill. Sweat broke out on their brows as they stepped forward and back, around in a circle, their blades ringing.

The door flew open, and Hawk appeared with Timothy at his side.

"Take him!" the captain yelled at Hawk.

I caught Hawk's gaze and saw his uncertainty, but he didn't move to help the captain, telling me all I needed to know.

A pirate ship was a democracy, and a captain could be challenged at any time. It was not up to Hawk to defend the captain from one of his own. The captain must be the strongest, bravest, and fiercest of them all. And if Marcus overtook the captain, proving he was better fit for the job, he would gain the respect of the crew.

As much as I wanted to help him, this was Marcus's moment to take back his life.

The captain's age was wearing on him. I could see it in the exhausted lines of his body. And when Captain Zale stumbled, Marcus used it to his advantage. He swiped at the captain's cutlass, and it flew out of his hand as the captain fell to the ground.

The captain's cutlass spun across the floor, stopping by my feet. I stood and grabbed it as Marcus put his foot on the captain's chest and placed his blade next to his throat.

"You won't ever touch the lass again," Marcus said as his chest rose and fell. "She isn't yours, or anyone else's, to command."

I could hardly breathe as I watched Marcus, my heart pounding from both fear and elation at his success. He'd defended me, as he promised, and he had not backed down or let my captor go like Lewis had.

"I suppose you'll kill me now," the captain snarled at Marcus, "so you can have control of my ship."

Marcus shook his head. "Nay. 'Tis time we both faced our fate."

Captain Zale frowned. "What does that mean?"

"It means that as soon as we lay anchor in Boston Harbor, we're going to pay a visit to the royal governor of Massachusetts. Just the two of us." Marcus noticed Hawk and Timothy and paused, probably wondering what Hawk might do. The two were friends, but Hawk had been under the captain's command until now.

Hawk turned to Timothy. "Grab one of the ropes in the outer room. Captain Marcus Zale is now in charge, and Edward Zale is his prisoner."

Respect filled Marcus's gaze as he gave his old friend a quick nod.

Soon, Edward was tied up, and the crew was gathered on the main deck to hear of the change in command.

Darkness had fallen, and with it, more rain. Boston Harbor was now in sight, though it was hard to see the city on a hill through the fog and mist. I stood on the quarterdeck with Marcus and Hawk, terrified that there would be an outcry from among the men. But instead, after Marcus made the announcement, a cheer arose that startled me.

I had not gotten close to the pirate crew and wasn't aware of the dislike they had for the ex-captain until that very moment.

"Prepare to lay anchor in Boston Harbor," Marcus shouted at his men after telling them the news. "There is much to be done."

The crew went to work as Hawk turned to Marcus. "What would you like me to do with Edward?"

"Keep an eye on him," Marcus said. "I must prepare to leave the ship at first light. We can take turns guarding him, but I doubt anyone will try to help him escape."

"Will you move to the captain's quarters tonight?"

Marcus glanced at me, a dozen questions in his eyes, but he said, "Nay. We'll decide what to do tomorrow."

Hawk nodded. "I'll start the first watch."

"Thank you." Marcus patted Hawk on the shoulder and then said, for his ears alone, "And I trust you won't mention anything about Miss Caroline to the rest of the crew? At least until tomorrow?"

Hawk's grin was wide. "I knew the truth about her back in Nassau. I saw how protective you were and how you had your hand on her back." He laughed and shook his head. "There's no fooling Hawk. I won't say anything."

Marcus smiled and then said, "Can you please have Timothy bring her a plate of food? She didn't get a chance to eat."

"Aye, aye, Captain."

I smiled at Hawk as Marcus motioned for me to proceed him up the steps and into his old cabin.

It felt good to get out of the rain. Marcus moved ahead of me and lit the lamp to allow a bit of light.

I was soaked and trembling, more from the excitement of the night than the cold rain.

Marcus didn't say a word as he took a blanket off his cot and wrapped it around my shoulders.

The moment his gentle hands touched me, I could no longer hold back my tears, and I clung to him.

He wrapped his arms around me, whispering into my ear. "There's no need to cry," he said. "'Tis done."

"Nay." I shook my head and pulled back. "'Tis only just begun. What will happen tomorrow when you take the captain to the governor? You'll be captured, Marcus. I'll never see you again."

He drew me back into his arms and held me for a long time. "This isn't how I wanted things to happen. But 'tis the right thing to do, Caroline. Tomorrow, I'll send Hawk along with you to Salem. I trust him with my life, and if I can't be there with you, he is the one I will send in my stead."

"I won't go," I said. "I'll stay with you. No matter what happens."

He shook his head. "Nay. You must go to your kin. Not only to find answers, but because they'll care for you."

"And what if they don't? What if there's no one left?"

"Then I'll instruct Hawk to take you back to your grandfather."

I grasped the lapels of his coat. "You speak as if you won't be with me."

He brought his hands up to my cheeks and kissed me. When he lifted his lips, he set his forehead against mine and said, "I don't know what tomorrow will bring, but I will make sure you are cared for. I've always known that my actions would have consequences. But I wouldn't be any sort of a man if I didn't face them. I hope you can understand."

I did understand, even though I hated every word he said.

Actions had consequences, whether good or bad. I admired Marcus for wanting to do the right thing.

But why did the right thing have to hurt so much?

28

AUGUST 31, 1927
MINNEAPOLIS, MINNESOTA

I didn't want to go to sleep in Boston Harbor. I didn't want to leave Marcus and know that tomorrow, when I woke up there, it would probably be the last time I would ever see him. But I couldn't stay there forever. Even if I had stayed up the whole night, as soon as I fell asleep, I would wake up here, to live this day. So, I had fallen asleep in Marcus's arms, though I knew he would be leaving to take his watch with Edward.

The day was hot and humid as I went through the motions. My birthday was only two days away, and then I would be twenty-one. Would I lose 1727? I just wanted this day to be over so I could be with Marcus.

But even then, what would be the point? If he was taken prisoner by Governor Dummer, I couldn't be with him. He would insist that Hawk take me to Salem. It was the reason we'd gone to Massachusetts.

"Are you ready?" Irene asked as she entered the foyer, putting her wide-brimmed hat onto her head. "Lewis just arrived."

I nodded, though my heart didn't want to go to the state fair.

The only benefit would be to take my mind off 1727 for a few hours, but the reality would rush back the moment I remembered.

Lewis bounded up the front steps and knocked on the door. Irene answered it as I lifted my hat off the coat-tree. Father and Mother were out for the afternoon, so the house was quiet except for the sound of Ingrid in the kitchen.

"Good afternoon," Lewis said with a big smile. "Are you ladies ready for some fun?"

It was too hot to go to the fair. The thermometer read almost ninety degrees, and it wasn't even the hottest part of the day. But we had agreed to this outing last week, and I couldn't back out now. Irene would be heading to Iowa in two days.

"Our first stop will be the lemonade stand," Lewis promised as he smiled at Irene. But when his glance fell on me, his smile disappeared. "What's wrong, Carrie?"

I couldn't tell him what was happening with Marcus while Irene was around, so I forced myself to smile and stepped out onto the porch. "Everything is fine."

The heat was almost unbearable with the humidity so high. It felt like I was breathing in warm water.

"Is this about the newspaper?" Lewis asked. "Because people have already moved on to talk about other things. Your father's tent meetings were so popular, they are still dominating the news. No one cares about what happened before."

"I care," I said a little too sharply.

He grew stiff at my response, but didn't comment.

Irene watched the two of us closely. She'd weathered the scandal with our family and had been a bright spot on difficult days. Her companionship had come at the perfect time.

Irene got into the front seat with Lewis, and I got into the back. Irene was chatty as we drove toward the state fairgrounds on Snelling Avenue. She had never attended it before and was excited to take a ride on Ye Old Mill and visit the carousel. She also wanted to look at the butter sculptures and then see the baby incubators. Since babies were rarely born in hospitals and hospitals saw no use in purchasing incubators, doctors and nurses traveled across the country with their machines to save lives for free. They paid for the machines with the ticket money and had saved thousands of babies. It was an exhibit I enjoyed seeing each year, especially because it was saving lives. Our last stop for the evening, before the fireworks, would be the performance of John Philip Sousa, the famous composer and conductor, who would premier the new march he had composed for the University of Minnesota.

The traffic on Snelling Avenue was thick as we approached the fair gates.

"I'll drop you off," Lewis told us, "and meet you by the lemonade stand after I park."

We happily agreed and got out of his Chevy near the fairground entrance.

"The lemonade stand is over there," I told Irene as I pointed to a tent on the right.

It was hard to find shade as we waited for Lewis. Irene was anxious to see everything, so I told her to start in the agricultural building and we'd catch up with her once we had the lemonade.

She waved at me as she walked away.

"I was wondering when I might get you alone," a woman said from behind me.

I turned, shocked to find Annie. She was wearing the same dress she'd had on at the Castle Royal, but today she was wearing a hat with a wide brim.

"I thought you left," I said. "I didn't think I'd ever see you again."

She shrugged and then took my arm and led me out of the thoroughfare to a more private area behind the tents. "We did leave," she told me. "But we had some unfinished business, so we came back."

It was strange to see her again, to know that this was the woman who held a key to my past—a key she didn't know how to use. "How did you know I'd be here?"

324

Again, she shrugged. "It's not that hard to find someone when you really want to." She smiled. "You found me, didn't you?"

It was my turn to smile—yet, there wasn't much to smile about. "I just arrived in Boston in 1727," I told her, sparing her the details about Marcus's plans to turn himself and Edward into the authorities. It hurt too much to think about. "I'm going to Salem tomorrow to look for Rachel's family."

She nodded and glanced around before she leaned in and said, "There's another reason I wanted to come back, Caroline. A couple, really. First, there is a woman you need to look for in Salem. Her name is Hope Abbott. She's Rachel's cousin. I don't know much about her, except that she was in the Salem gaol with Rachel when she gave birth to me. She was there when Rachel died."

I frowned. "How do you know?"

"I went to Salem," she confessed, "before I died in 1713. I learned a little about Rachel, but I also learned the truth about my father, too—your grandfather. After what I discovered, I decided to stop asking questions."

"You didn't approach Hope Abbott?"

"No." She shook her head. "Honestly, I didn't want to learn anything else. What I knew was hard enough. I didn't think it mattered. Maybe it still doesn't."

"Knowledge always matters."

"Not when it hurts."

"Even when it hurts." I thought of the knowledge my parents had about my siblings and me. Now that they knew what was happening with Andrew and Ruth, they were able to help. And because they knew about Thomas and Alice, I no longer had to keep it a secret. The truth had taken so much pressure off me. It also helped that they knew about my strange existence because now I could speak freely about it. And because I knew who Annie was, I could talk to her, too. "What did you learn in Salem that troubled you?"

Sweat beaded on her brow, and she wiped it away with a handkerchief before she said, "I learned that Rachel was not Josias

Reed's wife. She was his mistress. His wife stayed in England with their only son, and he came to Massachusetts as a merchant. He met Rachel Howlett, who was a Quaker, living near the town of Sandwich. She left her family and moved in with him, and that's when she became pregnant with me. When someone learned about her, she was put in the gaol and accused of being a witch. That's where she died, giving birth to me."

I couldn't believe my grandfather had done such a thing. He lived by a moral code that I couldn't even live up to. Had he really kept a mistress while married to another woman? "What happened to his wife and child?"

"They died on the crossing. Apparently, he took me to South Carolina to start over. And he never told me anything except her name."

"*Grandfather?*" I asked. "I can hardly believe it."

"I couldn't, either." She slipped her handkerchief into her pocket. "I didn't want to know anything else. I should have spoken to Hope, but I was afraid I'd only be more disappointed in my father and mother. Or worse, I'd be rejected by Hope and my family. I couldn't bear it."

"You and I have similar stories," I told her.

"That's the other reason I came back. I need to tell you something." She put her hands on my shoulders, her brown eyes meeting mine. "Don't repeat my sins, Caroline. Don't follow an unworthy man to destruction. Decide what you want, and go get it. I learned about your parents here—the Baldwins—and I'm so happy for you. You have the chance to really make something of your life. I wasn't so lucky. But that's not an excuse. Don't worry about 1727. Even if you lose it, you still have this life. Hold on tight."

I didn't want to tell her I'd fallen in love with a pirate in 1727.

"I can't stay long," I told her. "I have friends looking for me."

"Lloyd will be looking for me."

"Thank you," I said. "For coming back. I'm still going to Salem to see if I can speak to Hope Abbott."

"Good." She smiled. "Drop me a note if you learn anything helpful."

"Where do I send it?"

"My mother's house in Dallas, Texas. She keeps all my mail, and I stop in there from time to time. It's not a perfect system, but it works." She told me her mother's name and address.

As Annie started to walk away, I put out my hand to stop her.

"Yeah?" she asked.

"Do you ever think about what you're doing?"

She put her hand on my cheek and nodded. "Every day—but I'm in too deep to stop now."

I placed my hand over hers. "You're never in too deep. Please think about stopping—for me."

Something passed over her face, and she offered a smile. "I'll do that, kid."

And then Annie walked out of my life again.

It took me a couple of minutes to compose myself after she left. When I was finally ready to meet Lewis, I walked over to the lemonade stand.

He was waiting, squinting into the crowd, no doubt looking for me and Irene.

When he saw me, he smiled. "Did you talk to Annie?"

My lips parted. "How did you know?"

"She got word to me through the Green Lantern that she was in town and wanted to see you. So I told her we'd be here today."

Warmth filled my chest. "Thank you, Lewis."

"Anything for my friend's little sister," he teased with a wink.

Irene appeared in the crowd as she moved toward us.

Lewis's gaze shifted toward my cousin, and I saw something there that I'd suspected for the past couple of weeks.

He was falling for her.

"She's a sweetheart," I said to him.

He grinned but didn't take his eyes off her. "It's her fiery side I like the best."

"She'd be lucky to have you."

He looked back at me, searching my gaze for permission to move on.

I smiled and nodded.

He reached out and drew me into an embrace.

I hugged him back, thankful I still had his friendship even though I hadn't been able to give him my heart.

I prayed that he would find what he was looking for with Irene.

29

SEPTEMBER 1, 1727
BOSTON, MASSACHUSETTS

I awoke on the *Ocean Curse* with dread. My heart was so sad, I could hardly lift my head off the pillow. I didn't want today to come. I didn't want to face whatever God had ordained for Marcus. I prayed, once again, that a miracle would happen. I admired Marcus for his honor and conviction—yet I wished there was another way.

His cot was empty, and he was not in the cabin. My heart beat so hard, I felt like I couldn't breathe. I pushed aside the covers, needing to see him. To be certain he was still with me.

It was dark outside, but a slice of light on the eastern horizon told me it was morning. I could see the dark outlines of other ships in the harbor, but I didn't have a view of Boston.

A small, unfamiliar chest on the table caught my eye.

Gently, I lifted the curved lid and my breath stilled.

Inside was a beautiful burgundy gown, with all the trimmings. Stockings, undergarments, petticoats, panniers, shoes, and a hat.

I slowly lifted the skirt out of the chest, marveling at the beautiful silk creation. Where had it come from? I could only assume it was for me, but how had Marcus found it?

I didn't waste any time discarding my old clothes and binding. The gown was exquisite and had a cream-colored stomacher with burgundy flowers and green leaves embroidered in silk thread. There was a matching lace tucker to be worn around the neck and chest, and the ruffled cuff of my shift peeked out from the ends of the elbow-length sleeves, adding a bit of elegance.

Even with the gift of this gown, the heaviness of today was like a bucket of water, dousing the flames of happiness. I tried not to cry as I styled my hair. There was no mirror to see my reflection, but it had to be a vast improvement from what it had been.

The sun had just crested the horizon when I stepped out of Marcus's cabin. Timothy had told me that ever since Ned left, the whispers about a Jonah had died away. Even though the crew would realize I was a woman, there was little they could do about it now. My presence—or my real identity—would come as a shock, but none of it mattered since I would be leaving the ship, most likely forever.

The storm had passed in the night, and the salty sea air felt fresh and clean.

Every deckhand on the ship stopped their early morning chores to stare at me. Some even removed their hats when my gaze met theirs.

I walked down the steps from the poop deck to the quarterdeck and found Hawk standing guard outside the outer room.

His mouth slipped open at my arrival, and he smiled. "You look lovely, Miss Caroline."

"Thank you, Hawk. Do you know where Marcus found this gown?"

"He sent Timothy on a mission into town overnight." Hawk's eyes glowed with happiness. "Said he woke up the proprietor, but paid her so nicely, she didn't mind."

"I'll need to thank Timothy and Marcus."

Hawk nodded toward the crew staring at me on the main deck. "I've got some explaining to do."

"Do you mind?"

"Not at all." He laughed. "Are you hungry? I'll have someone bring you breakfast."

"I couldn't eat a bite." My stomach was in such turmoil, I wasn't sure I'd ever be hungry again. "Where is Marcus?"

"He's putting his things in order. The launch is getting ready to take us into Boston."

"I know Marcus said that you'll take me to Salem today." I swallowed, hoping Hawk wasn't upset about the request. "But I want to stay in Boston to speak to Governor Dummer on Marcus's behalf."

He tilted his head and said, "I don't know about that. Marcus might not like it."

"I know he won't, but I cannot leave him."

"You'll have to speak to him about it." He opened the door to the outer room, and I entered without him.

The door to the captain's cabin opened at the same moment, and Marcus appeared in the doorway.

Our gazes locked, and I felt the connection in every inch of my body.

"You look bonnie, Caroline," he said, his tired gaze revealing the depths of his attraction to me.

"Thank you for the gown." I touched the fabric and shook my head. "'Tis too fine."

He only smiled as he closed the door to the cabin and met me in the middle of the outer room, drawing me into his embrace and holding me tight.

"Please don't go," I whispered as I laid my cheek on his chest. "I can't bear to part with you."

Marcus didn't say anything for a moment, but when he pulled back, I saw everything in his eyes. "I love you too much to run away from my responsibilities. I have been praying, Caroline, and I know this is the right thing to do. God has forgiven me—but I still must make amends for my transgressions."

"You're stronger than me."

He shook his head, his weary gaze caressing my face. "Nay.

You're the strongest and bravest person I've ever known. I admire you just as much as I love you."

His words were bittersweet, filled with love yet laced with the regret of his life before he met me.

"'Tis time we were away," he said as he pulled a small pouch of coins out of his pocket. "But before we go, I want you to have this."

I took the heavy bag and frowned. "What is it?"

"I long to care for you, but if this is all I can provide, it gives me a small sense of comfort. Please take it."

I slipped the bag of coins into the pocket of my gown where it sat deep within the folds of my petticoat.

The door to the cabin opened again, and two men hauled Edward out. His hands were tied behind his back, and he wore a scowl on his bearded face. When he saw me, the scowl disappeared and shock replaced it—but not for long.

"Take him to the launch," Marcus said to the men. "And watch him closely."

Edward fought against his captors and cast a slew of harsh words toward everyone in the room—me included—until he was out on the quarterdeck.

Timothy left the captain's cabin last, and his ruddy complexion deepened as he saw me. He shook his head. "They told me I had to get a dress, but they didn't tell me who it was for. Carl! You're a girl?"

Despite the heartache, I smiled. "You asked me why I kept to myself on the *Adventurer*. This is why."

"You're our Jonah," he said with a chuckle. "I never guessed."

I shrugged. "I wasn't the only one, but that's a story for a different time."

Soon, we were boarding the launch. Edward, Hawk, Timothy, Marcus, Dr. Hartville, who was being released, and a few other pirates that Marcus had chosen for their loyalty to him.

When we reached the long pier, Marcus turned to me as if he was going to say goodbye, and I shook my head. "I'm coming with you to speak to Governor Dummer."

"Nay. 'Tis not wise."

"Why?" I stared at him, ready to go to battle with him if necessary. "I can speak on your behalf."

"Caro—"

"I'm coming, Marcus." I wouldn't give him the opportunity to debate with me.

He sighed and then said his farewell to Dr. Hartville after giving him some coins for his troubles.

"I'm sorry Edward kept you captive all this time," Marcus said to him.

"I wish I could have cured his ailments," the good doctor replied, "but the mind can be the hardest thing to heal if someone isn't willing."

As the doctor left, Marcus said goodbye to the men who had rowed the launch.

"Hawk and I will see that Edward is delivered to the governor," Marcus told the men. "The rest of you may leave."

"What about the *Ocean Curse*?" Timothy asked Marcus.

Marcus turned to Hawk and said, "'Tis yours. You earned it. Just be fair to the men."

Hawk lifted his chin, his brown eyes filled with emotion, and said, "I'll take care of it until you return."

With a shake of his head, Marcus said, "I will never return to pirating, my friend."

"Then we'll become merchants," Hawk said, sounding confident.

"I'm casting my lot with you," Timothy said to Marcus. "No matter what happens."

Marcus put his hand on Timothy's shoulder and nodded. "Thank you."

So it was Marcus, Hawk, and Timothy who led Edward Zale down State Street and left to Marlborough Street where the governor's mansion sat. The impressive structure was four stories tall with ornate dormers on the roof and a large cupola with a massive weather vane.

People watched us pass, but no one stopped to inquire.

My heart was beating hard as we climbed the steps of the mansion and Marcus knocked on the front door.

I was standing so close to him that when his hand found mine in the folds of my skirt, I almost started to weep. It felt like we were on our way to his execution—and for all intents and purposes, we were.

The door opened, and a man answered. He looked at each of us and frowned. "May I help you?"

Marcus quickly told him who he and Edward were, and he asked to speak to the governor, to turn them in.

The man's eyes opened wide, and he quickly ushered us into the residence, which also acted as the governor's office. A beautiful staircase sat in the center of the foyer, but the man directed us into a waiting room to the right.

"I'll return with the governor shortly."

Hawk and Timothy forced Edward to sit while they stood over him.

I waited near the fireplace with Marcus, who, despite his resolve, looked grim.

It didn't take long for Governor Dummer to enter. At his side were two soldiers, their hands ready on the hilts of their swords.

The governor wore a curly gray wig and a black suit of clothes. He stepped into the room as if he didn't believe the man who had summoned him, but when he saw each of us, his surprise was evident.

"Governor Dummer?" Marcus asked.

"Aye, and who are you?"

Marcus stepped forward and said, "My name is Maxwell Mac-Dougal, but for the past fifteen years, I've been living as Marcus Zale, on the *Ocean Curse*. I'm handing myself over to you today, and I've brought Captain Edward Zale as my prisoner."

The governor stared at Edward, his eyes opening wide. "Edward Zale?"

Edward only scowled at him.

A look of joy passed over Governor Dummer's face as he said, "Edward Zale is the last of the pirates that we've been seeking these past ten years." He turned back to Marcus. "You know there's a reward for his capture, don't you?"

Marcus frowned and shook his head.

"Aye. 'Tis a handsome reward, I must say."

"But I'm turning myself in, as well," Marcus said, his chest rising and falling with the effort to confess. "I can't accept a reward if I'm to be tried alongside him."

Governor Dummer started to laugh, so it was my turn to frown. Why would he be mirthful at a time like this?

"Sir," Governor Dummer said to Marcus, putting his hand on Marcus's shoulder, "I don't care if you have been the most notorious of them all. You've brought me Captain Edward Zale, a coup that will please His Majesty the King. He has only just ascended to the throne, and I've been looking for a gift to delight him. Presenting him with the last mayor of the Pirate Republic will be just the thing."

"I don't understand your meaning," Marcus said.

"I mean that it is in my power to pardon you—and I am," Governor Dummer said. "As long as you promise not to return to pirating, then you are a free man, and you may keep your ship and all your plunder, with a handsome reward coming your way, as well. Tell your men that they are also free," he continued. "But if I hear that anyone from your ship has returned to pirating, they will not get a second chance. The king desires this mess with the pirates to be over for good, as do I. I'm choosing to be lenient to all, except to this one." He walked over to Edward. "Edward Zale has already received the King's Pardon once, and that is all he gets. Mr. Zale will be tried as a pirate, and I intend to see that he hangs." He called for his secretary to summon the gaoler while the soldiers took Edward into their custody.

Marcus seemed stunned and stepped forward, no doubt to question the governor, but I captured his hand and smiled, pulling him back.

"You're free, Maxwell."

"But I do not deserve it."

My smile could not be dimmed. "None of us deserves forgiveness. Just as Christ pardoned our transgressions, though we were not worthy, the governor has pardoned yours."

His brown eyes searched mine, as if seeking truth. When he found it, he grinned and wrapped me in his embrace.

"You're free," I whispered. "Marcus Zale no longer exists. From this day on, you get to choose who you want to be and how you want to live."

When I pulled back, I found tears in Maxwell's eyes, and before he kissed me, he said, "I want you, Caroline."

It was midafternoon as Maxwell and I pulled into Isaac and Hope Abbott's property in Salem Village, a little community about five miles north of Salem Towne. He had rented a carriage soon after we had left the governor's mansion, and though we'd spent the entire drive marveling at the governor's pardon, our anxiety about what would happen tomorrow on my birthday was foremost in our minds.

Hawk and Timothy had returned to the *Ocean Curse*, which now belonged to Maxwell, per the governor's orders, to share the news of the pardon with all the men. Those who chose to stay would become employed by Maxwell, who planned to become a merchantman, and those who chose to leave were warned not to return to their pirating ways. Timothy promised me he would go home to visit with his father and siblings once the ship was secure, and Hawk assured us that he would keep an eye on things until Maxwell returned.

But all Maxwell could focus on was getting me to Salem Village.

The Abbotts' home was beautiful. It was a classic saltbox house with a slanted roof and no eaves. The clapboard siding was painted a brick red, and the trim around the doors and windows matched.

A large barn and several outbuildings spoke of prosperity, as did the cattle in the nearby field, the pigs in a pen, and the chickens running loose in the yard.

I sat beside Maxwell, my hand in his. "I'm still in shock," I told him. "I had expected today to go much differently. I had dreaded God's plan, but now I realize how foolish I had been."

"Aye." He lifted my hand to kiss the back. "I'm still trying to understand it myself." He nodded at the house. "I pray Hope Abbott has more good news for us."

Even if Hope had answers, it might be that I had no choice. That my life would end here tomorrow. The thought terrified me. But I would choose to trust God's plan for me, as well.

An older man appeared from the barn, squinting into the afternoon sunlight as he wiped his hands on a handkerchief and walked toward us.

"Good day," he said. "How may I help you?"

Maxwell stepped out of the carriage and came around to help me down.

My gown was cumbersome, but I didn't mind. Not after months of dressing as a man.

"Are you Goodman Abbott?" I asked him, trying not to feel so nervous.

"Yes." He looked from me to Maxwell and back again. "And who are you, may I ask?"

I licked my dry lips and said, "My name is Caroline Reed. My mother was Anne Reed, and her mother was Rachel Howlett. I believe—"

"Rachel's granddaughter?" he interrupted me, his face revealing his shock.

"Aye. And this is Maxwell MacDougal. We've come to speak to your wife. Is she at home?"

I held my breath, afraid that Hope was not there, or that she had died, or that she wouldn't want to speak to me.

"Come," Goodman Abbott said with a grin. "My wife will be very pleased to meet you."

We followed him into his home, admiring the interior. The house was decorated with beautiful furniture, lovely paintings, and thick carpets.

"Won't you have a seat?" Goodman Abbott asked as he led us into a parlor with wainscoting and built-in shelves next to the fireplace. "My wife is preserving vegetables today, but she'll be much happier visiting with you."

Maxwell and I sat together on a settee.

Goodman Abbott disappeared, and I took a deep, steadying breath, trying not to fidget with my new gown.

Maxwell laid his hand over mine. "You needn't worry, Caroline. God has gone before you as He went before me."

I instantly felt calm as the truth of his words sank deep into my soul.

A moment later, Goodman Abbott returned with a woman who looked to be in her early sixties. Her gray hair was still thick, and her brown eyes sparkled with life. Even at her age, she appeared to be healthy and active.

And she looked vaguely familiar.

She wiped her hands on her apron and rushed into the room. "Are you Caroline?"

I stood and nodded, and in the next second, I was held in her tight embrace.

Tears rolled down my cheeks as Hope wept. Any worry that she wouldn't want me vanished.

When she let me go, she held me at arm's length. "I have so many questions for you—and I'm certain you have questions for me."

"Are you Hope?" I asked, though I was almost certain she was.

Hope laughed and nodded. "Yes, forgive me. And this is my husband, Isaac."

"This is Maxwell," I said, still trying to get used to calling him by his real name.

"Your husband?" Hope asked as she smiled at Maxwell.

He put his arm around my waist and shook his head. "Not yet," he told Hope. "But very soon."

"'Tis a long story," I told Hope. "But I have so many other things I want to ask you."

"Please, sit. One of our girls will bring a tea tray in momentarily." Hope and Isaac took the seats across from us as we sat on the settee again.

"My first question," I said as I clung to Maxwell for support, "is what do you know of Rachel? Was she—" I couldn't bring myself to say it, but I had no choice. It was the reason I'd come. "Was she a witch?"

"No." Hope shook her head, fierce determination in her brown eyes. "There were no witches in Salem Village—not then and not now. It was—" She paused and sighed. "It was a tragedy from beginning to end. Rachel was accused of being a witch by my stepmother, Susannah, but that is also a long story. Rachel was raised as a Quaker, though she was living in Salem Towne with Josias Reed."

"I know all about their relationship," I confessed to Hope.

"It was partially due to their relationship that Rachel was convicted of witchcraft." Hope clasped her hands on her lap, sadness in her voice. "I was with Rachel in the gaol when she gave birth to your mother and then died. She asked me to care for your mother, but I had no way to help since I was also being held on the accusation of witchcraft. Josias took your mother, and we never heard from her again." Hope studied me closely. "But I've always wondered—and I hope I'm not speaking out of turn—" She glanced at Maxwell, but then back at me. "Your mother had a birthmark on her chest . . ."

"Aye," I said. "The same as me."

She blinked several times and then leaned forward and said, "The birthmark means you're a time-crosser, too. Only those who have it cross time. What other time do you occupy, Caroline?"

More tears gathered in my eyes as I said, "Are you a time-crosser, as well?"

"Yes, though I made my final decision many years ago." She took Isaac's hand, and they smiled at one another.

"Your final decision?" I frowned. "What does that mean?"

"You don't know?"

"I know nothing about time-crossing." I said the term carefully, having never heard it before. "Until just a few months ago, I believed I was the only person in the world who had this burden. But then I found my mother's letter and realized she did, too."

"'Tis what we feared," Hope said. "That your mother wouldn't have a guide. We prayed she would."

"She knows nothing," I told her. "She died here on her twenty-first birthday and is now living in 1927." There was so much to tell Hope about my mother, but it would have to wait. "That's one of the reasons I'm here. Why did she die on her twenty-first birthday?" I gripped Maxwell's hand, as if I could keep him with me always. "Will *I* die tomorrow, on my birthday?"

"Your twenty-first birthday is tomorrow?" Hope asked, her eyes wide.

"Aye. Am I going to die here?"

"'Tis your choice," Hope said. "Whichever life you want to keep, you need to stay awake past midnight on the night of your twenty-first birthday. But that means you'll lose the other forever. 'Tis the worst part of this gift—choosing one and forfeiting the other."

I stared at her, both elated and heartbroken. "If I want to stay here, I must stay awake past midnight on my birthday? But if I do, I won't wake up in 1927?"

"No." Hope shook her head. "Tomorrow will be your last day there."

"What will happen to my body there?"

"It will die."

In all my worrying about losing 1727, I hadn't contemplated losing 1927. My parents, my brothers, Ruth and the children. Irene—and Lewis. I would have to say goodbye to all of them?

"I'm sorry you didn't know before now," Hope said, "but I'm thankful God brought you here in time, so you could choose the life you want."

340

"But I want both lives." As the words came out of my mouth, I realized how strange they sounded. Just a few months ago, I'd been praying that God would free me from this burden, and now He would. So why didn't it feel like freedom?

Maxwell squeezed my hand and brought my whirling thoughts to a standstill. I loved him, with all my heart, and knew that I couldn't leave him. God had worked so many miracles for us to be together. And as much as I'd miss my life in 1927, it was nothing compared to how devastated I'd be if I lost Maxwell.

"There is so much to tell you," Hope said. "I would love if you'd stay for supper, if not for the night."

I had many questions for her, as well. And so much to think about.

"And I long to hear about 1927," Hope said. "My twin sister lives there. Her name is Grace. She chose to stay with her husband, Lucas."

I frowned, remembering those names. "Lucas and Grace Voland?"

Hope's mouth parted at the name. "Yes, how do you know her?"

"Grace Voland is a time-crosser?"

"Yes."

"I met her in Washington, DC, when Charles Lindbergh returned after his flight over the Atlantic Ocean."

"Someone finally made it over the ocean?" Hope asked with a grin. "I was the first woman to fly an aeroplane over the English Chanel in 1912. I wondered how long it would take to get over the ocean."

"You're *that* Hope?"

She grinned. "I am!"

Now it made sense why she looked familiar. Her identical twin sister was Grace Voland.

Hope's face was shining. "Oh, but it feels good to meet someone who understands!"

"Grace has two daughters—"

"I know." Hope smiled at her husband. "Lydia and Kathryn."

"You know her daughter's names? But how?"

Hope laughed. "I have much to tell you. And though I've already said a lot that is hard to understand, there is one thing that *I* don't even understand. You see, Grace and I are identical twin sisters. Both our mother from this path and the one in the future were time-crossers, which is probably why there are two of us. But even more miraculous is that we both gave birth to the same daughter. Lydia was born to me and Isaac in 1694, but she was also born to Grace and Lucas in 1914. From the moment she could talk, she told me all about Grace's life in Washington, DC."

"You share the same daughter?" I could hardly believe it. "When I met Grace and Lydia, I had no idea. What about Grace's other daughter, Kathryn?"

"She is also a time-crosser, but she had a different second family. I believe she was born in England in the 1860s."

I put my hand up to my head. "There's just so much to take in."

"If you think this is a lot," Isaac said with a laugh, "wait until you meet the rest of the Howlett family. There are dozens of time-crossers. I can't keep track."

"Dozens of them?" I asked Hope, feeling surprised at each turn. I had gone from thinking I was the only one to learning there were dozens of others.

She patted my hand. "One thing at a time, dear. For now, we'll get you fed, and then I'll tell you all about them. If you choose to stay here after your birthday, there will be plenty of time to meet everyone."

My head was spinning, and Maxwell was sitting next to me, not saying a word. As much as I wanted to speak to Hope, I had more important things to discuss with Maxwell.

"May we have a moment alone?" I asked our hosts.

"Of course." Hope stood. "I'll see to that tea tray. Join us in the dining room when you're ready."

She and Isaac left the parlor, and I turned to Maxwell.

"You see?" he said with a sad smile on his face. "I told you that

God had gone before you. Your family is not cursed by witchcraft but blessed with a gift from God."

"But I must say goodbye to my other family tomorrow."

He still held my hand as hope brightened his smile. "Does that mean you know which life you're going to choose?"

"Aye," I said, incredulous. "I love you, Maxwell. I cannot imagine leaving you."

The grin he gave me was like a burst of sunshine on a cloudy day. It was full of the promise of more tomorrows. "Then today is truly the best day of my life." He placed his hands on my cheeks. "I love hearing you say my name, Caroline. It would honor me if you'd take it to be your own."

"Mistress Maxwell MacDougal?"

"Aye."

I kissed Maxwell there in Hope's parlor, reveling in his love.

I'd found the answers that I was seeking, and they were better than I had even imagined.

Yet, there would be great pain in my life after tomorrow. A pain that had already begun to twist my heart.

30

SEPTEMBER 1, 1927
MINNEAPOLIS, MINNESOTA

It felt strange to open my eyes on Dupont Street, knowing that this would be the last time. Tomorrow would be my twenty-first birthday in 1727, and I planned to stay awake past midnight. If what Hope told me was true, I would not wake up in 1927 after that.

I had never cried so many tears before in my life, but as I watched the rain dripping from the eaves on the yellow house I'd grown up in, I couldn't stop them from falling. This was what I wanted, wasn't it? To live like a normal person. To have answers to my questions.

Now that I did, I wasn't as relieved as I thought I would be. It only added more heartache. How was I supposed to tell my parents? Instead of celebrating my birthday tomorrow, they would mourn my death. It was too much to contemplate and made me feel panicked.

The smell of coffee and bacon wafted up to my room, so I forced myself out of bed and dressed in one of my favorite outfits. People often talked about what they would do if they knew it was their last day to live. In many ways, this was my last day, at least in this life, and I knew what I would do. I wanted to spend it with the people I loved.

After I was dressed, I went downstairs and found my parents at the dining room table. Father was reading his newspaper, and Mother was reading a letter. Irene hadn't come down yet, but I was thankful for this bit of time alone with my parents. And I was thankful they knew about my time-crossing so I could tell them what would happen.

I hated to think of their despair.

"Good morning, Caroline," Mother said as she looked up from her letter and smiled. "You're right on time. Ingrid just brought in breakfast."

"I'm not hungry," I said as I took a seat at the table.

"Don't you feel well?" she asked me.

"No." I felt like I was going to be very sick.

Father lowered his newspaper and eyed me with concern. "What's wrong?"

I folded my hands on my lap, trying to find the words. "I have some very important news, but I fear it will shock and upset you."

I had their attention as they set aside their newspaper and letter.

"What's happened?" Mother asked. "You look like someone has died."

I needed to speak quietly so Ingrid wouldn't hear. "I found a family member in Salem Village in 1727 who was a time-crosser. Her name is Hope Abbott."

Both of my parents frowned at me, but neither one spoke.

"Hope told me about some of the time-crossing rules. She said that the birthmark on my chest is what marks me as a time-crosser. During supper, she told me that some of her children have the mark and others don't. My mother in the 1700s had the mark, and her mother before her, and her mother before her. I don't know how it started, but through the centuries, time-crossers have learned many of the rules that govern the gift." I was talking fast, but I needed to get it all out. There was so much I had learned from Hope last night and so much more I wanted to know.

"This is all fantastical," Father said. "Is it really true, Caroline?"

"I don't know how, but it is." I took another deep breath. "Hope also told me the hardest news of all. She said that on my twenty-first birthday, I must choose which life I want to keep and which one I want to forfeit. Whichever one I want to keep, I will stay awake there until midnight."

"What happens to the other one?" Mother asked, engrossed in my explanations.

"My body will die in the one I don't want to keep," I said quietly. "My conscious mind will stay with the one I do keep—and that will be it. I will never cross time again."

Neither one spoke as they stared at me.

"If what you say is true," Father said, "then of course you'll choose this one."

I could no longer meet their gazes as I studied the fruit bowl in the center of the table. "I—I will choose 1727."

The only sounds I could hear were Ingrid's muted humming in the kitchen, the grandfather clock ticking in the foyer, and the rain tapping on the windowpanes.

"Don't be absurd," Mother finally said. "You cannot die here tomorrow, Caroline. I won't have it."

I finally looked up. "I'm sorry, Mother. But I'm in love with a man named Maxwell MacDougal in 1727, and he's asked me to marry him. I've said yes."

Her lips parted as Father straightened in his chair. "What's this?" he asked. "A man has been courting you in 1727 and you haven't mentioned him? What kind of a man is he?"

My hands trembled as I said, "He was a pirate, but he's now a sinner saved by grace, Father."

Ever so slowly, a smile tilted up the edges of his mouth. "I'm pleased to hear that."

"How can you say that, Daniel?" Mother asked. "Our daughter has just told us she's dying here tomorrow to marry a pirate!"

Father reached across the table and took my trembling hand. "Our God is timeless, Caroline, eternal. To Him, a day is like a thousand years, and a thousand years is like a day. So whether you live in 1727 or 1927, your eternal home is in heaven with Him. It is your soul, and the soul of Maxwell, that most concerns me. I will miss you, but I know that we'll meet again one day."

"Is that all it takes to appease you?" Mother asked. "This is our only daughter."

"She has never been ours, Marian." He laid his other hand on his wife's arm. "She's a gift from God, ours for a short time. We've never had a guarantee that we'd have her forever. She could marry someone and move to Africa, and we'd never see her again. Her life is in God's hands. And if this is what He is calling her to do, then we will have to make peace with that decision."

I could see the struggle in Mother's heart. It was written all over her face, but she was strong, and she would rally, as always. Father's strength would be hers until she could muster enough on her own. I had faith in both my parents.

A noise on the step told us that Irene was about to join us.

"Let's not ruin today with this news," Father instructed. "We'll invite everyone over to celebrate your birthday early, and you can say your goodbyes—but you won't need to tell them it's final."

"Thank you," I said as I took my hand back. It had not eased my pain, but knowing that Father would hold up the family put my mind at peace.

As the day progressed, I found joy in the simple things I wouldn't have in 1727. Indoor plumbing, electricity, the telephone, and the automobile. We went on a drive through Minneapolis and into Saint Paul, and then came home for an evening with my family.

Thomas and Alice came for a short while, but they left before Ruth and the children arrived. It was the only way my parents could handle the situation for now. I was sad that I didn't get to say goodbye to Andrew, but he'd made his decisions, and I couldn't force him to turn away from them. I would pray for him, as I knew my parents and Ruth would, and hope he could find his way back to Ruth and the children.

But it was the arrival of Lewis that I anticipated the most. As the children played in the parlor and my parents visited with Ruth and Irene, I saw Lewis pull up in his Chevy.

I excused myself and walked out onto the porch.

It was still raining, so I waited for him. He got out of his vehicle and raced up the sidewalk to the house. When he reached the porch, he looked up and smiled.

"Hello, Carrie."

"Hello, Lewis."

"I was surprised to get your invitation today."

"I'm happy you could come. Will you sit out here with me for a minute?"

"Of course."

We went to the swing and took a seat.

The rain fell in a steady cadence, dripping on the green leaves of the trees and the blades of grass in the lawn. Mother's mums were just starting to bloom, and they opened their petals to the life-giving rain.

"I don't know how to tell you this," I said to Lewis, "but today is my last day here."

"What?" He turned to me. "What does that mean?"

"I spoke to one of my relatives in Salem Village yesterday, and she told me that I must choose which life I want on my twenty-first birthday. I've decided to stay in 1727."

"For Marcus?" he asked.

"His real name is Maxwell MacDougal, and yes. I'm staying for him." I explained to Lewis how we'd gone to the governor, and Maxwell had been given a pardon. "He's a good man, and I love him very much."

"You'd have to, to give up all of this."

"It won't be easy, but I'm grateful I have Hope to help guide me. I also have other family members there." I pulled a letter from my pocket, one I'd written earlier in the day. "This is for Annie. I've explained everything to her. Will you see that she gets it? She deserves to understand this gift we've been given."

He took the letter and slowly nodded. "I will."

"Thank you."

We continued to swing, neither of us speaking for a moment. A gentle breeze blew onto the porch, ruffling my hair and the hem of my skirt.

"I love you, Carrie," he said as he touched the edges of the envelope. "I've loved you my whole life, and I don't think I'll ever stop."

I took his hand in both of mine. "I love you, too, Lewis."

"Just not in the way I'd always hoped."

"I'm sorry."

He let out a sigh and lifted my hand to his lips to give it a kiss. "I am, too. But I'm starting to realize it's for the best."

"Because of Irene?"

He nodded and smiled, then he stood and drew me to my feet. "Come on, Curly Carrie. Let's not waste this last night together mourning the past or the future."

He started to tug me into the house, but I stopped him. "Be good to her," I said.

His face softened, and he said, "I'll tease her incessantly."

I smiled and gave Lewis a hug and then we walked into the house and joined the others.

Saying goodbye hurt more than I could imagine, but Father would help my family and friends grieve. And someday, we would all be reunited again.

Goodbye wouldn't last forever.

31

SEPTEMBER 2, 1727
BOSTON, MASSACHUSETTS

I had not imagined that my birthday would also be my wedding day. As I walked up the steps of Christ Church, not far from Boston Harbor, my heart skipped a beat. If all had gone as planned, Maxwell would be waiting for me at the front of the church.

It had been a whirlwind of a day. My heart grieved everything I'd lost in 1927, but the reality of it hadn't quite hit me yet. We'd woken up in Hope and Isaac's home that morning, and Maxwell had told me that he was going to Boston to acquire special permission from the governor to be married without reading the required banns. He asked the Abbotts if they could take me to Christ Church at six o'clock that evening, and, if the governor agreed, we'd be married.

Hope had been a great comfort to me as I shared my grief with her. She offered me her love and promised to help me carry the pain. It alleviated my fears to know that she had gone through the same thing and had no regrets. She missed everything she'd forfeited, but God had strengthened her, as He was strengthening me.

I looked up at the brick building with the beautiful white steeple and for the first time in my life, I felt close to God. Knowing that I wasn't the only one with this gift, and that others had gone before me, had eased my troubled heart. I saw the hand of God in my life and knew, with certainty, that He had brought me to this time and place. My life hadn't been a curse, but a blessing, one I wanted to share with the people I loved.

Christ Church was only a few years old, and the Abbotts told me it had become a place for the new residents of Boston to find community. Hope whispered that it would one day become known as Old North Church and would be instrumental in the American War for Independence.

"Two lanterns will be hung in the steeple the night the British arrive," Hope said quietly about a future event. One I was familiar with from my 1927 path. "Paul Revere and the others will know to ride toward Lexington and Concord to alert the militia that the British are coming by sea."

"'Tis strange that the American Revolution is still fifty years away," I said just as quietly, though Isaac seemed aware of many things his wife had told him.

"'Tis strange, indeed," Hope said. "But there's something else you must know about your gift, Caroline. You must never knowingly change history. If you do, you will forfeit the path you try to change."

I paused as I stood on the steps of the church that would one day become famous around the world. I would heed her words carefully.

The large white door creaked as Isaac opened it. Evening had started to set, and the interior of the beautiful church was dim. White pew boxes dominated the main floor, and a gallery encircled the space overhead.

After Maxwell had left that morning, I bathed and dressed in the beautiful gown he had purchased for me; then I had gone with Hope and Isaac to meet some of the family who lived in Salem. It had been hard to wait, and harder still knowing I would not wake up in 1927 tomorrow, but the anticipation of becoming Maxwell's bride had fortified my spirits.

Now, as I entered the church, a new anxiety overtook me, and I was tempted to fidget. Instead, I took a deep breath to settle my nerves, and the urge to fidget subsided.

The certainty I felt that this was the right choice, and that Maxwell would honor me every day of my life, washed over me like a wave.

"May I?" Isaac asked as he offered his arm to me.

I accepted it, and we started down the aisle with Hope ahead of us.

Two men entered the nave. One was wearing clerical robes, and the other was Maxwell.

My heart sped at the sight of him, and when our gazes met, his smile was so brilliant, I couldn't look away.

The rector and Maxwell waited for us near the chancel. Hope greeted them and then stepped aside so Issac could deliver me to my groom.

I had no flowers, no wedding veil, and no maid of honor to attend me. But I had Maxwell, and that was all I needed.

The ceremony was quick yet heartfelt as I pledged my life to Maxwell's. It was more of a civil ceremony than a religious one, as was the custom in Massachusetts, but I was thankful Maxwell had asked me to marry him in a church. I wished Father and Mother could be there, though it pleased me that they knew who I was marrying and that Father had given his blessing.

When the ceremony came to an end, Maxwell smiled at me and said, "'Tis done, Mistress MacDougal."

"Nay," I said as I stood on tiptoe to kiss him. "'Tis just begun."

The Abbotts were staying with one of their seven children in Boston. After we walked outside, they said farewell and made us promise to visit soon.

As soon as they moved out of sight, I turned to my husband and said, "And where will we spend our wedding night?"

Maxwell kissed me deeply as we stood on the church steps in the gloaming. When he broke the kiss, he said, "I'm taking you somewhere very special."

He led me toward the harbor as we reveled in the newness of our marriage. He held my hand and stopped to kiss me several times, not caring what the passersby thought.

When we arrived at the harbor, I smiled to see Hawk waiting at the long wharf.

"Are we going to the *Ocean Curse*?" I asked Maxwell.

"Nay, 'tis now the *Redemption*, lass. And it will be the first of many ships in our merchant fleet."

Our fleet. I liked how that sounded.

"Welcome, Mistress MacDougal," Hawk said with a wide grin as he took my hand and helped me onto the launch.

The sun was just setting on the western horizon as the crew—no longer pirates—rowed us to the *Redemption*. It was the same ship, sitting in the same harbor, yet it was a new vessel, for a new purpose.

Just like Maxwell and me.

When we reached the ship, Maxwell helped me to board. It felt strange and wonderful to return to a ship that had once been my prison and was now part of my freedom.

The crew had waited for our arrival, and the second we stepped onto the main deck, a cheer arose from those who had chosen to stay. Timothy was there, cheering the loudest.

"Timothy went home to see his father," Maxwell said. "But he learned that his father's tale of the Queen's Dowry was just that—a tall tale."

"Will you ever return to look for the treasure?" I asked him.

"Nay." Maxwell smiled and lifted my hand to kiss it. "My treasure is standing beside me."

He placed his hand at the small of my back and led me up the steps to the quarterdeck. Everything had been scrubbed and was gleaming under the setting sun.

He opened the door to the outer room, and we walked to the captain's cabin together.

When he opened the second door, I caught my breath, surprised at what I found.

"Does it please you?" Maxwell asked as he stood close to my back and wrapped his arms around my waist.

"Aye, 'tis very pleasing. But how did you do it?"

"I came to the ship this morning and told Hawk and Timothy my plans, and they worked all day to make it happen."

The captain's cabin had been completely made over, from the new table and chairs to the curtain and bedding in the alcove. The walls were freshly whitewashed, and the floors and windows scrubbed.

A meal was on the table, complete with two silver candelabras with dripping candles.

But the most amazing gift was the wall of bookshelves that had been added since the last time I'd stood in the room. They were filled with all of Maxwell's books and others, besides.

"Timothy must have bought out a bookseller," I said with a laugh as I laid my head against his chest. "'Tis a new room."

"Aye. A new room, for a new life." He turned me around until we were face-to-face, and then he slipped his arms around me. "My hope is that you fill it with the beauty of your song, both day and night, because you never have to hide it again, love."

I laid my hands on his cheeks, tears of joy coming to my eyes. "Thank you."

He grinned. "Have I told you how bonnie you are?"

"Aye."

"Or how much I love you?"

"Aye," I said with a smile.

"Well, I'm telling you again."

I encircled my arms around the back of his neck, pulling him down to kiss me. "You don't have to," I whispered as I gave him the kiss I'd longed to offer since I'd fallen in love with him.

He lifted me off my feet, heedless of the weight of my skirts, and carried me to the alcove, forgetting about our supper.

Epilogue

SEPTEMBER 5, 1727
CAPE COD, MASSACHUSETTS

We'd enjoyed two days of an uninterrupted honeymoon in the captain's cabin in Boston Harbor, but on the third day we knew we needed to return to reality.

The *Redemption* had laid anchor in Provincetown Harbor at the tip of Cape Cod that afternoon as Maxwell and I stood on the quarterdeck. The salted sea breeze tickled the tendrils of hair at my cheeks, and the waves lapped against the side of the ship.

"You think your family is still here?" I asked him.

"I don't know, but this is where my father came and where my mam was heading when we were overtaken by Edward Zale fifteen years ago." He looked down at me, his brown eyes filled with unquestioning love. "'Tis a long time. They might not be alive, or they might have moved on."

"If that's true, then someone will know the answers."

As we boarded the launch, Maxwell held fast to his family Bible.

Before we left Boston, I had penned a letter to my grandfather with a postscript to Nanny, letting them know where I would be living. I spared Grandfather the details about Maxwell being an ex-pirate and simply told him I had married a

355

successful merchant and was living in Boston. I apologized for leaving without warning and explained that I had gone to look for my mother and found her family. At the end, I had included an invitation for him to visit if he would like. Hawk had posted it for me, and I was already anxious about whether Grandfather would respond. Only time would tell if he would forgive me and we could move forward.

We were soon on a long wharf, walking toward the main thoroughfare in Provincetown. I was still wearing my wedding gown, though Maxwell had told me that as soon as we returned to Boston, we would find a home and I was to buy as many dresses as I wanted. I was pleased with this one—not only a gift, but the gown I'd worn to become his wife. It would always hold a special place in my heart.

Hawk went with us, as was his custom, and we entered the first business we found on Commercial Street, which was an inn.

The innkeeper eyed us with curiosity. But in our fine clothes and with a bodyguard, not to mention my husband holding a large Bible, he probably believed us to be trustworthy people of means, so he smiled pleasantly.

"How may I help ye?" he asked.

"I'm looking for a family by the name of MacDougal," Maxwell said. "Liam or Alish MacDougal."

"Aye," the innkeeper said. "Liam MacDougal lives not far from here. Continue down Commercial Street and take yer first left onto Center Street. His home is the second on the right. The white house with the black shutters."

"Thank you," Maxwell said as he reached for my hand, and we walked out of the inn. It had become second nature to hold hands, to touch whenever we were in proximity to each other. I loved his physical touch. The reminder of his love and affection.

Commercial Street was narrow and full of businesses, most of them associated with the fishing industry that dominated the cape. The sound of the ocean crashing onto the nearby shore was another reminder of the daily lives of the cape's inhabitants.

"I'll wait in the tavern," Hawk said as he stopped at the nearest public house and nodded for us to continue.

We took a left onto Center Street, which was narrower than Commercial Street and lined with quaint houses. The second on the right was a one-story white clapboard home with black shutters. It sat on the street, with no front yard.

"Are you ready?" I asked my husband as we paused on the road.

"I don't know if they'll even want to speak to me," he said. "I've hurt both of them deeply."

I squeezed his hand and smiled. "Even if they don't, we have much to be thankful for."

"Aye." He returned my smile. "And they cannot be displeased with my choice of wife."

I smiled as he knocked on the front door.

It opened a minute later, and a woman stood over the threshold. She appeared to be in her midforties, and she had the same beautiful brown eyes as Maxwell. She had to squint into the sun to look at us, but when she realized who was standing before her, she let out a cry of delight and threw herself into Maxwell's arms.

"My son," she said as she wept. "You've come home."

He held her tight, lifting her off her feet. "Mam," he said, burying his face in her shoulder. "I didn't think you'd want to see me again."

"Maxwell, my love." She continued to weep as he set her on her feet, and she put her hands on either side of his face. "You've grown into such a braw young man." Her gaze turned to me. "And who is this bonnie woman?"

"My wife," Maxwell said with pride. "Caroline MacDougal."

She put her hands on my face next and smiled as if I was another of her long-lost children. "'Tis pleased I am to meet you, daughter."

I entered her embrace, feeling the love from a woman whom I'd never met, but who still accepted me wholeheartedly, because I belonged with her son.

"I have something for you, Mam," Maxwell said as he held out the family Bible. "You told me to not forget where I came from, or who my Maker is. I've come all this way to tell you that I haven't forgotten either."

Her joyful cry filled my heart to overflowing as she took the Bible and gave him another hug. "You don't know the thousands of prayers I've uttered for you," she said. "Hours on my knees, asking God to be with you and guide you home."

"Your prayers were answered," he said, "and Caroline is the reason."

Alish took my hand and tugged me into her home. "Come," she said, "and tell me your tale. I know 'tis a good one."

I turned to Maxwell as I smiled, and the look on his face was so tender, I would remember it always.

"Liam," Alish called toward the back of the house as we entered, "we have visitors!"

Maxwell's shoulders stiffened at the sound of his father's name. But Alish didn't seem to notice as she led us into the cozy kitchen where a table sat in one corner and a large fireplace dominated the back wall. She gently set the Bible on the table, giving it a loving look before moving a hook over the flames and putting a teakettle to boil. "You're just in time for afternoon tea."

"Mam," Maxwell said as he joined her near the fireplace. "Has Father changed?"

There was a sad smile from his mother, and then she said, "Aye, some things have changed, and other things are the same, but I think you'll be pleased with the man he has become. He's a fisherman now, in charge of his own destiny. That has a way of changing a man." She paused and then touched Maxwell's hand. "My greatest regret was the way things were. The reason you left. I can't change the past, or how he treated you, but I pray you can forgive him."

"I have."

Her lips trembled, and she nodded as she gathered her emotions.

I sat at the table, watching mother and son, my heart warming at their exchange.

But when an older man appeared at the door to the kitchen,

I held my breath. His hair was graying at the temples, and there were wrinkles around his eyes, but he looked like an older version of Maxwell.

Maxwell turned, and his father stared at him for a moment, clearly not recognizing him after so many years.

"Father," Maxwell said.

The look on Liam's face shifted from confusion to clarity and then joy. He took two giant steps across the room and embraced Maxwell in a hug that seemed to take Maxwell's breath away.

"My son," Liam said as he began to weep. "I didn't think I'd ever see you on this side of heaven."

It took Maxwell a moment, but he returned his father's embrace, and I had a clear picture of his face.

It was filled with relief.

When they separated and I was introduced to Liam, he embraced me as Alish had done, welcoming me into his life and his heart without knowing a thing about me.

Maxwell put his arm around me as we sat next to each other at the table, drinking tea and eating sweet biscuits, telling them the story of how we'd met. We left out the part about my time-crossing, but the tale was filled with adventure and the miraculous hand of God, nonetheless.

As I told the story, peace settled inside my heart, and I started to realize the gift that God had given to me. I had gone on a quest to find my mother and to learn the truth about my time-crossing family, but in the process, I had discovered a new family. The family I had created with Maxwell.

I was eager to learn about my other time-crossing family members, and I had so many questions that I would ask Hope. I wanted to know all I could about her and Grace and their beautiful children. I was also excited to get to know Liam and Alish and watch Maxwell's relationship with them heal.

As I sat with my husband, in a quiet little cottage in Cape Cod, I realized I finally had what I'd wanted all along.

Peace.

Historical Note

There are so many historical elements in *Across the Ages* that have personal meaning to me, and I loved sharing them in this story. I also loved setting one of Caroline's paths in Minnesota in 1927. It allowed me to mention my hometown of Little Falls, which was also Charles Lindbergh's hometown! My editor called this book my tribute to Minnesota.

Speaking of Charles Lindbergh . . . my love for storytelling, and especially for sharing history, came from the ten years that I worked at his boyhood home as an employee of the Minnesota Historical Society. Lindbergh went on to become a controversial figure in his lifetime, but in 1927, he was the most popular and beloved person in the world. He is a minor character in *Across the Ages*, but everything I shared about him, his flight, and his Goodwill Tour are true. It's estimated that one out of every four Americans went out to see Lindbergh on his tour. It lasted ninety-five days, and he stopped in eighty-two cities, including twenty-three state capitals, making speeches at most of the stops and promoting aviation as we know it today.

Another important man in *Across the Ages* is Caroline's father, Reverend Daniel Baldwin. Reverend Baldwin is inspired by a real preacher named Billy Sunday. Billy was born in Iowa and went on to become a professional baseball player who gave his life to the Lord. His charismatic preaching and his wife's managerial skills allowed their ministry to grow. Eventually, Billy was the most popular preacher in America, holding large tent meetings across the country. It's estimated that he preached twenty thousand sermons, about forty-two per month, to over a hundred million people between 1896–1935, and over 1.2 million people came forward to give their lives to Christ. He was well-received in all economic and social circles and lived a comfortable—but not extravagant—lifestyle, though his ministry was very profitable. Unfortunately, his family suffered because of his long absences away. A nanny raised the Sundays' three sons, and each one grew up to engage in the very activities that Billy preached against, causing several women to blackmail the Sundays to keep the scandals quiet.

Opposing Billy Sunday were the notorious gangsters of the 1920s. Many people don't know that Saint Paul was a hotbed for gangsters during Prohibition because of the O'Connor Layover Agreement. Just as I described in the book, Saint Paul was a sanctuary city for those who wanted to avoid the law. All they needed to do was check in with Dapper Dan Hogan at the Green Lantern saloon on Wabasha Street, pay him a fee, and promise not to commit a crime while they were in the city. They'd often tell Hogan where they were staying in case the feds came calling and they needed to be alerted. The Saint Paul police also turned a blind eye on speakeasies and brothels if they were being paid. One bit of history I had to change involves Castle Royal in the Wabasha Street Caves. Castle Royal wasn't established until 1933, but it's such a cool piece of history, I wanted to include it in 1927. The caves are still open to this day, and you can take a tour, get a swing dancing lesson, and host a party there! It's a fun place to visit if you get the chance.

The other character that is inspired by a real person—or rather, persons—is Caroline's mother, Anne. Anne's life in 1927 resembles that of Bonnie Parker, more commonly known as the female half of Bonnie and Clyde. In 1727, Anne's life was inspired by the female pirate known as Anne Bonny. As I researched these two women with similar names, their lives had way more in common than I ever imagined. Bonnie Parker was born in Texas in 1910, and a few days before her sixteenth birthday, she married a man named Roy Thornton. Though they didn't divorce, they were only together for a couple of years. In 1930, while staying with a friend, Bonnie met Clyde Barrows. From all accounts, it was love at first sight, and they were together from then until their deaths in 1934. Clyde had a criminal record from cracking safes, stealing cars, and robbing stores. He was arrested for auto theft shortly after they met, but Bonnie smuggled in a weapon for him to use to escape prison. Not long after, he was arrested again and suffered unspeakable assault in prison, which led him to kill his abuser—though another inmate took the blame. He was paroled in 1932, but everyone said he left the prison a different man, hardened and bitter. People believe that the killing and robbing spree he went on the next two years before his death was not for fame or money, but to take revenge on the Texas prison system for the abuses he endured. Bonnie and Clyde caused terror from Texas to Minnesota and were eventually ambushed by a posse of officers from Texas and Louisiana in 1934.

The pirate, Anne Bonny, was born in Ireland at an unknown date (perhaps around 1700). Her father was a lawyer, and her mother was his servant. He was married to another woman, so he took Anne and her mother to the Carolinas and set up a law practice in Charleston, eventually purchasing a plantation. Anne ran off with a poor sailor when she was very young, but when they arrived in Nassau, she met Calico Jack Rackham, who purchased a divorce for her. She lived with Jack on his pirate ship as his lover, and to avoid issue with the other crew members, Anne dressed as a man. Jack didn't realize it, but another one of his crew members was also a woman! Mary Read and Anne became good friends, and when their ship was captured a few months later by a sloop captain under a commission from the governor of Jamaica, Rackham was hanged, but both Anne's and Mary's lives were spared because they were pregnant. Mary died in prison, but Anne's fate is unknown. Some suspect her father intervened on her behalf and took her back to the American colonies. It was her story that first inspired my idea for Caroline's story. I wanted to know what happened to Anne and Calico Jack's baby!

And, finally, I can't end this note without mentioning my pirates. Many of the pirates who became famous had very short lives, but they were filled with adventure, drama, and intrigue. While Marcus Zale's life isn't inspired by a single pirate, his early life is inspired by a young man named John King, who, at the age of nine or ten, was on a merchant ship overtaken by the pirate Sam Bellamy. John was traveling with his mother, and he begged the pirates to take him with them. They were so amused at this offer, they had him pledge an oath of loyalty in front of his mother and took him away. Sadly, he met his fate less than six months later when Bellamy's ship went down in a storm. Some of the crew who survived the shipwreck were arrested and later hanged in Boston, which caused the notorious pirate Blackbeard to take revenge on New England's coast, making him famous. Just like Anne and Calico Jack's baby, John King's life fascinated me, and I wanted to understand why a boy would give his life over to pirates—and then what might have happened if he'd lived. Thus, Marcus Zale's character was born.

The Golden Age of Piracy is a fascinating time in history. If you'd like to learn more, I'd recommend reading *The Republic of Pirates: Being the True and Surprising Story of the Caribbean Pirates and the Man Who Brought Them Down* by Colin Woodard, and *A General History of the Pyrates* by Captain Charles Johnson, a contemporary of the famous pirates. No one knows the real author, but there is much speculation. If you'd like to know more about Charles A. Lindbergh, I'd recommend *Lindbergh* by A. Scott Berg, and if you'd like to know more about Saint Paul during the Prohibition years, you should read *John Dillinger Slept Here: A Crooks' Tour of Crime and Corruption in St. Paul, 1920–1936* by Paul Maccabee.

I hope the history in *Across the Ages* has intrigued you as much as it intrigued me.

Acknowledgments

The TIMELESS series was originally slated to end after the third story, *For a Lifetime*, but the reader response has been so positive that when I shared my idea for *Across the Ages* with my publisher, they were quick to agree to another story. I'm honored and blessed to work with one of the best teams in the business at Bethany House Fiction and Baker Publishing Group. When I visit the Bethany House offices, everyone from the art department to sales, marketing, editorial, and beyond tells me how much they love this series. They are not just publishing my books; they are reading them, discussing them, and are excited to share them with our readers. That means the world to me! Thank you to my editors, Jessica Sharpe and Bethany Lenderink, for your great feedback and help in making this manuscript shine. Thank you, also, to the rockstar marketing team of Raela Schoenherr, Anne Van Solkema, Joyce Perez, and Lindsay Schubert for all your efforts in promoting my book. And to Jenny Parker, the senior art director, and her team for creating the incomparable covers for my TIMELESS series. I'm grateful to partner with all of you.

Thank you also goes out to my agent, Wendy Lawton, and the whole team at Books & Such Literary Agency. I love being part of the Bookie family. Thank you, also, to my mastermind writing group who have come alongside me to do this writing life together. I can't wait for all the fun things we have planned! And to my other writing friends, near and far, for all your love, support, wisdom, and knowledge. The Christian writing community is amazing.

I always save the best for last. I want to thank my husband, David, for his sacrificial love and for the countless ways that he has encouraged me and supported my dream to be a published author. Not to mention how he continues to ease my daily burdens so I can make time to write (he's a phenomenal cook!). To my oldest daughter, Ellis, for her keen interest and excitement in my stories and in the history surrounding them. She challenges me to mine deep for the gold nuggets of information that bring my stories to life. To my second daughter, Maryn, for her unwavering belief in me and her emotional maturity as I discuss my characters and their lives. Her insights into the heart of my stories makes me love them even more. And to my twin boys, Judah and Asher, whose adventurous spirits give me ideas. Their observations about the world around them offer me unique perspectives that almost always come to life in my characters. I would not be the author I am today without my family.

Finally, I want to thank God for the gift He gave to me and the dream He placed in my heart to share stories. I truly believe that the highest form of worship is to create with the Creator. To use the gifts He has given us to bear good fruit in this world. It is my greatest honor to write stories that glorify and edify Him.

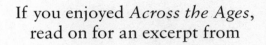

If you enjoyed *Across the Ages*,
read on for an excerpt from

Every Hour until Then

Available May 2025

1

OCTOBER 31, 1887
LONDON, ENGLAND

A cold wind rattled the window frame in my bedroom at 11 Wilton Crescent as the edges of a tree branch scraped across the glass. I jumped and looked up from the book I was reading. *The Strange Case of Dr. Jekyll and Mr. Hide* fell out of my hands and onto the floor. The story had been published the year before by Robert Louis Stevenson, but it was my first time reading it, and I was both enthralled and terrified. I retrieved the book and then buried myself deeper under the thick cover on my bed, trying to remind myself that the story was just that—a story—and there was nothing to be afraid of. There was no madman on the loose.

My candle flickered and then died out, leaving only the soft glow from the embers in my fireplace to light the room. I'd been reading for so long, the wick had burned to the bottom and would need to be replaced.

As the wind continued to howl, I lay for a moment in the dark room, wondering if I should set the book aside and go to sleep or if I should get up and look for another candle. It was after midnight, so if I went to sleep, I would wake up in my other life in 1937 and have to wait an entire day to return to 1887 to finish the story. I was working on an important exhibit at the Smithsonian with personal items belonging to George Washington, but not even that fascinating project could hold my attention if I couldn't finish Dr. Jekyll and Mr. Hyde's story tonight.

It was the strange reality of my existence, living two lives at the same time. When I went to sleep tonight in 1887, I would wake up tomorrow in 1937. After I spent the day in 1937, I'd go to sleep and then wake up in 1887 again, without any time passing while I was away. I had two identical bodies but one conscious mind that went between them. It had been this way since I was born and would continue until my twenty-fifth birthday in less than three years. On that day, May 20, 1890, I would have to choose which life I wanted to keep and which one I would forfeit forever.

But I wasn't thinking about my choice tonight. All I could think about was how the book would end.

With a sigh, I pushed aside the covers and set my bare feet on the thick rug.

The wind suddenly calmed, and the unexpected stillness allowed another sound to capture my attention.

I moved to my door and pressed my ear against the panel, the terrifying story of Dr. Jekyll and Mr. Hyde too fresh in my mind to find the courage to walk into the hallway without a candle.

Until I realized someone was crying.

My sister's room was next to mine, and my parents' rooms were on the floor below us. The house servants slept on the fifth floor, high above the rest. There should have been no noise outside my bedroom—yet I heard it again.

Slowly, I opened my door and stepped into the hallway. "Mary?" I asked. "Is that you?"

My younger sister's bedroom door was ajar, and the sound of weeping came from that direction.

"Where will you go, Miss Mary?" Sarah Danbury, Mary's lady's maid, asked in a desperate voice. "Especially on a night like this?"

Concerned, I walked to Mary's room and opened the door a little further. A candle offered a bit of light as Mary stood near a satchel, dressed in a dark travel suit, filling her bag with a few items of clothing. She wiped her wet cheek on her shoulder but kept packing.

Danbury stood nearby, helpless, as she wrung her hands together.

"What are you doing?" I asked Mary.

My sister looked up quickly, clearly surprised to see me. She had just turned nineteen, but she was delicate and looked much younger, especially as she cried. Her dark red hair, the same shade as mine, was caught back in a low chignon with tendrils falling around her pretty face. When her gaze met mine, her brown eyes glistened with fear. "Kathryn."

"What are you doing?" I asked again as I walked into the room. "Why are you packing?"

Mary glanced at her maid and nodded for her to leave.

Danbury bit her bottom lip and looked like she might try to protest, but she knew it wasn't her place to debate with her mistress. With a slight curtsey, and a distressed look in my direction, Danbury left Mary's room, closing the door behind her.

"Now can you tell me?" I asked Mary.

She wiped away her tears as she went to her bureau and pulled out several pairs of stockings before returning to her satchel to stuff them inside. "I'm sorry, Kathryn."

"This is absurd," I said to my sister as I investigated the satchel to see what she was packing. "Where are you going?"

"I can't tell you." She sniffed and swallowed hard. "But I can't stay here."

I frowned, truly perplexed. Our father was Sir Bernard Kelly, a renowned physician and respected author. Our mother was Mrs. Agatha Kelly, a leading member of Victorian society and a patron of the arts. Mary and I were rarely allowed to leave the house without a proper chaperone during the day, let alone in the middle of the night, alone. It wasn't safe, nor was it wise.

I took Mary's forearms, and I stopped her from packing her bag, forcing her to look at me.

Her eyes were swimming in more tears, and the anguish on her face broke my heart.

"What's wrong, Mary?" I asked gently. "You've been acting strange all week."

With a soft cry, she threw herself into my arms. "Oh, Kathryn," she wept bitterly. "I've ruined everything."

My lips parted as I held her close, a new thought gripping my heart. "Are you . . . in trouble? In a family way?"

"No." She shook her head and pulled back as she sank to her bed. "I wish it was that simple."

I sat beside her and took her clammy hand, my worry increasing. Mary was a beautiful, accomplished, and popular young woman. Her bright and cheerful disposition banished the darkest clouds and brought comfort to those who knew her. I couldn't think of a single person or situation that might bring her this much distress. "What in the world could be wrong?"

"I wish I could tell you, but if I did, you'd be in the same trouble, and I don't want you to get hurt. I have no choice. I must leave. If I stay—" She paused and shook her head. "There is no other option."

"I'm so confused," I said, softly moving aside a tendril of hair that had stuck to her wet cheek. "Do Father and Mother know you're leaving?"

Her entire body stiffened at my question, and she didn't meet my gaze.

"I can't waste another moment." She rose and wiped her cheeks again, her hands trembling.

As I stared, she closed her satchel and reached for a dark shawl before opening her bedroom door and slipping into the hallway.

I followed her, reaching for her hand, desperate to know what was happening.

"It's not safe out there for a single woman, especially at night," I said. The memory of Dr. Jekyll and Mr. Hyde was still fresh in my mind, though a fictional book was nothing compared to the realities of life on the streets of London. The Wilton Crescent neighborhood was safe enough, but we weren't far from Hyde Park, and we'd been warned since we were young not to wander there, especially toward dark.

Mary looked small and frightened but also determined as she pulled free of my hand and walked down the steps. She didn't hesitate on the second floor near my parents' bedroom doors, nor did she try to be quiet. I hoped my parents would come out to stop her.

I followed her into the foyer. "This is madness, Mary. You must tell me what's happening."

She paused only long enough to give me another hug, and then she said, "Goodbye, Kathryn. Don't forget that I love you."

I reached for her hand again, but she pulled away, and then I watched helplessly as she walked out the front door. Alone.

My heart was hammering as I tried to decide whether to follow her or go to my parents.

It didn't take long to choose. I ran up the steps to my father's bedroom door and pounded hard, doing something I would not have done under any other circumstance. I entered Father's room unbidden.

He stood near the front window, still dressed in his evening suit, looking down at the street that Mary had just entered.

"Father," I said as I joined him at the window. "Mary has just—"

"She is dead to us." He turned away from the window, his shoulders stiff with resolve. "I never want to hear her name mentioned again."

I stepped back as if I'd been struck. "What? Why?"

"Never again, Kathryn," he said in a loud voice, slicing his hand in the air with finality. I couldn't tell if he was angry or afraid, but his face had a fierce expression. "If you don't want to end up like her, I advise you to forget all about her. I do not want her name uttered in this house ever again."

"Forget?" Tears stung my eyes as I reached for his arm. "How can I forget my little sister?"

He pulled his arm away from my grasp and went to his door to open it. His gaze was hard as he said, "This is my last warning, Kathryn. Do not ask any more questions."

My legs were weak as I left his room, knowing I would not get any more answers from Mother. Instead, I raced down the stairs and returned to the foyer, desperate to catch up to Mary and talk some sense into her.

But when I opened the door and stepped onto the street, I was met with nothing but darkness and the swirling mist.

Mary was already gone.

Gabrielle Meyer is an ECPA bestselling author. She has worked for state and local historical societies and loves writing fiction inspired by real people, places, and events. She currently resides along the banks of the Mississippi River in central Minnesota with her husband and four children. By day, she's a busy homeschool mom, and by night, she pens fiction and nonfiction filled with hope. Find her online at GabrielleMeyer.com.

Sign Up for Gabrielle's Newsletter

Keep up to date with Gabrielle's latest news on book releases and events by signing up for her email list at the link below.

GabrielleMeyer.com

FOLLOW GABRIELLE ON SOCIAL MEDIA

Gabrielle Meyer, Author   @Gabrielle_Meyer   @MeyerGabrielle

More from Gabrielle Meyer

Libby has been given a powerful gift: to live one life in 1774 Colonial Williamsburg and the other in 1914 Gilded Age New York City. When she falls asleep in one life, she wakes up in the other without any time passing. On her twenty-first birthday, Libby must choose one path and forfeit the other—but how can she possibly decide when she has so much to lose?

When the Day Comes
TIMELESS #1

Maggie inherited a gift from her time-crossing parents that allows her to live three separate lives in 1861, 1941, and 2001. Each night, she goes to sleep in one time period and wakes up in another. She faces a difficult journey to discover her true self, while drawn to three worthy gentlemen, before she must choose one life to keep and the rest to lose.

In This Moment
TIMELESS #2

Identical twin sisters Grace and Hope are time-crossers who simultaneously live in 1692, as daughters of a tavern owner during the Salem Witch Trials, and in 1912, as an aviatrix and a journalist. As their twenty-fifth birthday approaches, they will each have to choose one life to keep and one to leave behind forever—no matter the cost.

For a Lifetime
TIMELESS #3

BETHANYHOUSE

 Bethany House Fiction

 @BethanyHouseFiction

 @Bethany_House

 @BethanyHouseFiction

 Free exclusive resources for your book group at BethanyHouseOpenBook.com

 Sign up for our fiction newsletter today at BethanyHouse.com